Strange Saint

Andrew Beahrs

STRANGE
SAINT

The Toby Press

First Edition 2005

The Toby Press LLC
POB 8531, New Milford, CT 06776-8531, USA
& POB 2455, London W1A 5WY, England
www.tobypress.com

Cover painting by Pieter Bruegel the Elder (Netherlandish, active
1551, died 1569), *The Harvesters*, 1565, oil on wood. Reproduced with
the permission of The Metropolitan Museum of Art, Rogers Fund,
1919 (19.164) Photograph © 1998 the Metropolitan Museum of Art.

ISBN 1 59264 124 5, *hardcover* original

A CIP catalogue record for this title
is available from the British Library.

Typeset in Garamond by Jerusalem Typesetting

Printed and bound in the United States by
Thomson-Shore Inc., Michigan

To Jim Deetz
and for Eli, always

A Selected Glossary may be found at the end of the book

Contents

vii

Part 1

Chapter one

I Wander through
the Old Points

I

The English Midlands, before 1620

follow the oxcart as it rolls south toward the Devil's Points, through orchards and the wrecks of old beehives. The sun speckles through fruit trees; the apples are ripening well, the pears better. Master Jacobs walks ahead of the cart. He's as mindful of the oxen as a baker is of spiced bread. The oxen and milk-cattle are his great pride—he holds close to Plato's right haunch, watching the roll of muscle under the good tawny flank. After we leave the orchards there are only brambles and thistles by the side of the road. Wheels creak, dusting the air, and my skirts, and scrub trees.

This is the last market before harvest, so we have no grain. Instead the cart is filled with all our summer's work—coppice poles we cut in from cropped stumps in forest clearings; two casks of malt, steeped and sprouted, dried on haircloth over a killframe; chickens I axed behind the lean-two, this morning. A headless hen rolls, leaving a spot of blood on a bundle of coppice. All these things I made. All these things might be mine.

Here's a question, I say to Patience.

What? she says. She's half my age and must take three steps to my two.

If you were going to the city and could buy anything you wanted, what would it be?

A back-laced bodice, she says.

Her legs flurry like leaves.

Priscilla Miller told me that ladies in the city always have their bodices laced down the back, she says. Where they can't reach the laces at all. They need a servant for the task.

So you want a servant as well.

And why should I not? she says.

There's no point to it, I say gently.

But I think to myself that she might as well. Myself, I want something that will make me notable. But nothing over-dear, that would be talked on. Just something to make me look well. Should I not look well, if I can? Something like a green ribbon for my hair, for after harvest—when my hair will be free from my coif, and seen.

Cho-ha, Master Jacobs calls out, stopping the oxen. They stand shifting, stupid, dimly sure from habit that they'll soon be goaded again. Jacobs stands beside the road, thistles and brambles around his best boots. He rubs his fresh-trimmed beard, peering off to the side of the road like he's never before noted this place. He has drooping eyes, a thin face, a slim small body, and I'm some taller than this sore-boned fox.

Like all those in the village, Jacobs names himself a Saint. Not in the same way as saints in the Romish Church—the village Saints do not claim any particular individual holiness. But their community, their congregation, follows the form of the first congregations described in the Book; and the Book says that any congregation in such form is blessed, and its members thus named Saints.

Look at that, there, he says, and gestures into the crammed green tassels.

If this was my first time here I'd not know where to look. But he stops here nearly every market day, or at least says a brief word to note the place. Still I peer in false confusion, forcing myself to be patient, giving him his wants.

Behind a cat's cradle of thistles and thorn and hopeful fern, behind stooping, elderly mandrake, through the stubborn deadman's digits of a few poor trees, huddle the remains of an old fire. Once-thick posts, long since burned to tapers, point tentatively heavenward. But they're cowed beneath the bracken, trapped under ruins of a spider's city. A dozen gingerline butterflies seek through. They light for moments on the posts, the points of thorns, and the leaves of scaled vines.

I bite my cheek, thinking that at night this'll be a hideous place. At night, all will be infested.

That's where the old tavern was, Jacobs says with quiet satisfaction. Before the husbandmen came and burned it all out.

I well know it. Though the charring coals are now shielded under the scrub of bad land, this old burning was the cause of my being put out with him, the source of all the years of my servitude. Those as lived here were all driven out and away, forced to the road south after they lost this tavern, their sometime home. And in their cowardice, those that fled left me, then only an infant, in the grass by the side of the road. None of the Saints would take me, then, for a foster child. But the Jacobs would take me for a servant—in their mercy.

My mother may have been among those who fled. She may have died on the tavern floor—she would not have been the only one who died in panic, though the Saints had intended only threat.

If she was killed then it was murder, whether by intent or no. Always I look at this place; always I wonder.

For a moment I close my eyes against the sun; and even more, against the sight of the ruins. But when I do, the sun's heat seems to redouble, aided by another burn—an echo of the old embers, that fell from the roof thick as hail, scorching, scarring, killing. And with that echo is another, the breeze softly twisting to a scream. I shake my head and open my eyes to the day.

I've rarely seen John Jacobs in such good humor. Often he notes this spot with only a few words—there, that's the site of the old tavern—as we trod by on the road to market. It's a wonder to me he never tires of it, but he always acts as though he's forgotten that he has shown us before. That's little better than a lie. It's one of his constant lessons—he thinks it necessary to show us the place. What happened here's important to him, as the Lord knows it is to me.

I can't think what might account for his added pleasure in the site this day. He gazes at the burned posts like a thirsty man afore waterfalls. Perhaps he passed good words this morning with Mistress Jacobs before our departure. Perhaps he's been reflecting on the healthy calves the kine dropped last spring, or upon his own coming increase—Mistress Jacobs is well into her carrying. Whatever the cause, I'm full willing to use his mood for mine own good.

That, sir, must have been a fine day.

A necessary one, sure, he says. His voice is pious, rightly judicious. They were only doing what needed doing, he's telling me. They took no pleasure in it, beyond what they would in any work of the Lord.

It's a good thing to think on, he says. Ah, I near forgot—you'll thank Sarah for me? I think that Frances is much improved, her force some restored. You'll likely see Mistress Hawkens before I've occasion.

I'll thank her, good sir, certain, I say.

A blue field bird lights on a post's tapered tip. It seems a sign to me and it picks at the post with its beak—quick, jabbing taps.

I wonder, sir, if I might take a bit of my pay early. There are some small things I would purchase, this market.

He glances at me, but his sharp eyebrows do not quite pull into the feared frown. He looks painstaking thoughtful. For an instant I think he'll stroke his tuft of beard.

We're not even to our harvest. It is very early, to think of pay. Have you naught left of the last?

I struggle not to laugh. My pay from last year vanished with two small trips to market. None of us are paid much and he pays less than is usual. He uses the pay to keep us separate—paying us makes us servants, not foster children. But I mustn't make it seem I think I have a say.

You should be more careful with it, he says. There is a lesson to be learned here, Melode. What the Lord gives us is not to be squandered. You should be more sparing with your money.

I will be, sure, good sir, I say. I know he'll agree. He enjoys dispensing punishments, lessons, and small indulgences, sometimes in equal measure. The only difficulty is keeping myself distant, whether he's imposing hardship or some small, fine grace. And that's a mountain to swim. It's an ocean to climb.

Master Jacobs wants to set his price; he's hopeful that this will be a good year, and desires the advantage that early bargains may give him over other sellers. Thus he's sent me to find his particular grain-buyer from the south among the swelter of the late summer market. I wander through people sitting on blankets, leaning on open oxcarts, sidling through the bustle with bundles on their shoulders, balancing on barrels to cry out their wares. Behind the trampled mart stand the market points, eight stones standing in a great half circle. They reach high as the collar of an open hall; their roots run deep as a well. Some say the Romans set them with curious engines. Others say they're fairy stones. Those people think the stones are not set deep, but rather raised up shallow, charmed out of the earth, meant for some kind of warning to us that live in the sun. Master Stradling says it was the men who came here with Japheth, Noah's son. I don't know. Once all called them the Devil's Points, but many think it no longer right to prolong that name—surely, were he asked, King James would be among those to condemn it.

There's a flash, sharply bright, in the corner of my eye. A man sells small, wood framed looking-glasses, something I've not seen at market for many years—it takes a hopeful man to offer looking-glasses to husbandmen. Though he sees my interest, to me he calls out no encouragement, and as I pick up a glass his mouth's a pinched line.

I've rarely seen my face, and when I did it was in still pools at the side of the river, my forehead and cheek stabbed through by reeds. Or else with my eyes shattered in mica on the back of a stone, or my nose warped and ears atwist in Master Stradling's turned windowglass. In the mirror, every brown hair escaped from beneath the tight bounds of my coif stands out perfect. My lips are fuller than I'd thought, my cheekbones higher, though my face is nearly round. For an instant a lazy animal stares back, some plump cat or mouse-dog. It's like listening to an echoed voice, recognizable but surprising, and when I part my lips for a look at my teeth—solid, not yet gone to brown—I force a smile, and the change is like a pebble in a pond. Somehow it's near shameful to think that no one knows my face less well than me. What ill have I done through the years, who have I unwittingly insulted or flattered, never imagining that I mapped my feelings wrong on my face? How have I been mistook, my intent twisted? I press my lips, one to the other. The merchant stares.

If I am to buy your wares I must see them first, I say.

I can't see you'll have means to buy, he says.

You'll risk that? I say. You talk so to a woman, and expect to earn your keep selling looking-glasses. Well.

After a moment he seems to decide that he'll take the chance, and leans back against his wagon. Again I look closely at the mirror, at myself.

Now the first surprise has faded, and I'm not so horrid on the eyes. I'm far better than that I smile, and my smile comes brightly. If a friend looked so I'd think her beautiful. I hold the mirror closer to my face. Now there is no coif, no hair peeking beneath it. There's only flesh to fill the silver surface.

A fine reflection, says the merchant. He's decided to treat me as a customer.

It is, I say absently.

Mayhap there's a fellow should like the changes a mirror'd prompt.

I turn my head a bit. The seller's words sound good-natured, a kind of flattery—but they return me to thoughts of my station. You'd never know I was different, to look at me. You'd never know I was different from any of the Saints. And neither would they, if they could look without cold judgments that wrap me like lover eels. The surprise of my appearance is not all pleasant; if I look thus, why must they think me so low? I chew my lower lip; the girl in the glass gnaws hers....

I shove the looking glass into the startled hands of the merchant and walk quickly away through the market, hoping that I seem to look vacantly for the blue plume of Jacobs' London grain-buyer.

Dogs snuffle the packed and dusty ground. Men sell sage-ale, mint-ale, scurvy-grass and sack, wormwood-ale that turns the world blue. The Saints cannot know they're saved. They cannot know they're among the chosen; they cannot know I'm not. They cannot know I'm not the best of them.

Very fine, this market wine, this market ale. So cheap and fine, all this. I'd thought to have a mere glass of what there was, but one brought another, and another after that, and this is none of the weak beer that at home I drink by the gallon. This is the better stuff, aged, steeped with wicked-weed. There's a dull fire under my hair. I see the market through warm glass, children rolling on the ground warped by the waves of the glass' turning, and I wander through it all trying to take pleasure.

Miss would you care to take a chance? says a dice-man. He's blind in one eye and leaves that wrinkled gray grape open to the world. Likely he thinks it mysterious, and I'm careful to look at both eyes in equal measure.

And why not, I say. After all I've not enough money left for another drink, and with a win....

The rules of his table call for three of a kind and a one to be rolled, out of six dice altogether. Uncommon hard, but the payback is well enough. For a long moment I grip the dice tightly, warming the cut bone, willing in my wishes. The dice scurry, then still. I count three threes. A four, a two. A one. I cry out my triumph, but almost before the dice have settled a pig's-bladder ball spills them about, sending the numbers awry.

No winner here, the dice-man says.

It was, it was, I say.

Nothing I can see, he says, and winks his dead eye.

With a growl of disgust I bend for the ball. Four boys scarce old enough for man's clothes stand behind me, keeping their laughter until they have their toy safely back.

And this piss bag cost me the last of my pay, I say.

'Twas an accident, one says.

We'll have that back, says another.

It's angering, but what can I do? I'll not keep their poor ball to scorn them. I step, kicking as hard as skirts will allow. The bladder flies like a goose, finally splashing into an open tub of milk, spraying a man standing beside with a ladle. The milkman turns, yelling like a boar. Likely it's a show for the customer. But the boys see only that he's scarce smaller than his carthorse, and scatter without excuses.

Though the milkman thought the boys to blame, the lanky, splashed fellow looks directly at me, holding a slight smile. With a start I recognize Adam Stradling—son of John Stradling, our own village minister. A thin scar traces a line from temple to chin. I recall, vaguely, that it's from the time he teased Henry Singer's dog—near ten years ago—seeking to bind its paws together. Finally it lost all caution and snapped him, leaving him crying in the road. Now, as I think of his father, Adam's smile seems a sneer.

He brushes droplets from a dusky green jerkin and pale orange trunk-hose, long past due another dyeing. Then he comes to meet me, his mouth pursed tight. But as he nears I see he's only trying not to laugh. Relief loosens me. Still I look direct at his eyes—the drink lets me do what I might normally shy from, out of wariness if not humility.

Melode, he says.

Mel, most commonly, I say.

Mel, then, he says. You against a pack of children in a game of ball. More of them, but then you've the hindrance of your skirts. How did the contest end?

In triumph, I say. We played to a single goal.

You found that one well enough, he says, and looks to his damp clothes. I think you've found the ale man, as well.

And should I not? It's mine own pay, I say. Though my voice is steady, nearly teasing, I'm inwardly wary—almost as though I face his father.

But he smiles again. Though his eyes are brown, the smile

lends a shimmer and defeats any threat of dullness. That was your only fault, he says. Next one's with my coin—if you've found one with wares you like…

I have, I say.

Well then. Let's wander to him, he says.

Soon we sidle through the crowd gripping new mugs. It's afternoon now and the points cast shadows across the wares nearest them—butter, bacon, coneys and cranes, ducks and eels. An old woman sits silently with the crowd streaming about. She's selling brown jugs with scowling faces etched into the necks and ragged beards hanging down over each belly curve. There are onions smelling of saltmarshmushrooms, carrots, cabbage, and turnips, almonds and walnuts and pears. City buyers appraise bushels of early wheat, sniff, and walk away on green shoes. Then they return, and they buy. There are all grades of bread, manchet and cheat, raveled and brown. Dancers from the south, jugglers from the west, husbandmen all, come to market to fling clubs at each other or themselves through the air. I watch it with pleasure as we walk through the smoke of roasting beef-belly and between blankets heaped with farm-ware.

A girl my own age sees us and calls out. Her dyes are heaped in bowls, the colors of the powders having scant relation to those they'll give to cloth.

All the finest colors here—logwood and cutch kermes for you, madam. Hottest reds from across far seas. Logwood and cutch, kermes for you.

Madam—it's empty flattery, she could never mistake my clothes for finery, but I grin at the thought. I dip my finger in a heap of yellow, lick it, and the powder turns pork-pink.

Four groats, and that enough to color a garment, she says, and rocks the bowl as though she thinks the tiny powder tides dazzling. I examine a few of the bowls, carefully, though I have no money left me. Very seriously I look over a brown dust, acting a fine lady that means to buy. With my spittle the dust turns precious daffodil. But Adam has wandered to the next table, where tobacco's lined in bowls. Pray pardon, I say to the dye-hawker, and leave her disappointed.

How's that?

There's more than one manner of stocks, he says.

And you'll not find yourself in any of them, I say. I thought it would sound a joke but the words come shocking bitter.

It's not so simple, he says. Not so easy. He mimes letting a book fall open on his knees.

Oh, I say. I look away, upper lip tightening against my teeth, eyes blurry from anger and disappointment. His honesty was a cool draught, and already it seems to run dry. Our interlude is passing, the gap between us again becoming plain.

Here, he says. His hand rests on my shoulder. A bird, nervous on a post. Would you choose to have my father?

I would, of course I would, I say. I'd choose any household that wanted me.

Our talk conjures John Stradling to stand before me; I curse at the knowledge of how readily he can be called to mind. He is no easy man; he stands over the stones, four horses tall. He shadows the market, a screening cloak. Beneath the shade, the redheaded boy who kissed the stone looks on with grave eyes as his furious mother knocks a grainbuyer's feather hat to the ground. Men with staves close on her, like ravens flighting to seed.

Would you, Adam says. Then you've given me no thought.

He flips the ground with curled fingers, crushing an anthill. He stares at that spot as though thinking on destruction, and breathes stubbornly, evenly.

Perhaps not, I say.

Well. Who were your parents, he says.

Ah. His suddenness is a way of not speaking. But I think he's not lied to me yet. And there's a great deal I could say of my parentage, though it is all confused by time and perhaps by willful untruth.

I could say my father was a masterless man. He lived for a time in the tavern on the road south, I could say, where he got me on my mother. He fled from the fire set by the Saints, who feared the tavern folk might be hired by the landlord to enclose their common fields. He fled from that fire that my mother burned in. She and one other woman died—so I've heard. So they say.

My mother, they've told me, died inside when the roof fell blazing. Her companion died after, from wounds that would have branded her bone-deep had she lived. The Saints sought for a time to give her care and comfort—they'd intended no lasting ill, but in righteousness and haste failed to think that some might fear them more than flame, and conceal themselves within. And I was taken in by them, a girl of under two years.

I could say to Adam that when I walk to market there are the poles of an old fire—I imagine you've near forgotten where, yourself. I imagine there's no one pointing to them every time you pass. And you need never wonder about the truth of your parentage; whether your mother died and wanted you, whether she forsook you and fled. You need never wonder if the tale of her death is only another shackle, proving that you've no place else to go.

I don't know, I say.

He says, I'm sorry for that.

A simple phrase, rightly uttered, has the force of a tumbling tower. I lean back against the stone. And now our silence draws us together, like stitches pulled gently closed. I feel warm, and whole, as though an icy spring in my spine has been sealed. For what seems a long time we sit in silence. The sun warms me, the stone at my back, the grass about my legs.

Adam says, It's a great fine world the Lord's given us.

And he's right, and although his words are a mere pass at forgetting what was nearly become a fight, I'm glad for them, and for him. With the afternoon sun, the ale, and the pipe of smoke, the trampled mart before the points is awash with colors bright and dusky. Woad blues like seawater and marble, yellows wrung from calendula and golden marguerite. The gray that's called mouse, the gray called dead Spaniard, those named milk-and-water, rat, and puke. An armless woman flips numbered cards with her toes. Reds bright as earth-dragons and rusty as dry blood, greens like popinjay and pine. A cape dyed the shocking orange of Ape's Laugh drifts like a toy boat. The colors sweat together, tumble apart, and melt once again. A bald man walks on his hands, dog's tether in his teeth, and grins at me. I squint at him and at them all, my chin drooping sleepily, happily, for my chest.

But there's a commotion from somewhere within the market, like a royal hunt charging through a wood. The people part, and four bear-wards pass, dragging their beast. It lumps along toward the furthest market stone.

Come on! says Adam, jumping to his feet. I follow as he weaves through the quickly gathering crowd.

They wounded the bear in taking it. It bleeds from both forefeet, on the pads. It sits before the standing stone, curled and chained, licking its wounds, brushing behind each ear. It moves as though alone in the woods, but within its thicketed face the eyes are fixed, wholly aware. A chain runs from a wooden, iron-studded collar around the stone, then back to itself where it's fixed with wire. The collar must have been crafted for the bear—it's too large for a dog, too small for a horse or an ox, and the studding gives it a look of armor that wouldn't so well suit another animal. After a time the bear backs to the standing stone and leans against it like an old man in the sun. It's the color of my hair; one at a time it licks its forepaws.

The dogs are coming.

Eager, a man says beside me. Burdenous.

His hood lays limp as a skinned rabbit. His face is like a ham. They're banddog mastiffs, kept always strapped to keep them from other animals and from men. There doesn't look to be much strength in their flanks or hindquarters but the muscle of their necks is knotted oak, their collars spiked in a weapon-way, no armor there. They're led through the crowd with leather sacks pulled over their heads and drawn tight around the throat. The sight or smell of bear must be kept from them. The air's full of desperate, formless lyre-song, jangle and thrum. The dogs are tied to cords much longer than the bear's chain. They can pull back when they choose, as the bear cannot. As they approach him, the bear stops his pretence of cleaning, sits on his hindquarters, and moans.

He wasn't wounded in the taking, I see now. They injured him intentional, to give the dogs some assurance of survival; at least their gaming chance of it. The bear's not meant to live through the day, and so they've sliced and twisted the pads 'neath his claws to make every blow hesitant. He'll share in whatever pain he gives. Sarah's told me that there are things one can give a bear to make him drowsy even during a baiting, or if not drowsy then slow. These handlers know their work.

Once the dogs are past and the length of their cords is clear, the crowd draws in and my view vanishes behind shoulders, hoods, coifs. I stoop and push my head between a loaf of bread and a man's armpit that smells as musty as a long-sealed cellar.

Can you see? Adam says. I can. I can see flashes when one man or woman or another steps aside. Adam presses full well against my hip. The heat of the day make me sweat and where he's pressed against me the sweat's a standing pool. I can see the stone and the first links of chain but a purple elbow bars the dogs from me. I shift as though I've been pushed, unawares, and firmly, against Adam. The hoods are whip from the dogs like moths. The banddogs roar. Bread near jabs in my mouth. Adam is pressed full well against me and they release the dogs.

From where I crouch the dogs seem near as big as the bear. The bear's backed against the stone, not bigger than a medium man, shifting on his feet, jerking his head as though to shake off water. The dogs flash across the tramped circle—will they not pause, size their opponent? My breath is cats in a sack. When the crowd surges forward I churn my legs so I can see. All that I want is to see. The dogs strike the bear, one at the legs to drag him down, one at the chest—or is it the throat? My tiny window shuts then, and absolutely. In that last flash I saw the bear's collar in the dust, torn free, never armor. I pull back, stand up. Adam stares over me, holding a half-smile, chewing on his lip. A bear screaming sounds a crashing wagon.

Tell me, I say.

Wait, now, he says. He's barely heard me and he stares over my head, sweat on his cheeks. Wait, now, he says, and he's a hundred leagues away.

I can hear when it is over. The crowd breaks like a pond's splintering ice. There's one dog dead and one dying and bear-wards drag away the corpse of the bear. They wear brown leather jerkins and black ribbons at the crowns of their hats. They drag the bear by the hind legs toward a cage in the back of a cart, leaving a stream of blood from its throat. The ground where the dogs fought for purchase is torn in arcs, like quarter moons.

Chapter two

I'm Punished with the Moon, and Seed Herbs

Trom his perch on the great beam Enry laughs and laughs. If I turned to see him, he'd vanish right quick. If I did that, Master Jacobs would have his questions. My tongue is thick from sun and ale.

He laughs and laughs. Enjoy the night, he calls down to me. Enjoy the moon. God speed you to the dooryard.

Master Jacobs eats in silence and he keeps a miserly hold on the salt. He'll give nothing to ease the pain of what he says is my wrongdoing this day. Without it there is nothing to cleanse my body of ale, I am weary and irritable and I curse myself for not staying to beer. Master Jacobs eats in silence. My doom he's already proclaimed, after a whispered conference with Mistress Jacobs behind the cracked gray closeroom door. It's been three weeks and more since I've seen her, the holder of the voice that guides my days. I bite my lip and eat in silence, quickly, yet striving to seem patient in my use of time. The faster I eat now, the sooner I can be in the garden, and the sooner away from it. The sun has sapped away my strength, and with Jacobs' miserly hold on the salt there's nothing to restore me. I'm scarcely hungry at all, and, after all these hours, only a shade of drunk.

Out to the dooryard, and alone, Mistress Jacobs says through wood with cobwebbed splits.

She'll to it, Master Jacobs assures her. Hold your strength, my love. Spend no force on this. She'll learn obedience, and quick attention to your needs.

And at least you'll not be beaten, Enry shouts. At least you'll not feel his hands on you this night. There's a cause for good gratitude! You want *my* word on it.

Enry is our house-spirit. He's lived here forever, since the house was made. His bones are sawdust; his mind, lost nails. He sits on the summer beam and laughs and laughs, there where the smoke's stained the beam black. It was years before he spoke to me but he was here all the while. Though he denies it, I'm sure he's sometimes earned me a beating. I'm certain it wasn't myself that lost the shuttle, or spilled the proofing to hiss aside the coals.

I've yet to have a clear view of him. From his voice and the odd corner glimpse, you would think he's taken the shape of an old man. But he moves sprightly in the corner of my sight. There's no weight of years on him—he's a drunken youth in a skin made of house and shaped for an old man, and he sways on the summer beam and laughs at my plight. At times he's been a help to me, if only by mocking Master and Mistress Jacobs when all I could do was blink at their cruelty, biting back a snarl at taunts that drifted like paper. At times like this I hate him and wish I could snatch him up without him fogging back to where he sleeps, down below the floor, where house posts grip the earth.

They keep me in the house until the last scrap of daylight is washed away. They keep Patience in the house and they give me no shielded taper. Only then—it being August and the moon come full—does Mistress Jacobs whisper me to the dooryard to seed the winter herbs. Master Jacobs swings the door wide; it thuds behind as though he's booted me to the dust, leaving darkness like that on the back of another's eyelids.

Some of these seeds I gathered my own self. But the most of

them come from Sarah's fine garden that's the mother for most village plots. She drove her body—solid as a stump—about her house, hands tugging at the air as though she was catching flies, declaiming against the ignorance of my Mistress Frances Jacobs. The black moon had fallen from her face. That left four lonely, staggered stars, the constellation of black felt she sets with sap on her cheeks, her forehead, her chin. When she came to rest in the corner beside the chimney, her callused hands picked, delicate, through dry herbs. She's had plenty of practiced care, but some cracked slightly, and their smells were free to trickle. Bear's breeches, yellow flag, honeysuckle, nep. Clarie and rosewort, Turk's cap, mullein—mullein, earthy and bitter, smoky and sweet, this special mix new but also familiar. She tipped the catches on tiny boxes, chose seeds for my particular wants.

But that makes for no comfort that I must be alone in our dooryard at night, even if the moon's come full. The seeds are from Sarah even though I know enough to gather my own seed if they'd trust me for it, and the moon casts shadows through moist summer air and the scratchy thyme seeding the earth where I sit with my ankles tucked under. Our dooryard's the familiar one I've worked nearly since the day I came here, but at night the sun blanket's been folded up, hidden away, nothing left to keep evil wisps from eyes and lungs. I tuck basil behind my ear, as I do when I sneak to the orchard. There's comfort in the orchard, where others will tarry with me. Here none crouch running beside me, none wait beneath the apple man with beer and plotting smiles.

It's late enough that the evening bugs are gone and I can hear the shrill wheedling of a bat, its leathery flesh chock with the soul of a dead and unbaptized child. A light breeze blows, shifting the moist warm air, cooling the slight sweat of my cheek. I've sat too close to the sage, crushing it. It leaks a robust, half-smoke smell. I pry my fingernails into the thongs on these small leather seed-bags, and I rest the bags beside me.

The moon rims the sage in silver. It soaks the yarrow full of dew. It coaxes the bears-breeches that will counter numbness should we have it, and I rake away the dried stalks of last season's herbs with my fingers and spill seed to spread widely across the furrowed dirt with my palms. And all the while I pray to the Lord that He'll bring forth wholesome herb from the seeds that only hint at the strength to come, that only show us what we may labor to cultivate. They'll not cause me to forget that, send me when and how they will. I know it's said there's no cause in praying at such a time, and who are we to ask the Lord for aid or to think he may answer. But I know also He gives us wholesome herb at his pleasure and it's frankly foolish not to thank Him or ask Him while planting. So I pray as I spill out the seeds: yellow archangel for warm spirits, and borage for comfort and the driving off of melancholy, and true black hellebor for mad and furious men and for women taken greensick. I spill them into finger-furrows, crossed by shadows cast by the moon and French lavender.

The door opens, and for a moment there's a pit of dull light beside me. But now I'm accustomed to the dark and the moon, and so this only obscures. The herbs between me and the door are sketched black. A pot of piss splashes. Patience has forced herself to go so she could open the door for me, spilling me some light. And I thank you, dear, though now I'm grateful when the door is again shut.

This is their fear, this doom of darkness. It will not be mine. I know this place; this place is mine. My time is theirs to command. Naught else. I'll take my thoughts, and I'll take this place; and maybe, the thought comes unbidden, someday I'll take him.

When all the herbs I have are seeded, still I sit, for the half of the next hour, more, watching the moon that's doubtless replete with Enry's cousins and mayhap mine own. Mayhap my mother, if she is ashes, not still vigorous and yearning for me—or else hateful enough to have left her daughter. A cloud scuds across that silver safe, blown by a sweet summer breeze full of the forest and bruised sage.

Mistress Jacobs sent me out here at night. I know there's labor to be done, but there's no cause for one to work alone at night. And I can hear another bat, two now, or three. Bats are shells for damned children all ascream, and honeysuckle smells special sweet in the dark. I force myself to stare only at the moon. I'll not flee as soon as I can. I'll be here for longer than I must, for then she's not ordered me in every particular. And with another prayer I crackle lavender off in my fingers as Sarah said to do. For lavender also will treat greensickness, when a woman has been too long alone. And though I never gave Adam no mind before today—though there are others more well-looking, and though surely he gives no mind to me—for now the thought of him makes me desire such a cure.

Chapter three

I Dodge the Stocks

Jenny Fulton was daughter to Charles Fulton and Goodwife Beth, said Master Stradling. When Jenny was sixteen she married Joseph Tiller, husbandman of a village six leagues distant. They had two children die during birth. Jenny's home filled with baby clothes, made during her lying-in when she had better have been at rest. The clothes were like rolls of cobweb, like grima silk. Jenny died with the third child. Master Stradling is friends with the minister in that village, and so knows the story. In our general meeting he attributes the deaths to Joseph's vain thoughts, and Jenny's unseasonable playing at chess.

This morning, of all mornings, Anne is late. I would not have word that I was late to haying return to the Jacobs, less than a day after my last punishment. But my walk with Anne is a rare chance to talk in something like privacy. I dearly love that, as does she. And so I wait, twisting the handle of my rake in the dirt, watching for her to come rushing along the road between houses that frown with aged thatch.

At last she comes, hurriedly swinging her own rake, and is speaking before she reaches me. Pardon, pardon. Fight-Faith waited until this morn to say I knew about the road-man, and Isaac'd not let me leave until I told him all. Not that he'll ever confess to being the cause of my lateness, should it come to that.

So he would not, I say. What manner of road-man, and why so special?

He was an ordinary fellow of the kind, she tells me as we make for the bridge. We see three or four of them a week here, which the Saint Elders think a mighty flood, and a threat to our being. The Elders call the road-men Strangers, as they call all who are not Saints. There is thus a plenty of Strangers, they being all the thousands of worshippers in the crown's church.

Anne was at the general oven at the crossroads when this tinker Stranger came, and so could listen as she waited for her bread. Like most road-men, he asked for a plain bit of dinner. Unlike most, he claimed to have news he might exchange for it.

Master Stradling listened, at the village center, where the path to the pastures and the fields meets the road toward southern cities, as the tinker claimed that our landlord George Pollack is dead, and foully murdered. Leaving a tavern in the city, he was put upon by a thief; being a strong man still, he took away the man's knife and, in a brave show of contempt, threw it to the ground. A bold move. But the thief again picked up the blade, and, being by then harried and in fear for his liberty, stabbed landlord George Pollack through the heart.

Listening to the story I hear the details only distantly. There is a meaning to this, but it's like a cloud portent, gone almost before I've blinked through the glare of the facing sun. Still, I know that any change in land tenure is weighty. The Saints are congregationalists; every one of their churches is independent, living on its own land, free of loyalty to any other. They are not Puritans, who hold empty dreams of bettering the Church of England. They are only men who would live free of those who think themselves holy, and able to wield control over gathering and worship. Thus, they believe, there can be no true church without land to give them independence.

We're to the footbridge and I snap fingers three times, it being my first crossing of running water this day. Bad luck loosens, parts, and sinks away into the river. It makes me feel lighter, and clean, as though I've shed a horse blanket from off my shoulders.

You think we can trust tinker news, I say.

I think so, she says. He'd not have risked a lie, asking for food and lodging as he was. What if we'd discovered he was lying while he was staying here? If lying, he'd have asked for food to take away.

He didn't get it in any case, I'd think.

You'd be right. The tinker was gabbling—he had a rotten mouth—I could scarce make it out. Master Stradling thanked him, all polite, then walked him through up the road and pointed him north as empty as he had been.

Four elm trees shade the path ahead; beyond that's the slope of the cow pastures and the meadow, split by the sharp angles of a snake-fence. Through two elm trunks I can see the crowded meadow side, full of men and girls all working at the haying.

I'm not sure this is right, I say. How would the man know about Pollack? Not his death, I mean. How would he know that he owns these lands?

Well, Anne says. Pollock owned lands all about, and wanderers like to know whose lands they walk. He might not have been anywhere near when it happened, but know the truth all the same. Anyway, he did know that Pollack owned these.

Girls are raking from the top of the meadow down, their backs toward the river and the village. They're brown against the warm white sky—the sun has crested the hill, shining with heat I've rarely felt so early and the girls are shadows harried into waves. We walk quickly, hay swooshing about our skirts.

As we approach, Anne motions to Susan Porter, a servant, who can be trusted not to call attention to our arrival. She smiles over her shoulder, a greeting made crooked by her hatred for this work.

A bit late, aren't you? she asks. She's teasing but also annoyed that we were doing something while she was at labor. The hay-raking is particular labor for unmarried girls.

I suppose, I say. That's how it is, when you have a dozen men after you every moment of the day. I had to let them down gentle, or they'd have been fighting the day away on my account.

Let them all down gentle?

Well, all but one—fine, you have me. Two. You want one? I can't keep up with both forever.

We laugh, and Susan's annoyance slips away. Fighting over me, Anne says softly, almost laughing. I shouldn't mind that.

You wouldn't, would you, I say. I can tell she wouldn't. Slightly she bites her lower lip, skewing a grin, looking sideways. She's joking but she's not, really. She's imagining men thrashing about, fists up, faces bloodied, risking their bodies for hers. I sigh with pretended reproach and shake my head as she laughs, delighted.

I slip into the rhythm of the work line. The raking is rough and tacky where the grass is cut low, tines bumping over warm earth and cropped stalks. Hay builds beneath my rake, heaping in heavy banks. I pull the wooden handle back but it's all pillowy, durable hindrance. We've missed the first cool hour, and the heat of the day is trapped beneath the layers of my clothes like flax oil. The handle is rough and unfinished, and grates against my hands. Sweat beads on my forehead.

So who was it after you, Anne says.

Ah, I was speaking nonsense, I say.

The sweat has plastered itching straw seed beside my eye, more on my arms, more still on my ankles. When I brush it off, I seem to press out fresh sweat to mix with the sour. Katherine Gardner, a younger girl, maybe ten, just old enough for this, works on the far side of Anne. She's listening, her head too steadily down, and although that shouldn't annoy me it does all the same. If there was any chance of my telling Anne about Adam, it's gone now.

I toss my jacket into the short empty grass where the hay has already been cleared. I work in shift and bodice but even those layers keep the heat. The air is full of sweet hay dust. The sweat on my forehead meets in streaks on my temples, drips down my cheeks, off my chin, into the hay. The hay builds until we cannot force it further. Then our line ends with unspoken consent, takes a general half-step, and begins again. The raking is rough and tacky where the grass is cut low, tines bumping over warm earth and cropped stalks.

I pause for a stroke or two and wipe my forehead. At the top of the meadow the men and boys have begun loading. They bind the hay into chest-wide bundles and heave them onto carts with two-pronged pikel forks. The sun glares above the haydust.

We rake in a regular rhythm. The unsanded rake handle rubs and heats my hands. From the far end of the line, someone calls out.

On the fifteenth day of July!
I'm grateful for the song, and answer:
Heave and blow, heave and blow!
A murder of crows down from the sky!
shouts the other. Others begin to take it.
Heave and blow, heave and blow!
They lit and let a mighty sigh!
Heave and blow, heave and blow!
To see the haying day go by!
Heave and blow, heave and blow!

Anne tries to take the next call, crying out something about a witch down in the riverbed. But another girl is also calling, and they cancel each other. Anne sings out again, louder, but the line follows her rival. And so it goes, time after time, the first call going to whoever is first to plunge in. Sometimes two compete in a flurry, sometimes there's a pause—full of heat, the scratch and whisper of rakes, and now a sneeze.

A cart rolls down the slope toward the bridge, heading for one of the village barns where the common hay is kept. Those on the cart are all my own age or younger—the older men are loading up above. I grin, and seize the next call—

When scattered by an oafish lout
A knot of toads scattered about.
They bit his balls off with a shout.
That ended their troubles, beyond a doubt!

My voice is damned loud, when I let it go like this. It feels so good, to let it go. But with the last line I feel a moment's embarrassment—I'm so much the loudest that it seems the line follows me hesitantly, stubbornly, dragged in by habit. I dismiss the thought. This is too good a feeling to sift through that sort of worry. The boys on the cart hear the song, and grin. The men above us sing, but the breeze whisks their words over the top of the rise. Their mouths blink silently in the hot morning sun.

I smile.

We stop work for noon dinner when our shadows are puddled at our feet, the wind dead, the heat furious. We drop our rakes and go down to the elms, forming small clumps in the shade, facing the river. It flows, slothful, through still reeds, but seeing it makes me feel cooler, as though a slight breeze is passing. As I unwrap my fare, a cart rolls past, dappled beneath the trees, the men trooping behind with the last load before they stop for the noon hour.

I sit beside Anne and for a time we eat in silence. My bread is stale but the cheese is firm, salty, and good, and pretty well the same thing everyone has. I'm not overly hungry. The sun and work suck out my strength, but also take my appetite, which of course in the end makes work even harder. But now I'm grateful for the chance to rest. I lean back on one arm and take a long drink of weak beer from a jug, my eyes closed and lifted toward the elm boughs. I breathe in deep through my nose smelling the reedy mud and water, beer, the sweet hay that clings all over me. Together they're the smell of summer, or the sun. Voices and lazy flies hum like a muffled millstone. For a moment I feel comfortable and quiet, and in-between.

Then the circle of speech breaks. A short span of the rim dies as those closest to the river fall silent. I look over, without sitting up—but I do feel a small tremor.

A half-dozen girls sit in an uneven group. They were drawn together by the shade of a tree. There are servants there and there are daughters. Their talk has been empty, reflexive, just filling the time away from work.

Now five are quiet, holding their food, like brachets surprised by a careless hare. They are watching Mabel. She alone sits with her back toward the river. Like me she's a servant, put out with John and Sally Hamilton. She thinks a good deal of herself for that. Why—now there's a question I've asked myself. I hate Mabel. She is dumb as anyone I've known, I think, and tries to make up for it by holding herself above the rest of the servants. That's brought the servants to hate her and of course the true Saint girls will none of her. She's always alone, even, as now, in the midst of a crowd. She's always alone, and people's feet trip her up more than accidentally. Depending on who gives them she takes her falls with rage, or else with a foolish heightened dignity that makes things worse.

When people are put upon, they shrink down to a pitiful noth-ing—or else turn mean as Mabel. Once she threatened to dunk and hold Patience under the river if she would not carry her tools. Patience had nightmares from that, thinking of sucking for air but getting only riverweed to clog her throat, Mabel's hammy hands between her shoulders. The threat wouldn't have worried me, overly. But then, I'm strong enough to beat Mabel. Of course Patience is smaller, and there's no telling what the nightmare will carry in her claws when she abandons the woods. I told Mabel that if she threatened Patience again I'd thrash her with an ax handle. She took my words with a stupid stare that I think was meant for defiance, or a threat.

She sits beside the river like a forgotten crate, her face plain as a trencher, hair dangling in thoughtless cords from beneath her coif. She takes a tremendous bite of gingerbread. Now there's trouble ahead for her, whether or no she sees it.

I stare scornfully at Mabel as she chews. Crumbs tumble and catch on her skirts. I feel malice rise up within me like foam in a freshly opened cask of beer. I want to grab that cake away just to erase the right merit from Mabel's face. I'm grateful when another of the girls does exactly that.

Abigail Smythe stands casually and walks to Mabel. Of the two, Abigail is the smaller, but also the more self-contained, with a sort of hard-packed confidence. Without her wide-brimmed work hat her hair stands out tan and smooth below her coif. Her teeth are yet very white in her sharp smile. Unusual, I think, and lick an eyetooth. Abigail's the true daughter of a prominent Saint, Benjamen Smythe, and from that thinks she has authority here. Whether they are servants or daughters themselves, many agree. That's what matters.

Mabel looks up, still chewing, a single brown crumb falling from her chin. Abigail smiles, and with a single sharp motion snatches the gingerbread from her fingers. For a moment Mabel stares blankly. Then her rounded features sharpen, like quickly sliced clay.

That's mine, she says furiously.

I just want to see what it is, Abigail says.

She takes a few steps, intently studying the firm cake. Her short walk draws our eyes like bees to milk. Abigail has her audience.

Mabel lumbers to her feet.

Give it back, Abigail.

You don't mind my looking, sure.

Abigail peers closely. She raises her head, pretending discovery. It's gingerbread, she says brightly.

Is that a fact, I think, and raise a dour eyebrow to Anne. I hate Abigail nearly as much as Mabel. In truth they're much the same, giving themselves the same airs. But Abigail does have the parentage to back them up. For that I can better tolerate her.

She's started walking again but now she stops. Mabel has none of Abigail's ready balance and has to step to one side to avoid her. Anger pools in the hollows of her face but she will not strike the daughter of Benjamen Smythe. I near hold my breath. I love it all. I want Mabel humiliated, I want Abigail taken down from her roost. Damned plumed bird. This is good. Whatever happens, this is good.

Gingerbread isn't everyday fare—gingerbread? says Abigail.

Give it me. Mabel looks at the cake, sullen and dull.

But where might you have gotten it, Abigail says. She holds it on her palm like a looking-glass. So well made, she says, and the smell so lovely.

She sniffs the cake. Above it her eyes are fixed on Mabel, but I can tell her mind's with us. She's measuring us and the way we watch her. It's as though her twinning ghost sits here, beside me, watching her living pair, always telling her how she looks.

Mabel raises her head in defiance, a foolish posture that forces her to peer down her nose. It's how she looks after one of the more privileged girls has tripped her up, and she cannot choose to fight without sure and awful punishment. It's how she looks before she walks away, leaving all behind her chattering, laughing.

Made by Sally Hamilton, she says. Made by her and given me after.

But quiet follows, and Mabel looks about, lost; surely even she can feel the general doubt at such a dainty gift. The Hamiltons are prosperous, she says hesitantly.

Surely they are, Abigail says, as though musing. Lucky you are to serve them, yet sugar is dear. Certainly there must have been some purpose to the baking? Some special time they wished to mark?

Ever since the Saints broke with the English Church, they've been diligent in seeking out those among them who would keep the feasts. It seems a small thing, but many think it our first defense against the corruption of Rome. Keeping a feast hints at a secret affection for things best left behind. Empty rituals, unholy observances. Feasts.

But I am not among those who hates the old ways; and it's taking Abigail so long to get to it. Her vile joy begins stealing my own pleasure, making me feel as distant as though I'm borne on a cart across the bridge. I wish she would just finish things; do what we all want done. I look about me, and my eyes rest on Rachel Hooker, a Saint daughter. On most days she acts my friend, at least enough for a nod and smile. But now she bites a side of her lip, smiles with the other, and the want in her eyes would fright a cat. She can't wait to see Mabel and her household punished for what her own likely does.

I wonder what day it is. The river's a still pond. It's so hot.

There's nothing special about today, Mabel says. Give me the damned bread!

Her face has gone red, even more so than when we were fresh from labor in the sun. Abigail gives an overwrought gasp that's echoed by her friends.

Swearing, and only a week since Sam Harper was whipped for it.

She's not the only one to swear around here, I hear myself

say. I was there when Susan harrowed your leg. You weren't silent about it.

Abigail snaps her head to face me. Then she relaxes, and looks away. Somehow she makes it seem that she only glanced. Now she ignores me. It gives me a sickly, rotten feeling, and I glare at her back. Anne clears her throat—a warning.

Surely they're not keeping the day, Abigail says.

Could be chance, someone says, tentative.

That's a fair bit of chance, says someone else. And although that's all that's said I can feel the downy assent all around. Is there anyone who doesn't want to see Mabel destroyed? For now that desire binds servants and daughters.

Mabel stammers. She could have used my interruption to order her thoughts. But Mabel is stupid. She remained intent only on getting her food back, and has only now begun to see what she faces.

It's not all sugar in it, she says. Most is honey. Sugar and honey.

Abigail's slight has let me see what it's like for Mabel. The girls swell like birds taking flight, filling her vision, clamoring, though only Abigail speaks. The stocks creep behind her, intent on crushing her throat in jaws of dusty oak. Master Stradling keeps that stubborn stock frame at the back of the great room we use for a meeting house. It's in the corner but can be seen all the better for that, for of course it's never covered. When the Hamiltons are in someone will ask, false-kindly, if there is anything they need. Perhaps a half-drunk man will pelt them with rotten things. Then, when the stocks are open, Mabel's master will beat her bloody. She'll work inside until the cuts fade from her skin.

And we've not seen either of them, today, Abigail says. Why is that, Mabel? Are they sick?

Yes, sick. Mabel nods once, like a collapsing table.

They must be very sick. But then how has Sally been at her baking? Is John injured in some way? Is she?

There are lots of things I could say, if I had the leisure or desire to think about them. Doubtless there are witty words I could string together for a whip. The other girls would gasp at the way they cracked Abigail over the head, leaving her weak and dumb. That is a pleasant picture. There must be something I could say, but I'm not that quick. Instead I push myself up, and punch Abigail on the nape of her neck.

The blow isn't very hard. At the last moment I begin to lose my nerve, as though pulling back from the full force of the blow will allow me to make some excuse—oh, I was just trying to smack that fly on the back of your neck, I thought it best to do it with a closed fist—but it still snaps her head back, drops her to the dirt. All the rest cry out; are on their feet. Anne is among their muddle, clear as a fall maple amidst pine. She pushes her tongue into her cheek. She'd like to help but it's already too late and there's no cause for her to risk the trouble. I wouldn't myself, I think. Mabel stares as though I've turned to a white owl. I feel I should shrug at her, make some small signal that this has naught to do with her, or very little. I give her no sign.

Abigail pushes herself raggedly to her feet and turns to me, her shock fading rapidly to anger, then excitement. She doesn't have to know why I've done what I have.

First blow, she says, a grin teasing the corner of her lips. She's tense and ready now. Her arms jerk slightly forward, testing.

I understand. Whatever happens from here, I'll be the one at fault, and the one to take a place in the stocks. At the thought my guts twist like wet cordage. I'll sit on the two-legged stool, forced to balance like a drunk crow, legs screaming, my hands and head though wooden circles, the holes fitting loosely, cut for a big man—but I won't take my hands out. I'll hold head and hands through the holes, a partner to my own punishment, or else out will come the chains and they'll be damned sure I stay there and this time for two full days. Abigail and the rest, they'll not taunt me openly. They'll just bring their food and their beer, and eat and drink where I'm forced to look, there beside the public beehive oven. I would close my eyes, I would sleep but my back is twisted, wrenching insistent pain from the base of my spine to my neck. The best thing, for them, will be

hadn't thought it necessary to convince him; her speech was more for herself and her friends. Now her face goes closed and distant, strange to see in one so flushed.

For what cause are you here, she says.

And why should we not be.

Because there is still the unloading, and that's where *men* belong. *Men* belong there. And here you are, on this side the river.

Her friends give a small, unconvincing laugh. Insulting Adam is a pauper's stratagem.

We're doing what we were put to, Adam says calmly. Seeing where we must harvest next, you know. One must have a feel for it, to know where to harvest next.

Daniel's hands slide around Abigail's waist, then snake for her breasts. She wrenches away, raises her arm over his shoulder like a hammer. Where to harvest next, Daniel says, laughing.

Now, says Adam, and steps between Daniel and Abigail with his hands up.

Listen, John and Sally Hamilton have prospered these last years, he says. They can take simple pleasure in that, without fear, can they not? We shouldn't fear the worst each time the Lord is pleased to reward one of our number with such small pleasure. As to her....

He motions toward me with his head, without looking, as though at a barn to be used for a landmark. He's taken on a voice that reminds me of that he used to mock his father at market. This time he uses it to make himself seem reasonable, and authoritative. But there's also a jesting current. It mocks his own speech, and any man who would speak so. I wonder if any but I can hear it.

I'm sorry for that, I say quickly. I thought I saw a fly on the back of your neck. I never meant to strike so hard.

I can't believe I actually said it. I bite my lip to keep from laughing; muzzled laughter wafts my worries away like chaff. In the end, Abigail's strength comes from those who want to do the things that only she will. With Adam's charity, her control has eddied; the other girls sit or stand silently, many already looking pious about forgiving Mabel. Now Abigail can only hold her crumbled, sweat-damp cake, in a hand dangling loosely at her side.

It's back to work for me, Daniel says brightly.

For us, Adam says. He smiles as he turns past me—good as a wink—and walks for the hayfield. There's a pause before Abigail's friends start talking, aimlessly, and too loud. Abigail returns to her place and sits. She takes a drink of beer, smiles at something someone is saying. She isn't listening at all.

It was no great thing that Adam did. Perhaps it was a whim, or an old dislike for Abigail. But some good spirit presses me above my eyes, between my lips, as I watch him walk away up the slope.

Chapter four

I Dance with a Notion

All the rest of the day we sing our songs as we rake our way down the hill. But there's no force behind our words; the midday quarrel hangs over all, the confusion it bred dampening every voice. It's precious unusual to find the right order of things so turned. There's sorting left to be done; debts some are thinking will have to be paid. Once I do take the lead verse, but take care not to hurl my voice. That would be a dangerous thing, and to no good purpose but mine own fleeting pleasure. A person may be pushed too far. Though Abigail seems subdued, I'll not chance increasing the hate she doubtless hides. She might risk annoying all our age, and inform, if I give her more cause for fury. I sing, my voice wrapped in padding, and all the rest of the day I think of Adam.

He has an awkward stance. He hoists hay as though with his elbows. He can scarce control the heap, but presses it between his arms until he's near enough to flip it into the cart. When he waves another worker to approach, his arm careens like he's signaling a distant ship, but his face holds always calm and friendly. He bends like a stork, flapping one foot in front of the next, laboring the hay up and into the cartbed. The man working there says something—a joke, a reproach? Adam turns away, laughing, and reaches for another load.

For all his awkwardness, I think him well-looking. There's a confidence to his carriage even as his arms flap at his sides, his feet slopping along and kicking up dust. He must be an assured man, to not be always measuring his gestures against his fellows. I can imagine his laughing look full plain, and his dog-scar takes nothing from it. It rather shows his careless happiness, as flames show bright around an andiron. I look at him for one instant, then away. I do so again and again, all the rest of the afternoon, whenever there's possible occasion to sweep my gaze across the summery hill.

Most days, haying on such a day should leave me weak. The sun should dry me as it cures the hay, soaking my inner clothes slick. It should suck out my wet for the use of the air, leaving me dry as straw. But today this work does not tire me. My muscles are full salted.

Does he think his help enough to bear me to bed? (Well, and it might be, says a smirk of a voice.) But I'll not allow myself to want him, yet. There's scant enough chance that my wanting him could lead to anything. Still, now I have seen him act, his scorn for the hierarchies made plain—though he showed it through faith, and perhaps only to me. Whatever his intent, the thought that he might have fought for me is sufficient to bring good feeling. Truly it's good, and that there's no denying.

Close to the finish of the day, when the sun at our backs is a mere two hands in the sky and all the field's burnt orange, we finish the labor that's our part of the haying. I lean on my rake. The warm breeze from the forest marks the turn from afternoon to evening as Abigail leaves, quickly striding down the hill, rake over her shoulder, a small group of loyal girls behind like bottles clinking on strings. The rest of us take our time, not eager to return to our households where we'll only be allotted more work before supper. On the way, the other girls give me small friendly trouble for what's happened this day. They say that none among them would choose to fight with me. They pretend they will serve me, from fear of my fists. I laugh along with them; and when Anne says that Adam must love me to come to my aid I only laugh, and never say they may be right.

❧

Hard words beat, distant and muffled. They sound a barrel filled with cream, pounded for a drum. I drift. Rats tunnel, scratching, through the roofing. My eyes are closed tighter than in sleep. The rumble rises, dies. They must be very loud, for me to hear them through two walls.

I will raise my own voice like that. I will shout loud, and sudden, and wake the house with a burst of declaration. I do it—I rise, and shout, and it being quiet morning my voice is a crash of water, or the thrum of wind through an oak. Nobody is awake. There is no sound from the closeroom. Again my mouth opens, wide as a well, and I shout loud and bright with my hands in my hair and over my eyes. Then my waking blear falls away and I again lie undressed. Patience breathes beside me, a lazy bellows. There is no fire built, no pottage made—and the Jacobs are up. I am as still as can be. As though that will hide me, or bar the door; as though the quiet will unman Jacobs and drive him in a terror from this house. I am still.

Lord let Jacobs not want to break his fast early. Let her drive him from the house quick, and without a look....

The voices have stopped. I listen to the silence. Soon there's a tramp of boots on the dusty dirt floor. He kicks something wooden— there's a hollow bang, a shuffling of dust and straw as he sidesteps, swearing, about the room. Then no one is talking, but the boots still stamp and argue. They are angry in the great hall and then outside. The door crashes, and the boots are gone.

I swing my feet off the bedstead, blinking toward the low light of the greased paper, running my fingers absently along a few sharp ends of chaff puncturing the sleeping mat, the chamberpot of nightpiss aside with my foot. My clothes are draped on field tools leaning in corners and all along the wall. Groping in the darkness, I drag cloth loudly from the handles of cutting-spades and bills and the molespear, signaling to Mrs. Jacobs that we're awake. Iron clinks, clinks.

I wrap layer over layer to keep away the summer sun and its heat. A shift to hang below my knees, skirts over that. The skirts hang from the bottom of a tight, front-laced bodice. A jacket the color of plowed ground. With a coif I trap my rumpled brown hair in a clump. As I bend for my leather flatshoes I decide that my request for Jacobs to leave was as good as a morning prayer. Jacobs would never think it enough, but I say that I'm as true a believer as him, and he's wrong if he thinks he may speak for the Lord's wants, even to a servant. I add a few practiced phrases, and an *Amen*, and that's all.

Living with Jacobs has given me some hard habits. I need to leave the chamber, to prop the door open, showing the tool-cluttered confines. Jacobs hates a closed door on any room but his own. Frances Jacobs might keep watch with her ears, but he wants to see us. Our door must be open always except for sleep. He's even smaller than I am, but holds himself as stubbornly erect as an iron tripod. The open room, empty except for that clutter of tools—that must give him some pleasant feeling. Peace, and industry. We're not there. We're tending gardens. We're brewing beer. I don't know. His eyes are like the soaked pegs used in building; they swell and hold fast wherever he drives them. I lean over and shake Patience awake.

Morning, and Jacobs is out already, I say.

She's sitting up in an instant, eyes flitting. Oh, God, she says. She's a squirrel before the furrier's club. Oh God.

He's out to the fields, I say. Most likely won't be back soon. But dress, quickly!

With the door open the hall is all a vague press, gray on gray. Crossing to the hearth, I sidle between household trappings piled and stacked and hung. It's all a muddling of overlapped shadows, though I can see well in the dark. Sarah tells me that nightseeing comes from a right mix of roots and anger. I don't know. I trudge past what I know is a wooden table and stools, stacked chests, a box of drawers, a bench. The fire is still down and they're all shadows, the color of mud.

I kneel and blow away the ash that's kept the fire through the night. Three small twigs across the coals. They smoke, blacken, and with my next breath flame a sanguine red. It's the first honest color of morning. I add larger wood and rock back on my heels, waiting for the flame to rise. There's no chimney and smoke rises to open rafters and a hole in the thatch above. Some filters through the thatch, but rats still claw out their roads. They tickle the straw. This house is soaked in old smoke.

As the flame rises, the brickabrac of the household grows around me. Sacks of carrots and onions, guns on the walls, herbs; the tables hold a dusty gaming board with pincer pieces, jars of pins and ball-shaped buttons, combs, scissors, nails and pipes and fatty soap. For a moment I feel I've made them. See what I can do with my breath.

I hug my knees close and rest my cheek on my shoulder. The smoke splits on the summer beam that runs the length of the house. Over the hearth the beam's stained black, where smoke flows, and where Enry sits when he comes out from his hiding in the thatch.

I listen quiet, feeling for his peculiar air. When he is there I know it, like an untouched boil; else he spreads all through the house as mist dampens dust. But before I feel him, he speaks.

Had best have left her to her beating, he whispers. Had best have left her to the lash.

He listened last night, when I spoke of my day with Patience. They would only have put her in the stocks, I say beneath my breath—near beneath my own hearing.

Had best have left her to those, then.

I would not see her stocked.

His chuckle shudders overhead. She has ever been a dear friend to you? he says. Had better think of your place here, your duty.

John Hamilton should have lost pasture rights for the season if they knew he was keeping feasts, I try. That should maim him, and his house.

Then maim him. Maim him, Enry says in a hiss. He has him enough wealth, he has him a son.

I shake my head. Enry's hate for the man near shakes the air about me. But the hate's more for the healthy newborn, the like of which Mistress Jacobs fears she may never have.

It's John Hamilton's misfortune to believe in Saint doctrine and yet find himself unable to abandon all the practices now thought ungodly. That's common enough, which makes it all the worse for a man who's caught. Though none will confess, to others or themselves, that they tolerate such things, to many it seems frankly foolish to abandon the feast days—they mark out the year. And in a year filled otherwise with famines of rain, with sickness, bad seed, burning autumn sun, and the ill will of grima and birds, how many will surrender a chance to ask for help?

But I say nothing of this, not even in a sheltered whisper. Surely Enry knows I care no more for the Hamiltons than does he. And when his mood is thus, his mind holds worse than mischief; I can feel him bending like a crow overhead, his gaze shackling my limbs.

You will never deceive me in this house, he says. Nor without it. Never and nowhere will I and mine hear your lies for truth.

Though I strive to ignore him, his words do stab, and I see in the coals before me a mass of crumbled gingerbread, Abigail's vicious face, my hands flying for her. I see Adam's scar.

Melode.

A new voice from behind me; faint, wavering, much weaker than that raised in combat against Jacobs.

Ma'am? I'm almost unsure that I heard, and walk hesitantly to the closeroom. The door's a weatherbeaten gray, with cobweb splits, as though it was left in the sun, and shut, always shut. I have lived in this house for as long as I can remember, yet know the room behind the door only from snatched glimpses and sounds that escape like fingerlings fleeing a spilled fishing bucket, talk, grunts of love, moans of illness. Screams of childbirth and grief. I imagine that the closeroom is big, nearly as big as the hall. But that can't be.

Mrs. Jacobs' voice seeps through tiny fissures. Mushrooms, Mel. I must have mushrooms today.

She said as much last night, and knows as well as I that there will be no more mushrooms until after the next rain. But she goes on, perhaps even quieter.

Alice Manning, she had them when her blood was bad during child-carrying. Said it cleared her up, balanced the phlegm of the boy growing within her. God knows I need that today. I've enough phlegm to stop me up entire.

I rest my forehead against the grain of the door, breathing in soft, warm sighs. She may be filled with phlegm but it has not brought her any courtesy, as it's supposed. It's easy to imagine her body gnarled from fear of the coming birth under blankets, eyes closed as she commands me, face always going flabbier and paler, stomach swelling. Her voice tangles me, drags me to thoughts of her looks. It had best be a boy you carry, if you speak so to your husband, I think. He'd not take that disappointment well. And if the lavender has failed you, how can you know it is phlegm? A mix of blood and bile might feel much the same.

You know enough to look at the monk spring, don't you, Mel? I want them whole, stem and cap together. Alice did not know which it was that done her good, she ate them whole and boiled.

Yes, ma'am. I'll look, certain.

But I want to pound the door down, and scream at Mrs. Jacobs—haul yourself up and out of this damned room! There's no cause to start a lying-in so early. Your envy of Sally Hamilton and her healthy babe Kenelm's no good cause. Likely you lost your own babes from too much care, not its lack. Don't do the same again, now. Up and out!

It was a robin sent her to bed, tapping at her window, a horrid portent.

I'm not hopeful of finding mushrooms until there are more rains, I say. Saying it feels good, but if she calls for it I'll still have to go.

Look anyway, she says, her testiness strange to hear in a voice so quiet. That should do, Melode.

Her voice is going soft and bitter as mold. I turn for the door, slowly, as though weary. She always does that, beginning and ending with my name, as though it's a handle locked into my back. It isn't something I can rightly complain about. She's just using my name. But as I step outside, relief strikes me as cool and immediate as the morning air on my face.

❧

The monk spring, the mushrooms, I'll put off 'till noon. Thus the sun will give protection in the forest, and the forest itself will shade me from what looks to be stifling heat. Of all today's tasks, weeding is my favorite. Thus I may order the garden, in a manner apparent only to me. I sit on my stool and bend to tear up each small blight.

My back is to the house but I can feel it there, gray and massive, a snail's shell for Enry, a cocoon for Mistress Jacobs; both of those for me. Ivy clambers up the side, suckers thumbing their way to pinch and split old wood. There's only our one greasepaper window on the front; the fine turned-glass windows of the closeroom, where the robin tapped, are of course on the side, where I never have cause to be. And when I have snuck there, there has always been a green cloth behind.

But the good herbs billow, before and after. They puff high about my head. Rosemary, a good high hedge. There's a delicious, spicy smell that speaks to me of food and a balanced body. I could use a balanced body, and an even temper, and I slip a leaf from the borage to chew. It tastes like someone has siphoned down clouds to use that fresh rainwater for mulling. Borage is fine for exhilaration, and to make the mind glad. It may not balance me. But in truth most days I would forsake balance, in favor of a glad mind.

I splash piss from the chamberpot about the garden. Not too close to the herbs, lest it scorch the thyme, burn the sage, brown leaves, rot out roots. Rain and riverwater must filter the good salts through the earth. Mrs. Jacobs says that human salts are best, better than chicken's or cow's, and men's salts the very best. Sarah mocks the notion, and says that corn and herb will never know which piss they drink. I imagine that's right.

But the earth is dry. It'll need a good soaking today, that the winter herbs I seeded may better nest. And Adam's work in the hayfield's not yet done, I think. He'll be by the river, or passing on his way to the storehouse. When the chamber pot is empty, the weeds out, the garden's order again clear to my own eyes, I go for water.

Standing on the footbridge, lowering my bucket, I see that a burgundy cow has mired herself. Doubtless she was hunting for reeds.

She and her sisters have long since eaten those closest to dry ground, and she lows a mournful low with water lapping at her flank. The ripples around her trace a pollywog. Four men pick their way toward her, quietly cursing. And there is Adam's lank stance.

I let the bucket dangle in the river, from the end of my hook-and-rope, and watch him wade. With water to his knees Adam even more resembles a stork—he walks with his arms rigidly balanced, fingers near skimming the water, as though he's fearful of it yet hopes it might hold him when he stumbles. I glance his companions over to see if there are any there I must treat formally. But they're all his friends, none over seventeen, and none of them are of the temper that will demand I call them Sir.

David Merchant is fat and tall; that high weight makes him uncomfortable, and he teeters slowly from side to side as the water threatens to pull out his legs. James Patters eyes the water as though the cold's a slippy-haired water sprite, ready to splash for his mouth and take his tongue. Only Adam seems calm; only he sees me. When he does he straightens, grins, and looks me over, one hand on his hip, the other out to his side, unconsciously holding himself balanced. The cow lows, sounding in pain. Even mired, she longs for the reeds she couldn't reach. They're luscious, untouched, and in today's good wind flash green like banners.

I smile a reply, turn, and begin my saunter back toward the garden. It may be in part the borage, but my mind feels ever glad.

⁊⧓

Anne has stopped by on her way to fetch some hops from Mistress Jenkins. Well met, she says. That was quite the day.

She squats down between the house and a fine stand of thyme, and pretends to examine a stem of double feverfew. Anne is no great gardener, but she's good enough at looking busy.

In what way do you mean, I say. Part of me wants our usual play—the greater part hopes she'll simply answer.

Well and didn't we see some uncommon interest in you, she says.

51

And am I not well-looking enough to deserve a man's interest? I say. I pose very straight on my stool, hands on my lap, chin turned slightly away.

Well enough, I suppose. There must be some men that would overlook your hunchback. Some might even love your baldness. And you have fine eyes, enough to make up for your sad lack of an upper lip. Was that an accident in your youth or were you born without it?

Harridan, I say. You can only dream of having what I've never wanted for.

She tires of pretending to look the herbs over and sits back on the warm earth, legs crossed under her skirts. When she's happy like this she reminds me of a sunning turtle, shell glinting, head happily resting before her. Usually she's more drawn into the netting of her clothes.

When I want what you have, I'll know how to have it, she says. I'll shave mine own head and strike myself thrice on the nose with a flatshovel. But stay this—it must've been a surprise and for true, having him come to your aid.

Who? There were two of them.

I pour water shallow and broad, only wetting the top earth so the next buckets can soak it well. Some noxious white powder dusts the orpynem, and there's a curl to my chamomile. The curl has the bubbly look of pox. I strip away the leaves. It's passing odd that the chamomile is so vulnerable to curl, for it's the finest of herbs when fighting shrinking sinews.

Oh, two of them, Anne says. And you looked at both of them equal. You were taken by both of them, equal. And both were equal taken by you.

That's not the same as saying he was coming to my aid, is it, I say.

I think you hope so.

She smiles at me confidently. She's always been able to read me well; I hope it wasn't obvious to all.

This is empty talk, I say. What matter, what I hope?

Well, what you want's what counts. All must follow from that, true?

True, I say. But I don't know that I want anything from him, yet. He's well-looking enough.

True, he has a certain quality…

She speaks as though dreaming of taking him for herself, and I lean to slap her thigh.

I think Benjy Butler'll be enough for you, for a time, I say. Is he not enough man to keep you sated?

He's well enough, when the moon's right, she says with a sly grin. That's not to say I can't cast eyes at another. He does himself, sure enough. If he thinks Sally Furbur well-looking, that's his own deficiency. That's not what we're talking about. I'll ask it plain. Do you want Adam Stradling to bed, or do you not.

I think about that. I remember a sermon given by Master Stradling, when he warned women against being loose, or wanton, or given to lasciviousness. When he was done I wanted badly to be loose, and wanton, regularly committed to lascivious action. It was not his words that moved me. Rather it was a churning that'd begun in my own body, in the months before, that left me as greensick as I'd ever been. My greensickness took my strength and made me irritable, and I spoke to Sarah about it as soon as I could. She gave me herbs and told me, impatiently, the best manner of moving my hand to cure myself. That was the best cure, coming without a man who might bring diverse trouble. Night after night I waited for Patience to sleep so I could do what I wanted, listening for her breath to go regular so I could hasten mine, to a lope, to a sprint like live steam. I had no special man in mind as my hands slid over my and all women's best possession (measured against any man's full soul, ours are all incomplete). I had no more in mind than my own pleasure, and with a gasp and a bite of my lip something did open in me and my greensickness did, for a time, end.

About that time the bees died in the hives. Master Jacobs drove his eye into me. He wondered aloud if one in his house was dirty, quarrelsome, or unchaste. But what was he to do? I had no man, then—if I was unchaste, he could not show me so.

And I later found my own touch better than Jonathan, who was a nephew to Japheth Hooker and put out with him after the death of his parents. Jonathan was the possessor of a fine form, but in bed offered me only pointless rubbing. Though he seemed to like it well I told him there would be no more of it, after I realized I'd never have even fleeting pleasure from him. He was a boy of fair looks, I told him in the stables, but there was in him a certain lack of substance. When I saw his disbelief I told him that I know greensickness, well enough, and know what to do for myself. I can cure myself better than he ever managed. So he told me that he'd been meeting a girl from his old home at the market points, and would do so whether he was with me or no. And thus we parted, as equal as we might.

But to Anne's question. The only true answer is that what I want does not matter. There are no laws forbidding servants from marrying those they serve, nothing written down in one of Master Stradling's great books, to be consulted and accorded with when the elders think the time right. Nonetheless, in my memory there's been no such marriage. There are unwritten laws that all in the village know. The choice to marry is never given the servant. If a certain quality of man lays with one and wants his actions ignored by the village, well then so they shall be, whatever she may say. What man could be a full man here, marrying so, and all knowing the source of his children?

But of course servants and masters do lie together, and the most usual end is that of Jane Higgins, who has been gone this year and more. She left with a swelling belly, down the road, one half-moon night. She stole from her household when all were asleep, robbing some food to wrap in a blanket. She hurried through town and barking dogs, the blanket slung carelessly over one shoulder and perhaps a shred of dried beef or a half-loaf of bread slipping from the folds and onto the road. I wonder where she was going, and if she looked back. I imagine that in leaving at night she was half-hoping to be taken by spirits, or grima, or a vagabond. And it seems to me that I'll never be with Adam. And I tell myself, near convincingly, again that I'm only thinking on what might be and not on what I want.

Pluck some of that lavender, there, I say.

This here, how much, she says.

Three stalks for now. And I'll add some of this, I say quietly, holding up a sprig of marjoram. Not enough that she may taste it 'neath the lavender, I say.

And to what purpose will you do that, Anne says. She's hoping to hear of some plot, that I intend to loosen Mistress Jacobs' fundament to a painful point.

Ah, and you should learn more of herbery, I say, in my best imitation of Sarah's scolding. Field marjoram's a fine thing to please the outward senses.

I'm to believe you'd choose to please her outward senses.

A robin pecks the path. That seems a great insult, and I cast a stone to drive it away.

Well. It also helps to ease singing noises in the ears, I say. I'd say she has those, constant enough. Mayhap it'll ease them until she can hear the sounds of the world outside her own damned shrunken head.

My last words come harder than I had expected. We are still close to the house; I need speak with care. Of a sudden I feel Mistress Jacobs standing beside me, for all that she's yet shielded behind old wood. Now I feel that walls mean no more to her than to a witch's stoat. I lean to pluck more marjoram, and leave the lavender to Anne.

I don't think we've spoke yet of the headstones that were overturned? she says.

It's for this that I love her. She moves us away from this talk, without asking why. And it's the perfect thing, and time, to lift my spirits. This is how news passes, down narrow and trusted paths—open gossip is rare, unless you're a householder or his wife. For servants, choosing whom to speak to shows friendship, and trust.

And so we speak of petty mischief, until she must go. Then I finish my weeding, and linger. The garden's warm, full of tussled forces that helps hold the world where it had best be. The Lord has made these for us. There's steam in the bulb of a winter daffodil, something like coalsmoke in a bud of balm. One must know what airy blood was knitted into each plant during its birth in Eden. One must study what was borrowed for their making, and where there's a crossing of inner stuff. This leaf here, this was made for the floors of mighty forests, where bears rut up purple mushrooms, and some of that beasty strength has been carried in the seed. The Lord's plants hold to his order, and those who know can turn for aid to that leaf, or to this like a sticklebacked fish, or this that embraces the air lazily as a stretching owl. Here, where I seeded them, my plants grow splendid. I've not ordered the garden in the way of a straight road, as some are beginning to do, laying their plants in clean plots. I watch my herbs, listening to them for news of where they had best grow. The most of the time I let them be and only coax them stronger. I've been from the house too long, but I linger.

Chapter five

I Discharge a Cleansing Armament

There was a congregation to the north that held meeting out of doors, the whole of a long summer, while a new hall was built. They'd torn down the old meeting house and planned to build anew, on the same spot. They met beneath the trees. Summer rains dripped from the leaves, soaking their shoulders to remind them of the fault in one of their own. The old building was corrupted by one Kate McNeer, who snuck in, at an indecent hour, to give birth to her bastard son. She'd cunningly concealed her condition. It was fortunate that her unclean deed was discovered at the last, with her biting a rag to keep any near to hand from waking. James Tilman discovered her—he passed in search of his troublesome boy, and heard her kick a bench. Being found so by a man, her offense was compounded. Days after that discovery, she took to the road.

Borage to drive away melancholy, and to make men merry and glad. Over it pour water, distilled from yellow archangel, to liven the spirits. Weave in jasmine, against raw humors. Knot around a sinuous rose-root, that'll ease pain of the head. All together they're a balm to raise love. Not to set love. Mind that. I only want it raised and not set, now, I tell myself. There's time for the other later, if I choose.

Sarah wreathes the herbs for me, standing in the storage place beside her hearth. Her door's wide open to the sunny day. Though it's hot there's a smell of dried leaf that tells me autumn is nearing.

He should want you, now, she says. There's no cause to think there's a counter magic, anywhere about.

She's amused at herself, and sly. Today she's set all her stars on one cheek, the moon at her chin. It makes her look off-balance—stubbornly so.

Have you been countered of late, I say.

I have, she says.

She leans close.

My chickens, she whispers. I begged the dark man to make them stop laying. To give them a rest, I said, but in truth it was so I could roast the birds in clear conscience. And this now the best laying season ever! Eggs, eggs, eggs, all about the house. My magics countered, and worthless. Damn that witch to blackest hell!

She shakes her fists at the rafters, gives a little jump.

And when you're done with your mocking, I say. Is there a witch near, in truth?

No witch in this village, love.

How do you know that, for certain, I say.

My stoat should tell me if there was, she says, and winks. He'd tell me when he comes at night to suckle this wart 'side my nose.

Away with you, I say.

This is no magic we do here, she says. None do magic in the village, whatever good Master Stradling may call it.

I never said it was magic. I know the ways of herbs, I say.

You thought it, she says.

You think you know that, I say stubbornly. Well, I know what it is to want. Yes, you thought it, or wished it. Wouldn't you like to think I have that certain power, enough to teach you. But forcing earns you nothing—not in a household run by a woman who waits for a child. And magic's a forcing. I coax.

One old palm, on each of my cheeks. The pads 'neath her fingers rough as bark.

And you'll coax, too, she says.

Her hands slide slowly, sweaty, over my face. Almost drawing me toward the stars and moons set on her cheeks. Her eyes are fixed, bright, determined, and I can't tell how much she's joking.

You coax him close, she says. Never seek to command the world. Then you'll order it the better. Coax it. Coax him close.

Unwillingly I draw away, only a hair. Feeling it she lets me go at once, and laughs.

That's my labor, she says, studying what'll coax what. Where the Lord's put what good stuff to draw and bind. Place them together, the right stuff and hour, and that's right enough like magic. The world'll warp itself drawing to you, when you tempt its parts the right. I'm not fool enough to command the Lord. I stay accorded with the world He's made and given. I study His elements close.

She stops, considers.

'Course he made the witches, too, and their magic, she says. But I think he takes no pleasure in their rebellion. Would you?

I would not, I say. On her loose face the moon and stars are black as continents. In my head Adam whispers, quietly, insistent: Do you think her light minded?

I flip open the chapbook on her table. It's the one called *Mary, Jewess of London*. When I was younger I'd make tales to match what looked to be black bird-tracks. It seemed then that those tracks might one day widen, become a road. Now I know the pattern of this one full well. There will be youthful misadventure. Punishment. Defiance. In the end enlightenment, and conversion. You can see that last on the page with the woodcut of Jewess Mary lifting her eyes to heaven. On the first sheet she stands with a star at her throat, skin sallow, eyes on a dead dog lying with tongue on the cobbles. Around her wobble toothy merchants, fat landlords, sickly whores. Fiendish children.

There are other broadsides Sarah keeps hidden, in her poultice-cloth chest, under the mortar. There's one with a woodprint of our Lord on his cross, squeezing his own bulbous tit, sending milk to shower the happy crowd below. Their mouths are open, and put me in mind of sparrows. Not all writings accord with Master Stradling's sermons, though they are not so distant as he might think.

And what's the purpose of your stars and moon, I say.

Still I look to the page, that I may seem to speak absently; I run my fingers across a dog, a cart, and end by Jewess Mary's necklace.

Fashion of youth, she says. Wealth's no protection from the pox, but it makes for a finer way of blacking over the scars and these grew popular.

And why did you keep them after?

Well, it's not so easy to give everything up. I'll keep what I can. And are they not passing lovely?

I'm grateful for the herbs, I say. Have you anything for me to do? I'd thank you for them with some work, before I go.

You can sweep—after I clean my chimney. Let's clean it now?

I grin at that, knowing Sarah's notion of cleaning. Now she's like a little girl, fair bouncing at the thought. Probably she has waited some months between cleanings, thinking the ash cloud will be all the bigger, and the more fun.

The fire's put aside? I say.

This morning, she says, and nudges with her foot the pot where she's kept the coals—an earthenware cylinder, thin smoke drifting from the slits. Then she moves to hang cream-cloth, draping over her herbs. Now all's ready, she says. Hand me that musket, there.

The bore of the musket is big enough that her husband used it for a fowling piece. It's meant to be supported on a metal rod, but now she uses it only for cleaning. I heft it to where she squats beside the hearth with the other charges wrapped and ready, and laid out orderly on the stones. Sarah knows this had best go quickly, once begun. She dips the long match into the firepot until a yarn of acrid smoke says it's lit. On her back she worms into the cold, swept hearth. With the musket set firmly against the stone, the barrel stuck a good way up the flue, she touches match to pan.

Boom. I jump back—before I've touched ground Sarah's near disappeared under a cloud of smoke and ash. I cough, I laugh to break my back. Sarah is a quivering, choking, laughing pile of cinder.

You'll set it afire, I say when I can breathe.

You'd know enough to cut it away, she says as she brushes off her face and spits.

By that she means I would chop out the support poles on the side of the chimney away from the house, bringing the shaft crashing away, leaving the bonfire on the ground. A wise design, except that her neighbor Midge Thomas lives no more than eight feet distant. Her house would go up in an instant and no doubt toss flame straight back.

Hand me that charge, there, Sarah says. Brushing off her face has loosened her half moon, and it hangs by the tip, loose among her stars. She loads with motions she probably hopes and thinks look practiced. They look well enough to me. When she lays back again the moon flops onto her cheek. *Boom.* The room's full fogged. If not for the heat I'd think her roof had been torn free by a winter storm, her tables and bedstead all covered in a quick blizzard. Sarah stands and shakes like a wet dog. It's enlivened her, she's up and pretending to be all serious as she reloads, her movements snappy though she looks a scarecrow capped with dirty snow. The sulfur of black powder mingles with the old gray woodfire ash, as though this harsh new fire has woken the ghost of another. Sarah works busily over the muzzle of her musket. The light from the doorway hardens floating ash into a wall. It's a chore to see anything but the pace of Sarah's working. Outside there's the sound of hurrying footsteps, and shouting.

That'll be Midge Thomas. Just close that door, there, Sarah says, and I do, without looking out, so I'm not so rude as to slam it in Midge's face.

A knock on the door. Bang, bang, bang.

Who's there? Sarah calls.

You know that very well.

Midge! Sarah says. I can't ask you in, just now. You're well I hope?

She finishes loading, lays back down.

Midge cries that she was right fine until this morning, when Sarah set about her chimney again which is scarce better than attacking Midge's living outright. The Lord provides for her with the milk of her good Dawes goat. That's the Lord's provision, that's the workings of good Providence, and though the goat's a good fine goat she's a true sensitive one that Sarah has sent leaping the fence to the garden which is bothersome in itself, though Sarah can fix that well enough and Midge trusts she will...

Sarah pushes herself back into the hearth, leaving a streak like a snow-angel in the ash behind.

But now the milk'll all be sour for a time, Midge yells, and what am I to eat and drink with the milk all sour? The milk is my trade, the milk's my means of bread. Sarah? Sarah?

Midge is knocking. The musket's set. Bang, bang, bang. *Boom.*

Now I have a sure mind, and I have the coaxing plants. But my chances are so few, so few. For the next month I'm near always kept to the house while the grain seasons like steeping ale on the slope between village and forest.

And at night, I think that a small servant is no longer enough to warm my bed. I fight to hold still, until to keep from thrashing against Patience I think I must bite the sheets. What heat she brings, what we have from summer, only makes me feel more strongly the cold that is the lack of him. I've wreathed myself with borage, arch-angel, jasmine, rose-root. I must stop this thrashing or my wreath will full dissolve. I'd have it whole. I'd have it true, and robust, I'd breathe the good sweet and honest scent until it's rooted in the dust of my lungs. Then my breath will be enough to coax him near, laced with scents of hot promise.

Mel, Patience says, insistent.

I lay still and silent. The blankets have weight, are easily shaped. They turn atop me, dense and inconstant as clay. They're him. Patience, she's him. The blankets are a chest, legs, his yard. They're him. Patience is his impatient breath. I'm ready for his turn. He's here.

Chapter six

I Seize a Green Egg

Janice Healdstrong trapped her husband in consort with Timothy, a servant, Sarah tells me. Janice chose not to take her revenge on Timothy, reasoning (for she knew her husband's gentle ways in bed) that Timothy had suffered enough. Rather she came upon her husband in his sleep, severed his yard, and tossed it to the pigs. For that treason she was burned alive, two months after, which time was the soonest visit of a Justice to their town.

Harvest is the last time all will be in the fields together until Plough Monday ends winter. But before harvest can begin we need a choosing. It's always by decree, never by lot, and thus will likely annoy me. I stand by the path to the fields, holding a sickle, smelling dry leaves and tawny grain.

The Saints are a jubilant, ready army in torn brown skirts and mouse-chewed breeches. The towering clouds that threatened rain at first morning are disappearing over the eastern pastures. They yet shade the rising sun. The smallest girls carry burlap bags for gleaning; many of them are still young enough to be eager for the choosing of a queen.

Look at them. I remember when this was such an exciting thing, I say to Anne.

And now it's not? Anne says.

I'll wait for the choosing of the Maid, myself, I say. That's where a woman has a chance. They're all thinking it may be them, this season.

Adam stands with Daniel, and fat David Merchant. They laugh, shifting like horses feeling their strength. Always, before it starts, men think this work will go easily under the force of their arms and backs.

You'll take no more than your proper quarter of *my* wheat, Sarah shouts. She stands close by to Richard Hall, hands made fists on her hips, leaning close as though watching a wasp settle on the end of his nose. He smiles uncomfortably, hands half up. Those around them pretend not to watch him fade before her.

Anne motions down the road with a half-nod. Master Stradling is approaching. From the set of her jaw I think Anne may dream of being chosen herself, and I wonder if I've been too dour.

Well, and she may as well stop that. There's no point to such.

Master Stradling has a staff. With each step he thuds it to earth, as though he'll set it in the ground for a flag. Beneath the pale plane of a forehead his hat can never quite cover, his eyes stand out like blue wells. His jowls seem too broad for a man of his mid-age; in concert with his brow, they make him seem larger than he is. But for once he wears broad wings on the shoulders of his jerkin—under the assertiveness of the fashion he's somewhat eclipsed. There are bulges of rusty red above his tremulous knees, green hose on his calves. On his staff a small bell jingles beside a feather, and thin orange and yellow ribbons blow back in the breeze of his walking.

Adam watches him approach. He could as well be looking at blank paper. But from the deepening shadow of his scar I can see he's drawn in his cheek, and bites it, ever so slightly.

My girl, there, she'll have that staff, says Benjamen Smythe.

If you've paid him half as much for the honor as I think you'd be willing to, I've no doubt you're right, says William Dover.

Shush, says his wife. That's not a proper matter for a joke. John Stradling'd take no money.

It was meant in fun, Dover says.

No fun, she says. Once such a thing's said there's those as'll believe it, no matter its truth.

Very well, then. Good luck to you and your girl, he says to Smythe. But I think there's been no check on his thoughts.

Master Stradling reaches the outskirts of the crowd; the steady talk diminishes to breeze. He thumps his staff with a jingle, lifts his chin appraisingly toward this year's harvest. Since earliest memory, the rise where all our grain is grown has been divided into hundreds of thin plots. At each season's start the Saints divide and apportion the strips between the husbandmen, with a few plots left behind for widows. This year John Jacobs was given three pieces by the woods, one in the center, two nearest the orchard. The combination changes each planting season; it's meant to be fair, and weighted by the size of a household.

Of course there are disputes. This plot receives an abundance of sun; that one less, but, being toward the river, the watering of it will be immeasurable easier; this one was wounded by three seasons of poor tending by a drunkard, and will demand the new holder be uncommon diligent in the ordering of his cow dung. Every man argues his preference, and each has his own manner of work. Though the plots are marked by thin bulwarks, scarcely more than ankle high, this late in the season the practice of each husbandman's marked them as though they were splashed with watered paint. The grain is over-dry, or too fully soaked, or perfect; it was early neglected, or else tended from the first as with a lady's comb. The slope's a spilled basket of ragwork, ready to be picked over by the quickly blushing fingers of the woods that crown the hill.

How much will the next season cost us? The nameless voice sounds meant for a jest, but wrenches all into a moment of quiet.

For now all understand the import of landlord George Pollack's death. He lived in a distant, southern city, but there was an understanding between him and our congregation on matters of rent, and of religion, which he cared not at all about so long as he was paid. He cared not at all that our congregation was unlawful, and never swore fealty to the church of the crown. But now his son's our master. All feel naked. None here know the son's intent. If he wishes it, soldiers or masterless men may come to enclose our lands; if he wishes it, all here may be cast to prisons, their houses seized, their families split. Burning could provide no better warning to those who would worship in like fashion.

It begins, again, Master Stradling says loudly, quickly. May it be a good one.

He holds the staff by the lower end, stretches it over us. It swings slowly back and forth, a sapling in high wind, its bells softly jingling. Slowly, Master Stradling lowers it to hover over Margaret's head. She hesitates until a smile breaks on his face, a smile determined and awkward as a robin's first flight. Then Margaret flushes, and takes the staff.

Girls crowd around her but now she's intent on her task—she brushes through and strides confidently up the path toward the fields, bell jingling with every second step.

With her as the guide of the girls for this week, I know I'll never hold a sickle. The harvesting is done by men, and women deemed strong enough to swing the blade, and now Margaret will choose the latter. No doubt I'll glean, picking grain for the general store that guards the old and ill against hunger. All this week I'll follow the sickles, working beside girls so young and small they scarce need to stoop. I'll bend, pain clambering up my backbone like a rat.

But if I must do this work, there's nothing that can lead me to do it perfect. I'll leave a stalk, here and there, for the birds. That will do no man any harm, and the jays'll thank me for it.

Five days and a thumb of blisters later the fields are cropped. The grain waits in the barn for threshing. We've cut and bound the wheat much as we did the hay, although the long wheat grass is thick, rich with seed. The gleaning's been done well, almost better than I'd choose, only a few stray stalks left to be taken by crow and thrush. But some straw has been cut and spread in a thick blanket, as big around as ten wagon-beds, midway up the rise. The time for the second choosing is nearly here—and this second will not be decided by a lone man.

The sun is hours past crest; at last there's only one more swath of grain, one more swing of the sickle. Fallen deadwood is stacked in heaps along the northern edge of the fields. The fires are always in the same place, for they bake the clay in the earth hard, uncommon unbreakable—in planting time it may halt plows and harrows.

Some Saints have stayed out of the fields to slaughter chickens and an old bull, to roast and bake in faith of spring. But now all return, and gather, close beside the last wheat that stands like a wicker man.

Girls in, girls all in, says Master Stradling. He means for us to stand bunched together, within the three sides of an open square formed by Saint men. He stands burn-faced across an expanse of cut wheat and freshly naked earth bulwarks. In his left hand's a russet sack, tied with ribbon and with blue-and-green dyed feathers stuck all about. He smiles broadly—but even from down-slope I think I spy in it the old bird's flutter. Waves of straw look to lap his feet.

We're old for this, I whisper.

I thought this was the one you liked, Anne whispers.

And it is. I giggle, there's no fighting the old pleasure I take in it. But underneath that pleasure there's naught but pure want, like a beetle under a mossy log. *I'll have the egg.*

Master Stradling surveys us, then intones the words he uses every year: Green as wheat before gleaning, pressed in under white upon white. Girls all in, and come for it!

The sack lofts, a confused owl. It lands, heavily, and at that signal we're up like a hail of doves.

Sarah's laugh brays over the rest. I'm near to the front, far ahead of the younger girls, but I stumble—drop to my knees, crawl forward, and root through the straw. Already girls are finding eggs. But all the eggs they have are white, nothing's yet decided, and I fight my way close in. Wrestling for a place, an elbow in my eye, heavy clothes pressing me all around. A foot on my hand pushes it down against jabbing haycuttings and the sharp quill of a green feather fallen from Stradling's sack.

I muddle through the hay, desperate to find the hidden gem—the hope in winter, the laugh in sorrow. But none of the eggs have been boiled. I must force some care in my search. Already the found white eggs are flying, smashing against backs, the year's battle breaking out even before we're done. I shuffle my hands through the straw, grab an egg with each hand, and force my way from the crowd without waiting to see what I clutch. When I'm well away I look at last. One egg is white, the other green—dyed with Sarah's best woad and weld green as first buds cracking winter clays.

I stand, and shout. It feels so good to shout. But as the village turns to me I feel a loss, surely as I'd feel garments torn from my back. It's not me they turn to, and not me that shouts. It's the harvest maid, borrowing my body for this season, and it could be anyone, but oh, I'm glad it's me! I whoop again and loft the egg, a doused star against the swirled sky. When it comes to earth it breaks, green and yolk. The villagers have moved back from its flight but when it falls and splits they move back in, over it, and past. Boots and flatshoes crush wet shell.

They rush in on me, on the maid, and I cannot pick out faces; there is only the whole group of them coming in fast. They rush and push, almost carry me down the slope, the press of them near holding me off the earth. A dozen hands on me, arms around, elbows crushing my ribs. Children run ahead, to a solid storehouse set between fields and the first houses. They swing the door wide as the crowd approaches, dragging me. The door slams shut. I'm alone with their fading laughter; they return to the stripped fields.

It's quiet. After the clamor, the paltry remnant of talk and laughter trickling into the storehouse seems only to brace the general hush. I shake my head, look about. The storehouse is built on two levels, with a ladder leading up to a loft that's filled with bins of wheat and barley. In the aisle between the ground bins, a candle burns in an orange dish. Beside it, a suit of man's clothes lies neatly folded on the floor. I take a deep breath and strip down to my lower shift, then pull it off. I'm naked but for Sarah's garland—alone amid the year's grain. I think all minds are on me. What would they do if I refused to dress, I wonder with a grin. Imagine their faces if they came on me like this—naked, and draped in blossoms.

But I do dress. Though I try to move quickly, it takes some time. I've seen these clothes all my life and know the mending of them well, but have never put them on myself, not even for a fitting. Nothing like them—even the unsexed clothes of children are more like a woman's dress than a man's. Men are made, Sarah's said. Women just are.

Someone's beating a cowbell. There's a tentative drumbeat. I pull on hose, then trunkhose that bulge like baggy, yellow-and-red striped onions. A ridiculous, oversized purple codpiece; a doublet. Everything's loose. They've left me the clothes of a big man. Last year Abigail Williams took the egg, came from the storehouse with garments hanging dead around.

Dressing done, I much wish I had a mirror. I take off my coif. My hair falls in rivulets, like rain from a thatch roof. There's a dumpy worker's cap I pull over, though I still let the tresses hang loose. Then I wait.

They give me plenty of time, and as the minutes pass my stomach clutches. Again I hear the distant cowbell, and now others join it. Finally there's the approaching trod of oxen, and the shuffle of feet. All stops. A brief hush, marred by barely held laughter. Then the doors burst open and they all rush in, a flood. Their hands on me are clamps.

They carry me to the waiting oxcart. The oxen seem indifferent to the rush and the noise and then the cart's moving, led by a boy who looks back at me and grins. I don't remember his name. One of Butler's sons? This rare energy's all about me but I'm above it all, and at its heart.

The cart bumps over earth balks, the oxen tramp up dust. Open barrels of ale stand above heaped deadfall aside the forest. Villagers drink from great wooden bowls passed freely from the barrels. A drunk man points at me, shouts without sense. The Saints yell, they bang on cowbells, tambers, little drums. Benjy Butler tries to stand on his hands—but Susan Porter leans, and with her head to his stomach bumps him to the ground. I stand in the front of the cart, bending over to support myself on the driver's seat, and wave with one hand. Someone hands me a drover's staff. I plant it on the floor of the cart to hold me up. The cart's all surrounded. Now Master Stradling leads the oxen. The bells are everywhere, clank and clang.

The harvester stands by the last of the wheat, carrying a sickle, wearing skirts and a bodice stuffed with straw. The feathers from the signal-bag are all through his hair—it seems uncommon long. Then I see it's a horsetail wig that hangs to his waist. That horsehair near obscures his face, and the thin scar that runs from his chin to beside his eye. I catch my breath.

My cart rolls up beside. The harvester raises the sickle high. Pauses. He swings as though to carve the earth. The sheaf's cut cleanly, and a shout goes up. I'm surprised at my relief—Adam is awkward, but not so clumsy that he might fail to cut three handwidths of grain.

He gathers the wheat into a truss and gives it me, the last truss of all the year's work. I step into the back of the cart, bind it with red ribbon. The harvester climbs into the cart; we sit at the front, the ribboned truss between. Then we smile at each other, as the drover and Master Stradling begin turning the oxcart in a wide circle toward the storehouse.

Light from the deadfall bonfires flashes against the overhang of the forest and the loomscrap thicket below. Fresh-killed beef blackens on sharpened sticks and leaves rusty blood on the roof of the mouth. It's washed away by cider pressed from windfallen apples. There's perry, and strong ales. Around the fire pipes lilt, and dusty strings thrum themselves clean. Patience runs by in a race. Behind her arrows rush for a firelit target. It's made up like a royal warden, the kind who forbids right religion and the hunting of deer. Master Stradling's arrow strikes the yellow, cut-felt heart. He has always been a fine archer. But he laughs too loudly at his victory, and the competition turns sourly away.

I swig beer from a wooden bowl and pass it to Anne, but I've drunk too much and as she takes it I cough. Ale dribbles down onto my chest.

If you were a man I'd have no difficulty taking you now, she says.

I am not at all drunk, I say with mock pride, and stride away. After a few steps I collapse in a stumble I hope looks drunken, and laugh. But as I stand from the fall I see Adam. He stands upslope, out of the first light, watching his father collect small coins.

No better time, Anne says.

Hmm. I dip the great bowl full of beer, lean to her, kiss her on the neck like I'm her man. Then I saunter up the rise, undecided between playing at filling my man's clothes and walking in a way I think will draw him.

Harvester, I call from a house length away. Cutting's thirsty work, I'd think.

It was a surprise, seeing you, he says as I near.

Seeing me? You should see yourself, I say. When I reach him I hand him the bowl. I'm confident, full of beer, cider, abandonment. Everything is upside-down. Everything right.

He looks himself over, grins, and drinks. I want to hold his gaze, but something makes me look downslope toward the dancers. They leap in the flickering firelight to the strains of pipes, their faces glistening with sweat. They've none of the ordered salutes and side-retreats of practiced market dancers. Caper after leaping caper, disorderly as flame.

Down there? he says.

I nod. We watch at the edge of the flickering light, where the fire fades into shadow. The outermost circle. Fire, dancers, us. Our arms touch, blown branches clashing. It seems a momentous thing.

Others might see this. They will—and might see me rejected. But now I can know, and I think that I have to know. I can't walk away from this fire and lie in my bed, next to Patience, waiting and wondering and waiting and wondering. I lean in to him, then closer. Adam smiles, looking over his shoulder.

I'll to the woods, he says, and he's gone away from me. I'll wait, and follow. And, after the light has sunk from his shoulders, I do. I walk through darkness compressed, made weighty by my sudden loss of firelight, my quick turn from the flame. I feel my way along a path

I'm sure he's taken, somehow certain as though on a trail hammered from brush. And when I come to the edge of the woods, far from the fires, he is there waiting, my certainty proved sound.

He grips me tightly. He kisses me, and I him. Then I can scarce breathe, my lips are so crushed against my teeth. But I press forward, against his. We're away from the bonfires, the music and laughter coming to us distantly as through water. The far clanking of cowbells, the wistfulness of dry leaf. Adam tastes of his own good self. We're across the field where the straw is left to dry in loose rapes. I clutch him, tumble onto it. It smells dry, and sweet.

His clothes are those I know, mine are his. I kiss him, and open what I can, tearing past layer after layer. We're kept so fully wrapped. I feel myself near shedding, for he is quick with these men's garments as I am with his skirts. Garments bunch on our bodies and suddenly we're open to each other—at last, also so quickly.

I pull him onto me, the heat this time altogether different. I've been told since birth that woman is man inverted, incomplete, and as we come together I might believe it; through the slip and shock it's right, and us whole. He shudders, my chin against his neck. And I look up through sparks and smoke that drift from the harvest fires, wrested between a moan and a laugh for stars that shine so starkly, and clear.

Chapter seven

I Laugh, and Think
Ice Warm

This wondrous winter—this fine, white time! This good, honest season.

This winter's come sooner, and stronger, than I'm used. The first flakes chased the last leaf down to the forest floor, ice-white baby butterflies after an old, orange mother. Soon they grew to a swarm; since then the snow has lain thick, even during sometime warmings. We've taken to ladders, and raked it from our roofs in puffy, blustering clumps. Dry old Josiah Flynt stood direct on the thatch, shoveling, and the fall he took would have snapped his bones if not for what he'd already mounded below. The snow lies in banks beside the iced road, so deep that were I younger I'd be carving out a cave, as Patience does when she can rush through her work at the chicken house. When she returns, smiling, to the fire where I mend, pads of snow pressed into the folds of her clothes, I remember the peculiar warmth of a snow cave, how under my breath the walls would turn slick ice.

Master Stradling would not pray for good harvest—we must not, in arrogance, ask for aid we never deserved—what he did was only speak his hopes aloud. If we do merit help then it'll be ours, ask for it or no. But prayer or casual wish, his words have fallen true. The harvest was good enough that none need fear hunger, and only the very poorest need pick the gleanings. Though early, the snow did come late enough that all fruit and corn was brought in. Now we need only hope that an early start means an early end. If it does, all is perfect.

But the Saints think the snow a plague. They tread steaming about the village when they must, snow crimping in their boots, melting about their toes, making Sunday meeting a damnable chore, adding to labor to no good productive purpose. There are slushy yellow holes in the dooryards where they toss their chamberpots. But this year, though the snow makes our roof sigh and Enry giggle, heaping in honeycombed walls about the road, for Adam and me the blinding white seems that of a binding cloth.

We meet in the storage house, coming together on the same floor where I found the clothes for our first meeting. We meet in the stables, on the far side of a heap of hay one can't see past without a clumsy climb. I clutch him in the smell of grain left on the stem until spring threshing; I seize him amid the musk of cattle.

Once we met at the mill above the blank hayfield. Daniel might look a puppy, but he has more strength to hold back his words than I should have credited. And more, he fetched Adam the key for the mill's gaped iron lock, secreting it from the hook where his father hangs it, replacing it with another that should never be thought different at first glance.

The body of the mill's a shed, passing small, balanced atop a post chin-high from the ground. The mill-post's pegged straight in to an old mound we call Mistress Rachel's Tit. When the mill's working, Master Williams' hunched legs frame the iron-bound stones, like a dream of great wheels turning on needles too delicate to hold them in course. The mill was cold and breezy, not sealed proper for winter habitants, the mended, folded sails all tucked away. It was a close space beside the millstone housing and we only shivered, and talked, and looked for false corners and robber's chutes, means by which the miller might steal his bit of each grinding—but if they are there, they're done cunningly.

Adam has told me gossip: that the new landlord is known to be no saint, or Saint, neither. He told me that his father fears that the terms of our rents are now subject to the will of a questionable man. Master Stradling watches the congregation closely, and prays we may hold true to our covenant. Of course it's little I've not heard from others. But as Adam talked I could trace his scar with my thumb, like I was blotting ink.

Fondly, absently, I told him of the broken pot-piece that melted from Mistress Rachel's Tit after a rain. It was etched in with stamens and curlicues. I think the mound was, years ago, a grima place. What looks a dish to me would have been for them a tremendous kettle for their draughts. I've kept it, for Sarah says it might serve as the heart of a shielding charm against them.

When we left the mill, Adam walked ahead: we stayed within the single set of prints we'd made in our approach.

Of course we can never meet so much as I'd want. Already it's a wonder that none have seen us coming variously to these places, and makes me feel our blessedness the more. Always I wait to be with him. The times we're together are like a roasted root, wrapped in cloth to warm my hands—I may cling to the memory of our last meeting, my hope of our next. When Master Jacobs curses me for failing to lay dense manure at the base of the apple man, as though I could do such with the weather so, I nod with grim mouth. Yet inside I smile, and am far from his house. Adam's the lone story of my season.

But in truth we need hurry, as though to douse a rising fire. There is scarce ever time to talk, as in the mill—to take each other in a clutch. I strive to set him in my body's mind before we again part, lips giving final words and a kiss as a door swings into the snow, then shuts against the shine. I know from the mill and like instances that if we had more time he would hear me. He would listen. And I want him always, and for this time I am happy enough with the prayers I give to his neck and shoulders—yes, Lord, God. Being with him is the finest prayer I know.

We cannot ask for gifts. What arrogance, to ask for gifts from God. We can only repent, or offer our thanks, and now I give Him thanks as never before in all the gray times of my life. He has given us this solid wall of winter. Behind it Adam lifts me, I never thought it so but a man may lift a woman's soul with his own. Almost I think there some truth to what is said, that a woman's spirit needs completing from without. A man of full Grace may fill hers, and lift hers. I thank Adam—and I thank Him.

Then Master Stradling leaves for London. He takes his dappled mare, a black cloak slung beneath his nose and a hat pulled down to his eyes, wrapped tightly as a swaddled babe. There have been occasional warm days, and on them wagons passing carved various ruts in the slush. Now those ruts are frozen, and the mare picks her way over a road turned a briefly numb, muddy river. Master Stradling is off to London, to take meeting with our new landlord. And when his black cloak vanishes behind the glassed limbs of the southern orchard, his great house is only Adam's.

Of course we have no more time than before. The strictures are all on me; that I return swiftly to work. But the wondrous luxury, of taking him in a bed! It's true I never saw until now how much pleasure I had from the most fearful expectation of another girl coming upon us, in hay or straw. But much is gained from laying with him in his own, private bedstead, that has been always his alone. There, we're how we might be. Even the mare is gone from where she's kept stabled below his loft. It's quiet, without even the threat of an opening door. Once a man does knock. Then we giggle, never stopping, laughing as though there's a chance he might enter without invitation. Adam gives himself to me. From want for him I take his scarred skin between my teeth.

Then, after each time, each the snapping of an eye, and a hundred years, and perhaps the half of an hour, I'm back to the Jacobs' close, smoky house—flushed, and clutching an excuse. The excuses make Master Jacobs impatient with his neighbors. I'm the one he shouts at, but he holds most Saints in small regard, and believes me. It's only that he must shout at something. He sharpens his beard, and with quickened, sulky casts spreads moldy seed to dry.

The whimpers from the closeroom are quieter. It's but a matter of weeks now until the babe should come. Both the Jacobs can feel the time loom; both think of their late losses. There is here a heavy air, as of illness. It seizes Patience. Once as we dry malt over the killframe she turns an eager face and asks if I don't feel anxious over what's coming. Perhaps I should, I say. I do not.

That night I look for a long time at the darkness where Patience's face must be, and for a while it seems that there is no great difference between that dark and what I know of her. What affection I have for her is all tied to this place I may abandon. For so long as I am kept in this house, I'll defend her as I may. And if I could leave and take her with me, I would. But if I could leave this house, and by leaving doom her to remain…though striving to see her, I think I must look to myself.

I hear Enry through the door. He sings, his own soft song.

Chapter eight

We Trudge to the Monk Spring

T here is but one blight on this time; I've not spoken to Sarah for weeks. After one of our lessons, when the other girls were gone and I was helping her stack and tie her chapbooks, I asked her (foolish, foolish!) how a woman may dodge taking child. It was one of many questions about herbery, and I thought I spoke casual. But what's casual, to a crooked woman who wants news? Now she thinks the success of her own coaxing charm might signal the wreck of my life. I wonder if she hadn't had such faith in her own crafts—or else believed I'd be satisfied with his wanting me, and never take him once I could. She worked herself to a froth about it, shuffling about her house, fists pumping at the rafters, shouting as though to warn me about a careening horse.

If I find myself with child and I'll not name him, she told me, I'd best not think her my friend. I know what she means—she does the same with all in like condition. In the worst of labor, when tearing pain's everywhere and eyes are blurred, aswim in saltless sweat, when breathing's a backward scream, Sarah will lean in, and whisper, gently: Why do you fight so for him. He should be here for you, for the child you bear. A name, a name. One word, from all these screams he's given you. One word, and he'll share—*this*…

And then the public whipping, and the marriage. Seeing my face, Sarah asked how many of them would marry, unforced. And then how would their children find meat, beyond mean bread? But what I thought on was skin sagging around aged eyes, and lips, locked like ramps for chapbook siege engines, and blows taken behind closed doors, all the wages of an unhappy marriage. I was silent. At last Sarah gave me a nameless root to simmer and drink, to scour me, should the need come. But I left angry, and left her so.

Since then, at lesson time I've chosen Adam's house over hers. I've not felt so distant from Sarah since I asked her about the tavern fire, and she would say only that she did not go, nor did her Henry, nor did she know any else of who was killed and who lived. She had as well have said that I'd best keep in the present—as much the fire ate the tavern, the fire's been ate by time. I thought there was more Sarah could have told me. But I've never asked her since. Now I feel her house lost me, at least for a while.

Thus when Mistress Jacobs takes to cramping, it's Patience that runs to Sarah for the proper remedy. She returns with the word that the cure needs water from the old monk spring, that even coldest winter can't make freeze entire. Sarah has said she doesn't think there a sprite in the spring, or anything so useful in that water alone—it's not even so good for beer, valley clays making the river water better for that. But there's something about it that strengthens herbs left to steep in jugs overnight; strengthens them until they become something different altogether. So, after telling Adam I'll not see him that day, I fetch Anne. She escapes her house, leaving children's quarrels behind like burrs in a dropped blouse. Together we start the long walk through the woods.

There's a long neck of forest betwixt us and the monastery ruins. We could walk around it, through the fields and then the marshy wastes where we take reeds, but that would take most of the day and it's already late morning when we climb to the forest. Sun sparkles on ice glazing the high oak branches that overhang the fields. Beneath them the thorn is thickest, where the sun's pulled each plant up into a summer hood that thins in winter like a drying pile of nets. We sidle through the thorns and bare vines, and I'm true relieved when we're inside—the shade of the trees overhead keeps the floor sparse after that first daunting barrier. But always I hold a leather bag, full of sidley root and that old piece of grima pot, a charm against what runs free in these woods.

The path's not been walked since last snow, so it's a clean white ribbon draped between whips that stretch, black and ice-crusted, from the forest floor. All the great limbs blown down by autumn winds were chopped and dragged out by the end of that season, leaving only saplings. It's a warm day, and along with the smell of wet wood there's the crackle of ice flaking from high branches to flick holes in the snow.

So far from the houses, we need not restrain ourselves. In summer this is where the village pigs run. In winter, all's asleep but the nightmare, who oft drags her ragged claws in thin trails toward town. But we fear her only at night and now Anne complains about common dreads—her master Isaac, and her mistress, Judith, and their daughter Fight-the-Good-Fight-of Faith Rowe. Fight-Faith's a sallow girl, with stringy hair and a rat's face, well into marriageable age and true desperate about it. She thinks an ordered household will improve her prospects, and of course thinks it better to command Anne than to order it herself. She's jealous of Anne and Benjy Butler—most of all of Benjy's visible want.

It's not easy for Anne. But I've heard it many times, and don't want to today. Thinking of my own household, I ask what it was like in theirs, after the twins died. For weeks Mistress Rowe spoke not a word, until Isaac told her they had eight other children and she should be thankful, and show it. He said it at supper, before the children and the servants, and she soon started speaking. Then Anne's back to complaints about Mistress Rowe. I mostly stop listening.

We're near to the coppices. These trees were cut six feet up, and the tall stumps send up dozens of sprouting poles that may be used for thatch-binding, or chimney-weave, or handles for any tool. In the snow, the coppices look foreign as fairy trees. They've no thick crown of leaves, so no shade restrains the brush challenging the trunks. I peer in, looking for a rabbit or other hiding thing I can throw snow at. But then I hear crunching steps behind me, there are arms around my waist, and I'm swung into the air amid Adam's laugh.

I thought I might catch you if I ran through the neck, he says into my ear. I turn, and kiss him, and feel the leavings of snow on his shoulders where he's pushed past branches.

What's this? he says, feeling the bag that holds my ripe charm.

It's what you should have brought, before running through this place, I say.

Catch us. We could have gone another way.

Is there another one? he says, seeming rightly surprised, and slides an arm around my waist.

Well, there's not, she says, but it's unlikely you'd know it if there were. How much time have you spent laboring, in the forest?

I take his hands in mine and step back to draw him. Come. I'm pleased you're here, I say, and we continue on, Adam and I side-by-side behind Anne. With each step she kicks snow from her shoes, as though a small dog nips at her heels. A breeze blows flakes of ice from above. She shakes them from her head.

In truth, have you spent so much time in the woods? Adam asks. He's heard the sour tone to Anne's voice, like a drop of spring-wort in beer.

In early youth, she says.

We were like little weasels, I say. We'd look for salamanders. Under stones, and logs too rotten to be dragged out to good purpose.

What's a salamander like, he says.

It's a kind of in-between thing, I say. I'm right surprised at his ignorance, and there's no embarrassment to it—he seems only to want to know, and to make idle talk.

Part snake, part fish, Anne says. When you hold one, its skin leaks water in and out. They're born of the mulch like frogs in river mud, or maggots in old meat.

We'd look for toads, I say.

We'd split their heads with a knife, and look for a jewel within, says Anne. Ah, those were terrible days for the toads. Likely that they still speak of them as we do of the Flood, or the fires of Sodom.

What would you have done with the jewel, had you found it? Adam says.

Who knows? We were small, I say. Kept it, likely. I'd have kept it the half of the week, she the other.

And we tried growing rocks, Anne says.

Rocks.

Silver scaling. Mica, I say. On the back of a stone. We thought it a witch's moss that'd grow back thicker, if we took out small patches. I imagined it'd scale the rock in plates. But when we came back there was only the gray holes we'd picked, still ringed in silver.

We never feared to be here, then, Anne says. Oh we were young.

Have you heard what happened to Joseph Butler at the monk spring, I say to Adam. He shakes his head. Butler went to the spring when there was something amiss with his wife's mouth, I say. There was a bluish sort of fuzz massing betwixt her teeth. They tried putting three pink stones 'neath their bedstead.

And burying her usual spoon in a jar filled with piss, says Anne. Beside the one with piss and needles meant to keep cunning men from their threshold. I had that from Benjy.

But still the fuzz took on a greenish tinge, more Gooseturd than Lincoln, I say. After that Butler went to the spring promptly, too near to dusk for safety. When he finished filling his jug and turned to the woods something growled behind. A horrid noise, like brass sobbing. And there it crouched in the spring basin, hunched with black hair falling to the water, and it grinning.

Quite the sight, it must have been, Anne says.

And I think to myself that she's right. The monk spring's not hot, but it pulses through stone veins that are warm enough to keep it flowing in winter. It trickles from a rock crack into a mossy basin. That basin's carved for a skull. In winter, snow rims the open braincase, and the water grows a skin on the side furthest from the flow. Years ago there was a real skull there, and a flat rock with water that gleamed over all. After the skull vanished, the monks carved a death's head, with hearts for eyes, into the side of the stone. They scooped out the top for a basin. They had wanted a new skull but it had to be one from the Rilley family, and they were dead; buried, jumbled and indiscriminate, in the churchyard.

I think of the spring filled with black, hostile hair. I tell Adam that once Joseph Butler was into the woods, he turned and ran, the thumps of the thing bounding behind. All he could think was to try for flowing water, and he made right for the bridge. It hung close behind as though tied to his boot, but when he crossed that water it vanished yelling.

Stories, Adam says. Butler's a flighty man.

Doesn't mean he's a liar, Anne says.

No. But he'd have passed right through the village, and so been seen, says Adam. Do you smell burning?

For a moment I think that he's only trying to turn our talk. He used to do so when uncomfortable, before I knew him well. I'm annoyed to think it's a habit he falls into when others are about. But then I smell it as well—a sultry smoke, heavy with steam.

Anne stops and turns to us. The spring's no great way ahead, now, she says. Who would be there in hard winter?

And why burn a fire there, Adam says. Why stay so long, if one need go at all.

Well, it's quiet there among the old buildings, I tell him. Anne smiles nervously. It's true we've stayed there longer than we ought, at times, but only with larger groups sent to the wastes to gather aromatic bark. We would never have built a fire, lest it wake something we'd rather have sleep. And that was before we had heard Butler's tale, which is widely known even if Adam never heard it. Things live at the monastery that only a grima would willfully wake.

Let's not go, I say on sudden impulse. Let's go back home. She'll never know the difference between spring water and snowmelt.

But that won't cure her, Adam says.

I'd as soon let her cramp for a day and I look at him closely, searching for signs he's joking. But I find none; his face is serious, almost earnest, determined to go on. I never meant you need spend more time in the woods, I want to tell him. And is it not fine, that I know more about this place than you? But I say nothing. When he crouches against being seen and heads for the spring, I'm only a moment behind him, and Anne less than that behind me.

The spring is on the far side of a hillock that blocks our view of the monastery. Now I can see the smoke drifting like damp paper over the hump and through the wintered trees. As we sneak around I see what's left of the tumbling, twig-bearded stone walls. Some have summer-beams that have rotted well away, except for final decaying protrusions like lopped wrists.

Even when it was built, the central church here was at heart a dream, foolishly hopeful. The monks built it even as their sister churches moldered in heaps. The English Church did do the sainted faith that single service, destroying the homes and practices of those loyal to Rome. Now the walls are a cairn.

But tawny cloths stretch tightly between the best of what stone walls yet stand. There's life in the place. A fire burns, steaming, beside what was—what, I wonder? The buttery? A dairy for the goats they'd have run on the wastes, or a smokehouse for pigs they'd forage in the woods? Adam's hand warns us to silence, briskly, as though he thinks us likely to sing. A man squats beside the fire.

He's bearded, his face weary and cruelly used. Long hair spills from under a tight round hat. His work clothes are torn, rimmed with fur. I see deer pelt and rabbit stitched to patch the older cloth, and imagine him running the animals down, savaging them, taking their skins. He might have been birthed from woodland loam. The stitching is clumsy, hanging in loose loops. But when he wipes his forehead his gloves look to be of fine leather, better than anything I've ever owned. And beneath frayed trouser cuffs, snowmelt beads on new boots.

Anne's hands on my back are like the pads of a cat about to spring. I reach for Adam, to pull him back and whisper that this is no place for us. Before I touch him he stands and walks for the man. Well met, he says.

The man starts, but he's not truly surprised. Aye. Well met, he says, and stands, a mule resigned to returning to work.

Now Adam seems not to know what to do. There's a bit of me that admires his willingness to stand. There's a bit more that's angry that he has so much less to fear from this man than me. But I tell myself that I could do this man right injury, if it came to that. And the difference isn't Adam's fault in any case.

Adam is silent, as though his merely being there might make the man flee, or force him to declare his purpose. Of course he does neither. And now another man stands from beside the fire. Before, Adam's shoulder blocked him from my sight. This one's skinny, wearing the same good leather and poor stitched cloth. His orange beard's an intent hue that must be dye, cloaking a true, aged gray.

There is a common bearing in these men. Their manner speaks of a belief that they have right and cause to be on this ground. There is in them such effrontery that I long for a pole to beat them back down the road. They hold themselves with the air of householders, who should rightly be greeted first by an arriving guest. There is no good end to speaking to them, I think. They should only be driven out.

My name is Adam Stradling.

Mine is Kelly, the first man says.

Mine, Merchant, says the one with the orange beard.

Where are you bound to, Adam says.

Kelly spits, as though clearing his throat. Merchant holds a half-smile. He was proud enough to dye his beard, but now I see he recently tried to shave. His whiskers are scarce more than a finger's width long, and in places patchy. If he was full shaved he'd look still thinner.

You are welcome to hold your winter camp here, I would think, says Adam. Of course I am not one with power to say.

Aye, this camp'll hold us 'till the ground be soft enough to set new posts, Merchant says. His eyes're black beetles.

These lands are tended by a full town of husbandmen, Adam says. They hold them legally, as waste commons, and have through their generations.

Merchant bends and picks up a hoe. He leans on it, easily, as though he's finished pulling a season's carrots.

You're right young, to be the one we speak to of this, Kelly says.

So if any ask about it, you tell them we're not uninvited. You're the ones that oughtn't to be here, you and your women as think they're hiding. Shit. He waves his hand disgustedly, shakes his shoulders as though to turn away.

At that I stand, brushing my skirts to keep them straight and clean of any snow. A half-dozen more men work at the far side of the buildings, where the wastes begin, and beside them a brace of steaming oxen. It's frightening to declare myself this way, but in truth I only wish I'd stood sooner. I squeeze my charm, and wonder whether it has heft enough to hurt a man if hurled with force.

Fine women, says Kelly. Well met, my ladies.

Merchant did not try to shave. The whiskers grow around skin that was marred intentional. It is something like a D.

These lands are rented, full and legal, from George Pollack the Younger, in London, Adam says. What we pay him includes waste rights, and a surety that those wastes will remain uninhabited.

George Pollack the Younger? Well then ask him what he thinks of our being here.

At his words the ground might shake—it should so do. For though these men have tramped and fled about the country all their lives, they know something of our home that we do not. They know of how its destiny is molded in far cities, by landlords and their whims; they come with knowledge like a weapon.

At that Adam pauses for what seems a long time. And will asking him profit us? he says. He's mostly talking to himself.

There are great barrels on the carts, likely of food and beer. The carts are the heads of arrows; their tracks, shafts.

I was not hiding by choice, I say. I'd never be afraid of you and yours.

You'd not have to be, lady, Merchant says. Do you think us low as dogs?

Saying it seems to make him think that I do. And I do. Rage churns his face like a rabbit once I saw an owl take. Low as dogs, Merchant says. He looks down to his side, at the fire, shifting the rake as though to work it into the snowy ground. I want to fight this man.

That stands for deserter, does it not, I say.

Merchant stares at me with disbelief, then raises his head to the trees and shrieks, as he must have when taking that brand. It filters through the trees, dies, and he will not yet look at me again. Those loading the wagon are stone frozen. On the hoe handle glove-leather tightens, shines. I want to take Merchant's head in my hands, grinding my fingers, making mine own mark.

We'll away, Adam says abruptly.

A fine thought, says Kelly. And afore Ridley comes. God be with you, then. He turns, squats at the fire, tosses a branch to it. He neglected to knock off the snow and there's soon a goodly steam about both the men, like rude fingers, like rotten lace. They've learned to take what warmth they can. I lick my lips. One would think we never were there, except that Merchant still stands, sullenly, with his hoe.

Adam remains, as though he thinks his departure merits more mind. When no more comes he turns to us. I never thought we might be more defeated by vagabond's words than by their blows. Adam walks around me, toward the path, without a glance to my face. When we're into the woods, he says that Anne and I must be the ones to tell what we've seen.

Chapter nine

I'm Drawn
to the Closeroom

Why must you go?

I'm not given much choice in it, he says bitterly.

Did you dispute with him? I lead Hannah from her stall, then around the next pen to the milking ring. After a dutiful fight she follows well enough.

There'd be no good end to that I've seen him so before, but not commonly. Argument means nothing when my father is thus—I've seen him so only twice before, he says. Once when we put my mother to ground. Again when he berated me for letting a good butt of wheat go to rot. He faulted me for slighting the Lord's gifts, then. He said we should go hungry. Of course none would see him go hungry. Every Wednesday after, we'd find packets of corn on our step. And there were men who gave the fifth part of what eggs their pullets dropped.

I run my hands over Hannah's crest, rub her chine to soothe her. She's Master Jacobs' pride: a fine, glossy milker; and I look at her that I may not look at Adam. I'll not weep for his going, not openly, and before him. The air here is cold, and heavy with cow.

Adam says, When he told me I would go there was no thought in him to persuade. There was no wheedling like you'll sometimes hear in sermon. He said each thing once, and not again.

You will go to London, Adam says, and now his voice is his father's—quiet, weighty. He takes a step, as though to leave a sermon hall, putting an end to dispute. I sprinkle a line of salt between Hannah's front hooves, dab a single dot on each side. She paws at the damp ground, but never breaks the line. Now her milk will be sweet. You could refuse this, I say.

I could, he says. But the timbre of his voice says different. I glance and find him looking to the rafters, as though a swallow has insulted him in cloudless voice.

Behind him, Samuel Butler's ox Caesar lies with nose to the wall. He licks his left flank. That lapping tongue says the weather will be clear this week. I give no thanks for the news—clear sky, good travel. There will be no storm to keep Adam from the road. Bitterly I watch Caesar lick a slick brown patch on his hide.

Why must it be you? I say. I set the milking pail, and draw a stool up behind me.

Who would you have it be? he says. I am my father's son. He would have me trained in these matters.

Benjamen Smythe's wise enough to see such things done well.

He would have me trained in these matters, he says, and folds his arms before him like a breastplate. It will not be long, he says. We will see each other on the ship. That must be no later than late spring.

So soon, I say. I clap my hands three times, and Hannah's prepared for milking.

It is soon. If we are to leave this year it must be, or we'll land in dead winter. Could you countenance coming to ground with the weather so, in a land where all the country's forest? We'd need aid from savages, were we to live out a month. I think such aid unlikely.

When I told John Jacobs what we saw at the spring, he went on sorting gravel out from last summer's eye-beans, I say. Later he seemed more concerned with lack of spring water than he was about the cottagers.

He'll be thinking more on his wife, doubtless. With her about to drop a babe.

Of course.

But he was not surprised, either, Adam says. There's been enough talk about the chance of something like—never in general meeting, mind. But with George Pollack dead, what's to stay his son from making what changes he will? Nothing I can see. And so he's hired him cottagers. And so we're off for the western ocean.

He's right in all of that. By themselves, I know, the cottagers are nothing. But they tell us of the landlord's intent to seize our commons—and should we resist this time, all he need do is alert King's men to our presence. Our congregation is illegal. Defenseless.

Adam's voice turns tremulous, determined. He is once again his father, preaching to a dumb row of cattle. Under Mary, good congregations fled for Basel, or Frankfort, or Markpurge he says. Red-Man gives a snort.

The rulers there gave little thought or care to the manner of worship kept among their people, Adam says. There is safety, surety of life, in lands without principle. But there. Is. No. Satisfaction.

With every word his arms spread, until he stands like a sunning hawk.

There one must struggle against errors made more dolorous by their origination among professed Saints. And at bottom, those who flee to Amsterdam only borrow time, as from a Jewish usurer. There will come a day when there is no truce holds between them and Catholic Spain—and what then? What lands must they take to? What land will we take to now?

America, he says. America. America, he whispers. His hands float down, resting on an imagined, ghostly podium. The cows are too much idiots even to stare. I shake my head, turn to my milking.

There's little milk here, I say. And look, Hannah's speanes are raw. Something's been at her.

It is just winter, he says. He sounds annoyed to be interrupted. Or is it that I've not complimented him, or laughed?

I know what's common loss of milk in winter, I say. There, 'round the speane holes, all's red. It's like when your lips go scaly from wind. There's been a grima to the cowshed, or a stoat. Or a changed witch's come as a cat. You can see the toothmarks, near.

Here, he says, and his hands are on my shoulders.

We could use new-milk cheese in the Jacobs' household, I say. What we have left's much faded.

I roll my fingers along an udder, squirt a splash into the pail. Hannah's flank is a map of islands. It's like a wall.

There will be food enough to keep you, he says.

I would not have you go, so soon, I say.

Sooner depart, sooner return.

Scant good that'll do us when we're hungry, I say, and stand to kiss his neck.

I will see you on the ship, Adam says. His words have the cadence of a pledge. Then, gently, as though testing the soundness of a bake oven washed by rain, he turns me from Hannah. My back presses the planking of a cowstall, between the common hanging crucks and pails.

I think about the necessity or madness of removal from this place. I think of fights shouted. Until the cottagers came, those spats were like arguing over the situation of clouds. Now they seem verses of a true old debate. Snow that can hold the print of a cottager's bright leather boot has proved weightier than a season's words.

When Master Stradling returned from London his face was drawn. By then none were surprised that he'd brought with him an adventurer, who might lend money to those who find themselves willing to take passage. Many are so minded. There were those men who, after they were told of the cottagers, returned to their homes and put at least a single shirt in a trunk, in token to themselves that this will be no longer a home for them.

The choice to go is not mine to make. But now we're like a warren of rabbits in fear of dogs and plows, and there's no great dif-ference between two rabbits when their eyes roll and their mouths spit foam. I put neither shirt nor shift in any trunk. Still the ground threatens to sink away beneath my feet, leaving me floating, and I see no place for me to fall.

It may be that this severing from the village earth has been coming for some time, like when you build a fire in a hole. The coals take hold in roots, patiently powdering them to glowing, ashy paths, between worm-roads and the sealed kilns of grima homes. Then one day the old apple-man, the greatest of trees in an orchard, grandfather to all the rest, falls, and what seemed a wooden foundation's shown to be smoldering stubs. Mayhap it's like that. I know what Adam thinks.

Strange, I said, that the cottagers should take hold on ground once forcibly emptied of priests. There seems to me a judgment in this—a flagstone will hold on ground that the Saints once forcibly emptied of priests. But Adam returned, in a short, sharp voice, that I was foolish. This is a matter of rents and law, he said, and the way those things may serve wickedness.

That was the start of a fine row. Though we made it up, at times since I've felt towed behind a vessel he pilots. Except for his mocking of his father, he's not been as troubled about the coming removal as I'd think, or would like. Quite the thing, to be chosen for a matter of such import! Maybe it keeps him from thinking about what it will be like for us to depart this place.

America, Adam said. That word's a bag, to fill with lead or gold. I imagine what the forest would look like, if never touched by Japheth's fire. How wildly the green branches should claw, when tamed by nothing more than the tramping of savage feet. I know only more tempered ground. For all that it's full of delight, my garden is full tiled; some of those tiles are bright, pleasant as Dutch or Spaniard's stuff; others black like tar. All of them are mine.

But in a brighter mood I imagine what could be in land that is not so storied as this. Who's to say what a woman's condition might be across the ocean, where there's no such weight of years? I imagine herbs and plantings hid for my own discovery, that when grown will be like clouds and light on the tongue. Savages speak like a clatter of

pebbles, or a weasel's growl—but they must take from their forests as
I do from my plot. They take what they need, what's there for their
sustenance. Surely some of that will be also good for us.

I will clear away those pine trees, black as their own distilled
pitch, and defend my place from savages or Saints as needful. I have
heard Virginia called the Englishman's tomb. Now I have cause to
think of it, that phrase takes on new meaning, one that might hold
good promise. What is an Englishman, without England? What might
he do, what changes find or make?

Adam is gone for London.

I will sacrifice him for this time, though it will seem a score of
seasons. I will bear it willingly, and with love in my heart. Nobody
knows what I surrender. I hold my sacrifice close, feeling my heart
noble. He's near become a full Saint man, gone off to do his duties
for our congregation and the Lord. There is much I would change
about our congregation, but I would not have change come at the
point of a Queen's soldier's lance. I will see you on the ship, he said.
I can wait for that. I can wait for when we go to sea.

With the loss of Adam, work becomes a good balm. In wintertime, I
dry malt over a killframe, grind it in a wooden mortar, and brew it
into ale. I cask it for keeping in the lean-to buttery at the back of the
house. I rub oil on the iron that sheathes the wooden hoe-blades. I
tinker with axes and knives, fixing the blades on the handles with an
occasional neat nail. I mend, and stitch. Winter's a time for drawing
together all that frays apart during spring and summer labor. We eat
pottage with great dollops of butter, striving to get fat. Our English
bodies burn hot within, allowing us to bear our winters, and need
that fuel. In winter I cut ice from the pond, and ensure that burlap
covers the most delicate of my dooryard plants. I knit all together,
in winter. Today I am making brooms.

It takes a deal of strength to make a good broom. Patience
draws straw around the coppice pole, then wraps a turn of hemp
rope around. The other end is tied to a hook in the doorframe. I
pull hard against it, leaning back, slowly turning the handle, binding
the straw tight. Patience cuts the line to tie off, and we start again,

a hand further down. When I'm done Patience cuts the ends of the straw clean with a cleaver. She sweeps a bit, as a gunsmith might fire new ordinance to see that it is sound.

That's the one to keep, Enry says. I bend to take a broom. Not there, that one, he says. There!

This's the one we'll keep, I say.

It's not the best of them, Patience says.

I shrug at that, and say that to me one seems much the same as another. Enry has his likes. Defying them is rarely worth the trouble. Pick another broom to keep, and soon enough we'll find it in the fire. But he'll not ride me much longer. It'd be a rare thing, for Enry or his kin to travel. Like as not he'll be here waiting when the cottagers take this house as their own.

Who will he speak to, then? Will they have a daughter, who he'll think worthy to hear his voice?

But my thought breaks. A dog's caught, whining, in a neck-trap. It's in the closeroom, with Mistress Jacobs. The cry comes again, louder, and this time before it fades it forms my name. The backs of my hands prickle as I hurry to the door and say Yes, good Mistress.

Now she can speak, but her voice is a caged doe. It longs to fly leaping from the house, and she bids me run to Sarah Hawkens. I'm to say the babe is coming. I tell Patience to fetch Master Jacobs—he is at a neighbor's, talking over combining their labor in keeping bees—and I am out.

The newest snow's not yet cleared. My shoes have flat, smooth soles. I slip on hidden ice, near twisting my ankles in the frozen ruts. Two thin dogs, failures at hunting, bark as though I'm prey they can snare. But when I pass they fall silent, holding their ears at attention, looking to one side.

Their barking rumbled the air. Now that they're quiet the whole world is peaceful, crystal silent. Every roof is frosted, every rail, each small shed. I'm tempted to stop, and breathe. Just that, until I've taken all in like a draught of fine cider. I do stop. The air before me billows steam. In the stillness it comes to me to ask why the Lord has made this quietest of seasons both hard and lovely. What lesson are we to take, that the time we spend closest to others is that when the world strives to kill us with cold? Under snow, these houses're much alike—whether a creaky hall where men shared space with goats, or a new, tight home with discrete passes, each lets slip warm smoke from chimneys or holes in white smocks of snow. I could stay, and watch as I would a hatching chick. There is much beauty here.

But in the Jacobs' house a woman sweats, and a babe's ready to come to this world. I head on down the white road, between houses like sleeping hives.

Sarah usually meets me at the door, voice booming, nose wrinkled, seeming to overfill the frame. This time I enter without a knock and find her before the fire, small as a black kitten in a snow-field. She looks up at me without surprise.

Good morning.

Good morning, I say.

She looks back to the fire. It's her time, then? she says.

It is.

A bit early. Not to fear, I think.

She heaves herself up, rummages through a chest. A moment and we'll go, she says. I've had this made up, these weeks. I'll not be accused of taking my sloth. When Sarah turns, she holds a package of brown cloth and a stoneware jug.

We walk back in silence. Sarah holds to the edge of the road, shuffling her feet to find the flat stretches. She clutches at her bundle. I realize she wears no cloak. I think it passing strange, that with all her speaking out against the Jacobs she's not taken time for that. I shake my head and walk always a few feet before her, as though I might draw her along on a string.

When I open the door, men's laughter floods over me. Master Jacobs is in his glory. His fear of what may come is buried beneath a loam of hope and pride. A woman reproves him but she's laugh-ing too, her face lit like a good bright flower. As she goes into the closeroom I hear more women, who will leave this house only to bake food for the celebration of another born Saint. This is the last act that surrounds a birthing, a gathering of friends and neighbors for the joy of it—and, sometimes, the mourning. There's a high clear blaze on the heart. A joint is set to roast, and after Master Stradling leads all in good-natured, earnest prayer, black tygs of beer pass from hand to hand. With a modest smile I walk to the closeroom, and follow Sarah in. Some of her force has colored me, like dandelion's dust that tints your nose. Today I'm permitted in to the closeroom, to give what help I might. The other women are there, quiet, happy, waiting for Sarah to speak. Mrs. Jacobs is quivering fearful. But at the sight of Sarah she calms, as a pond stills under dying breeze. For once I understand this woman's wants, and the green buried in her. For once I forgive her all.

That's how it should be. But the house is cluttered and hollow; the fire, dusky, and my view of the closeroom imagined. We're greeted only by a mess of loose straw, and hemp rope that hangs from the doorframe. The Jacobs will have no festive time until there's some surety that this child will stay. This house's colder than the street.

Sarah hands me her package. Boil up a pot of water, she says. Bring three spoonfuls from it when hot, and throw these leaves in what's left. They need steep for an hour.

I go to the woodbox at the back of the house and pick out the driest wood I can find. I must not send sparks to the roofing. This day of all others, I must not fill the house with smoke.

But all the while I gather the wood, build a hutch around the coals, and blow to watch it take flame, I think of bringing Sarah her spoonfuls of water. She's told me to come to the closeroom. At last I've been told to swing wide the sun-split wood—but not by the holder of this house, nor his wife. And when Master Jacobs returns, I think, the time when I'm welcome will be over.

So instead of a heavy pot, I take up the small iron pan I use to fry perch, and put in a spare four spoons of water. Even without the fire gone to coals it soon steams, then giggles. Enry has nothing to say about it. Is he even here?

When that little water is boiling hot I take up the pan with an old skirt I keep for a rag, and go to the closeroom door. There I find, to my wonder, that opening it and walking in is no simple thing. I stare at the gray wood, as though that might pry the cobweb fissures wide. Suddenly it opens and Sarah's face fills the doorway, twisting in aggravation. My hesitation was ice on her back.

It's no very special room. But for what lies sweating and gasping on the bedstead, this is a common place. I realize, with a snap of recognition, that I expected such, and hoped for it. Their space is not so damnably different from mine. How could I think it would be? Even the joinwork's the same as in my chamber, the timber unfinished on the sides facing inward. Perhaps it's a hair bigger on a side. Of course there are no field-tools. But there's a little occasional box. There's a little green rug on the floor. In the corners, heavy trunks.

And there's Mistress Jacobs. Her face is red, creased, but under the contortion and color of labor she's pale as spring's new moon. She's been in this room, this bed, since summer. She looks through me, past me, as if I'm shadowed by a grinning, malformed giant.

Sarah kneels beside the bedstead. The topmost blanket is ragged with age, and the orange of the blanket below shows through the blue. Sarah rolls both gently back. She strokes Mistress Jacobs' forehead with a weathered hand, talking quiet, regular nonsense, the kind of talk one offers a bull before gelding. She says something I can't hear and Mistress Jacobs snatches at her shirt—she's dying in the river, she has found a rope. She pulls her shirt up below her breasts. Her body is a splotchy hill. Sarah still strokes her, still speaks her sooth. She motions me to come with the water, and pour it into the stoneware jar. With her first fingers and thumbs she draws out a whole soaked plant. It's a kind I don't know, something like a cousin to bear's breeches. The small berries on it are soaked plump with some infusion. Mouth at Mistress Jacobs' ear, Sarah holds the plant by the roots. She draws it across her bulging stomach—it trails blue streaks. Mistress Jacobs whimpers.

I don't hear her husband enter. He grabs me by the arm from behind, wrenches me around as though to rip my shoulder. I cry out. Meaty breath fills my face.

Out, he says. You act as though it's only since this morning you've lived here. He is a slave to fear, this man, and to quick rage when he sees his orders slighted—he must command something, he can command me. He drags me to the door, spins to throw me. My chin hits the floor of the hall, my teeth clack together. It's torn my tongue. Blood blooms, rusty. Unseeing, I push myself to hands and knees. Straw's bedded in my chin. It sticks to my cheek.

Sarah shouts at Master Jacobs. She says that it may be his house, but she'll need help and it's no help he can give. Mistress Jacobs moans. Her voice is a horse she hopes to rein in. Master Jacobs is silent. This is no ordinary day, Sarah says. He's to pick me up, brush me off, invite me in to his wife.

I stand, and with two sharp whisks of my hands clean myself. Whatever he decides, I will find my own feet—I will not be lifted, not from the ground he put me on. And when he comes from the closeroom, eyes expectant on the empty floor, I am fiercely glad.

Chapter ten

I Hear of Bees, and Baptism

An iron kettle of brawn and clove is a good, warming dish. Bubbles wrinkle about the stone-gray meat. A cradle's creaking. But Steven, he's in Master Jacobs' lap. He coughs like a spike scraped on granite. Master Jacobs rocks the empty cradle, absently, his foot against a runner, eyes haggard, humming a song he likely knows from when he had young brothers.

Mistress Jacobs is out under the stretched sky of late winter. She returns with her face cuddled by cold, red where she rubbed herself dry after cutting pine boughs that snapped and spat kept rain. She binds the five branches with red ribbon, sets them in a stoneware jar with brown curls glazed about its rim. She takes Steven. She says the brawn smells fine, does it not, and Master Jacobs says it does. Soon Patience comes like a soggy gopher from the common oven, where she baked a loaf with the best wheat left. When she takes the hot loaf from under the cloth, the steam of it meets the brawn and cut pine, and together all smell secure and hopeful.

He's stronger than the rest, Master Jacobs says from nowhere.

He is I think, says his wife, though it's clear she wishes he'd said no such thing. He'd as well have spoken outright of their babe's fever. I also wish he'd held silent. I don't want another loss in this house. I must live here until our passage. If there's another loss the Jacobs will be like the wax armor some bugs leave picked into bark—when they've cracked through that brittle skin, and flown.

We'll drink the beer made on his birth day, this night, says Master Jacobs. A fine thought. A month since he's come, she says.

But it's been a month like hillocks. In the dank days after the birth the Saints came, and the small snow that clumped to their boots would melt to wet the floor as they stood over the babe. They carried small gifts—some intended to heal the body, others only for comfort. Chicken stews, herbs boiled with honey; tiny blankets; plain, draping clothes right to robe a boy or girl. An orange time, when my acts were never thought wrong.

But when Steven began to cough, the long line began, slowly, to crack. Their visits were shorter, then. They'd come chirping good hopes—but soon scuttle for daylight, so quickly that I imagined them with hands raised against hail. They left the house hollow.

At least Sally Hamilton had the good grace to stay away, and thus keep the sight of her young Kenelm from Mistress Jacobs. Sally must know her healthy child a dagger.

When all had gone, and none came any longer, I feared the Jacobs must think it plain that our work had been wanting. It's fortunate that her husband had already drawn in like a snail, with never a spoken chastisement. His blaming thoughts stack silently for keeping. I do my work right, so when he climbs from where it is he's hid this place will not be so wretched, and I to blame.

When she takes Steven from swaddling his hands wave, blind and aimless. These are fever-dream flailings.

At table Mistress Jacobs eats half as much brawn and bread as she ought, and drinks twice as much beer, though when he asks she says all three are good. Master Jacobs sits above the cone of salt, watching it like it's a hill in his own hunting park. He seems deep in thought. When he says something, when his wife does, it's about today's work, or tomorrow's. Never, *The cough is no less.* Certain never, *We'll lose this one too, sure.*

Mistress Jacobs pulls a chair to the cradle, rocks it with her foot, hands folded before her where she sits. She says, does he not look fine today; today the cough is less; we're beholden to Sarah Hawkens once again, and will be sure to thank her for it with more than words. Master Jacobs agrees, and says he'll think on a good gift. He chews his brawn, then turns to us sudden—he asks do we know that brawn's a good thing done well only in England.

I'm right startled that he's spoke to us at all, and say, I did not, good sir.

He says, Here's a true story for you then. Those outside England know not what to make of brawn, and oftimes think it foreign fowl. There was a good English Saint who fed it to a room of popish Spaniards, on a Friday, and they never knew they'd eaten what they oughtn't, under their horrid filthy faith. And what he served them, served them right, for they'd tried to keep that man from supping on honest meat.

Patience laughs, though I'm sure she doesn't know that Papists are not to eat their meat on a Friday. Master Jacobs says he's heard of Jew men who ate brawn, believing it a heavy deepwater fish. After, they puked up all they could, drinking water to wash out what was left until they nigh pissed blood. Then they prayed forgiveness, though it passes reason to know why the Lord would give us pig, if not to eat.

My laughter is duty; this man put me on the floor, and only one month past. Still I confess it is a funny thought, to not eat pork when you have the chance to do. I near think of asking has Master Jacobs ever seen a Jew, and what did that Jew look like? But before I open my mouth there's a knock at the door.

I rise from my seat. Greeting at the door's my task; Master Jacobs would show himself a fine man, and have visitors see a servant. But tonight he's up himself, so quick that I think he must expect this caller.

But Mistress Jacobs snatches up the pine branches from the table. She tosses them behind a tub of rope. Those outside are not expected after all; this must be some feast the Jacobs keep, and they would block the visitors before their trespass is detected. I stand beside the table, wondering whether to sit.

Fair evening to you, says Jacobs. He speaks to Master Stradling, who fills the door; but from Jacobs' formal stance I know there must be another man there.

John, says Master Stradling. I present Colin Farnsworth of London. He is a man of admirable family, which in spite of considerable station has not allowed its eyes to be drawn off the path.

Master Stradling gives a flourish that opens his cloak.

You are welcome in our house, Master Jacobs says. He gives way.

Well met, Farnsworth says. His voice commits him nothing. He has worn a great wide hat against the rain, and pulled it down hard over his head. Rain has beaded on his cloak. When he slides it open I see there are gold threads twisted into points along the bottom of his green jerkin. A sword hangs from his belt. It's the first true fighting sword I've seen worn, although there are those men who keep one in their households as relics of old war. With his hat pulled down and the sword visible his smile seems feral as a falcon's cracked beak. There are dark places under his eyes. I've never liked that look in a man. But it may be only lack of sleep—for he's doubtless accustomed to feathers, and here must bed on bolstered straw.

Well met, sir, says Master Jacobs. The Mistress has begun to rise but Master Stradling waves her down.

Do not trouble, Frances, I beg, he says. You will be tired, tending to Steven.

She forces a smile. You are good, sir, I thank you, she says. I'll not deny it's tried me.

I feel Master Stradling's consternation. For a moment I see her with his eyes. Mistress Jacobs looks flat, as though the shadows of the hall refuse the hollows of her face. She rocks the cradle gently. There's a tiny, crippled cough. Even after it fades it hangs, as a moth's wings might catch on grass. Master Stradling stands over the cradle, and looms, I think unwittingly, over Mistress Jacobs. Without looking he holds out his cloak for me to take.

I see no great resemblance between him and Adam, and wonder about the looks of Adam's dead mother. Was she young, awkward as a colt?

The cloak drapes on a nail. I wonder if Master Stradling thinks that Mistress Jacobs' close watch hints at a discreditable belief in changelings. If he does, then he knows her not at all. Steven is her son. If ever she confessed that not all with him is well, doubtless she would say that a cunning man has witched him. She could never doubt his parentage.

He looks strong, Frances, Master Stradling says. You can see such in his eyes, in the set of his wrists. I have seen many children with that look about them recover from worse maladies.

Truly? she says, her mouth slightly agape. I wonder if she can really believe that he could have any honest answer for her. He does not strike me as a man to watch a babe closely. Though in truth he's seen many come, only to be buried. But she does think he might know something, for she says she is glad to hear it, and Steven has been better, this last week, and when the spring air comes the phlegm and black humor will be much reduced.

Still Steven's lips are pale. His eyelids are splotched; the sides of his nose webbed, like tangled thread.

I agree, says Master Stradling. It much pleases me that you nurse him yourself.

I think to myself that that is a great fine compliment. Many Saint women rely on others for nursing. So soon after birth, the strength and purity of their milk may be suspected corrupt. And Mistress Jacobs does, I think, believe that the fault's in her. There is some hard tumor that pollutes her milk. There is some wrong nestled in her blood.

It takes time, said old Temperance, Master Jacobs' mother, when she came to call from the south. Years, before the Lord saw fit to give them their John, she told him.

But there's been no churching for this woman. Her childbirth clings to her, venomous.

As he walks to Steven, Farnsworth angles his sword between chests and a tub. A pleasant looking child, he says. Mistress Jacobs thanks him, though not so gratefully as she did Master Stradling. When Master Jacobs asks if they will not sit, Farnsworth thanks him, and without a hitch of hesitation leans his unbuckled sword against the table. He takes the great, armed chair above the salt. Patience gasps a bit; I glare warning.

Master Stradling now looks to us for distraction. He asks if I was not one of those who came upon the cottagers.

Good Sir, I was.

He thanks me for my calm bearing, courage, and presence of mind. All are indebted for news of such import. And though I know he only delays to his own purpose, his words warm in me like leather left in bright sun. I think perhaps there's something of him in Adam after all, and thank him with great pleasure.

As he takes my normal seat on the side bench, Master Jacobs asks if there can be no other defense against the cottagers but removal. That, he says, is no good resolution. I kneel at the hearth to build up the fire. I listen.

I am surprised you should ask, says Master Stradling. They are a sign that there can no longer be a life for us in this place. You have heard in council of elders what I learned of George Pollack, Pollack the Younger, while in London. A mere word or sign from him and we will see King's soldiers standing about the bakeoven, the dogs.

I think that he's right about that. Surely most Saints would believe him so. There's no royalty as would allow a congregation such as ours to thrive, refusing fealty to the royal church. If the king learns of us, soon after we'll learn the means and extent of his force.

Would you have me tell you what they do, Enry says from his beam overhead. Above him is a slow, smoky mold, that Master Jacobs has sworn to Frances he'll see to come the spring. I lean to blow a stalk of smoke into flame. I mean it as a nod, and Enry takes it so. Very well, he says.

But, says Master Jacobs, there were those, before, who fought.

When I hear that I think of him pointing off, into a green tussle, at old burned posts.

Master Stradling sighs. He says our days have changed, and what can defend the right in one age will not, in another. He says one should know that, having had to take water from the spring like a thief. But before the last words are true from his mouth he says he's sorry for them.

John Jacobs' lips, there, went a shade whiter, says Enry. He was in no wise pleased to be called a thief.

The hive is over full, says Farnsworth, like he's pronounced something for Jacobs to inscribe in the family Book.

The hive says Jacobs.

Oh, that's made him no happier, Enry says. I do not think him glad to have another man here, tonight.

On the way from the south I noted the orchards outside your village, Farnsworth says. John Stradling gave me to believe you were once among their keepers.

He has brachet's eyes, Enry says. Eyes of the hound, when it thinks on whether to strike.

That's true, says Jacobs.

It must have been some years past, Farnsworth says. The hives are in sad disrepair. I cannot believe that they have been used for six seasons.

Seven, I think, says Master Jacobs. There was a blight and we lost them all. We found another king in a hive at the edge of the forest. But the blight took that swarm too, and the one some years after. I didn't see the profit in going on. They were a profit to me while I could keep a hive, but it's no simple thing to keep bees while living plain, as a simple husbandman.

He said that last like he was tossing a broken bottle, Enry says. But Farnsworth, he seems pay no mind.

Yet you observed the motions of the bees for as long as you kept them. Their motions, their manner of labor.

That's Farnsworth drumming his fingers, Enry says. Master Stradling's looking to end this talk.

The fire's taking. It gnaws the edge of the wood I placed.

When I could, Master Jacobs says. There was not oft time to sit and watch them hum about the apples.

I am of the mind that there is naught better for the study of human society than the close observation and consideration of the various bees. There is there pure order and labor, a great pyramid of position, all subordinate to the king.

I am no philosopher, says Jacobs. I worked the hives, I did not read them.

That time would have been profitable spent, Farnsworth says. Consider that when a hive is filled to its limit, removal is the lone recourse. Some part must become a seeking swarm, probing glades and hollows—it finds one proper for its artificial transformations, its glorious artifice.

There is no hierarchy among our people. If you take that to be an impediment you will be disappointed, here.

I think you take his meaning wrongly, John, says Master Stradling.

Perhaps there is no hierarchy between your congregation and like others. Within, it must surely be another matter, Farnsworth says.

We have no more than we cannot do without, Jacobs says dourly.

I bite the inside of my cheek, look doggedly at the coals. If he asked me I could name hierarchies here we had better do without. I could point to changes that should not disorder the Lord's world, or not unpleasantly.

No doubt that is so, Farnsworth says. But men need a great deal, I think. I have found no society where one man does not defer to another.

I am no philosopher, Jacobs says again.

One need not be greatly learned, to be called philosopher. One need only have enthusiasm, a desire to observe.

Then I say men are not bees.

Enry tells me Farnsworth's body is become a plank, in that armchair above the salt. All men will think as they will, Farnsworth says. His voice, at least, is certain stiff.

It is a poor thing to live without consciousness of the world's patterns, he says. There is in them a deep meaning. Thus it is artful to

see through shallow materials to what is hid beneath, or writ behind—
for a daffodil or mourning dove are mere letters in a mighty volume
for those who may read. If you will heed me, you will reflect deeply,
and at length, upon your time spent working among the bees.

An excellent notion, says Master Stradling. We must observe
all that the Lord has given us. We cannot fail to profit from such
observance.

Though he speaks mildly, I think he also deems the models
of Master Farnsworth foolish and corrupt. But he needs to keep the
support of this man—without him, without his goodwill and treasure,
there will be no passage. This is no time to debate theology. I feel sure
he'll give Farnsworth no chance to speak before general meeting.

Abruptly, as though stumbling off a blind step, Master Jacobs
says there is a matter he wishes to speak of.

There is nothing that cannot be spoken before Master Farnsworth. We will depend upon him for passage across the roaring
ocean, Master Stradling says.

For a long moment his only answer is the creaking of an empty
cradle, a pop of flame.

I did not intend to cast doubts upon your discretion, good sir,
says Master Jacobs. It is only that this is a tender thing.

Please, John, says Master Stradling.

Yes. It is a tender thing. But it would give Frances and I great
pleasure, if you might baptize our Steven.

Already he sounds defiant. He knows what the answer must be.
Baptism is not for the voiceless—it's kept for those who ask. The souls
of those who die before finding their tongues flee into lower beasts.

Frances makes as though she cannot hear, Enry says. She feeds
him mixed cow's milk and honey, with the corner of a soaked rag.
He will not suckle. It bubbles by his mouth.

I cannot do that, John, says Master Stradling. As you know
as well as any. I cannot baptize any man who has not asked me for
it in his own voice.

I think of Steven, red skin squeezed in around his eyes, and
think it passing strange for the word *man* to be spoke in connection
with him. A bench scrapes back. Look, Enry says. When I glance

back over my shoulder Master Stradling is full tensed, Farnsworth's feet drawn up as though ready for a spring. But Master Jacobs' fury is not for them. The knots in his jaw are for me—for being here, and hearing refusal.

Get from the hall, you cow, he says.

I follow Patience as she scurries to our chamber. When the door is closed behind she asks what was the cause of his anger. I whisper her to hush, and to blow out our taper so that when I crouch to listen there'll be no shadows between the door and the swept dirt. Now words seep there, like dusty melted butter.

I know that and the cause for it, Master Jacobs is saying. We've grown full attached to him, I'll tell you plain. You were good to speak of his strength, and it was a kindness to Frances that she might hear that.

I think: She's still there, you sodden idiot. She's not deaf, and now you've burned whatever she heard that was a help to her.

Master Stradling says, I understand. But I pray you remember, baptism is no sure step to heaven. No action of men on earth may aid that trip. Certainly, no act can ensure it. Baptism is a sign only, a symbol of entry into a worldly covenant.

I know.

The worldly covenant between a congregation and the Lord, Master Stradling bears on, that provides the earthly conditions amenable to Grace; that allows us to labor as He wishes us to. Baptism is no assurance of Grace. You would make the judge of that which no man may judge—the truth and devotion of a man's heart.

We've waited long, says Jacobs. I know what baptism is and what it is not. It would be a comfort to Frances.

I cannot do it, John. I would pretend to an authority I do not possess, speaking for one who cannot speak for himself.

I'm his father. I'll speak for him.

You cannot, nor can any man rightly speak for another on this matter.

There is a long silence, then. The door is black and the light of the hall glows under, like a sunset horizon gone topsy-turvy. At that Master Jacobs speaks again. He says—I think—that he does understand.

I never doubted it, says Master Stradling. Be comforted. This is a great struggle, for the continuation of our congregation in perpetuity. There could be no finer gift to your son than that. Look on him. Think that the waters we'll pour over his head will be dipped from fresh streams. Looking on him, see rank on rank of Saints sprung from American earth.

Soon after, they take their leave. From the spirit of this quiet, I know that the Jacobs sit, silent, in the hall. I lie in bed, and whisper to Patience what has passed.

I don't want to go, she says, in a voice that cracks like glass.

In a whisper, in a voice I hope gentle that yet comes too fast, I tell her it will be all right. We will build a mill there, I say. It will be beside a river. It is true that there will be forests, thick as the one that stands above us now. But we will cut it back, and make houses, and fires. Those fires will burn hot and bright. Who will need fear a lessening of wood?

There will be fields, cattle, deer for the taking. There will be glass windows on every house. The dust within will shine in columns. Outside, wildflowers. Daisies, and dandelions. Primroses. From them we'll make dyes, so bright that in spring you'll stand before the meadow, and seem to fade away. You'll hide in plain view, so little difference will there be between God's colors and the ones we make for our clothes.

Then Patience laughs through tears but still she cries, and says she does not want to go.

I ask her then if change is all to fear, and what do we lose of so great value, in taking our feet from this ground. Could there not be some to gain? Think, I say. How could there be servants, with so much good land, and so many ways for a man to build a household? When we go, all will be different for those who stay behind. There is no chance that all will stay the same forever.

She says nothing more; after a time I turn to the wall. Then she turns to me, her hand on my side. Feeling that tiny anchor there, I cry with her toward sleep.

III

Chapter eleven

I Find Cause for a Burying

I tell Sarah about good Master Farnsworth and ask her about the ocean and then, with her lap filled with rags stitched for a scarecrow's head, with her eyes cast off to nowhere, she tells me this:

I'd labored that season by the ocean, for a mast-maker whose name's lost me. He and his guild hired promiscuous when they'd timber in from Baltic forests, for that needs seasoning, and steaming. When work was done, I'd go down to see the ships with all their worldly frickafrack. It was spring and the barnacle geese come in numbers to muddle the channel, giving the launches a going hard as through a marsh. The barnacles come yearly, to those harbors, their flocks a great Lord's gift. They come in braying mobs, cap the sea until they go west in a flush of wings.

Their dung dapples rope and dock. But until they go, the people row out to catch them with hemp nets they pull back near to bursting. Then they'd boil them in iron kettles, to loosen the feathers, before roasting. I liked them best prepared in such wise, gutted and stuck on sticks over the fires. It was like at once eating flesh and the sea. And the smell of crackling goose and fires burning in holes on the beach—that that was true rich.

While we ate, I asked idly where the barnacles'd come from, and where they'd go. That prompted much glad debate. One man said they were native to Orkney, where his cousin'd seen them roosting in pine trees. The people there would set those trees afire and wait below with trenchers, catching cooked goose for their evening's board. Another man said they were from Spain, where they fed on olives and thin wines. Many thought they came from the south where the sun stands straight over your crown, hot enough to burn the black that's streaked between the birds' eyes. It warms the seashells that cling to stones near the surf, and from those seashells the barnacle geese hatch. It was something to talk about while we laughed and drank beer, and paired off in the moon-shadows streaked below the docks.

But there was one, named Cudman, who thought the question less casual. He wore a purple cloak, and a codpiece—that last stitched elaborate with silver thread in spins and twirls. He used the codpiece for a pocket, to hold small foods and sweets beside his cock. You didn't see that much, even then. Of course he stood out like a mallard among goslings.

Some mocked him, calling him a fop, and a whore to birds. That last should've prompted a fight. He seemed never to care. He was greatly insistent in his questions about the geese, and who among us might have seen them at their proper roosting. He listened eagerly while men made up stories about the birds, that they had seen them vomited by whales or pecking their ways from sodden moors, and you could not see what he credited and what he saw for a lie. I rather liked the man. But what mattered to me was that with him came Henry his servant, who was later my husband.

My first memory of Henry's him saying *Manna* with great satisfaction, grease glistening on his frumped beard. He told me about their lives out of doors. They walked or rode from town to field, driven like oxen by Cudman's confidence that there was wisdom to be had through the study of birds. They tramped over hills and through flat champaign meadow-country, sunk into flooded fens, tore through thorny woods, burned red during high summer with the grass around them going brown. Hearing that, I thought Cudman's face odd, for what should have hardened through all that time under sun was pasty, loose as dough.

Henry, now—he was wholly a bull, with bright eyes, a shaggy black beard, a windburned cork of a nose. I could feel his strength from the start, and thought it made him gentle. Strength will do, for some men. Before the night was over I tested his force under an overturned launch. Oh, he wanted for nothing. We were happy, there.

For me, the shore seemed a special time. I thought then that anything new was fine. When Henry told me of roaming I thought I understood why he stayed with Cudman, though it would've been an easy enough indenture to shed. Then he said, casually as offering a cup of milk, that I might go with them. It seemed natural and right, that I would say yes. I said it with hardly a thought.

Cudman took the news with ease and grace. I thought him a generous master, not to voice an objection. Then I thought maybe he saw that, if I did not go, then Henry would not. I swelled, that Henry would hold me so high.

But later Cudman asked him to go into town to buy him some small sugar. When he was gone Cudman asked if we might not speak of coming plans. Then under a pier he took and forced me and fucked me, whispering *Soft*, muttering *Hold*, his hands to my throat the while—only the part of an hour I think now but that was the longest season of my life.

After, I thought of reasons. In the end I saw they do not matter, to me, and if not to me then to no one.

I cried beside the great seawall, in a slick and rocky nook. Henry found me there. What is wrong, love, he said to me, and that was the first time he'd called me so.

I said to him, Nothing. He laughed at that. But so gently that I spoke again, and said, I've been forced. He was very quiet, then, and I was glad for it. I said, It was your master.

What would he do, at that news? Would he rage, would he blame me for it? Would he take me there, whether I would or no, to show me and himself that his force was no less than that of the master who ordered his days? Henry was no common man. He grew seeming cheerful.

This wall, here, he said, and slapped stone with his palm. This is a sea wall.

Well I know it, I said.

A seawall holds back waters from the folk, he said. So they can live their lives calm and peaceful, with never a flood.

Are you so great a bastard as to speak so to me. I have no care for a seawall, I said.

Listen, love. Last night with you I felt all sheltered. Now I do not. Much like a townsman must feel, should his seawall breach, in a storm. Think you so?

I think yes, I said. There was a warmth begun to spread in me.

And when a seawall's found lacking the proper care, that's a horrid crime for him that's charged with keeping it. Letting another's peace fall to hazard, through his own sloth. In these lands they have a treatment for such a man. They place him in the breach and build the wall above him, so his bones might form a good foundation. Is that not a fine cure?

It is, I said. That blaze in me had took.

So that night we came upon Tim Cudman where he slept alone. Caring nothing for great comfort, he had taken a room in a shabby house where sailors had chambers. There was Henry and myself—only us.

Henry held him with a fishknife to his throat, whispering, while I bound him with rope we stole from the wharf. Soon he was muzzled with an old shirtsleeve. We bore him across the street. A drunk whore laughed to see us—a game, good mistress, Henry said. Down a flight of wooden stairs, and we stood beneath the pier.

Henry stood with his ankles breaking the rising surf. You'd scarce have credited his strength. He raised Cudman by the feet, and with his shoulder held him smashed upside-down, against a piling, with hair sweeping the sand. I bound his legs tight, his waist, his chest, as you would a pig you mean to bleed. I left no play in the rope, so when Henry stepped back Cudman slipped only a finger, a shade.

He hung thrashing, humming into his shirtsleeve, back hard against the wood. The water'd rose to wet his hair. Barnacle geese cried, and I thought they sounded right glad. I cut away Cudman's codpiece. Do you mean to take his yard? Henry said, and sounded alarmed at the thought. But I only sprinkled nuts and sweets about his head, and left him there with cock flopping in air.

His head bobbed like a float before the rising water. He hoped to keep his nose in air. But on the piling the shells that marked tide grew at his waist. Henry spit on him. We left him there—I was furious, and young. We went up the wood steps to the street.

There, love, Henry said to me. His bones'll be a fine foundation. You may think of the fish that pick them, and find peace I hope. I will, I think, I said, though I knew it a middling lie. But you, I said. Will you be calm, with me? It was no easy question. Likely my voice skipped on it like a flat stone on a lake. But he took my face in his hands, and kissed me, and I thought that the devil had one less claim—for he would never tempt me with another man.

I want to take Sarah in my arms. She's told it without a note of shame, but she waits to hear what I'll say. I know this: whatever pleasure she took in seeing the world with Henry, she is done with seeing more. This is the place she'll never leave. I sit, my arm heavy on a broadsheet, and I say: It was Lord's justice.

I wake to the sound of slapped cloth. Someone is beating out blankets, and in the house. Someone is tanning leather.

Come, says Enry. Come. He's speaking through a scar.

The fire's built up higher than permitted, higher than is safe. The room is dense, huddled with bright smoke. Sparks flit for roofing. Before the hearth, in that one clear space, Mistress Jacobs paces, clenching her hands like hammers. She strikes herself on her thighs. That sways her forward in a bow. With every second step she strikes. Her course is regular, as though she's set in a trench. Five steps, turn.

Five steps. She's a housecat with certain knowledge of wolves, and her hair falls free—black with white, salt and dust. She looks naked. When I cast my eyes about for her coif it is a moment before I see it by the edge of the fire, blackening, crisp.

I stand in the chamber door, biting down on my lip. Smoke sucks at my eyes 'til they tear. Oh ho ho ho ho, says Enry. A chortle; a sob.

Mistress Jacobs might fall in the fire. She could lash out to wound. She could call me her daughter; hold me tight. Mistress Rowe did so at the loss of her girls, and after was poisoned toward my friend. Frances Jacobs might do anything. For Steven is gone, and she hopeless.

Her eyes glisten, broken and blood-edged. He was never large enough to teeter his cradle, but I can see nothing in it now with force of breath. Now the cradle is empty as soapbubbles, as still as lead.

Frances sees me. She drags to a stop. We watch each other across red silence. The air is stinging mud. Oh, she says. She crosses her arms against her stomach, pulls on her elbows. I think that she'll step back to sit on a chest but she only stands, arms crossed, and watches me. I cannot leave. With that, I should confess to seeing her. The smoke is smoldering. It is full. This is no decorous bereavement in the burial yard. This is not like the deaths of the other babes, when Frances kept to the closeroom, grief to gut a woman locked away like a bird fluttering in a chest.

Master Jacobs is at the door, and with him a small clean billow of air. His short sharp beard is combed. He wears his best boldly colored clothes—fine pear green, and a stitched border of purple. Without looking to me he crosses to his wife.

Dear, he says. His arm is out straight, to stroke her shoulder. He will calm this calf. She chokes a bit, falls to him. Their arms are ivy.

As though I'd only paused on my way to work I walk quietly for the front door, then out. Without the smoke the morning smells fresh and clear. The eastern sky is lightening above the pastures, and the smell of recent rain seems to promise dryer days. Mistress Jacobs is crying. She is crying out. But a few steps into the dooryard, and there are only sounds of early day. Some of the mint is spotted brown. I'll have to do something about that, I think. What could kill mint? A chicken comes pecking into the yard. She snaps at the ground, under rosemary.

I should feel this more strongly. But without the sounds of them I feel only empty, and clear about my place. This household is not mine. Their losses are not.

Chapter twelve

I Spark a Dissolution

aster Stradling's house is the last before the burying ground. We wait for him grouped before our households, early as on a workday. He passes, staff tap-tapping dust tacked to the road by dew. He walks south, through the village. He nods, and smiles. He's past the homes, the outbuildings. He's where the orchards and wrecked beehives begin. A bright breeze twists last year's leaves about his feet.

Master Jacobs and Mistress Jacobs wait. The days that their Steven is in the ground don't make a week. Their shoulders are loose doors. Their heads, propped drums.

Master Stradling turns deliberately. This time each household follows when he passes. He walks slowly, purposefully. Any child may match his pace. We fall in, house by house, melting to a clumsy serpent. Our clothes are of the best; pond-green bodices, blue skirts. We flow north.

Mistress Jacobs has been in the ale this morning and she lurches as though crossing a brook stone to stone. Her husband may also have been to his drink. That's common enough, these past days. Their drunkenness sews my mouth shut (I feel I've not uttered a word, since the loss). If he is drunk now, he hides it better than her. Wise—it is a great offense to go to meeting filled with strong ale. So that her gait may show the less strange, I walk as though the road ruts are perilous, and need special care. I wish they might show me similar mercy when they are right in their heads.

Master Stradling's house is a hall, once meant for beasts and men together. Now even his dear mare is kept in the cowshed, so only the slightest fall in the floor marks the old stable space. When I file in, Master Strading is already in place behind the podium, his fingers bunched to tripods. There are two blocks of benches with an aisle between. Men to the right, women left, servants to the rear. I smell ancient sheep, and musty cow. Since midwinter that scent has put me in mind of Adam, of our private bed, and as I sit I mask a smile with my wrist. Though there are windows of wavy turned glass, most light comes from the open door. As Saints enter the hall dims, brightens. Dims. The men look unfinished, for this is the only time of the week they go bareheaded. Hair drapes to shoulders. When the door is closed all colors fade as under a layer of fallen dust.

Anne lives closer to this house, with Master and Mistress Rowe and their brood. When Fight-the-Good-Fight-of-Faith Rowe passes down the aisle with her mother, I know Anne must be here as well. I feel her, like a quiet laugh against my neck.

The Jacobs sit each on their side of the aisle, each in an edge seat. Today they permit no body between them.

Before Master Stradling burns a single taper. He surveys the last shuffling and settling of his congregation. Beyond the men is a fire, its coals giving warmth but little light. Master Stradling looks a perfect stone troll. When all are seated his fingers flex, and he begins.

He says that there is in this land, all across this kingdom, a hierarchy of caterpillar landlords. The enclosure they threaten is destructive of our good life and its method. There can be no right community when all labor for the good of one man, and his sheep. There is no long time left, before we must set out from this place. We may give thanks to the Lord this day, for making the course of our coming passage, and its desperate need, so plain.

He says the progress of religion can be seen in the turns of history. These have been revolutions, and are greater than revolutions of arms. What acts of martial men, he asks, what clash of fleets and cannon, could compare to the most tentative step in the progressive restoration of His true light in this earth? True that there have been times of decline; and those, though lesser than advances, are nonetheless greater than the men who live out their lives within those sad ages. The progress of His will is the great argument of the world. It must surely overwhelm men, whose bodies are the stuff of its rhetoric.

There was a time I should have thought this text a thorn. All here would say that none can know the Lord's wants. And yet he speaks with such certainty, when all the Saints are certain of is their position here and mine among them. But more recently I've felt these words different, as a fire once built may warm a stranger unintended. Though they were not meant for me, I feel grateful for them. And so I rock beneath those blanketing waves of words like an egg simmering. I rock, rock with the rest. And these words are worthy less for their meaning than for how they bind us—there are days I believe that Master Stradling would make a fine ropemaker, should he try that craft.

He tells us it is an error to look for the origin of right religion in rebellions against Rome. For as Eusebius has written, true religion came with First Man, to be corrupted and sundered by first sin. What was the First Man, but a congregation of one? And with his woman, our General Mother, to serve him, there was found perfection in worship. Simple life—First Father, General Mother, first household, first church. Man and woman sustained by God's garden, bound together in love of God. Bound to the land, they held to their own hierarchy, simple and perfect. They were, then, as all right congregations have strove to be since the late, horrid sundering from earthly Paradise.

But the newer cloth was sewn with weaker stitches. The younger pot was not full fired in the kiln. She was flawed, with intended imperfections. She allowed another to intrude into the peaceful realm, bringing our fall into a state transitory, and wounded. Ignoring the authority over her that was given as a condition of her being, she was cursed. And the Lord decreed that her daughters should pay that debt, ever after, with the agony of creating new life, for in pain you shall bring forth children, Master Stradling says. Yet in perilous condition your desire shall be for your husband, and he shall rule over you.

And on my pew, this bench, I sit, and think it an amazing thing that he should choose this day to speak this text. Steven is in the ground these five days. Is Master Stradling so consumed with what we'll do that he can speak so thoughtless, or cruelly, and seek to teach her? I will not look up, to see her head, and think of the frantic springs it cups. Will there be other men who will hear of her plight? Will they speak of it, in another hall of husbandmen, on another Lord's day?

But I believe I feel the room draw close in silent tumult, like skin touched by cold metal. Perhaps he has not read this place right. I think that a cause for hope. He has only been thoughtless.

Soon after, he is done. Now comes the part of the village council that may be done in full view, before we women, and we servants, and the boys. Then we will all take our leave, so the church elders and men will speak what we'll strive to hear later, from sympathetic lips. Now Edward Adams claims that the timber work done for him by Henry Smith was done untrue, the framing lying weak and skewed on his shed; John Barnes accuses Christopher Holman of refusing to honor an agreement between them to mend the common fence betwixt their dooryards; Isaac Rowe requests, on behalf of his wife, that Elizabeth Trevor replace one churn she did borrow and break. While Isaac and Anthony Trevor debate, their wives sit nodding agreement, or humphing dismissal. It's all in the common run, thus exasperating. I think all refuse to confess that these matters will be meaningless, once we depart, thought they know it within themselves. The debates are uncommon anxious, as though a churn's is of mighty import.

And one other here, at least, thinks as I do. For when the matter of Mistress Rowe is near resolved to her satisfaction, Frances Jacobs stands, and with a voice like a broken blade says that her husband and her household will not leave this earth.

It has happened before, a woman speaking out in meeting. Once last year Midge Thomas would not be silent concerning money she claimed was owed her by the miller Williams. When the next week she pursued that same matter, and in so doing cast doubt upon his manhood, and the identity of his children, she ended in the scold's bridle. That iron mask has a backward iron tongue. Once in, a woman cannot speak nor close her mouth for the horrid rusty check between her teeth. Midge was kept in it the whole of a day, with the provision that she must remain all that time out of doors. She has no husband to silence her. But when I saw her eyes behind the mask, I knew they'd never need bridle her again about such slight concerns as loss of labor and food.

Now Master Jacobs should remove his wife—cover her mouth with words or hand, lead or bear her from this hall lest she end in like condition. But he is silent, and to me his silence testifies that they've spoken this out between them. Their household will not go.

Thus I will not. My stomach's a dry well.

John Jacobs sits mute. His wife stands, striving to look solid but swaying like a tree before a rising wind. Made vulnerable by Master Stradling's ill-chosen text, middling complaints struck her like ax blows. She must now fend them, or fear perishing before us.

Walter Haggard is adamant. His lips quiver as he shouts. He says, this is no time for you to speak! But I think he takes pleasure from it. So strange a thing, to hear a woman speak in general meeting!

Still he is right, this is no time for it. There are those among the Saints who will not go, but they have not spoken their doubts openly. Surely no woman among them has. Now the enterprise is cast in question, rejected open and in general meeting, and the half of me says: Silence, good Mistress. For I would take this passage, I would not have you stop me. I will kill you if you do. And the other half of me says to her: Speak. Speak. Speak. Speak. Speak.

But she has said all she will. Now she is weakened, and may be dragged down. If her husband will not do so, the congregation's here for the labor. She stands but there are hands on her, like vines that in an instant creep a month's growth, women's hands striving to rot her roots and bring her to their plane of earth.

Richard Hall, his black beard like a cottager's, calls John Jacobs coward. And doubly so, for he will not speak his fears outright but would have his woman do it.

John Jacobs sits with his head sullenly down. I wish you a pleasant journey, friend Richard, he says, a landing profitable to your purse and soul.

Master Stradling stands with his hands before him on the podium, as though leaning on a low rock wall. His forehead is wrinkled like blankets. He looks everywhere but at Goodwife Frances Jacobs. She looks only at him. The Saint women strive to draw her down, the men speak only to her husband. Her voice is hardy, it is barbed, and cuts through muddle: You refused me so little a thing. Why should you refuse me small kindness?

There were times when I'd have taken great joy in so confused a meeting, in being there to hear it—and indeed Josiah Flynt says again and again that this should not be done, and we should divide out those who are not to hear such debates, we should send away the children and the women. But Master Stradling knows it too late for such niceties. He looks to Mistress Jacobs and says he did not refuse it to her, but to her son; and it was not him that refused it, but the Lord.

I can take no joy in any of it. They would have me stay here, in this place ghosty as the monastery, while Adam goes before me to a country I'll never see. He said he would see me on the ship. I would keep that pledge for both of us. But still I cry in silence to Mistress Jacobs, that she should speak.

Speak, I say. And I stand, and I do. I shout that I will go with them. I say that it is the right path, and none should be kept from it that are willing. Good sir, will you permit me to go, I say to Master Stradling.

Oh, in his eyes there is such blessed relief. This is what was needed, though he never saw it before I came to him like a blessing, like a shameful prayer realized. A good word—entire unexpected—from one who speaks in the name of good and righteousness.

He says that I may go with them, if I will. And I feel free, as ever in my life.

Chapter thirteen

I Quit This Ground

As long as I keep this coming, says Susan Porter, in her best scolding goodwife's voice. She hikes up her skirts and shakes her hips, stumbles back, thumps to the ground. Lying on her back she laughs with the rest of us. As long as I keep this coming, I run the place, she says. Householder, I am!

It's the last night. I sit with my back to the apple-man, that wracked old tree's father or grandfather to all the rest of the orchard. It rained last night, and damp soaks through my seat. The moon's past full, yet the skirting ring looks solid enough to slip a finger through. When we came to the trees, the new blossoms shone in the moonlight, beautiful though there's not light enough to show their fine pink and from below they only look dark. A cool breeze blows, shaking leaves and blossoms to scratch the moon. I drink deeply through a grin, and pass the jug. The beer chills my skin but warms the muscle below. Happily, I draw up my knees and hold them in a tuck.

There are five of us here, tonight. We crept past the sagging hives, squinting at other creeping shadows, until we knew all that we saw were expected. Of course we're fidgety about being found out by any Saint. More than that, we thought of the time Gwen Hastings was rushed by a shadow stitched to no body, its own uncertain edges flying free. It wisped away like a winter's yawn. Since then, when we come to the orchard we tuck sprigs of basil behind our ears, and tonight I carry my little bundle of sidley and grima pot. The ground about the village squirms with ghosts, and sometimes they crack into the air. One can only be careful.

It's the first time Patience has come with us to the orchard. I know she's been angry since I spoke out in meeting, feeling that my leaving was somehow aimed at her. But if I can, I'll leave with her still my friend. So I've brought her with me, this first and final time. Now she giggles and rocks over her folded legs, hands on her knees, face round as a belly bowl. She's been quiet, listening and laughing, nervous about saying the wrong thing, in love with this night.

And he'd pulled it out himself by then? says Alice, laughing and gasping for breath.

He had, Susan says solemnly. She'd come back drunk from the Lord knows where. I thought I was sure to see a beating. But when she slobbered over him like a dog, I could see his anger was pretended. Then he pushed her off him, and to the floor, and pulled out his yard. She answered with the match. And as well she might, when offered such a fine gift! Ah, there are those that find having another there to watch them to be a fine and pleasurable thing. It much pains me to find my master and mistress among that number.

Though I laugh, I think to myself that fear of being caught was enough to give me some pleasure. Cold loneliness twinges me like a needle.

Susan looks about us, her face consciously set and serious. When we're alone her voice and laughter booms as though from a hollow body. Like many others she was pulled here by twisted kin-threads—her parents were dead, her uncle unwilling to take her, and someone remembered a husbandman cousin…. It's a strange thing, to be called servant by your cousin. But she never tries to insist that she's above common, and for that I like her, a good deal. She came to the orchard with Alice, servant to Sam Putnam, and Susan's particular friend.

Anne says that story puts her in mind of Tom Fullworth. He went calling to Walter Haggard's, who had been his friend from long before. Haggard's wife was there, and Gwen Taylor who was servant to them. That family's not known for humility. They had wines, and strong ales, and after much was gone Haggard asked Tom if he were well provided. He'd meant to ask whether there was wine left in Tom's cup. Tom took his meaning different—leaped to the table, and dropped trunkhose. For a dare, Mistress Haggard asked Gwen if she would not take a closer look, which she did, but got too close with the candle. Tom's cockhair went up in a flash and he went falling out into the street with balls gone bald and smoking. He had to be whipped, later, for the indecency of it, before he could yet stand straight. They had to help him to the pole.

At that Susan and Alice laugh near to cry. Patience giggles like a sparrow. Tonight we form the most of a circle, beneath the apple-man. Tonight she can pretend it will be a common thing, oft-repeated.

Patience, you pup, I think. All glad tonight to be brought out among us, feeling it's much like being brought to womanhood. I'm glad I'll not be here, the day you realize that that seeming open gate's long been walled over. But perhaps you'll take ship, one day soon. Perhaps I'll see you on that new earth. Laugh tonight, and drink, and when I bid farewell tomorrow I hope it's not for the whole of our lives, for what are you but me, less seven years? I would keep you, yet. I would be your sister and friend, and see that Sarah gives you charms to make you feel set in this world. But tomorrow, I will go.

When the laughter's gone it leaves a hole. Our casual liking fades to occasional swigs, overly contented sighs. I'm not inclined the break this quiet. The moon flashes, new leaves waving over her face, and to the north a mastiff barks. I drink.

I'd never heard that, says Susan. I think it too long after the tale, for her to remark upon it. Any harm come to the Haggards, then? she asks.

None I know of, Anne says. She might as well say that Susan's a fool to ask. Walter Haggard is an elder. Since that time he's been right staunch in his support for Master Stradling.

Part II
The Ocean Mount

Chapter fourteen

I Cross Much Country

Red-Man is a muddy brown, Caesar black and old, with drooping dewlap and sheath, tough crest and chine. We roll east over grass, in land too thin to hold a crop. Where something can be grown, a village will puddle around a river or brook. Sheep dot the hills like lice, and cows seem afterthoughts. The fields are freshly planted. A few sprout a pale green. But these seem vast, undistinguished tracts, without familiar striping. Caterpillar landlords already enclosed these lands, leaving sheep and tenants. .

Most often we skirt the villages, but on the fourth morning we cross a bridge mired between buff-clay homes. There Josiah Flynt recognizes a cousin he's not seen since his middle age. The cousin's a much younger man, but has the glazed eyes of a desperate drunkard. Off to America, we are, now, says Flynt, and shakes the man's hand warmly. We'll see you there in the years ahead. All of you!

The laughter that follows squeezes me, and I wince. Before we left, I wondered why Flynt thought he'd the strength for a new country, with his belly like an alepot, his kindling limbs. But this journey's infused him with new strength, and he talks constantly, as though he tastes his words as savory treats. He says the weather is bleaker than he would have thought. That's nonsense, in this season. He says that only he and Sarah have lived long enough to true understand what we're doing, and now there's only him. He says that nothing can stop us. He wishes that his departed wife could be here, and that she had not roasted to ashes when his house took fire. An accident, he says. He says he wishes that she had borne him sons. As the days pass, his talk gives me blisters as grating as those that grow on my feet.

My farewell to the Jacobs passed without ceremony. Except for the chest I dragged behind me like a harrow, I might have been going to the cowshed to tend to Hannah. I struggled to look sincere when I said: Thank you, good sir, and Lord keep you, good mistress, and I left their crumpled house behind me, a filthy garment that Enry will force Patience to wear. Enry will not ride this swaying cart. I thought I could walk a thousand miles.

At the bridge oxen stamped, and cartwheels rocked grooves into the road. It was before dawn, and dark. Patience clung to my arm—under the flash of torches Saints prayed, clustered in kneeling knots. I wept for the sight of Patience. Her face twisted like a drying apple. She scurried to the edge of the crowded crossroads, she would not look at me. My own mouth bent. I looked to the purple sky and wandered the crowd, giving her respect.

I heard Daniel Williams puking last night's drink into the reeds below the bridge. David Merchant went trundling to his aid, and called to James Patters for help. Good master Williams made as though he heard nothing at all.

Midge Thomas had a firepot, full of coals from her home hearth. She said to anyone who would listen that she intends to mix her coals with those of the galley fire, for keeping until we have need of flame.

Richard Hall studied the sky. The village will be empty, brittle as bubbled glass.

Isaac Rowe fought his way through, bellowing for Anne. Though I had also watched for her, I did not know myself whether it was to make amends or dodge her until she had time to cool from my blow. Laying hands on a friend is a true breach of trust—as much as her words had been. I looked down at a wicker chicken cage and thought, stubbornly, that I'd not speak to her until the shore. In that flashing light it was a simple thing, to avoid—perhaps she also avoided me. The bustle of departure was no place for amends.

The men were stubborn, judicious, as they checked cords they'd already checked thrice. Their wives were more honestly distraught, their children silent, transparent as foam. Sarah stomped up, a dour messenger. Without a word she handed me her Bible, her Book; the weight of it like a pail of cream. I looked at her in astonishment. Seeing my face she said she had another, that will hold together years more than this cracked thing.

I know of no one my age who's owned the like, I said.

Nor your position? she said.

I nodded. She'd said what I wouldn't.

You are doubly peerless, then, she said. You'll journey alone and sundered. You'll bear a Book of your own.

Sarah, I said. I clutched the gift to myself and made to kiss her on the cheek. But when I neared, she jerked. Our mouths met. I smelled chewed walnuts. I thanked her then but not, it seems to me, enough—for my words were awkward, and limped.

When she walked off, swinging her arms like staves, I knew already that I would regret our so brief leave-taking. I'd have chased her but Master Stradling was there before me, brow filling my sight. He praised me for my good part in this. He put his hand on my shoulder, turned halfway from me, and praised me to the heavy Saints. When I was called so to their attention they seemed indistinct as smoke, a swirl of faces without bounds. Still, that was a good fine feeling.

There were prayers fragile as glass, and, and muffled weeping. It was light, and the torches vain, when we took to the road to the ocean.

Our cart was sent from the village alone, the better to dodge notice and King's soldiers. Every cart will travel alone. The ship waits for us in a secret harbor. We will take to the sea. Master Stradling has thanked me for my good part in this. I stride toward Adam, and the ship that holds him like an egg ready to hatch. The ship holds my love, and a promise of bed. My passage has the making of a chapbook about it.

There are times when Anne seems to walk backward before me. On her face there's sad condemnation, and the marks from my fingers. But I think that when I see her on the shore I'll say I'm sorry, and then all will be right. This land drifts past. I imagine our carts, though unseen and spread over miles, to be a joyous processsion—the more because they are a secret thing.

Josiah Flynt is much taken by the grandeur of the passage. He huddles in a corner of the cart, wrapped in our grand purpose like a calf in a blanket. He prattles on, scratching his baggy hound beneath the jaw, infecting my own sense of the good thing we do. After a time I walk ahead, where the clanking oxbells at least pad his shrill voice. Now I lead this cart.

Farnsworth rides with us. I knew he would never be permitted to address the general congregation; perhaps he did not wish to, for he has never been to sermon. But Master Stradling must be greatly annoyed by what he says in private, for them not to travel together. For a time Farnsworth tried talking to Flynt, but the fellow was all ignorance and sideways glances when questioned by a London man. Then he tried with Samuel Baker, owner and drover of this team and cart. He has hunched shoulders, and a gray beard that drapes over his gut. His usual silence stems from satisfaction with his family and his own sound judgment. Farnsworth was bound to failure when he spoke to him from atop the finely brushed mare he calls Horse. He said to Baker that we are doing a great thing. That beyond the service of the Lord, that we will all surely remember, there is the fascination of seeing a new warp in society. There will be transformations wrought through climate, and the particulars of social design. Did Baker not agree? Baker grunted. Other than him and Flynt there is only myself, and Mistress Baker with her tiny, red-head twins. No one Farnsworth will speak to, so he is quiet except to admonish Horse. He rides off from time to time, to look at villages, or slumbering beehives, or to note the patterning of crops.

One day there is on a distant hill a city, with crumbling walls and fields like worn patchwork. Those walls must once have been a mighty fortress. Now they mark the limits of houses. As we pass the sun falls behind us, lighting the walls and houses the burning red of baked clay.

Flynt's dog drops from the cart. His spindly hindquarters won't hold him—his rump thuds the road. He struggles up, jogs slowly ahead. He passes the cart and Farnsworth's horse without seeming purpose, then veers before the hooves, and stops. Horse jerks to a halt. Farnsworth lurches, and grips her mane with a glove of fringed kidskin. The dog pants happily. Farnsworth glares down, as though he'll check for brains, or their lack, by opening up his skull on the spot. The cart rolls even with him as he kicks Horse forward. The dog wanders off just before being trampled, seeming in no way to mind his near jeopardy.

You have a degenerate animal, there, says Farnsworth. No kind to bring along.

Degenerate? Flynt cries. For a moment his mouth flaps. Never. He's the most generous beast I've known.

Easily said. Better to kill him here, than see him breed unencumbered.

His balls're long past that, Flynt says. He'll never be killed in my life. Some neighbors have said as much as you, before. Two winters past, Benjamen Smythe asked that it be done. Said it would be best to take care of his pain quick. Well there's been some good living for him, these past two years.

Better for a dog to bleed, than to unwanted breed.

I'm glad I never took those years from him. Dog! calls Flynt. The dog comes trundling up beside the cart, nose to the ground, eyes blankly up.

You are well suited to him, says Farnsworth. He kicks his mare forward.

No insult, that, Flynt calls after him. And you, sir! You're handsome as a dog, sir! Proud and loyal as a dog, sir!

Flynt is fortunate he's so old, or he would take a blow for that. I walked ahead when this dispute began, out of the dreary dust, and listened to their raised voices through the tramping and clanking bells. There's some kind of tight and vicious fly the oxen kick up, in flights lit brightly yellow by the lowering sun. Ahead of the oxen the flies hold to the grass. When Master Farnsworth rides up beside me, he's near muttering to keep his anger, pressing his ankles hard in the stirrups, resting one hand on his fighting sword. Still, I could use talk. And if there's ever a time for it, it is now. Empty agreement is a sound method when a servant would open speech.

If I may say, good sir, it's not the first time Master Flynt's denied someone asking him to rid us of that dog, I say. Probably past the proper time, I should say.

Farnsworth glances down at me, hesitates, seems to shrug. You had lived in your village long? he says.

All my life.

Which means.

Seventeen years, about.

Ah. I recall your history. You are a child of the tavern fire. John Stradling spoke of that, the night we came to your master's home.

Farnsworth looks at me strangely, as though seeing me for the first time, the pouches beneath his eyes slimming as he peers. His feathered hat has a long brim like a beak, that casts an angled shadow on his face. His mention of the fire and my origin there would commonly annoy me. Today I hear it with some slight pride—see how I have risen, to be part of this great venture.

That was hard, sir, with the baby so ill, I say.

Of course, he says.

He's slowed Horse to a steady trod, keeping to a pace even with mine. He rides closer than I'd like, his boot and Horse's flank seeming likely to nudge me aside. The mare smells of hot earth. She drops balls of swat into the road behind.

You are the girl who left without master or mistress, then, Farnsworth says. You must have strong resolve. Leaving was no small matter. I would imagine you thought as deeply as any about your home, in the time before your choice.

I suppose yes, good sir, I say, and find it flattering that he would think so.

Might I ask you about the village, then.

Sir.

What are your habits of breeding?

I'm startled, but he only peers, inquisitive, without threat. I'd thought his asking my leave to question me a courteous thing, even a kind one. Why ask, when I could not refuse?

Breeding, sir?

Mating. At what age do you first fuck?

I gape at him. There are ways of asking such a question in fun, that might have drawn me as into condemned sport. If such was his intent, he's not managed it. He looks at me as physic might at a set leech.

Come, there must be some answer you can offer, he says. I know well the habits of Londoners, and of some of the surrounding parts, from students who originated there. You yourself?

I say nothing and he waves away his question. If not yourself, then what is the typical age? he asks. How many lovers will a girl take, before taking the one she means to keep? How many after? I might ask John Stradling these things, but leaders may be among the last to know the practices of those they profess to lead. Hey?

Although he holds her back, my pace has increased to hold abreast of the mare. The oxbells are not so close as they were, or I'd like.

Then, sir, it comes with marriage, I say, and that at woman-hood.

That is what your reverend leader should say. Nothing you say will be passed on. Better, I will ask for no names. In the event, I am concerned only with generalities. I find in London that fourteen is usual, and that marriage comes several years after that. Unless the girl is unlucky, the boy unluckier still. I have made a study of this—and as I say, you may hold your answer to the common run. There will be no betrayal of past confidences. Does that suit?

He ends almost generously, and I bristle. If you will not hear the truth, sir, I cannot offer else to please you more. It comes with marriage.

He wheels horse sharply, near knocking me over. I take three stumbling steps, thrashing my skirts. When I've righted myself I glance back—the cart is yet further behind than I'd thought. The sunset's colored apple. Baker is a black patch; he puts up his arm as though to saw rope, and Caesar and Red-Man haul to a stop. There is no aid from that fool, whose silence comes all from fear and a head filled with hair. I turn back, try to pass. But Farnsworth backs the mare to stop me.

Look at this beast, he says reasonably—also absurdly, for I can scarce see else but her flank. Look at the fine gloss on her shank, the brightness of her eye, he says. These features will be passed, to a calculable degree, to any foal she may bear. To a greater degree, also calculable, that foal will possess the features of the sire. King Henry Eight had directives drawn on how to breed him horses, for war. His counselors had found the features predictable, as was the age at which mares begin to breed, and the age at which they do so most profitably. You think yourself, your friends, so different? You are a fool if you do. God has provided us with the beasts as lessons, and as models. Now.

If I would not be beaten bloody for it, I would drag him down from Horse, and maybe crack his neck. Less than men, they tell us. Well, we are more than animals, immeasurable more. An oxcart of eyes weighs on my back. I stand here to defend Saint women, one of them, yet that damnable oxcart holds damnable still.

I will not look to his face. But that refusal sticks my eyes on his leather switch. The wood handle's carved with even, hollow diamonds. He fingers it, with a kidskin glove. He tells me that all he need say is that I answered back.

That's a mistaken threat. Beatings and whippings in public need explanation. But then I think that such explanations are commonly made to master and mistress, that they may know why they'll lose their labor for some short time. To whom will they be made now? Who call for them? I cast about for a grip. There is none in those behind me, these cowards who shy from conflict with any man of the higher stations they claim to scorn—they think I stand here alone. There is none in good Master Farnsworth's regard for Saint women. I find one in my voice.

Fifteen is usual for fucking, I should say, good sir. Younger for some, older for many. It is a small place, and difficult to hide. Some plan to wait for marriage but with one thing and another it is rare to wait so long.

You yourself?

Good sir, you said you would not ask such.

Yes. Thank you. I am glad to have an answer before night.

He nods down the road. Above our path thunderheads huddle like collapsed castles. All the while he harried me, he held himself composed enough to note the sky. The clouds are sickly lit by the sun deepening behind me. There's a flick of lightning across a bulge of cloud, a web of curt power that vanishes as soon as it is bared. I catch my breath.

It's night and we crowd beneath the cart, vying in half sleep for the dry strips, nudged into trickles of the downpour. I toss about, among castoff fools I thought a grand parade. Until they see me with Adam they will think I stand alone, never walking with them but only among them. Through the hairy blanket of rain I think I see the shadows of men. They form from windblown water, and bow beneath it. Lumpish, and hopeless, but they seem to labor. They pass beneath the torrent. They are plowing. This earth will never take good seed. Farnsworth lays himself beside me—through the night I lie awake, pinned unwilling between him and drenching rain, waiting for lightning and a creeping hand that never comes.

Chapter fifteen

I Come to the Sea

The first seabrush is straight as border posts. But as we roll further east, leaving the blown, barren grasslands, the brush begins slowly to craze, the new flats of gray pebbles scarcely able to hold their roots firm against the wind. Here we walk through miles of stunted brush, dragged by the wind into frozen, pleading poses. Salt clutches the air and above us birds crank in tightening circles. Their black-and-white heads are the starkest color of this gray ground, this sky.

The last hill is highest. From inland it seems a wall, built to shield dry ground. A road cut from light, sandy soil jogs back on itself, cheating the slope. With growls and curses we drag around the cart, and crest. Beyond, the land slopes for slow miles toward the last, cracked rocks, and then the forever gray of the sea.

The wind here is a shrieking thing, soaked in desperate salts. The coast, a far white line, holds my eyes like a bolt. This is no sight to love, yet I cannot look away. The slope to the ocean seems a plunge and I put my hand to the side of the cart. I hold myself, against the wind. I hold myself to earth. An anchor is needed, here.

The ocean is a stone giant, that's took on life and crippled breath. I had thought it would be placid, a pond swollen to cover all in sight. I grip tight Sarah's mightily generous gift. A deluge, a flood, a cap of the deeps—the ocean of this Book rises and falls, conceals, makes a calm, watery road, until the Lord speaks it different and brings fury to those waters. *And the Lord hurled a mighty wind upon the sea, and there was a great tempest upon the sea.*

But before me all the power of a storm is made visible in water, heavy and perilous as iron cannon shot. As we roll along the last of the road, the land coarsens into tumbled boulders, punched by pools that ripple under oncoming tides. The little twins sob, they bury their heads. Though Mistress Baker strives to hush them, tears leak through her voice. At last the road is done. Our cart clunks forward, in sharp starts, over rocks and the gaps between. The oxen are at hazard. Baker stays close beside, whispering, calming them, as they're squeezed between waves and clattering wheels. Then, with a grating crash, a wheel splinters to an oval. I sigh, and go to help prop up the body of the cart.

Driftwood fires burn about the furthest reach of water, cupped by Saints who guard them from ocean winds with their backs. The sun's near to setting. Slowly, graceful as stars, four wagon lamps swing down the distant hill. Their twins are on the sea, in the ship. Each of those tiny flickering points is a promise, of Adam, his arms. It will be harder than ever, I think, to be so close to him and no place to hide, our affection never openly known. But though it will be a furious hard thing, it's a burden I burn to bear.

We sort our gear in piles. Already there are chickens and geese, a pregnant sow, goats and cats, all caged among crates of shoes. This place is all the stranger for these homey beasts. A few sagging sheds, near collapsing, adorn the higher packs of stone. They are poorer than they were this morn—their stripped boards burn, in six fires. I set down a trunk and a Baker girl perches on it like a soaked duckling. The cart is empty as a cold oven. With grieving face Baker looses Caesar and Red-Man. On our vessel there will be no stall adequate for an ox. They hump away, searching for fresh water and a place from out this wind.

The bonfires of driftwood and shed timber are now like to

houses, that Saints visit as they would a home after harvest or a birth; a pause beside one serves for a knock. Like a welcoming door a family swerves, admitting the guest. But there is a last flame, closest beside the water, built by folk unmarried and near to my age. Among their shadows is Susan's. Her laugh thuds to me, cut off quick in the wind.

I long to see a familiar face, but feel a twist at the thought that Anne may be with them. I had rather come upon her alone, that I may offer simple apology. And whether she has arrived or no, the others may judge me for the night in the orchard. I fear they'll find me wanting—I might find myself so. But I hold my breath and walk to them, forcing care across the rocks.

I join the circle wordlessly, bending as though it was the fire that drew me. Briskly I rub my hands together, and smile hard. Then I look up, into Abigail's clean face. To my surprise, that is no wholly horrid thing—seeing her is like finding a dirty blanket in the cold. Her cutting lines remind me of common labor, summer sun, and despised tasks that now comfort me to think of. A familiar face may guard against flat, probing wind.

Abigail smiles wryly, draws in her elbows tight, and shivers. Here we will not dispute. If we are not sisterly, we may at least leave old grudges for a time.

Mabel sits closest to the fire, hunched over like a fat, aged goat.

Well met. This is a bleak place, I say to all.

Well met. Well met, it is, they say.

Night comes on. The wind pinches words from our tongues. But in Susan's voice, at least, is warmth and no care, and my fright about this meeting is gone. She smiles at me roundly. There is no need for challenges, tonight. There is only relief that we have safely come, and fear about what's yet to do, and the hiss of water.

Were your journeys glad ones? I say.

Ask Susan, someone says.

Oh fine, says Susan. She tells me about golem boys, who threw apple cores from behind a pen of black pigs. I think to myself that I have a better tale than that, what Farnsworth said to me would make for warm gossip. But something holds me...

This weed gives a horrid stench, says Abigail. She presses some with her toe, drags it from the wood.

It does, I say, and squat to pull away a tendril that curls like a burning spider. Now the drifting stars are near to us.

Ah, now there's a fire, says Abigail. Without the black weeds air reaches to the heart. The wind presses it to the stone, like kneaded dough. It swells, guarded by Mabel's stubborn body.

There may've been a hint in Abigail's words that there's none more fit than me to make fires for her. I say nothing, but it does give me a small, sickly rap. I could hear the coming wagons, if not for the rush of air.

Water sluices through channels that broaden to flat slabs. There is only a single narrow fan of sand, below the lichen covered shed-frames. Then there is black water, and on it, somewhere, is Adam. Seawater heaves behind. To stare upon it might seem strange, for all here wish to ignore it. They plant their eyes willfully on blown fire.

When did the ship come, I say, and turn from them, from Abigail, to watch the swaying lights.

The *ships*, says Alice. She saw them when they arrived, shortly after noon. Now they are anchored across the teeming inner waters, behind a spit that gives semblance of shelter. When all are here the launches will come so we may begin final lading. Already the ships hold our base needs, purchased and laden in home port.

But I listen only a little, scarce noting even that there is more than one ship. Hearing of them, their situation, makes me feel that I tread the planks of the deck on this instant. I am there with him, watching the fires on shore beacon farewell to this land, and hope for a new one. On the bulwark his hand caps mine.

There is the *Neptunus,* and the *Prosperous Joan*, says Abigail. She sounds mightily impressed that we should need two. It speaks well for the dedication of the Saints that so many should have come.

So great, this water. Should you have credited it? I say, and walk down to look. In the little sand are set rotten pilings, old enough that no chain nor wood's left between.

Do not drown, says Susan.

A wave slips to meet me, and I dip in my fingers. Under the

wind it seems cold as an icehouse. With ill-thought haste I suck my hand to warm it.

And then there is such salt! Before me I see the miser Master Jacobs with his pitiful cone, that he would dole out to each of us, at his pleasure, in pinches. Here there is a world of seasoning for meat! I forget that this water may carry all manner of illness; I laugh at the taste. The lights across the water are too distant to reflect, the sea too uncertain. They beckon over a deep valley. But now I feel I know what they ride upon, and am carelessly happy as never since we left.

To think we wanted for it, at home, I say to Susan, near giggling. She looks at me as though I'm mad. But I care nothing for that and I listen, happy, as she turns to argue with the others about Daniel Miller's looks. I could tell them that though his looks are wanting, he can sew his mouth closed when it is right. That marks him a finer man than I would once have thought.

Isaac Rowe's beard and pug nose are cast marigold. He hulks, he rakes his gaze across our faces. He leaves like a barrow let slip down a hill.

And what was that, I say.

That would be his search for Anne, says Susan.

Well, he should find her soon enough, I say, casually as I can. Susan and Alice, at least, must now think of the orchard. I will not call attention to my next meeting with Anne, that they may cast their gaze there, and make light talk of it.

Susan looks at me strangely. She says that Anne was not to be seen, on the road.

There were a great many of carts. It's not strange you didn't see her.

She was not to be found by anyone.

Abigail says that Isaac looked high and low, before we left. It passes understanding, to think why he should think to find her at the end of the road. The faithless are long behind us, now, she says.

My hate for this petty harlot is a grima come prancing.

She ran, you mean. And as I voice that question, I know it is no question at all. She did run. I know that Anne did run.

Something is said in answer. I nod, and agree. But I am watching Isaac.

He eases to another bunch. He is hopeful, shamed, a dog begging bones. That's a familiar gait. That's mine own thoughts, visible here on earth. That's the look of a lost lover, seeking out his mate. Roots ball in my muddy guts. I breathe faster. Isaac's face was like a mirror, for it held the same need in it I feel all through my body when I think of Adam. Anne would be for me like cleansing water—but that she may never wash me.

All come!

All come!

All come!

They've torn one shed out almost entire, leaving only a few strakes of framing work. The rest burns, drawing us. When we are gathered, Master Stradling stands on a barrel, and speaks. There is a black kettle beside the thickening coals. His arm stretches east to the water. We will cross these watery depths. We will take to ship, on the morrow.

So, Isaac, you took Anne in the night, for your own. You took her from me. The last time I touched her was to strike her face and when I strove to comfort her for it. I thought her bitter when she spoke to Adam in the woods. But she would have been aggrieved at any man coming then, any woman. There were chances to speak to me after but it is no simple thing, saying outright what you most hate, or best want, in the world.

Isaac, you would say I cannot know this, of your sin and crime. But I do know it. It is like blood that fills my eyes and ears. There are pilings here I would lash you to, Sarah's old wrath come fresh, and made mine, on an empty coast.

Hot wine simmers in the kettle. Master Stradling ladles it out by the cup. It is right. He knows always how to bind us, at hard moments. He has known what to do from the first.

Isaac takes a steaming stoneware cup. His smile is forced—I know what he means to mask with it. His crimes have took my friend from me, made forgiveness impossible—our petty quarrel may grow unbounded in my thoughts, becoming my last memory of her. And standing there on shore, waiting for dawn and the launches that will bear me from this land, I wish of all things that I might kill him for it.

Chapter sixteen

I Board a Mighty Contrivance

Out across the crests that rise so startling are the ships, each flying a lone, slanted sail to keep hulls hauled strongly against anchor lines. They're sheltered behind a long spit of rock that angles for the shore, but vanishes below water before it can reach. The spit's too low for surety. The tide brings over raven sheets that then foam white. The ships are far away, and look to float calmly, like old shoes tossed to drift downriver for a race. Yet the closer waters still flood and course, swirling an uneasy inner sea. The spit should give succor, but when the waves reach us they seem still untrammeled.

It is scarce dawn. Our things are sorted into stacks, neat as they may be on this jagged ground. The launches are broken looms—they are wounded beetles. The legs are gripped by men who must have labored each day from birth, for they have not even the small belly fat a husbandman may take on in winter. Though their skin is aged with sun, none are old; the ocean strips men to death before the world can sag their bones. On some of them skin moves loosely over muscle in first retreat. They have not much longer at this craft. Their skin is cooked, but I think them raw of spirit.

The Saints board in order of precedence, never saying they will do so, perhaps never noting it even to themselves. Some hesitate before climbing into a boat, others stride in with carelessness that speaks of kept fear. A few weep—for the intimacy of the foam, for the scarcity of wood beneath. When a launch is full the broken loom swiftly mends; the beetle legs lower, and scrabble the launches away. Master Stradling is in the first prow, his back to the ships, twisting to face them as he might.

Hours, hours later, my time to board has come. The shore is at last empty but for a lone boatload of us, the tide shifted. We need wade out—they will not pull up for fear of waves, or so they say. I think it much pleases them to see Saints labor in surf.

I have run my fingers through chill foam, and the clean water beneath. Now I step into the ocean. It wraps coaxing tentacles about my ankles, a delicate, slender-fingered surge that would draw me to a vast, monstrous chasm. On the eddy, remnant sand slips from beneath my feet, leaving me in shallow holes. I cannot stay in this pool of illness. I jerk for the launch. With a gasp I put out my hand, but the boat dips away, a nervous calf. I'd expected constancy, a cradle's rocking, and I near fall. But it swings back. I catch the edge with a ridiculous, panting bleat. Weathered splinters pierce my palm.

Someone grabs my wrist. He draws me up, twisting my elbow, stabbing me with pain. Beside my flailing he seems most regal, and grins at me with great good humor. I clamber in—mouth tight, but I am grateful for the platform. Below is naught but black, wet tumult.

Flynt stands in the play of surf, his dog snuffling at ankles wet again and again by scurrying foam. His hand lifts slightly, as though he could draw the boat to shore if only we would reach for him. He looks a boy who knows it's wrong to ask for something. With each wave the launch drifts closer to shore and a sailor drops into the water, on the ocean side, not wanting the boat between him and the oncoming swells lest the launch plow him under. There must be a sharp slope to the bottom, for he's wet to his chest, and true disgusted.

I will not look at the other Saints, for fear their faces will hold the same contempt as the sailor's. That would breed contempt in me. Already I see Flynt leaning on my shoulder during a long stumble through the surf. We'd end dumped in laughter, and frigid foam. Suddenly I long to leave him on the shore, and pretend we never knew him as we sail away.

But the man who grabbed me from the water has his own leg over the side. He is a tall man with narrowly slanted shoulders, and has the look of an underfed horse. He wades to shore. All the while Flynt's mouth works, but his voice is smothered.

They return to us like a three-legged man—Flynt lurches on the leg away from the sailor, as though he must be a perfect cripple to deserve aid. His dog barks on shore as Flynt moves with short, dangerous hops, leaning with both hands hooked over one stooped shoulder.

The sailor has loamy eyes, and hair that was likely much the same until the sun took it. His skin's gone tan in places, but in others it burned. There, it shows a young man's plague of tiny pits. He shows little expression until Flynt's in the boat. Then I catch a flash of embarrassment as he turns to fetch the dog.

The masts casts slim shadows under *Neptunus*. I hold up my hand, against the sun. We pull up heavily under the wooden flank. For jagged moments the bundled sails block the glare. I drop my hand then, but the light flashes back stronger, blinding me.

Our river-craft were babes. *Neptunus* rolls with the waves, but it is like a mountain, and under the rolling may avalanche. The center deck's lowest, front and back rising as though they strain to escape the navel. Cords and lines are drawn tightly to the edge of the decking, like huge woven nets cast down on the masts. Salt veins gray, barnacle-spackled wood. When we coast into the final massive shadow the sunken hull is green, indistinct with weed.

I climb a rope ladder, a line running from the deck to clinch my waist for surety. Sailors flow around bunched Saints who have lapsed to terror or determined silence. The Saints stand with hands at their sides, clutching children before them like Romish crosses. They are slippery rocks in the sailor's stream.

The picture I hold of my meeting with Adam has been a fine, full one. I have seen his lanky body, felt his weight against me, run my finger along his chin without any reprimand that I come near to pulling him by the beard. I've smelt his loosed, tussled hair. Being so clear, the picture is more readily thrown away. Not seeing him at once, I know I am not to see him at all this passage. He is on the *Prosperous Joan*, two hundred yards, an eternity of sea away, and I laugh out loud, a sharp, bitter bark.

Candlelight strikes the walls, too strong. Wood cuts light before it may fade as it would in Master Stradling's great hall, where we packed in congregation as we will here. No piercings, no windows give even a lie of space. A covered grate leaks a vacant square of light to lay at my feet. The grate is scarcely above my head. Most men will stoop. When they enter they add their stifling breath. I muddle along a broken track of chests and huddled, quiet bodies, to where stem-post meets deadwood, where the mate with the salted crust of beard told me I must go. I sit and rest my head where the beams make their angle. There is the wasted smell of meat, the rotten, chewed smell of rat. From overhead comes a dull, ordered tramping.

Captain Beechwood's jaw tapers without weakening. His nose is too broad for his face. He's made of odd parts, joined by a willfulness that spurts from flat blue eyes. The browns and reds of his tunic have bleached away to show the first cream cloth below. He had better have used some fastening. The brim of the hat hung carelessly by his waist is whorled with lines of dried salt. Footsteps overhead thud, and beat.

He says this hold was filled with meat for the Baltic. I knew that I smelled beef. This is the first time it has borne passengers, he says, but we are without Writs of Passage. Without writs, this cargo is much the same as meat, for now no lord can say that our journey only rids the land of rubbish, and that it may yet turn a profit for them on distant shores. Without writs we are beholden only to him, and he to none.

He wonders if we know what it is for a man to own his own vessel. *What profit has a man from all the toil and strain with which he labors beneath the sun?* he asks. It is startling to hear scripture from this stringent mouth, and seems vacant punctuation, serving to mark out the passion he feels for this his property.

These are our laws of conduct, he says, and holds his hand up with palm to himself. First, he says, and his thumb vanishes. He says we will be divided into watches, eight or ten persons to each, three to eat at a time. Most will sleep on deck except in the worst weather. Second, and his hand is a shadow-play crown. Twice weekly we will bring our bedding to air. We will take from the casks of vinegar, and scrub to the very corners. He says we will thank him for this, when we do not end as the *Dove*, with one hundred thirty of one hundred eighty lost. Or the voyage of our own Elder Blackwell, with like numbers of fluxed dead.

Third, he says. But now I am drifting, seeing behind us a trail, hundreds long, of dead let fall in the sea.

Finally the captain drops his fist like a fishing weight. There will be no intercourse between the crew and our people, he says. His use of that word is plain. I raise my head, crane about. There must be others that wish to whip him with their tongues. But all are indistinct, massed in cloth and warm breath, oppressed by fear of water and need for what this man knows. What need of laws, if there are none to break them? he asks. He wishes us a pleasant voyage, ladies. He is gone from the hold, like hot tar spilled out.

I am below when the ship's aborning, the anchor pulled to sea breeze with muffled shouts, leaden footfalls, and a dim rush of foam near by to my head. I rise and fall, a leaf in a stream. An earthen lamp lights the timber grain. The shadow of a 'scaped hair shifts like a sundial. Prayed words are uncommon even. Surely, the hidden wave pumps me full of filthy liquor. That spirit gropes, it slides. I squeeze my eyes tight, lay on my side with my head propped on clothes. My arm drains of blood. I clench my fist and bury it in dirty skirts. How familiar their smell. Behind me Daniel retches. His gut-stink floods the hold, drowning more Saints. Many gag. I bite my lip; I bleed copper.

Think what men have endured, when given grace to endure it. Think of those on open sea, when God brought rains and made sea of all the earth.

Chapter seventeen

I Endure a Passage

First. Youths, and a Fool's Plot.

Daniel Williams and Jonathan Hooker plot ill. Beechwood's cabin is often empty, they whisper. It is the only space on board that is so. It is true at the stern, close by to where a pole leads from a tiller to the deck pilot. I long for sleep; a small dying of wind has opened the deck to many Saints, leaving the hold as free from their sickening swelter as it will ever be. But the murmuring rubs me, and I say in aged voice that I should not press for entrance to a captain's cabin. These are fools, these boys who know nothing of a closeroom.

Daniel tells me to hush. Jonathan threatens to mark me a scold. I am silent at that. But their scorn leaves me angry, and steals my sleep. They crouch, whispering, planning some play.

Second. A Text, Challenged.

John Henders was the sailor that dragged me into the launch, and helped Flynt to it. Now he chews salt meat to spit in the dog's gummy mouth. He runs his hands over the fur, like it's a coat he's

a distant man, the destruction of their congregation follows not far behind. The wise woman builds her house. The foolish plucks the structure down with her hands.

Now his voice is in steady flight, in spite of the plaguing imp. I raise my eyes to him. He's found a calm place within mockery. It is a matter deserving of all our pride. However spoke, I now feel this prayer a good thing. Only the foolish would let such a shared text pass by. Now, when I pray aloud, I speak clear.

Third. Leviathan Encountered.

A fine, fresh sun. The sails are new-hatched wings, tethered yet to the shell by strings of white. This is all a fine knot I cannot begin to unravel. The sailors pull on the strands, sure as initiates.

Sometimes the *Prosperous Joan* sails close enough that I can tell her misnamed. Her planks bow; her flank is a raft of shallow furrows. The tits of her figurehead are yellowed, sea-stripped. But now she sails at a goodly distance, and might be a toy.

I lean out, a bird, plunging to the next trough with beak down for fish. But to see only churning water there—slipping, falling onto itself—it leaves me dizzy. I cling to a line. The feel of it hauls me to memories of making brooms. That gives me some welcome foundation. But again I lean out, testing how long I may bear it.

I imagine us anchored, standing starkly still, amidst a world-circling river striving to sweep us toward our abandoned home. If the anchor lets go, the wind will still give us a shade of grip. We may think we ride forward while we're borne invisibly back, one day crushing against old land. I shake my head. Again it seems that on each rise we hold steady, that every fall is a plunge toward America.

From nowhere, the bright water frames a black stone. A moment past, there was nothing. I think a sinking wave must have bared the tip of a sea-mount. But before I can shout warning to the pilot, the rock blows out steam. It sinks below the swells.

I cannot credit it, that so great a thing should live! My cry of warning turns to amazement, nearly a laugh. Again the whale surfaces. This time it swims, leviathan gentle and regular, a slight fifty feet from our flank. Under the brisk wind the waves are sharp as flame. Well, there are those that should think this thing fit for a lake of fire.

Behind me feet come rushing, and I turn to watch all come to see the beast. Alice's fearful, tipping along as on hot sand, as though afraid that it may lurch from the sea and for her. Behind her Master Stradling clambers to the deck, his face tight. I wonder what was said to him below, to spark such blue anger as I see in him. Elders climb up after. Captain Beechwood follows the Saints like a drover. But I have no time to think on dissent within these men, or on councils closed to me. The whale's breath blasts like signal smoke—what roads does it follow, this thing of warped, inhuman, yet kingly soul?

We are no cousin to you, no matter our bulk, I think. Do not come near with eyes of love. Saints crowd, gasping at a creature that seems to them like to a heaving barn—full of meat, and blood, and windy breath. The *Joan*'s too distant to recognize features on the tiny, wavering poppets that clump her deck. But I imagine Adam among them, across the watery expanse. Our eyes may fix on this same astonishing thing.

Fourth. Slumber.

I lay in my humid angle, in a half-dream of love and straw. Slowly, swervingly, I stroke my legs, the one against the other. They heat like rope drawn through the palm. Lightly I grate my teeth. Daniel and Jonathan have called to mind this vessel's sole hidden room. I will take him, in the cabin that gives us our course. Hidden. Away. Our own small thing.

Fifth. Geography.

These things are said of where we go:

That it is a wild land, empty as a dry skull, save for men with furnace bellies, who need not build external fire.

That those men have no cities. They call *town* any place they may gather, and stretch skins above their heads against the rain. Prester John once sailed there. He scorned to speak with them, or have truck. Yet he left with full cargo of fat birds and green stone.

That they do have cities, each laying beneath its mountain. The savages visit the cities once in each year, when they pay their respect to the dead. They dance without tune. They know not the name of the Lord.

That it is none of it enclosed. The forests are vast, and make our poor woods look like to an ordered garden. I was born in a green, gold country. We go where colors are lost and bewildered.

That there are as yet no grima. But the beasts are awash in savage souls, replete to their bones with them. A savage lives unbaptized. The ghosts of their children rest in shrews and bats. Those of their elders stick in harts, in hares; in the paws of martens, and the beaks of cranes. That the savages slump like badgers. The first grima will look like stunted weasels. With our coming they'll twist from hewed trees, and charcoal, and the splinters off a cooper's mallet.

That the stars are rain in sunlight. That the moon is a babe's palm.

Sixth. *The Actor and the Orange Girl.*

Henders stares at his food as though to guard his pink, pitted face from more sun. He is right to do so. I think he would look finer, if only he shielded his skin. His thin, burnt hair parts at the top, drawn back to a pigtail he often looses. His words come slowly, as through he must structure each from found twigs. At times he's speaking more to himself than to us. Now he chews salt beef for himself and Flynt's dog, and tells us tales of whores.

He knows Saffronhill, he knows Turmil Street. He remembers every whore he's had, or he is a right fine liar. He says that the Queen of Morocco was a Spaniard, and not a bit of African. Long-Haired

Mistress Spenser was bald, but had plenty 'tween her legs. Welsh Nan Peg the Seaman's Sister was a field rat. Near all gentlemen like to think they're stealing a woman from under a sailor's care.

Mistress Osbridge's scolding daughter, Henders says. As he says that he laughs, rocking his head up, spitting bits of food. The walls in that place were thin. He could hear insults, slaps, and each gentleman's meek, harried pleas. Their faces were proper, dignified, often slightly bruised. He notes her fee. It's right amazing—it would make close to my season's pay. To be given such, and for slaps…there have been times I would have thought *that* a tolerable good condition.

I cast eyes for the *Joan*. But my view is blocked by a slung launch, and Jonathan Hooker's annoying stance. He stands, consciously careless, beside two Low country brothers whose speech recalls guttural pigs. It passes understanding that there was a time I chose to be with this sallow boy. It is scant wonder I may envy a scolding daughter.

Young Nan Orange was the death of John Churchill, Henders says.

How was that? I say.

He wipes his mouth, seeming surprised that any should ask. Our mess has been quiet, through all his tales. I look at him straight. He can take my words, if he will, without my repeating them. A long moment later, he does, offering the tale to all equal, never noting that it was I as asked for it.

He tells us that the girls to love best are the orange girls. Betty Orange, Nan Orange. Orange Mary. They have their baskets, their pushcarts. They sell fruit brought in on fast ships. They keep thick knives in their belts. Their fingers are sticky. The better kind have cones of sugar. Wealthy children lick them, then suck on lemon. But the greatest part of their money is not in fruit, but in the rooms they let, behind the curbs they work. All he'd need do is wink, when the children had gone. Orange Mary made him buy a piece of fruit. He passed by Nan Orange, before the show, in the courtyard, where he watched John Churchill die.

His words have been tentative. Now, though they thud like turf, the clumsy clods make a plot where pictures may bud. The theater is round as a kettle; the play bloody. The audience fills the pit, they lean against the rails, they crack nuts and chew sweet dainties.

Churchill's boots hold the feet of a true player, practiced in traipsing and the pace of farce. Though he does not care for this work, it is by a playwright he honors; he gives what he may to the words and acts. He prances and deals out death to a baker; to a treacherous midwife; to a Duke of France. The kettle theater's full of bored, squinting eyes. They have seen this manner of death.

John Churchill is fine as a hawk, and as far above the coney public. When he looks to them his eyes never rest. He kneels, and blinds the baker, leaving sawdust in circles on his trunkhose knees.

When there is a cry from the courtyard, jolting him upright, there must be few that do not think it part of the play. It is only from the silence of the other players, the men in horsehair wigs, that one could know something is wrong. Another cry turns his feet to lofting ravens. They bear him to the passage out. He is half through before he knows it himself. He never sees the gaping burrows that are the mouths of paid customers.

Nan Orange lies in the dust. Over her stands a man of noble birth. His cloak's draped in purple trim and silver points. He struck her, in dispute over price. Likely he's disputed with her for the pleasure in it. Nan Orange was never precious, nor thought herself so. She's readily bargained down.

As the owner of the theater, Churchill has regular small coins from her and from any orange girl to work his courtyard. But he values her for more than her groats, and with the fury of a broody thing he strikes the noble back. The man stumbles. In disbelief he summons a blade, dancing in crimson tassel.

They fight above Nan Orange. She lies with broken nose, blood on her chin, blood on her scalp where a tuft of pale hair was torn away. Oranges and an empty basket lie tumbled about her. There's scarce less audience than for the stage—and now, no need for stillness. They shout and stamp. All declare their favorite.

Off of the stage, Churchill's shrunk; he feels himself an old bull that has lost the strength to fight. He had never learned proper combat, not even in his vanished, voracious youth. He fights clumsily, sword hesitant. His fear and weariness grow. Betty Orange cries for them to stop and, perhaps, if Churchill had not struck him, the noble would be willing. He parries mockingly. Churchill is stubborn, and flails at him. He's pushed, by all there, down a fickle slope. Churchill is an actor, and owner of the place. Nan Orange is freckled. Her hair's like pale wheat.

John Churchill strikes furiously and well, below the armpit. But his blade is dull, meant for play-acting. It scarce cuts the weave. The noble laughs when he sees his shirt will need repair.

Churchill feels something tear him—rending as silence, easy as ale. His world's burst a new horizon; his navel's the rising sun. He looks down at a lazy edge that tickles the back of his stomach. Before there is pain he realizes what's been done to him, the nature of the play. He doubles as though struck by a club. Then the sword is at his throat, only the tip, so—Henders presses finger to mottled neck, as though testing water. But the noble steps back without giving the threatened cut. He berates Nan Orange for a miser and a whore.

She crawls to Churchill. She is over him, clutching at his shoulder, unwilling to touch him beside a wound. But he dies choking on his blood, curled like a babe, amid oranges they have broken and trampled in their fighting. Their juice draws the dust.

Henders is done with the tale. He unbinds his hair, lets it fall forward before pulling it tightly back and tying it with his head up, eyes shut tight.

You show little sense of that story, I say.

And how is that?

You said she killed him. She did not, at all.

And how did she not. He was well enough, before taking up with her. Owner of a theater, and more.

That's not at all the same thing. How are you to blame her for another's acts.

Likely she made to claw that fucking gentleman. Without that, her fellow'd be alive.

Come, tell the girl more, says Jake Macauley. His voice is light, his arms smooth as beech trees. You and she may as well be cousins. No cause to be rude or stingy with a tale.

At that I look at Henders closely. He mashes his lips together, turning them pale in that red face. But now I see things I did not before. Stolid men taught him to hold himself. He looks underfed, for he brought his stomach to sea late; in his youth he fed on butter. He does not threaten quick movement, as a vagabond would. He was a husbandman—at least born to one, and raised for a time. Before I can stab him with what I've seen, he is up and away to the rear of the ship, the dog staring wistfully after.

I shake my head and look to sea, away from sailors and the troubles of orange girls.

Seventh, and Last. A Doom Proclaimed.

Daniel Williams and Jonathan Hooker are taken up for drunkenness. In the hold they broke into a cask of good beer. They would not have been found out, had they stayed to the deck, where the liquor on their breath would have been swept away, or had they lay in the hold, enjoying the deep, numb comfort of much beer. But of course they would not stop at that. When they were drunk, they went to the captain's cabin with a fine collection of three dead rats. The rats dangled from the ceiling like hanged men. Surely that was not part of their first plan. But I wonder how they thought it should profit them, even so far into drink.

Their backs are white, the lash brown as Beechwood's mood. Daniel struggles to hold his face. But it twists fearfully, and is from his grasp.

At home he would have received a lashing of nothing harder than a tongue; his father should see to that. But now his father is not to be seen. He and his family cling to the hold, for they will not see theirs beaten—and need not, for this whipping was not called for by Saint law. In their place stands Master Stradling. His brow is creased with squinting, and perhaps a hint of grief. He will not speak up for the boys. It may be that he has great respect for particular authority.

My pity is for Jonathan. We did not part well as lovers, but I do remember the feel of him. A memory of another can leave a tender bit of feeling, whether or no the memory's worthy of it. Jonathan follows easily. Today he trailed behind one of poor judgment and humors. His back that once I clutched is smooth, trembling from touch of air and fear of what's to come.

There is none of the ceremony the Saints should have brought to this, no words to begin or sanctify. The lash falls, and slaps like a book slammed shut. A welt rises on Daniel like a skein of red yarn. He yelps, sucking in his lower lip to bite and stop the cry. But had I not seen the lash drop, I should have thought it struck Jonathan. He seems near to crumbling, strangely attired in hat and no shirt, and squints at the deck as though there's much there of interest.

The Saints have determined not to show themselves disturbed, and watch as from a great distance. They will show Beechwood that they have seen whippings before. It is no great task to stay distant—I suspect the mate was told to not cut flesh. He does not lean into the blows, only striking with force enough to sling out loops on those he already dropped.

Christ, Jonathan says quietly, his head drooped between arms that stretch rigid to the mast.

Three more for that, if you would, says Master Stradling.

I watch the Saint elders closely, wondering if they'll resent Master Stradling's naming a penalty without general consultation. But in Joseph Butler I see only satisfaction that we can be party to the judgment. He pulls in one cheek, smiles slightly. They should thank Jonathan for giving them justified cause, I think bitterly.

Hawley, one more for that, when you're to him, Captain Beechwood says. He speaks casually, as though he'd always meant to punish the curse.

Master Stradling says nothing. His arms cross before him, pulled tight against his body as for warmth on this mild day. It was not grief I saw in him. He does not turn from the whip that slaps again and again on Daniel Williams' back, and it is not to show that he will not. There is in him a passion for this work, that he would learn to master himself. Beechwood did not need turn to a muddle of Saints before he laid hands upon the lash. He only took it from a cloth bag, and gave it to moon-face whose name is Hawley, and told him to use it well, five times, on two boys' backs.

Chapter eighteen

I'm Betrayed by Leaks

The waves have hardened, twisting together into butts and kegs that tumble in drawn, rolling lines. Now the water seems hard as flexing oak. Waves march in ranks, thudding against keel and deadwood.

The *Prosperous Joan* looks a hard, shriveled gourd, and threatens to crack. A launch hauls raggedly between us, bearing requests for instruction and the terse replies from off *Neptunus*. There is nothing for them to do but pump, and no need for help for so long as the Saints on *Joan* are fit to hold a handle. I watch anxiously, fearing that the seawater may bear illness into the sink of Adam's hold.

Our sister ship lurches against waves that run east. They scorn the south wind that drives us. It is colder. The crowds on deck tighten as the gray sky lowers, pressing cold between. The Baker twins drape blankets over their heads to catch warm breath. In her weeks on *Neptunus*, Abigail has shriveled to a cruel, twiggy core. I think it's been days since she ate anything she didn't retch straight back. She only sits staring, face pale under a blue hood, turning a useless bowl of oats brought her by a sore, smitten Daniel Williams. Many are ill as she.

Once she catches me looking. Then her face turns poisonous,

in an instant, as though it's me that has sickened her. I turn away, holding that same hate. She's wrong if she thinks this passage does not touch me. My own body slowly softens, loosened under the rocking and thudding that turns flesh to soggy paper. My nostrils and lips are chafed raw, and stinging.

I might creep to the hold. But it is close, rotten, damp with bilge water and rat's filth. Breathing there should spread sticky waste on my tongue, without relief. I chasten myself to wait. One day this will all seem short. When we have come together on a green shore, this will be an instant. This is how it must be. Good things need their suffering.

There is right penance in these thoughts, yet I know them ridiculous. They are but foolish echoes, flicks off the walls of remembered sermons. I wait for the end of our passage and for what it will bring, girding for more weeks of wind, jarred wood, and the stench of spilled inners. What a tale I'll have to tell, to my future babes—of an ocean that seemed boundless, and a new land that one day rose in the West like a swimmer's brow. But the end comes sudden as the edge of the world, when the seams of the *Prosperous Joan* loose, and give way.

The first launch lowered from the *Joan* is heavy with Saints, the cables swaying like the arm of a mill in fallow season. The launch nudges aside floating cages. Their denizens have been slaughtered; the knotty sailors who return the *Joan* to England will first feast well on chicken.

The launch struggles through wicker refuse, and across the chop. Treasured iron wares splash from the uncaring hands of mariners into the clouded sea, spraying their eyes shut, loosing the hull to loom graceful inches higher.

Rachel Hooker is the first to our deck. She leans against the bulkhead, gripping the oak firmly with both hands, as though to push herself further from the waves. Working the pumps must have been exhausting, the steady leaks of icy water oppressive; soon the deck before her crowds with embracing, joyful Saints.

Midge Thomas offers thanks to the tip of the masts. She forgets, for the moment, that our hold has not near enough air for all. For now she and the rest are filled with hope, seeing cousins and friends who had as well perished the day we took to ship. But if rain comes, it'll find many of our heads, while those below wrestle to breathe.

Jake Macauley lurks between crates. This is a different ship than that he woke to this morn. Now the sailor's common paths are fettered by husbandmen. The seamen must feel this no longer wholly their ship. When I see Hawley leaning morosely, twisting a dropped poppet into the deck with one booted toe, I think that feeling a dangerous thing for us. There are none as enjoy exile.

But there's no time for such concern—I stand by the rail, making as though to help with the unlading of cheese and what roots pass for pot-herbs at sea. My hands threaten to betray me, nearly letting slip a crate of onions into the swells, as the thought constant beats that Adam must soon come. I steal glances at the coming launches and their cargo, praying I look uninterested.

Near half the year since my eyes touched him. But when he moves to board his boat, it is not an instant before I pick him out across the impatient furrows. His dear, lanky, awkward way is not something I must recognize, as I would a half-forgot passage once often read me. There's no need to remember; I carry his manner always with me, have taken his being and motion to heart. When he swings his leg over the edge of the launch, it seems a fine, welcoming wave. Unseeing I pick at a stubborn knot, until Richard Hall tells me, sharply, to let those provisions alone.

Last night I lay on deck, and though I did not sleep there came cold, wind-tossed dreams to chill and bathe my face. I stood beside a hill covered in gray, shifting grass. A giant hand rose beckoning, and in beckoning traced a crown. The hand rolled and blackened, becoming slick sea animals hurtling endlessly behind the gray grass hill. They stretched to my horizons, east and west. I opened my mouth to shout.

When I look again, the launch has half crossed to our vessel. Adam holds himself as he always did, without elegance, with surety that his bearing is a matter for his own counsel. I see now that he is not entirely the same. Once-soft whiskers have thickened and browned, their color like to his hair. He may be some heavier. Though they are of simple enough fashion, I think I've never seen the clothes he wears. But beneath them is the demeanor I cherish, and it is a sore trial not to call.

Feeling that I no longer own my feet, I flee across the deck, struggling between Saints. Windward of the vessel's naught but open water, and birds diving for their daily board. But beyond them, at the very edge of the sky, is a shred of darkness. It's like a sunken spot in the horizon—there's a hint of distant, rocky peaks settled in the tiny gash. When I look at it straight, it's gone. The birds dabble. With marvelous ease they pluck up shining fish.

When a good time has passed I know he must be on deck. Our shoes press the same boards. The thought harries me, urging me to turn. But I do not, for a long moment more. When at last I do I smile broadly. I must look right pleased to see the crowd. What play we shall have, what joy I shall take in this company. But in truth the crowd seems a mere unwitting audience to this dance of two players; through them, somewhere, is my partner.

Adam is bold as a standing stone, as real. He sidles confidently, taking Josiah Flynt by the hand, greeting Mistress Baker with generous care. I hold my general smile, thinking of the perils he has already weathered. Of sickness, and foul water. His father grips him by the shoulder; proud, pointedly he leads him toward the hatch. They will have much to speak on. There has been much of import, doubtless, in the progress of the *Joan*, and the only words passed between the ships have been between Captain Beechwood and his people. I imagine Adam will answer his father's questions honestly, but with distance. He is a man possessed of his own mind.

As his foot touches the ladder he straightens, and looks about him. For me. With playful inspiration I duck behind a mast. While he's below I'll wander the overrun deck, turning here and there, twisting among the crowd, waiting for the time I can lay my hands where I will. All the while I'll steal him with eyes and mind, a thief in night—for the Saints will never know what I've stolen, nor that they possessed it to begin. I have waited, and for so long. He may wait this little time more, I think—I bring hands to mouth, catching a laugh.

But the laugh I thought to capture still comes grating. I look up, embarrassed, and find Henders hanging above me. He's slung from the shrouds, letting himself dangle from one arm as he watches. He grins, knowing he's caught me at something. He cannot know what it is, yet takes pleasure in my small humiliation. I calm myself, and make as though I was only wiping spray from my cheeks.

Men must be made, Sarah said once. Women, are. She said that pridefully, and with scorn for things that must make themselves over different before they're thought worthy of honor. Now I think, happily, my hands full of cable, that women are like a stage covered in bellowing players—whether they think of it or no, the players' steps are guided by the platform where they stamp and declaim.

I'll hear my words pass his lips in meeting, and feel myself full, as woman can be full among the Saints; with feet on a dusty floor, back raising up hay and straw, breasts for sweet milk, head in general congregation—my presence there a spring of strife but of balm for me, words I had spoke private at night said openly by him.

A woman must know which secrets to keep, which to cup between her palms, which to raise to the world. It is a hard thing, to hold back such wisdom as you possess, and I do know more than most of them of hard, unreasoning thoughts. There is much they should be shown. They are scarce ever the receivers of hard reason. When they are, likely they will not bear it. Frances Jacobs did not. I will speak to them, I think, and twist a cable round to bind the facking.

When I meet a servant whose condition is alike to that of my own youth, I will talk with her. Then, knowing her mind, I'll be an opening—for a girl who never hoped to be free from another's blacking on her fingers, or from scouring soured milk, or making provision for another's house. Thinking of it I feel cloaked in clouds. Men must be made—women, are.

Sarah was half right. For I am, and yet will make myself. In my hand ropes twist and knot. My sight fades away and I see a hearty congregation, meeting under a hall of fresh timber, ready to be shaped by my hands, my tongue.

Adam is a scant outline, in a miserly place, where the ladder drops into the musty under-deck and the smell of moldy food. He is near past before I see it's him, and then I cannot be sure I truly did see—I may only have sensed his whole generous, particular being through a thousand seed-small signs, for I was myself coming down from the deck, eyes yet blinded from the loss of a sun that at noon broke mightily from behind a seeming pure, stubborn wall of cloud. In my hand's a length of facking. That's what Henders named a mere strip of line, when I helped him with his labors to draw his mind from my foolish play. While we worked, he took pleasure in naming all manner of ropework. But my mind was always elsewhere—scolding me for having regard for what a sailor should think, or exploring Adam's every contour. When I was done I kept this piece of facking, that I might look busy. For what should I do with facking, if not to labor?

I was coming to the hold to lay there, and, maybe, to catch a glimpse of Adam, my someday man. But now I'm sudden struck by the whole of him. It's as though I've rapped my head on the ship wall, hard enough to thrum seawater behind the inch of oak. Adam is here.

We are alone in the passage. That will not last—there is a better place. At once I know where I can drag him for a moment of dear, perilous quiet. I seize him by the wrist. In my hand's the facking, and his wrist, the first part of the body I've needed these months. He is here, like a homey beast escaped from a wild burrow where it wandered, lost.

I did not sleep last night. I have been dreary, slow, confused. Now my senses join and form him whole, like fingers curling in to touch.

The captain is on deck, giving weary commands to sailors who for once long for something to do. Through determined labor they'll show the Saints that this is yet their place, no matter how many of us there be.

In here, I say, and draw Adam toward the blue cabin door. For an instant I think he'll protest, fearing to follow—his arm drags, leaden with what I think is reluctance to chase his wants so plainly. But he'll say nothing in the passage. A moment later and the cabin door closes behind him with a snap.

Though stacked high for storage, the captain's cabin is snug, with nothing in it so disorderly as a shock of corn or herb. All is neat. The walls seem made of boxes—iron-bound chests with locks like clenched fists, crates strapped with rope. A lone piece of dainty work, a lady's thing, colored like an ideal of pink complexion. The window is turned glass, big as two spread hands, flecked with water that dulls the little light.

Now at last I can smile broad and honest. Well met, I say softly, and reach to cup his cheeks. I would feel the new beard that's thickened there, to place my palms where none other may without insult. Beaming I lean to him, and believe I smell, beneath the salt and grime of long passage, the sweet air of harvest ending.

But his hands are on my own, holding me away. Come, there'll be no one to come upon us, I say, and again push for him.

His hands, they are stubborn dogs. In what light can force itself into this dire chamber, I see his mouth is a niggardly line. There is no desire in his face. Blood balls in my stomach, a dead weight.

Don't you, I say. It is meant as the beginning of a protest; it sounds a question. My face flushes, slow and hot. There is that in me that knows the answer, before I believe it, or hear it spoke.

He is nervous at being here. But under that he is sure, horribly calm as he watches me. His lips just purse. I look close for a weak line in his whiskers, for the scar where no beard will grow. It's like the trail of a snake. I shake my head as though loosing a hat.

Adam smiles forcedly, but he has not the strength to hold it. It becomes a dismal look. He has not spoke a word. But I have seen this face, when he played with grass, watched a crushed anthill, and said I had given no thought to him. Then, it was aimed in part at his condition, and now, all at me. Now he has gripped my mouth. He has stole my tongue, and packed my gums with clay.

How can this boy pretend to ignorance? For without a word he does pretend, holding me at bay as though I'm an unbalanced woman, or clutch him for a fee.

It is fine to see you, he says, with what seems like cheer.

With that my voice returns to me, quick as a fish.

Adam. This is not the first time we have been alone, I say.

It is not, he says, and releases me. Still he looks at me with as little desire as he would at a chicken shed, or a fence.

I want to take him in my arms, and feel him take me in his—to taste the peculiar salt of his skin. I want to grab his face, drag my finger along his scar, seizing him by the beard, holding him with as little regard as he regards me. Part of me thinks, madly, that *that* might wake in him the old joyful spirit. But in seeking to wake it I would surrender my right to explanation. That, I will not yet do. The cabin smells of copper, and well-kept coats.

You said, I will see you on the ship, I say. Now it is an accusation, and though I feel myself tearing in twain, I am still enough myself to hear it sounds pathetic. I had imagined saying those words to him, but in a whisper, a soft jest given, a hot sigh as I clung to him with all the strength the Lord gave my hands. *I will see you on the ship.*

And I was right, he says, with a quick half-smile that vanishes with the knowledge that he cannot, of all things, joke with me. I did matter to him. He cannot jest with me about that, nor tell me it was ever untrue.

He takes a deep breath, puts left hand to hip, with the right rubs his thigh. Then he speaks, with the honesty I valued in him above all else. Though it seems that he begins with things of little purpose, I let him. For he is telling me of where he has been. And it is no simple thing, somehow, to halt someone from placing in your chest an anchor of iron.

Before ever they reached the city he was exhausted, as much from being forced to the company of Benjamen Smythe and simple Joseph Butler as from the long journey. Smythe grated with his arrogance, Butler with stupid prattling. When there was any inn to be found, naturally they slept all to a bed. Then Smythe's dumpy body worked like a bellows, wheezing and huffing, banishing all sleep. When they were two days from the city, the road curved to flank a flat river. A dusky smoke drifted up the shore, leaking away through the trees. Beside the main road stout horses walked easily, keeping even with the broad barges they would soon haul back upstream. Still their owners quarreled over pace and right-of-way. Two fought with staves, clacking and shouting until one stumbled back with broken jaw. The barges were heaped high with grain and pigs. The smoke made Adam think of a burning hive. One day they passed a stand of elms. Then there was a broad plain, and beyond it a city like piled stirrups. Later, Adam thought that the smoke was not from kitchen fires, nor pleasant industry; instead the air darkened from a welter of hate and the Lord's displeasure.

While yet at home, Adam had thought he'd wander the streets of a city easy as on a village path. But the streets of the city were clogged with dogs, rumbling carts, fat men, children with bare, black feet. There was there a rank, sinuous anger. He felt it in its many parts, crammed into districts that would hold five villages. From so close the houses looked built without order or sense; they were too narrow, too tall, built right on to the street, making all the blue sky a poor trail. We have none to cling to but our own, he says.

They had meant to stay in the city only a short time. A day—but Beechwood was late coming from the Baltic. In the end that proved a good thing. For they had money and Beechwood was in need of it, being weary of hauling meat through the same old seas. But it meant that they needed wait for him for a week at an inn near by to the docks. On the third night, Smythe and Butler sent Adam to buy wine. They felt themselves badly in need of cheer.

The houses had high, gray fronts. He was walking a roofless passage. The cobbles were worn under years of horse-hooves and flung piss. After a time Adam found a tavern—it stunk of fish, and soaked leather. A painting on the wall was once of a woman, now gray and shapeless. Three bottles, he said to the tavern man. The man had the blond hair of a silversmith, the narrow face and precise fingers. Without a word he vanished behind a strip of wooden paneling.

A man that means to make much merry, said a voice from the end of the bar. The man was piled under gray hair. He laughed and said it again, low and fast, slurring the *m*'s, nearly humming.

For my uncle, Adam said, though in truth he was kin to neither man. In fact they had asked for only two bottles. He'd thought to hide one away for his own later joy.

Your uncle's a man of fine parts.

He is.

I have nephews myself. They're drinking here tonight, with me. Boys.

There were three others there, at their own rear table, spilling out bone dice from a cup. One looked at the old man and snorted a bit. He turned back to the game.

What are their names, Adam asked, not knowing what else to say.

John and James and Henry and William and Miles and John and James and William, the man said. He stopped and looked at the ceiling, blowing through brown teeth with a sigh.

The barman came from behind the paneling. He placed the bottles on the bar lengthwise, the corks facing his customer. Here's our best, sir, he said.

Adam did not like the *sir*, neither the word nor the way it was said. A drink for this man, until his nephews return to him, he said.

What manner of drink.

Rum. Of course Adam had never tasted nor seen rum, and was startled at the price. He paid without a question.

The old man looked at him unsteadily over the cup's purple rim.

That's touched me. A fine thing for you to do. You tell your uncle he has a nephew of fine parts. His nephew'll grow to be a gentleman in manners, whatever his worth in coin. A worshipful young sir, from up midlands, no doubt.

From up midlands, Adam said quickly. He was afraid the old man's eyes might begin to glisten. His clothes had never felt other than natural, simple and fit enough for a laboring man. Now he pulled his rain cloak tight. In quality his clothes were not greatly better or worse than any there, but his jerkin was tighter about the neck. It seemed to have more fastenings. He took up his bottles and left.

Outside a woman clutching a bundle begged him for coins. The bundle might have been a babe. It might have been a dead cat, and he walked quickly past. The passage of tall gray homes led to their inn.

Give us a drink, then, said a blurry voice. Adam's stomach clenched. Of course it was the dice-players, of course. The one closest was missing many teeth. It made the right side of his jaw look weak, tentative. The man reached up quickly and pulled on his own hair, making a neat point by each temple. His tongue was slightly out, like a mole. The others stood behind, seeming idle. Probably they had not many more years than he did. It was a challenge to say, with the weathering given them by sun and wind. Fishers, he made no doubt. He felt himself very small, hesitated, and gave over a bottle.

The man passed it on to his fellows, without opening it, without looking. Give us another, he said. Adam did. The man grabbed him by the wrist then, and jerked him forward.

Call you a Saint, someone said. Papist fuck. The first blow came from behind, and though there was at first no pain it felled him to the street. Before he struck ground, he wondered how they could know so much about him; that his people named themselves Saints.

He was sore hurt. They pounded him with fists and feet, though never weapons. Later he thought that wielding a tool would not have given them the pure satisfaction of boots and fists—of skin on skin. His head filled with color. He tried to stand but another blow took him beside the eye, crushed him down into the lamps that faded fast to nothing. When he woke, he was of course without even small coins. His teeth were gritty, his mouth tasted of blood and old piss. His rain cloak was gone.

Butler gently cleaned his face with the corner of a sack. Smythe said, again and again, that those who beat him were simple roust-abouts. Some unsuspected gentleness had been touched in him. You'd have thought he'd speak in grand tones, of sacrifice, and righteous-ness. Instead he seemed to think a chance attack less likely to fester, and so insisted on calling it so. He wanted to bandage the wound however he might.

But Adam did not believe him. He had a good deal of time to think while he lay healing on a padded bench. It was his clothes, his manner of speech, that marked him as an easy take. It was the same things that led all city people to watch him with wolfish eyes. He'd never been true beaten before. No village fight had the snap and blister of that day. It proved a mighty thing.

We have naught to cling to but our own people, he says to me. When we spoke of the flaws in their thoughts, well that seems a hundred years ago. We are alone in the world—the right path is nothing you can take and leave as you will. You may wish it, or think some things wrong. The world will strike you back to it soon enough.

They hate us, he says, each word sharp as though he would stick it to the wall. I don't know if we make them feel their own lives paltry—but they hate us, that's plain. It is hard to feel yourself the aim of such, whether from fists or the scorn of a merchant. I'd thought to walk there unnoticed—we didn't walk the streets proclaiming ourselves. There was none among us inclined to preach. But they saw us and knew us; they scorned us as husbandmen before they ever knew us Saints. After, I thought a good deal on our people, and their worth. They are a finer people than you know.

You spoke of them before, without so great love, I say bitterly. He near bites his lip, and for a time does not meet my eyes.

I love him well. I have never failed in that, he says.

I know that is not so—I know his mind better than he knows his own. But he slides backward, slowly, as though to deceive. His hand will reach for the leather doorclasp.

You cannot deny our time, I say. If you will, I'll speak it to all.

As I say those words, I know they end my hopes. But they do stop his hateful glide.

I've much repented of those days, he says earnestly, with a probe of his chin, wanting to convince me, or at least for me to believe he does.

It true great, he says, to know that you labor for the Lord on the earth, and feel yourself in accord with His will. There is such strength in accepting our places here—holding to such is the lone defense against those who would tear us down.

Oh, he has repented of our days. But he knows, in his deepest self, that he need not repent. God will elect who He will, he will curse who He will, and these Saints know, with sunny confidence, where they fall. All the old mockery is vanished from Adam's voice; he repeats himself. Once he would never have spoken so, without scorn in his voice for any who claim to know all below heaven. I loved that in him. Now it's vanished I see only a boy, who thinks to make himself more.

You're but a brawling fool, I say. You'd arrayed yourself against pompous fathers. Now you'd battle the devil where they think to find him. Where do I fall?

His face draws inward. I do not see that I ever arrayed myself different, he says.

Fearful boy, I say, and strike him full across the face. That awakens him, at last. He eyes me warily—angry, but not enough.

I wish he would strike. I wish this a contest of blows.

Coward, I say.

That slaps him damply. A coward fails to chase what he wants, he says, precise as a dirk. Then the door closes, and he is gone.

This drifting is only the ship, the waves. I step back and sit heavily down on the captain's cot. Such luxury to have your own cot, in close quarters. The cabin tilts beneath me; the floor's a cliff. I look to a distant door. If I slip from this ledge I may burst through, if the wood be thin. My hands are on my knees, palms up. Slowly I clench them, nails to palms. I will have me eight bloody cuts. They'll be like crescent moons.

Oh Lord, I say. I'd thought of wisdom I could impart. But in all His world, there is none other so stupid.

I slide my hands along my cheeks, twisting down my face. Sarah's laugh can reach me here, seeking through wind and over the sea. She has always laughed at proud error. (There is, in her, a cruelty.) Should I be different.

I will find Henders. It will take a lusty man, to defy his captain's inner place.

You look right ill, Abigail says meanly.

You foul, fucking thing, I say in a low hiss, my face turned to shield reddened eyes. I push past. Henders is taking more stores toward the true stern, where they mound about the pilot's place. He moves as little as he can, and will rest often. I come up behind him. Chin by his shoulder, I whisper.

To the cabin.

What?

I smile sickly as he twists. The cabin. Am I not as fine as an orange girl? Without waiting for an answer I turn from him, go back down into the hold.

In the cabin I pace, and punch my legs. With each blow I strike deeper. The bruises will rise black, just where my legs come to my body. The pain must surely mark me, but there will be none save Henders to see the black and purple patches. And the bruises will not come up sooner than he, if he does come. I stop, look at the ceiling, run my hands up through my hair. My coif falls off, and to the floor. My hair falls free; I drag my fingers through it and hold my arms to the sides, stretching out my long, earthy, constantly bound locks. I hold them until the door opens and there is Henders coming to me, pushing his face against mine, pushing me back against the cot. However great his fear of his captain he has wants that are greater, for he has come.

His kiss has naught in it to warm me. This is right, I think. This is how it should be, and what a dismal thing that is to think. He moves as viciously as a child, as eagerly. There is only one way this ends. That is now fine. His hands are andirons between my legs. I pull him closer and on to me, opening to him, he need not put those horrid things between my legs. A mole on his neck is shaped for an elbow.

He thrusts forward, mindlessly as an ox. I am quiet. I do not cry out. To give my mouth labor I lick his neck. His eyes are like a bug's; forward, blind. I take his throat in my teeth, and silently moan. I can bite to blood. He had best pray I do not choose to do.

He moves in me, such a small bond between us but from it waves course to my fingers, to the tips of my loose hair. I fight to take the waves over for my own, to take some pleasure from this; there could be no finer revenge than to take pleasure in this. And I do, I think I feel the beginnings of warmth before he spends in me, so that when he does spend I've bit him on the neck, keening, crying.

Henders sits up, on the edge of the cot, quivering. His joy's drained, his buttocks press me heavily against the wall. I cry on my back. Maybe I will spit on the floor. In the light of a lone, water-specked window he looks at me, without fully turning his head or opening his eyes.

The door opens slowly as though dragged through honey. For a panicked instant I think that Adam has returned. He will see me in this bared condition. I start upward, pushing down my skirts. But it is not Adam, come to make amends. Captain Beechwood is like stacked animal cages.

Henders pulls on his breeches. I cannot believe this hour. But the captain is real as a wasp sting. There's an old, rusty stain on the left collar of his greatcoat. In his eyes is wrathful expectation but no surprise, no pause before the anger. He was informed I came here, certain as my life. Abigail's gaze bored into me like a weasel. Her ghost swells behind him—flabby, scolding, unkind.

Captain Beechwood's eyes are blue; fearing to fall into them, to drown, I blink them away.

Chapter nineteen

I Behold a Hideous Place

The ocean runs over the cobbles like grease. It leaves them clean, dark as walnuts. The water here is silver with glare. The smooth swells hold rings of light, like blinking eyes. At the edge of land they shatter—they run through cobbles like grease, they slick them to jelly. A riot of screeching pinches at my ears, a sharp, probing stick. For though the inner swells may be smooth, beyond them the water is caked with foam like foul beer, and the foam is all of birds.

The birds croak and flit for fish. White bellies, black heads, white eyes. Though they are fat and well fed they seem fearful, snapping constant glances at nothing I can see. They drift like cakes of froth, melt and split over hidden schools. They dive by the dozens, boiling water. They shake to heaven gullets full of fish.

Behind me is the launch, and nests that spot the shore like aged pox. Only a few are full. The other birds are putting on final fat, vixens readying for the den. When I walked past a rare, full nest, the tenant twitched to eye me, then again looked to empty air. There is nothing in me for her to fear. Nothing she could see, I tell myself. Her slim wings are tucked below the cobbles, in the ashy dirt. In the water their wings knife them though turns, driving them like hail.

I squat by the water and watch a swell shatter in. When it reaches me it's flat as dropped pane-glass, flecked in chips of old eggshells. It spreads, pauses. As it hisses away, tumbling the cobbles with a sound like frying, I duck in my fingers, sudden as a snake. Here is a world of seasoning for meat, I think, and eye the bobbing birds. I press my fingers to cool my bruised eye.

They cry like sick dogs. But dogs are kept beasts. They will lay beside fires, when permitted, until driven out that they may drive less profitable beasts from the fields. They know to bite my leg, or else let me alone. They know I am not nothing.

The birds crowd in packs, swelling the breeze with squeals and grunts that sound obscene in their variance. Their concern's with oily fish. They do not see my Saints. My Saints drift, circling the island, creeping to the rim of my cracked sight. They are confident and loving, everywhere yet never here. I shake my head—they smile at me. Slowly, just beyond vision, they pass and turn.

This is a poor dance. This is a hideous poor place for it.

When I look at the mountain, that fat, titan's tit, I must know myself here. I look to sea. Between the birds and the breakers, the swells are not greatly different from what I could see to shipboard. But the stench of men and women in a close, stinking hold is gone, replaced by a hundred years of rotting eggs, of offal, of filthy birds. The air stings my throat. It's softest at the edge of the water, where most of the foul fog can blow behind me. It crams our sleeping crack like poison.

Drops of dung plink around me, then grow to a brief blizzard. I shield my head, look up at the passing flight. Their shrieks swell like the crest of a wave about to crash over its barrel. Their lofty flight is some obscured by fog. They shift it into a simmer.

> *Little bird of Paradise*
> *She works her work both neat and nice;*
> *She pleases God, she pleases man,*
> *She does the work that no man can.*

A bee, a bee, a bee, I think as the flight heads for high, rocky cells—and for that right answer I'll have a honeyed cake.

Dried piles of dung heap around the mountain, pierced by scrubby, shredded brush, up where waves will never cleanse and rock shields blown rain. It cracks under foot; I thought of crunching through frozen pack and into powder, feeling the hard crust of ice against my shin.

There's a cut in the rocks—less a cave than a crack like a pried mouth. There was only a thin layer of filth to clean there. Some oily feathers, two skeletons. Now sailcloth stretches tight over the cut, weighted down at the edges by cobble piers. We spread more of the cloth across the bottom, and blankets on that. On those he took me, without question or contest. Some small light speckled through a sail heaving with his piggish grunts. The troll thinks himself deserving of me.

My knees ache dully. The sun here sets for too few hours. Over my shoulder it looks a late fruit with poor, watery color, and casts dim shadow into the play of surf. The birds cluster. They surface dripping, and fishtails slip and vanish in fortunate beaks. On each eye is a great white spot. The beaks look knapped, like stone tools.

The northern distance is broken by rocks, jagged teeth above a sunken jaw. Once I saw them as a gash in the sea. They rise and fall. I think this snake must loop the world.

The ship was a barnacle. It was a crab's dried shell.

There is a pale, rounder stone, some closer. There. But steam bursts from it, and it sinks. Another creamy whale rises behind, then another. In line they're like a single stretched creature. They turn and head for open sea. I shudder. I press the heel of my hand against my bruised eye, shaking, squatting on the rocks.

My palms are on cold cobbles. Do I pose a hazard to the mountain? An unchaste woman come to rest beneath a slag hive? I think of it sinking into the swirling waters. Then I'd tumble down the ocean slope, skirts floating round-about, a gray and drifting rose.

But there is no need for the land to sink before I find that doom. I can stand. I could step forward.

There's a crunching step behind me. I twist, lose my balance, and catch myself on one arm with a jolt. I struggle against a snarl. The sun is behind Henders' head. Where his head should be is white, his face flat as blank paper. I squint, shrinking his head, melting away his neck. He's a lessened face floating over shoulders. Behind him is the hulking mountain, a pillar through my eye. Then he squats beside me and his rough face comes clear. He is again a man.

Get your feet wet, and that's all we'll have to do for the day, he says absently, intent on outer rocks or the open sea. He rubs his nose and slips a bit, rocks into the fall. He ends seated, arms around his knees. I think he wanted to make the slip look intentional. Licking his lips, he stares over the birds at an empty patch of horizon.

You could get wet just as quick, I say. Though he may have spoke casual, I feel driven to answer a stupid complaint.

I'd know what to do for myself.

And I would not.

Couldn't, is what it is.

I've heard this note to his voice, once before, and will not tempt it now. But if he could see my mind he'd recoil, as from a hackled beast.

What kind of birds are those, there, I say, turning a stone with the tips of my fingers, half hoping that anger will stain my voice, that he'll hear it. There would then be no need for talk.

Which ones, he says. On the instant he sounds different. He will make this a boast—that he knows the names of birds.

I don't think they can fly.

Nor can they. Pinuins, they're called by those as don't know them, auks by the rest.

Awful that he should speak with such authority, so soon after telling me how readily I might die. How helpless I am. Beyond the swimming flocks, flying birds are fishing. As they dive they twist, as though following the threads of a cider press. Their splashes seem impossible modest. May be it's the distance.

You think I could not dry myself, I say, and feel I've stumbled off a familiar step.

Your feet would fall off from the freeze.

It's not even so cold, I say. He grunts. I would fail to find myself a blanket? I ask, voice climbing. The skin around my eye is hot metal.

Quicker than I should credit he turns, and snatches my shirt about my neck. He half drags me to my feet. My knee strikes his leg—he pulls me close.

Might as well be here alone, for all the good you'll do, he says furiously. At least you brought your cunt along. I'm glad I'll make right use of it.

His face is a crushed toad, my head full of dry charcoal. I'm on my toes, off balance. But if he looses my neck I'll fight him. This time I will fight him.

There were two of us there, I say through my teeth.

Bad as one being paid for it, you desperate bitch, he says. His lips quiver. If you were any else but a buggered Saint, I'd have no worse than a bloody back.

Cloth squeezes my throat; my breath is cutting. I told the truth, I say, gasping. At that he drops me. My head strikes rock, jolting me through, filling my head with sparks. For an instant all goes dark. Then light returns as though a veil's blown from my face. I start to rub my head. But I will not, not before him.

He stands over me, fists clenched into gunstocks. The only thing to do on these rocks is die, he says. Not much more to do, on a heap of stone and bird shit.

I would dispute any words of his. I would dispute that the Lord made the sea, that it is gray.

There's nothing to keep us here, I say. There's the launch.

I push myself to my feet, for he's done looking at me. The water's become a vise for him.

We are far from, he says, and stops. His shoulders tense like a cornered cat's. Then he cups his hands to his mouth, and howls. A few auks twitch their heads toward him, then away. No matter how little their interest, the white circles about their eyes make them seem to stare, and thus to ignore him willfully. The wind scatters his yell like dust, leaving only the sharp shoals of bird cries.

Henders stands in silent fury. He bends for a rock. It splashes between a clump of auks, breaking them for an instant—but they spin and mend together, scolding.

As he bends for another, I turn, disgusted, and walk back toward the mountain. The soles of my shoes slip on the cobbles. A small voice says I may wrench an ankle, break a foot. But I only clench my teeth, and rub cold from my hands.

Beside the mountain I fling open one of our chests and lay the topmost clothes on the ground. Beneath are knives, flints, more blankets, a few tapers. At bottom, powder and lead balls. They would not risk my taking a final, spiteful, just and deserved shot at the ship as it sailed away. Those two guns and, leaning against a rock shaped like a flipped, broken pail, a hoe. A wooden rake, a sickle. The tools look lonely and pointless. The Saints gave me the things they think of, when they think of a home.

The hoe has good heft, and a blade. I raise it high, thud it into the pile of clothes. I strike it from the side, I burst them into the air. Most fall to ground like pigeons under lucky arrows. Others catch an eddy in the wind, and scatter. After a time they settle, rubbing to rest.

From beside the taut sailcloth I squint, twinging my bruise, and watch Henders throw his stupid rocks. They burst helplessly. Many birds seem able to dodge them without looking. They read signals given by their spinning fellows.

Standing in the junk of last year's eggshells, Henders looks wrong as a mill in a cave. His fury slowly fades and he tosses a final rock. He stands with hands on hips, looking at the water where the spirals from his throws should be.

I begin gathering up the clothes. I mean to have them folded and back in their piles, before he returns. But it is not fear of him that commands me. Never for him. The only thing one can do on these rocks…he's right about that, I think.

It's a simple thing to catch a sleeping auk. At night, when the sun has set for what seems half the proper time, I take one and bury it alive.

Though taking her up was simple, the binding is more trouble-some—she twists, trying to stab me. I'm glad I chose to wrap her trowel beak while holding her wings tight beneath my arms. But finally I lose patience and whip her by the feet, stunning her against the ground.

I dig a narrow cone, working it out with the hoe, then my fingers. The bird is wrapped in rope. When she wakes, she lies croaking. Her head needs to go in first. I dug the cone to fit, so there will be no means for her to thrash about like a worm. But she twists as I lower her, catching the edge of the hole with her beak. Again I whip her down, this time against the mounded stones I dug out. That leaves a spot of blood on them, and a wet patch on the side of her head.

Sarah would have used a cock for this, and complained about the worth and quality of her lost bird even as she was burying it beside the thyme. Sarah's not one to apologize for thrift. But she would have confessed that using a fowl of such value might better draw attention to one's need, and make other things the easier to call. A killing may clear your mind to see how things are sewn together, in a strange place, or in weird condition. Likely this practice will neither aid me nor clear my mind. But it makes me think of her, and may draw her thoughts to me.

Henders knelt at the mast, hemmed by Saints ordered as before a podium.

The sailors drew together tightly as a thistle bloom. Jake Macauley leaned whittling; Hawley stood beside him, face shadowed, until all the crew was ordered to the mast. There was not one among them who would not have done as Henders did. The captain well knew it, and moved with a badger's calm surety, running his fingers through the lash to separate the tails. Then Master Stradling's voice stopped him like a spear.

Leave them, he said. I had handed him a squirming, uncertain sack. But he knew that there was, hid in my matted, wormy treachery, a golden kernel that could be his. He probed my face, seeking it. When he found it, and his voice, he said to leave us.

And with those words I felt myself alter, surely as when the

Harvest Maid made me for a time both less and greater within a thicket of eyes. The Saints feast on stories; I stood within them alone, without a household, a grantee of their trust found criminal. Through me Master Stradling could craft a tale of seeming righteousness, of betrayal, of determined justice—a verse in his greater song, that had been humbled for a time under shipboard command.

Janice Healdstrong. Jenny Fulton. Kate McNeer. A dread fellowship; a new member.

The captain would have had Master Stradling silenced. He would have had him carted below, and maybe assigned him a penalty. Even him. But there was, to back Master Stradling, a swamp of Saints. With hands of root they dragged the captain down as though to drown him. Ten to seize him, ten to hold each mariner fast. Jake Macauley dropped his knife to stick upright in the deck; Saints rushed below. They fetched up muskets they had meant for deer and savages, and never threat to Englishmen. The Saints had force enough in numbers to force the ship to do their will. Still they primed the arms—surely less from fear of resistance than from love of their own power, and its increase.

But it was their journey. Authority over it was theirs. Ownership of the words that would shape it, and what would become of us, all theirs. Around them was water, water, the Lord's great sea. Where were the villages and fields, the things that at home fixed the law? They were nowhere and there was nothing, only vast ocean, empty, and savage. The land they will come to is no more a homey place than the depths below. But they will cut their laws and traditions into the land; they'll not be distracted by ocean waters, nor ever corrupted from within.

A wicked affliction, though it stem from only one, may collapse general strength. They would cut it out, lest it spread. They would not leave a reminder on board the ship bearing them toward a free and righteous life.

And what could simple mariners do, when confronted by Saints who had sudden found their force, who crowded the deck with rage and black powder?

Midge Thomas folded clothes, all of them worn, salty at the seams.

Most all were for a woman. The sailors had few they could give to Henders, and the Saints few they'd choose to. They would put me from the vessel with the greatest seeming goodwill in the world, with a few barrels of small beer. Midge laid blankets over my Book, carefully as though dressing a child. Behind her, Captain Beechwood argued with Farnsworth. He said to stop this. Farnsworth smiled wryly and watched Master Stradling with great interest. He found it remarkable, he said, that Captain Beechwood should think him in any way our master.

I studied Adam's scarred, familiar face. He would not look at me, not true. It seemed to me that all there knew his offense, and mine, so there were moments when I was near to screaming out that I have been with him. That I will bear his child; for it would have been three weeks more before my moonblood came, and they could know my claim for a lie. By then we would be on shore. There would be open land, and no fences, and sometimes, maybe, fishermen—means to flee them, and live.

The Saints watched me with love, with lies of forgiveness and charity. Adam looked through my body to the ocean. When his father called him he dragged his eyes across me like a harrow, and to the ship's far side.

Susan was rapt, and watched me as she would a dog gone mad. I glared black death back at her alone. I chose her as my lone target, among all those who looked at me as she did. I needed choose one. Richard Hall insisted on giving us guns; they are no murderers.

I climbed the two rungs of a stepladder, swung one leg into the launch. Then Master Stradling's hand was on my shoulder. He looked at me, intently as in loving. He asked if I was forced.

Startling, to be told there was something I could say that they might hear. Master Stradling peered into me, seeming to measure me with agitated hand.

The deck seemed a closed tunnel. Want dripped from his eyes like springwater. He was not looking for true words. It was a ritual, though only he and I might know it. For that brief time we seemed alone, all others deaf and blind. Unwillingly, he had gestured to me. I could go there or fall away, at my pleasure. Whatever I said, he would have more words arrayed for his cause; he would cast me out whatever I said. But I would not be forced. I would not be, and in fury for him and his son I answered. I was not, I said clearly. And for a moment, for an instant as we stood there, public yet in strange embrace. Master Stradling smiled.

They lowered us in the launch. Henders screamed at men who did nothing to help him. Amidst the attentive village heads Macauley looked over and offered a sickly, apologetic smile. Above him the sails lifted; the hull soared by, slow and relentless as an eagle, dragging away all shadow, leaving us in pale noon sun. The groan of rigging, of lines, the chatter of sailors, shifted to the distance, fell away. The stern sank like a drowned hand. We were alone. Distant seabirds shrieked over invisible schools of fish. Blind water lapped wood.

I sat hunched, hands on my lap. I was sticky between my legs. Henders watched the horizon. He seemed for a while almost to think it a jest, as though they might send another launch to tow us, or even turn the ship entire. But he might have saved the force he spent in his first screaming for our coming labor, for there was naught there but the wind; what mattered was already past.

I saw rocks, before, I said.

I can see them now, he said, and sat in glowering silence. He has a seaman's sight.

Finally, with darkened face, he began struggling with the long sweeps. Each was meant to be handled by a man, and he thought to grip two. So handled, they seemed to jerk with unreasoning will. He flailed awkwardly, his anger such that I feared he would plant them in the bottom of the launch, splinter each with a stamp. But abruptly he handed one to me, and with the other knelt in the prow. We'll paddle, he said.

Foot by foot we dragged the launch through the foamy sea, running on a current I'd never known the ship was fighting. It bore us toward the southern rocks. We never disputed over our destination, nor ever spoke a word of it. It was the only place we could see not made of cold water.

The sunken, dark place on the horizon plumped, rose like a

blister, finally split into distant, shattered stone. As the rocks came more visible they seemed to draw our boat. I stroked, stroked. The sweep was too big to use as aught but a lever. Henders leaned into his, like a pole for a river flatboat. I gritted my teeth, and sought to do the same. I think we only squirmed the boat along a course that we must have followed, whether we would or no.

Hours later my strokes'd lost their force, become a useless reel. My guts were grown poisonous, treacherous ugly. The sweeps made small, spinning cones in the water. Being so close to the sea was altogether different; every whim of the surface seemed to sway and wrench us. There were times I could near forget it, and think only of the rocks we labored for. More often it filled my head, deep and black, a dread matter that would soak out my life if the launch did as threatened, and turned. My sickness grew in me until I dropped the sweep in the boat and leaned, heaving, over the side. I felt my body scraped out upward, from my hips—I puked it all, clouding the ocean. Gripping the gunwale, I spit, and felt Henders' scornful eyes.

The water was black. But there was, deep within it, something shapeless. It was a sort of vaporous spot, gray, as though some slip of breath leavened it and showed it different from all the dark water around. I peered down through tears, fearing to be ill again. The spot billowed like yeasted dough. It swelled further, turned light blue, grew near as big as the launch. I started back as it broke surface beside us. There were horns, and furious spikes. I screamed without hope, the edge of a sea chest cutting at my arm. The beast turned from us, going, I was sure, to dive. It would surface again, spill us out, rend us to pieces. I scrambled for a knife. If I was to be consumed I would first wound my murderer.

Then Henders hit me beside the eye with an open hand. He grabbed my by the hair as he would a puppy and twisted me to face it. It rolled lazily, slowly heaving away. Henders said it was only a valru. When he let me go I lay against the side of the launch, last puke on my chin and bodice. Empty.

We rested fitfully. During one ragged sleep a wind came. It aided the current. When I sat up to watch the rocks at last drift by, I thought

I saw another launch keeping ready pace with us. Then the boat turned, and I knew they would follow the vanished ship. I woke, and was unsure if I had before. In the moonlight the rocks rose and fell, stealthier than sails.

Soon I heard the island. There were screams and gibbers, distant but very plain, a riotous crowd. Through some trick of wind it faded for a while, and I thought it part of a dream. But in the morning it returned. We were closing on the feeding waters. At first we saw a few birds through the early mist, then dozens, finally hundreds and more of fat, diving auks, their squeals tangled into a single shriek. Then the mountain eased, darkening, from the fog.

For a thing so vast it seemed almost comical quiet, calm among the tumult, made with perfect artifice—a child's mud mountain, shaped by cups and handslaps, left to dry in expected sun on a day it rained instead. Before I believed in it I thanked God, with numb head, for giving it us. I prayed thanks beneath my breath.

Before the island birds fished, screaming for their meat. They swarmed, an unbelievable plenitude; I thought that some among them could have walked dry along their fellows' backs. Gannets dove twisting into seeming empty water until auks saw them. Then they crowded over the schools of fish hid beneath.

Great wealth here, said Henders. He spoke as with admiration—a man who knows what can be sold, and where, and for what. But I thought I heard in his voice a tremor, a thread of fear at so very much abundance. The island holds a thousand thousandweight more of bird than man.

We pushed through the birds, our oars shoving them aside until they learned, one by one, to dive. It was like paddling through mud. As we moved on I began to smell them and the island, a forgotten chicken coop, a charnel house, a bog of ocean filth. As it struck me harder I gagged, and breathed through my teeth that I would not again be sick before Henders. Our launch seemed lower, as though we sank among the feathers and black backs that came near to the gunwale. Beaks tipped up; black eyes in white patches peeked to see us, then away, their curiosity readily sated. Finally our boat was through them, among the clean swells, broken only by drifting feathers and birds passing lonely from shore to sea. The launch rode a breaker, then flat, foaming water—it grounded heavily, still eight feet from land.

Cobbles ran to the base of the mountain, and in places piled against it, mixed with slides of slag. I felt the ground rise to meet my steps. Waves rolled invisible through stone. I rode them for the mountain, hounded by the stink of a rotting barn, following a thin trail of clean water that dribbled between the only clean rocks to the ocean. My eye swole up to a squint.

From close the mountain seems a wall of grainy rock, its color like rotted brick. Far above there look to be layers of darker rock. The face is broken by thin terraces. Gannets vanish when they land.

At the base of the mountain is a spring. It gurgles lightly between stones, and into a few small sinks. They're scarce larger than footprints but without so much order, cleansed by the small, steady flow.

We should have feared disease, but Henders bent to the first sink like a horse. I wet my hands in the next catch of runoff, and pressed them over my eyes. I pressed the water on my face.

Chapter twenty

I Glean the Nature of Ghosts

A soggy, lumpy lode grows in me, until I cannot stand true. I stand straight, not true, and wander, away from him, alone. He is done with me for this morning. I never had use for him. I've a leaden rootball in my gut, a knot of oil. It heaves with every tread of my foot. I cannot bring it to center; it pulls me false.

The auks are nesting. They ride in and land on their stomachs, then hop to their feet and waddle up the shore. Their strut makes them look solemn, like market clowns that play at being landlords. Some of their nests are still tiled with shards of year-old eggshell. They trundle by me like geese passing a tree stump, fat with the season's fish.

There is some pattern in how they choose their nests. Some are fought over with quick, vicious blows that seem meant to blind. Others they leave empty. There is a certain pattern. I am damned if I can see it.

Only the hoe, now a makeshift shaft, keeps me upright. Without it I would sink to cobbles. Beside the horrid weight that plagues me the cobbles are airy things, husks of fallen stars. I force myself to the ridge, and sit. My burden skews, pushing me to lay on side or back. Then it will leak to my every tip and tarn. I sit forward, leaning on the handle of my hoe. With eyes closed, I press my forehead against the wood. It's nothing I can vomit up, this weight that fills my every gutter. It is personal, and repulsive.

There's no longer even the tiny check of my presence to stop the Saints from saying what they will. They'll think I was a pitiful hanger on, a runt long past drowning time. I was a breast's black growth. Coal-fire in a foundation. They'll speak me up until I seem to stand before them, lash me with words and charges until my face is bloody, and I pathetic.

Slowly I sink, depressing around my leaking burden; around me there are only wild ghosts.

The auks come to shore in waves, twitching and rolling, eager to claim their plots. They waddle confidently, seeming surprised when challenged for a given nest. It is a mystery, to me and maybe to them, what land is good, what merits sharp combat. One nest that brings a hateful fight is surrounded by five more, all seeming the same, where auks rest sedate and unchallenged.

The ship will come to harbor near a green shore, where oak trees stretch knotty wrists over the water. But forests are a horror that can be carved. Soon stumps will lay in barley, like footprints. The wood will be sliced thin for house timber, also a palisade to seal Saints off from unwholesome savage pagans.

Within the pale, listening, weary from labor and replete with bread and beer, is Adam. His face's burned with snow and cold. No rest from killing the forest, in these first days. He speaks with a mild woman. They have a guest from down coast, and tell the tale of their passage. Their speech is smooth and practiced. He is safe.

I rock back and forth. With every sway my hoe lifts off the rocks, then barks back down with a clang. That's the most regular sound amid the nesting birds, their windy coos. A few look at me, and away. I suck in my cheek and clang the hoe down. They twitch their heads. They never look.

I watch myself stand and walk toward the nearest homey nest. Now the auk twists around. She hisses. I swing the hoe like a sickle.

Her head snaps to one side; her body holds still as though glued in the nest. Her skull is collapsed. Blood spreads across a cobble, splits and narrows into dribbles. The shock grows in my imagination, until I seem to remember that it thrilled the wood in my hands and that it felt wonderful.

By the time he returns I've a good fire burning, and there is some base of coals. Finally her smashed head's off. The knife is dull, as though commonly used to hack cordage. Some tiny half-ovals have broken off along the blade. With it I made a jagged cut to drain what blood was left. I sat beside the fire and found a joint between the neckbones, but it was hard going and I ended by near tearing off the head. At home I'd plunge her into boiling water to loose the skin about the quills, but there is not near enough wood to merit boiling water and with the butchery I'm grown right hungry. In any case the feathers are tacked down on the breast like fine, oily fur, and I'm not certain how readily they would loose. Better, probably, to cut her up and roast her straight.

But my first cut goes only an inch before striking bone. The second is the same, and the third, the auk coming to look ragged and bloody. I take a deep breath, and again try to cut. This time I make it a hands-breadth before striking something hard as a stock-lock. I near throw it away in frustration. I've cut up chickens and roosters, capons and geese, ducks. The bones of any seem common to all fowl, but in the auk they've rattled about, taken on weird, cat's-cradle places, making my practiced strokes vain, forcing me to rend her apart. I kneel for better steadiness. But the knife slips, cutting my hand on the thick part below the thumb. I cry out angrily and plunge the knife in the breast. Now it punches through.

Henders sits down across the fire and watches me suck my bloody thumb. That's a right fine cut. A dull knife's the danger, he says.

I close my eyes for an instant, let out a thin stream of breath that I'm glad doesn't escape with a hiss. I know, I say.

Even the wooden haft looks ready to crack. I wrest it out of the bird and ready to work. But it is slippery, blood dripping down onto the iron. There's no cloth ready to hand. In frustration I press my bloody thumb against my hip.

There's a trick to it, he says.

And what is that.

I'm no birder.

With my good hand I toss the auk on the fire, sending up a quickly dying fountain of sparks and smoke. There, that'll cook it right enough, I say. Henders shrugs with one shoulder and I lean back, frustrated, against a rock.

At first the flames die a bit about the bird. As I calm I think that I'll still be able to scrape off the charred bits, make a meal of the good roasted meat below. But then the first fat renders from the rough cuts. It feels its way to the coals, for a moment tickles at the edge, and flames. The heat brings a growing flood as thick, warming fat melts, runs, and burns. A greasy black smoke rises as flames bury the bird. She looks the black spot at the base of a candle flame. I gasp, then laugh in surprise. Before I can stop myself I say that I've never known a beast that'd burn like that.

Nor I, he says. He stands and walks around to my side of the flame, away from the smoke. Might have guessed, he says. Oil's what birders come for. The eggs are good enough, but profit's in the oil.

So much of it. A fine rich fowl, rich as a pig, I say.

I heard once that when Turks assault a castle they'll dig out a tunnel below the main wall, then make a fire with a couple pigs for fuel, he says. The heat knocks out the base stones.

We grin at each other. The flames are soft, greasy and black—a surprising, hopeful thing. The shore below me is filling with more than food, that I thought I might need eat raw. It fills also with wood, and fire, roasted meat and eggs, many necessaries of life. Now the nests seem ten thousand waiting bonfires. For the moment the world seems a welcoming place that I'm meant to live in.

Coming to this feeling with Henders there makes me feel an unexpected flick of warmth for him. We are all that we have here, we must survive this place together. We may well do so. I reach out, and touch his face. He is still until my fingers reach him. Then he recoils as from a burn.

I'm sorry, I say. I mean it—I should never have touched him on the beard.

He reaches for me, for my body not my face. I hold fast until he takes me, and draws me in.

For the first time with him I want something for myself. Beside the salt and foreign birds, the smell of his hair's familiar; I feel myself dying into him, a surrender that somehow makes me feel my whole self the stronger. When I return, and lay once again beside him in the blanketed cut, I know my own outlines. He lays asleep as I trace my flanks, slip my hands gentle, take full account of my body and the pleasure it can give. After a time I lay quiet.

But I cannot sleep. I crawl out and beside the last, sparking birdfat, fumble through spare clothes for my Book. Then I open it at chance, and begin to read.

At a lodging place on the way the Lord met him and sought to kill him. Then Zipporah took a flint and cut off her son's foreskin, and touched Moses' feet with it, and said, 'Surely you are a bridegroom of blood to me'. So he let him alone. Then it was that she said, 'You are a bridegroom of blood,' because of the circumcision.

I know the words well—not only their sense, and order, but the very form of the letters that make them. The type is sure, stout, wider than most, a spendthrift of precious paper. Why should it not be, I think—are there not matters where thrift is imprudent? Should some things not be written on a banner shouting in the wind? The words transport me, the letters fill my sight. Then they vanish. I'm in the thatched house where once I read them; I'm in the dry desert tent they speak of.

After a time, dark threatening, I throw some more brush on top of the lone, charred bird. It flames like a puff of whale breath. But there's no long force in it, and the orange webs playing quick on the sheer wall of the mountain die before I tire of watching them. I close my Book, sit with legs folded beside the embers, and listen close to rocks and air and water.

At home ghosts exalted in mad glory. They howled as they bounded down from the forest, or burst from the spring with eyes tendriled red. They crumbled up from earth, twirled beside the river banks, misted from the air—a scaly, one-eyed dog, a red man who shook an ax on a midnight rooftop. One who looked a girl shrieked laughs, twisting herself to nothing at the crossroads, leaving a pair of naked eyes staring up, moonlit, from the dust. Beneath the forest were caverns forsook even by grima, now filled with the echoes of ghosts. They pulsed through veins beneath my feet, down under the grain fields and to the river.

Master Stradling would sermon about them. To suppose that they were human spirits would be a Papal error, based on supposition of a Purgatory. The soul cannot persist in any other wise than heaven or hell. Papists think of a place or condition where they might atone for the sins of this life. But this is, he said, no world of half-measures the Lord has given us. What period of penance could be sufficient to alter the judgment of God? A thousand years, a thousand thousand, would count for less than a pebble tossed and meant to overflow the sea. The Saints would nod, and agree until they saw the next ghost.

Here, I feel Master Stradling only ignorant. There is much to fear in night, black stretched to my horizons. But any ghosts here, though wild, are like to toys, pipeclay animals with the line from the mold yet on their spines—lions, bears, wolves, all furious but still and silent. The ghosts of birds must be that small, that harmless. Only in their vast numbers do they birth fear, and confusion.

People, the old ghosts were, I know beyond all doubt. All of them people, at least those who guarded or desired. They were torn in their passing from life, turned and broken when they died. Without their like I feel the island empty.

The mountain hulks mightily, roots set to the heart of the earth; it is as puddled ice. The fogs are only fogs, disguising naught but coming birds.

Chapter twenty-one

Much Butchery

The fog burns off in holes. It leaves the sky like a gameboard. Brown and yellow seaweeds hump at the tideline, nudged by waves carrying in more loose scraps. I look down and look down, dancing to the side and back a step, watching the water, dodging it like a child in metal shoes.

I've taken to walking the circuit of the island every day—it lets me take the measure of the place. I'll brush each turn and stone until they're familiar, until they're mine. Henders is indifferent to the habit. He prefers to stay near by to the shelter, killing birds for food or sport. He eyes the launch as a hungry man would an oven. But he knows, full well, that the current that bore us here would only carry us south, yet further from shipping waters. Once I also thought of making sails with the cloth left us—but there is that current, an invisible, coursing river. I know us prisoners here.

Near our shelter are two stone ridges, like swollen streams that run from the mountain and into the breakers. I followed one down to the water, above the densest nests. The air was full huddled with fog, so I could scarce see the waves until I was upon them. Now auks wander past on their way up the shore. They gag out fish beside particular nests. Each's quickly snapped up by what I suppose must be their mates.

The shore's like a garden as the nightmare would have it—the plantings seethe, snapping skyward. There are no longer any empty nests, save for those we've emptied with killing. If this is a garden, then what a diseased mind must have planned it, and planted it. What I have for my own ground are the crevices, filled with limp weed, visible when the tide rolled back. I brush them with my eyes, my mind. I feel the slimed weed there, pop the hard bubbles at the ends, and wonder if it might be eaten. In such manner I seek to steal the ground from birds.

Though I walk above the tideline all I see is Adam, bound before me. A cord pulls back the sides of his mouth into a grimace. His arms are tied tightly behind, knees wrapped like a boar readied for slaughter. I have a knife in my hand, a club. He grunts protest. With the point of my knife I trace his scar. The knife is heavy, the kind I'd use to butcher pork. His eyes drown in fear, and knowledge that whatever I may do with my blade, it will be just. Any blood of his will bathe, will give a churching.

A smile teases my lips. I dance to dodge a crushing wave. Squawking surrounds me like a flurry of damp leaves. But as I walk, intent on vengeance and dry feet, the squeals and hoots thicken. Far before me, hundreds of auks crowd about a huge boulder set in the last, highest, flat foam. Then, as I approach, I see it is no stone, no part of the island, but a beast.

Realizing, I near cry out. It's like a rat, but naked and long as the launch, the pale hide streaked in blood. The auks jab my ears. For a moment I almost expect the thing to heave at me, but the flesh is exhausted, bloated. Dead.

Dozens of auks clamber about, tearing off what they can. This is no solid spirit from the deep sea. It's no huge, deformed valru. I approach it slowly, cautious even now. It's a whale, with head and tail colored the gray that the ocean soaks into black things. Everywhere else the skin's been rent off viciously, down to muscle and narrow, stubborn strips of fat. Lying on shore, waves lapping then sliding away, it's more compacted than I'd have thought, a terse word when measured against the lush verse of a seagoing whale. And yet in death it's more real, every line clear—there's no longer need to dream of what might surge beneath the water.

The mouth is an open horror. There were once something like jowls there, but someone cut them away with an ax. Now soggy meat hangs loose and gray about the jawbones. Only the jawbones are white. The eyes are chewed out; nothing in the mouth but the tongue, flabby, as big as me, in places chewed by fish. The tail is yet in the water. It rises and falls, gently, with the tide.

The auks tear at what little they can reach. They pull strips from the thing, raising their beaks to gulp as more fight to snatch the morsel. I push through them, stand beside the body. My fingers brush a ridge of muscle. It's begun loosening. The whole's marred by rips of butchery, and tears left by fish, and birds, and whatever ocean things have had at it. Gannets scale the back. They spread their wings—for the sun, for a threat? One wins a good piece of whale and flies, chased by his fellows.

I run my palm down the side. The softening ridges once held force enough to drive the momentous thing through hidden byways, or through upper surf, swifter than ships. Now it looks like brawn, some old, cured meat, and smells of salt and musk.

All about me auks attack, as though they seek to undermine it, causing a collapse. Soon they'll be at the ribs. Cautiously I smell my fingers. I think the flesh fit to eat. But it will not be, much longer, out of the sea. With the knife I add my own scars—below the waterlogged gray it's red as fresh beef. My blade is poor but I carve greedily.

When I have two great fistfuls I leave the whale. From even a short way it fades in mist. Still it is monstrous, and hounded by the frantically feeding auks. I grip the strips of meat tightly, and walk quickly back the way I came.

It smells like greasy beef, and fills me with regret. The rich smell brings to me cowbelly roasted at market or harvest, feasts of meat. It fills me like a rolled quilt, banishing my daydreams of a purging kill—for now Adam is entire faded, his cries silenced. But as I tear away bites with my teeth and swallow hard, grief for what's lost lies hard in my gut, a dead thing.

The whale is gamy. It smells more like to beef than it tastes. I stop eating for a time, and breathe deeply for that dear, unsure scent.

When Henders crawls from the rockcut, I have the rest of the meat sizzling on sticks above the fire. Whale, I tell him—casually, as though that's been a common dish for me. He squats on his haunches and with clear pleasure reaches for a shred to chew. He asks where I found it. I tell him. Then he says there should be more fat on it.

It's greasy enough, I say, though I know what he means—my favorite bits of any auk are the crispy bites of fat, just below the charred skin. There's a thing to make one feel well-fed, and homey.

Needs more, he says. But it'd been butchered?

It had. Someone cut the teeth out, mayhap with an ax. It looked horrible.

Likely it didn't have teeth to begin, he says. Their mouths are filled with hard hair. No bone to it at all, except by the jaw. All the water's full of fish, smaller than you can see without—there are thousands together. I knew a man once who'd speak of it. That's what the hair's for. They'll open their mouths and it drapes down, then they push through and strain whatever's there. That hair sells well enough, in any city.

He chews, swallows with great satisfaction.

It was huge, I say.

None but a whaleman can proper guess a whale's compass—until it's out the water. I remember…

There must be men, some close, I say.

What? He says it as though I've begun speaking Spaniard.

The ones who killed the whale. The meat's still good, it could not have been so long. They must have killed it nearby, for it to have drifted here so quick.

Could have been weeks, and further than where our blessed fucking friends left us.

It's still fresh. It's good.

Well I've seen dead whales on an outbound voyage, passed them on the return two weeks after. They swell up and can hold the surface a long while. Some fools take them for rocks, they hang to the top that solid looking. I saw one bastard start to sketch one on a map, thinking he'd seen a shoal out where we were deep for true. Stupid man, whether or no he knew his college geography.

He pulls a string of gristle from his teeth, tosses it aside.

The meat's still good, I say stubbornly.

Water's cold enough. See how long it holds up, now it's out. A lucky thing it blew up so far from us. We'd have to move, else.

A damned shame that'd be, I think, and reach for a sizzling stick. Where Henders crawled from the cut, eyes bleary with sleep, the tarp has pulled free of the rough stoneheap piers. In the breeze its corner flips lightly. I bite on greasy meat.

Henders was a husbandman once. Now he would forget that. Should he remember it, he might offer me more generous speech. We must share this island. Why will he not see that our captivity is not all that's common between us?

But whatever he says, tomorrow I'll again go to the whale, and see for myself whether or no it still be good.

In the afternoon I read my Book. Henders tells me, peckishly, that I had better work. Fine then, let us ready the launch for the sea, or else break it apart for timber and build a proper hutch, I say. He hears the mocking in my words, and that I think him both stupid and lazy. This time he only spits. Then he goes down to the shore and kills a stack of auks, with a musket, for sport. The hard booms come regular. Sometimes he wishes to see what a ball will do to a bird from close at hand, and at others from what distance he may strike one. Even from afar a lump of lead will rend and ruin a bird. From close, it leaves little you would choose to name auk. Those nesting around his feet scurry a short way with each report, then back again when a fleeting time's passed. This is ungodly waste. We do not have such surplus of powder.

I sit and read my Book, fighting against the feeling that I thus give him his own cause to complain of wastefulness. There is no time to spend reading, if we would live. My eyes move unseeing over the text. But he himself chooses when to work, and what he will work on. Much of the latter is foolishness. These killings are pointless, doing nothing to strengthen us or our condition.

There are no echoes here. The shots burst flat. But finally I grow accustomed to them, and they seem charges set to mark the hours. I read of famines, bestowed on sinning communities by the Lord. It comes to me that those visited by such hunger are always took unawares; whatever they may say, none know themselves sinners until they find the larder empty.

The Saints may cut the wilderness, but it will be no easy nor quick thing, there, to find a means of bread. They must wait for corn to grow, and without stores such as sustained Joseph in his desolation.

From the south a flashing noise burgeons, like thunder, like applause. Birds pour around the mountain. They slip beneath the sun. Their numbers eclipse it; they begin as a turnpike, then broaden to a plain. Beneath, all's dusk.

Henders fires overhead. Eight birds fall around him, the size of open hands. He whoops, and quickly reloads. I feel tears coming and I close the Book, holding it to my chest with arms crossed around. The sky has turned night sea-waves; we breathe the only air between ocean's waters and heaven's.

Sarah, this is a finer gift than you could have known, for there is here no replacement for it. I may here live out all the short days of my life. Henders is below me, laughing, killing birds. The auks are coming to ground. They are laying. He kills only to see them change, to mark this place as his. I am so, so afraid.

He said the whale will like as not be gone with the tide, and what's left will likely be spoilt. Nevertheless I'll visit it, and see if there is more meat to be had. After just these few weeks I am dead sick of bird, whether auks or those little handwidth things, like thrushes, that came and went so sudden. But even if the whale has drifted, I'm happy enough with the walk.

I woke to a roof of blankets speckled with pricks of light. There were tan stripes in the overlapped cloth. Seeing them, I climbed eagerly from the cut and into bright sun. The fog skirts have all dropped away, and wet cobbles glint soft and light as bubbles. Standing atop a boulder I can see to the outer rocks, and beyond them. From my vantage I believe I see cousins of the dead whale spouting lively in far distance. Maybe it is only spray off of sunlit waves. But wonderful, to see the sun, and the world so expanded! My chest swells with a kept laugh, warming me.

Wind blows over the far ocean, over the shore, and rides up the mountain. There it thickens into cloud, looking finally like snow extended impossibly off the mount. Even so, the lower faces seem less sheer, the whole somehow less imposing. If I had a mind to, I think I might climb it. The auks cluck softly, safe and useful as chickens.

Rounding the mountain, I see that the whale, that amazing thing, is still there, though a bit further down shore. The tides have turned it slightly in the night. Before, you might have thought it died in trying to reach the mountain; now it looks to have begun a slow, ponderous turn back toward the water. It's not visibly diminished; for all their frantic feeding, it will take the birds weeks to strip it.

But as I approach I see there are no auks. I wonder if it could have gone to rot so suddenly, hating to think that Henders could be proved right. A few determined gannets pick and gulp on top, but the auks seem all in their nests. Could flying birds love carrion more than those that walk? I walk forward slowly, still a good long way from the beast but bracing myself for what must, even in this dung-heaped air, be an appalling smell. I fear it's become a swollen, gassy corpse.

One bird stands strangely still on the whale's back, making no move to feed nor to fight over scraps. The rest hang some feet away, as though fearful of this, their confident ruler. I peer closer, and start. It is no white bird, but the head of another dead thing, hairy and horrid, rested on the whale as a savage offering. Then it is not dead, for in the white face black eyes twitch. Now the head seems big as a barrel. It drops from sight and I realize it was a bear, standing with forepaws on the far flank, watching me.

Slowly it lumbers around, as though wrestling free of the torn mouth. The fur is white as an egg, that around the jaws stained bloody. It tosses its head, sniffing. It sits heavily, then seems to reconsider, and wanders back behind the whale. I could scarce be of less concern to it and the knot within me begins, slowly, to unravel.

Slowly I walk backward and to the side, up the hill and through nests. Finally I reach a good vantage on a knobby outcrop. The breeze come brightly, and sun and distance ease the threat of the hidden bear. I stand with hands on my hip, waiting.

When the bear again appears it is chased by one smaller, with yellower legs. They game like pups. They roil and roll, sending auks waddling up the shore, easily knocking aside rocks the size of heads. Seeing their speed in play I tense, thinking of how quickly they could cover the ground and reach me. But they have little interest in what must seem poor prey—they rear, batting each other with paws, gnawing harmlessly on each other's necks. I think of the bear baiting, of the change in that one when cornered—and it was a beast well versed in the company of men. These would doubtless think any close approach a threat.

The smaller one sees me. He stops as though sniffing the wind, but that cannot be; it comes from the ocean. For now he is not concerned with water. He stares across a field of cooing birds, to me. He is far enough off that I can scarce make out his eyes, but they lock with mine. I could turn and run. I do not; I stay, and find myself slowly squatting, kneeling, making myself small. I cannot make any claim to force, not before something that might have swum—greedy, and replete with spirit—from a far, savage's land. The bear licks his lips, brushes his mouth with one paw. If I were close, maybe I could hear him murmur.

Now his mate stares at me. Before she was only curious. With her companion disturbed, her gaze is direct as a hatchet blow, her shoulders like great guns. With a shudder I defer; I look away, to an auk combing herself beneath one wing. Maybe she is cleaning. Maybe she's hungry for bugs. But then, from the corner of my eye, I see the bears running.

They splash into the sunlit ocean, swimming with smoothly jerking heads, like dogs chasing shot ducks. They sink, turn to light patches, and are gone. I wonder how long they can stay under the sea. I wonder how long they will.

On the walk back, I search nests, prodding auks aside with my hoe. I find one egg the size of a drinking cup, snatch it up and put it in my bag, then walk away quickly before the mother can attack. She fought hard for the ground; there's a ragged patch beside her left eye where tufts of feathers were torn away. She seems more concerned over her nest than the egg.

Eggs, eggs, eggs, all about the house, I say to no one.

The ocean looks different to me now. The sun that glistens over it makes a shield; beneath it live beasts of mighty appetite. The bears made no threatening move at me, but the force under their white fur seemed beyond the speaking of it. They could come dripping from the waves, up the shore, at me. Somehow it's worse to have them out of sight. I no longer have their play to check my fear, and can think now of gnawing jaws, of claws like murderous knives. I shake my head and lose myself in looking for eggs.

At home we would sometimes roast eggs in the coals. A pleasant meal, and simple to prepare. But many nests are empty. This must yet be early in their laying season. After the first treasure, there's naught to fill my bag but birds' shrieks. I work faster, working around the island until I can see the rockcut ahead. Henders has a fire going. Else, there would be little to mark the spot. The flames seem cleaner than the birds' usual black smoke. I slow, taking longer between nests, in no wise eager to return.

Something like a red moth rises from the fire, frantic and resplendent. It climbs, sprinkling dying dust from its wings. I gape as another follows, quickly, seeking to seize the first. It crinkles, holding steady for a moment, becoming rubbed soot. It is burning paper; finally it dissolves into black, powdered down. I drop my bag and run with my hoe through nests, breath furious, a flaming pressure filling my head, cobbles clacking underfoot like galloping goats.

Henders sits on a boulder, his back to me. The cleanest fire we've made burns before him, but the light is muffled by that from the sinking sun. Several twisted, shrunken bird corpses are burning.

But he's also used a great deal of the scrub about the mountain. That's made a bed of coals, like the hot, brief ashes that come from bark.

He must have heard me approach. I near stand over him. But he does not turn; he reaches for the fire, as though offering food to a dog. A page slips from his hand, then slicks sideways on a thin pad of air, and into the flame. It blackens. Words twist, clenching. Henders jerks his arm back and I hear paper tear. Enraged, I snatch the Book away over his shoulder. Before I have it fully away I hear him laughing.

Nothing like a fine fire on a cold day.

A fire. I need this! I shake the Book at him. A loose page falls out. A prankster breeze slices it to the flame, faster than if balled and tossed. I gasp, and crawl through his laughter to beat the paper with the heel of my hand. What hasn't burned has blackened to a blind confusion. Beating out the flame thumps pain back into the cut on the pad of my thumb. I squeeze it tight, not looking to see if it's bloodied.

I turn on him, Book in one hand, ruined page in the other. You burned it, I say. He nods. Though I have hated him before this, I never thought him possessed of such cold malice.

I may burn your coat. Your clothes, I say. I sound a child who would be pettily revenged, and curse myself that I do not have a voice of thunder to lay him on the ground.

His smile fades like a cave collapsing. That'd be the last time you'd walk for some weeks, he says softly.

I need this.

I take a few steps, and sit. The cobwebbed binding is broken, and where he slammed it open is violated with a large scar joining two old, severe cracks, near severing the whole. I scan the pages quickly, seeing what I've lost. He moved through without seeming order, leaving some passages whole, tearing others to parody.

You planned this ahead, you bastard, I say, seeing the thick bed of birds and brush. At least he saw the need for a torrent of flame, and did not carry out his destruction with petty fire.

He took a page here, half a page there, leaving more torn and meaningless. I leaf through quickly to see what I yet have. But from behind he bats my head to the side, and snatches the Book from my hands. I stumble to my feet. He smiles at me through pursed lips.

Need this, eh. Will it keep you warm, can we eat it. I've watched you peer through it when you'd better have been working, looking like it has a single answer we need. Did it?

He flips through pages in clumps.

A true and faithful discourse of survival on northern isles by Christfucker, Esquire, he says. Reminds me of my old ma reading to us. Helpful. And a good thing it is, summer won't last forever—we'll need good guidance afore we can live under snow.

I grab for the Book but he jams out one arm to hold me away. With the other he dangles the Book over the fire. If I did not fear he'd drop it I'd scramble for my hoe, seek to brain him.

Why not? he says, taunting. Tell me why not.

Reasons patter like dropped tacks. There is the need for order, and the necessity that he not tread upon what's mine. There is the need to hold a gift. I know he'll think whatever I say frail, contemptible. There is nothing I can say to stop him. But my need for the Book is a simmering growl.

I lunge and this time he lets me come, bringing the Book courteously to meet me. I grab it, glaring, forcing myself not to strike him. Even in my fury I know there is a better way.

He watches me as he would an old steer—though furious, there is scant chance I'll strike. When he sees I will not, he is bored. I hold the Book close to me, both arms tightly around it, looking fixedly at it, as though I watch a child for signs of sickness. For many minutes I stand there with the torn gift. But I think only of Henders, and his body that he thinks stronger than it is. When I look up he is wandering off toward the water, kicking birds aside.

Shreds and knappings of the text, holes that leave nonsense. At least he didn't burn the parts I need, I think. A wry smile; hot tears.

Chapter twenty-two

I Loose a Hound

A mouth of chipped teeth sullies my face, and behind it is no mind for me. The air is trapped like netted fish. The smell of him is a rotting hollow; below, I'm deadened as mud. It makes no matter. He does not come to me for liveliness.

He is a dull hammer and a wretched man and he finishes quickly. He comes, and rolls away. Soon he lies asleep. He is sure of his safety. But me, I lie awake, arms crossed over, gnawing on my lip.

My legs yet shiver. But I tell myself that he was never there. It's only me, my own fingers, that have been in me. I sought to give myself pleasure. The mood was wrong—my touch, joyless. But when I slide hands to legs, to rub them and give a caring warmth, I feel I've slipped into a nest of baby snakes and pull back. The jerk will wake him, I fear. He only shifts.

I think on what he has done, and squeeze shut my eyes. Tears leak to my hair as I hug my chest, legs loose, near where he sleeps like a hog. He is only appetite.

Outside there's a rolling blunder of calling auks. I think of a white bear, come galloping through their pauper's nests. But the cries end quick, as though they only briefly warned of coming clouds.

Before it seemed quiet. Now that I've heard them squall, their hoots and coos rustle in and fill our cut. The auks cry softly, waiting for mates to come faithful up the shore, bringing them chewed fish. At times they may fight and howl, but there is among them order. They warn each other. They provide. Another wave of screeching passes. Perhaps the cloud they warned of has dropped lightning or other sign of storm.

Sweat cools. The sweat is most his and it leaves my skin clammy, like turtle meat. A rib of stone turns my shoulder inward, urging me to turn toward him. I stay on my back, draw up my knees for small relief. I should sleep, gain strength. But I clench my teeth. Patience gave me a piece of glass made cunningly, to toss rainbows on the ground or across a watching face. It was a clever thing, but in the end a mere passing fancy. Any book is a mighty precious thing in itself and mine was more so. He knew it, too—when he sought to make his mark, write his story, he chose its pages. My body tightens, a ball, my fists knit, my veins turn copper ribbon as the mare finds me even here and I dream, awake, of what I might do to him.

I dream the manner of his death: I'll tell him of new whales, blown in close by to where the old corpse drifted. I'll tell him there's a great surety of meat, rich, sweet smelling, plentiful enough for a feast. But I will not go back. My moonblood is come, I will say. I'll say it makes me a cripple, and it is true that I feel myself a crooked woman though he will not know that, nor that he is the lone cause of it. And, from gentleness toward his own pure humors, he will not wish to use my bloodied body. When my moonblood is come he risks me bottling his heat. He will go in the end to the whale, and there meet the beasts I met and shared a moment's communion with.

It may be I drew them here.

I did draw them, with murderous will.

Then I deferred, showing right respect for inner force and grace. They ran, they swam like free thunder. From respect for me they'll tear his throat beside the whale. I'll laugh at the sight of his heart ripped bare. My chest is an iron plate. I smile crookedly, readying words to send him into hazard and, I pray, to his doom.

But I know with a sudden draining that this is vacant fantasy, floral dreaming. If he did go, he should sure see the bears. And if he did not see, well they are no partners of mine and would not aid me, no matter that I gave them respect. Henders laid out dead, slaughtered by animals hungry for his many parts, is a pleasant, restful picture. But only that.

We are alone here. Perhaps we will not always be so. And as I think of that I search myself, for as I search myself there's a twitch in my blood. May be it has been there some time. But now it draws my mind like thread. Skin frozen, I search my body for the needle. There is none—but there is a kind of spark.

How long has this been in me? It cannot be more than a pair of months, or a bare few. Maybe it is hours. My fingers are turned to stone, hemmed in black ice, and I think frantically that there are those who would call life a gift but it seems not so to me. Something new has seated firmly, as my liver. Something has formed in a hot, silver mold. A babe, a babe, no bigger than a thimble, weightier than the world.

Henders stirs and turns, curling up, drawing blankets close. I lay quickening. Memories come like panicked cats—of a frozen road, of soaked herbs that streak blue. I pass hands over my stomach, making small swirls with my thumbs. I am increased, I am multiplied. He has blessed me. Bearing is a woman's useful duty to the Lord, to the world, to this fine place He's given us. I never thought it my duty to further this man, to extend his blood.

Henders' back swells, falls. A gift must be given, and received, and when he gave this he did not give but flung it, to land in me or on cold barren ground he cared not at all. He did not give, but took. If not with the viciousness of open force, then with vile threat of it—if I did not fear him he would never have lain with me, not after the first time, not with a whole cock left him.

My body is cold and sweating, but the rock beneath me seems suddenly hot as brick. Neck and eyes clenched, I bite hard enough to break chestnuts on the knuckles of two fists. Blood. I should leave here, and flee him, and would if there were stars. But I know that there are not, there is nothing here I can see. I remember stars of light, others of black felt. They dance around me mocking me, strangers talking foreign.

Oh Lord, I would say, but I fear to wake him. I will not have him wake and know that I am weak. I cry quiet, with wheezing breath.

Oh Lord I whisper, quiet as spiders sewing. I think of him lying there, a mound of sleeping man who has commanded my dear parts through fear of what he could do. From nowhere I see a bear sitting in the remembered sun, haunches below him, and a studded collar.

Where is his armor I whisper in the same nothing voice. There is nothing to answer me, nothing to steam from the stone walls or fling aside the sailcloth with wicked shout. There is only a vanishing whisper of ten thousand birds and, yet fainter, shushing water, no ghost nor mocking grima nor household thing to answer me when I whisper again to tell me where is his armor. But this time the silence seems my answer, that comes blazing, and silent, and from me—that he has none.

Slowly, quietly, I sit, and seek through bunched clothes for the knife with the cracked haft, the dull edge, the point that's good as a spear. A spear's a sporting weapon. The sheath's tied with rough, tawny rope that finds my hand before the sheath or the blade. I pull it to me like an eeljig, I have the cracked haft. Then Henders begins to wake, and to turn. But it is too late for him for the knife is to his neck and plunged, his naked throat brought me.

I cut straight and deep with my knife like a spear. Blood fills my hands like clear water and he gurgles, swings one arm, knocks me against the rock. My head pushes up the sailcloth roof, and it pulls from cobble pilings, sinks across half the cut like a washed sheet. Henders thrashes but I think he is going and gone to hell deservedly for holding me with so small regard—I cry jaggedly but should be stronger than to cry, for what could be better than to be here alone save for my own increase; alone, if he does not haunt.

This bastard would have killed me in time, he would mark the island how he can, with pitiful stories—here is the place he killed birds when first we came, here is the place he burned a book, here is the place he murdered me. He would have ended thus or forcing me again, and I would not have survived either, the killing or the constant taking. He thought himself a banddog but I am here, roaring with the hood from my head, and no mere cub or cur. The tide of blood rolls steady and never checked, for I have cut him as I would a beast bled for food. This is not very different for when I slaughter for food it is life for me, and with him dead my life can take its own poor contours but with him alive there was naught for me to do but wait for death.

Chapter twenty-three

I Learn of Parentage

It would be pure dark if not for the snow. Today, the sun did hang above the sea for a time. But it was weak, and sank down sickly behind the distant rocks. It's only an usurer's pound.

The snow's thick, wet. In the village, I would have thought its coming a harbinger of winter's dark. Here its stubborn whiteness leavens the night.

It's dampened by the ocean, I think. There is a blessing in that, for dry snow should mean cold. It's not near as bitter as I should have thought. Of course I cannot stay outside for long; the wind strips me, forces me to my house. I only come when my legs cramp, crying out to stretch. There can never be a fire. The only auks I've left are dried, and their fat won't so well drip or flame.

I catch a flake on my tongue, open my mouth for more. Below me the shore is pure white, but for the few lines forming my name. Even those I can scarce see. They've filled with fresher snow. I walked the letters out a week past, when I couldn't bear the clean cold white. I thought I must do something to mark it, and did, stamping out *Mel.* A passing bird may read it, or any eyes in heaven. Perhaps tomorrow

I'll write it out fully. *Melode.* I won't today. I need something to wait for—something to break my days. Their sameness is a scream.

The light from the snow is like that from my old greasepaper window. There must be a moon, above the clouds; the light must come from somewhere.

Whether or no it's full dark, the ocean is always with me. I can't see it at all, now. But it crashes, moaning.

There's no snow about the house; I cleared it all with my hoe, clanging and rapping on the rock underneath. I do so again whenever there's more than an inch. Do it less often, and my feet should be perilous wet; do it more, and I'd have naught to wait for. My days would stretch more unbearable. Sure I no longer wait for rescue, nor any outside succor. Since the auks left the shore, I've slipped further into a murky dream. This land is formless in winter. Even the tides seem to have no ready order, but come a foot more or less each time against the shore. They brush back the snow irregular, making the island greater, then less.

I am greater, I think, and hold my hands around my middle.

I shake my head, take up a handful of snow for a ball. It flattens against the side of the mountain, leaving a white pad. My hand is red, painful with cold. Worse, stooping sent a jab up my back. My legs feel so weak, drained by sloth and a tedious board. And their force drains into the babe. Perhaps I should walk my name more often, walk it bigger. But not today. My head's full of air—I need gather strength.

When I kneel, and crawl into my house, my belly sags near to the ground. This is a house, for I built it with boards I stripped myself. I wouldn't stay in the rockcut. That's filled with bones, and my memory of him. I tossed the bottom blankets to cover all. The rest, the rower's benches and sailcloth, I took away and used to build this house. The mountain is also part of it; I found a flat place, near a cliff, with an abutment like a stone knee. It was a simple thing to prop the planking there, and brace it with gathered rocks. With a morning's work I had a better dwelling than ever he would make. Now I have a house, one clean of him.

At the base, it's big as the bedstead I shared with Patience. In places I can near sit up straight. But I lay on my back, breathing deeply. A voice tells me I should move later, go out to the air again, lest I turn mossy. Another voice tells me: No—I had better lay still and quiet, storing all the force that can be had from dry and smoked birdmeat.

But the loudest voice, the muddiest, filling me ear to ear, says it makes no matter. I'm crammed with a mournfulness I can't shed. I'm growing great, yet thinning, my humors stolen to make a babe. But it seems years since I've felt care for life, or hope of it, or dread at thought of its loss. All here is heavy, silent, thunderous. The world is lead.

This inside me was nothing I ever wanted. Certain not from him.

But it is mine, I think, trying.

But it is his.

It's quiet beyond reckoning. I can speak, I say aloud. But that only deepens the silence; it's plain there's no hope of an answering voice. My ears are clogged with quiet, and an almost unheard thrum. Perhaps it is my heart, my blood. Or the creak of the mountain, a rumble, near below hearing.

The babe kicks—a companion to my heartbeat, or its rival.

If I could, I'd fill my head with welcome things. My head is mine, and should obey me, as does the rest of my body.

Raise, I command my arm. It does, my hand placed slowly before my face.

Turn. And all my body does, pressing my stomach against stone until I bid all turn back.

All obeys. Why should I not so order my head? But it's a barn filled with swallows, hunting owls, bats—whatever may find its way in, and choose to nest.

The stars on Sarah's face, I think. The marjoram crushed on her floor. The times I scorned her; those I thought her lightminded, and cruel.

My garden plot, that was always mine—Patience must tend that now. She serves the Jacobs, and alone. The cottagers must have come. What manner of life can she have, with them all about?

The Lord. His charity. His love for the world—Adam. Adam. There's nothing so cavernous as an empty word. My head fills with cries. Where do they come from? Where grow?

Often, I pray, and sometimes, very rarely, do find a moment of peace. Then the world falls away; I am quiet within and without. The house no longer seems a fortress against this place, but only a sign of the truth that if a woman would live here, she will need shelter, and food, and must bring both with her or else make them. The snow does not attack—it only builds my walls thicker. I am warm, complete, happy that my humors are right to build a babe.

But the swallows sleep only briefly. When they do Anne is before me, or Sarah. And I long for them, my peace sudden fled.

Something is happening. This is no kicking—it is lower, and from me. I bite my lip, pull elbows across my breasts. Always I shiver. Though seldom bitter, the cold here seeps bone-deep. I wonder if the babe can feel it, and if the cold may harm it before ever we meet.

I may find such sooner than I knew, for the pressure in me builds, shudders. Then it breaks, a hot rush down the inside of my legs, such relief! I hadn't known I so hungered for this. With the relief comes shame as though I've fouled myself—as though there are men here to know it, as though I'd care. Then the first pain comes, high in my thighs, but further in, near to where the head of the babe must be, squeezing. I cast about me wildly—somehow I'd never believed I would live to do this, not alone. I've never known anyone do this alone, no matter what their station; only women in tales, who find themselves in forests.

If Sarah were here, she would bid me walk. She tells women to lie fixed only when they must. I go to open air.

The sun's a bare sliver. Or so I imagine from the light, for the sun is shrouded, its blaze masked. Somewhere it is hot. There are lands the sun never leaves, where all is burned to black. But here the wind rushes me. It is only a breeze, salty, without the living stink of the auks, but it cools me uncomfortably, my ankles most of all. I must pull out those blankets I burst onto. Else, I'll be cold when I lie there. It must be as healthful a place as I can contrive.

I pull the blankets from my house, leave them rumpled in the snow. There are still more inside than I need. Blankets, at least, they left me a plenty of. The wet ones can freeze, and later cleanse with snowmelt. I struggle not to think of what is coming.

The hours pass forever. The jolts come faster, harder. The last are rapid, hard as spikes. Finally they begin to sink. I think of the babe. I will meet the babe. Its name will be John, or Mary.

Beside me's a jug of lichens. I sweat; I drink deeply, spit some back. I think it is John. This is John, and I will meet him soon. I think it is a boy.

Blankets tangle in my hands. Those below my waist are soaked, though I'm most numb there, and know it only from clutching of cloth about my hips. My skirts are pulled high. Somehow I never thought to be clothed. Mistress Jacobs was. But this is a thing a woman should do naked.

Come, John! Drop from me. I seethe, and hate this boy.

This cannot be right. I struggle to empty, feeling the great mass still within, smelling gore. It must have been more than a day. If the light here was just and proper, I would know, or have a notion. I don't. Have I slept? Surely not.

I would give all to bring Sarah here, for her to make blue streaks across me. But what is there for me to give save us, us that I'd have her come to rescue? It hurts so, an ache that steals me, no longer in one place but run entire through. This cannot be right.

But some woman bore me. I was born. I suck air through my teeth, eyes squeezed shut, and that woman comes before me. She's a small thing, and comely. The old fear returns me then—that my mother did not die. Why should she die in that fire, and I live? That this thought should come bludgeoning, and now, seems the Devil's jest. But it will not leave me. It rumbles through my head, this doubt—crying that I was abandoned, never orphaned.

You did this thing, I say, I think, I shout to her. You who bore me fought thus, and maybe had a man waiting, and maybe you did not. Maybe you died in that tavern—they fucking burned it. Maybe you made your way from it and away, and now labor, living with a husbandman who needs a season's work, sharing his bed. Maybe you hate anything that puts you in mind of this pain. And never thought me worth it, nor longed for me once gone.

Drop! I scream, rigid as rock. Come! It makes no matter whether I scream at the babe or my own body, I need to scream. It does bring some relief, some slight lessening. But it's only made me a shell, not hastened the hatching. I am hard, maybe brittle, and strain that I may crack open. It is coming and I hate it so.

Oh Lord. Help me.

The prayer comes without hope for justice or mercy, as a raw, forbidden plea. What matter that I ask the Lord of all the world for help? He will do what He will do. But I've lost all hope of pleasure returning, hope of life. Desire falls as into a pit. There is nothing but me, but us, here—no history nor future. The pain's a quick razor, a ravening dog.

There is no world but this. Sure there is no escape from it.

Thinking so, I have a moment, never looked nor hoped for, of lying easy. And at that, something begins to open, to spill out. I see the way before me, push ferociously—and yet, somehow, give way. There is nothing here to fight against. And I empty.

It is more water and it is me. All drops. I'm emptier than ever in my life, empty as death, sobbing, exhausted, joyous.

My hands fumble blindly between her legs. The babe's a girl. This is Mary, upside down and screaming.

Holding her close, heedless of the cord that yet binding us, all strength fails. I fall back, sink into my body. But my body is gone. There is naught to sink into. This is more than weakness. There is her wailing voice.

Mary. There is me crying in answer, calling her name. Mary. The house near drips but I am voided within, and torn. Mary. There is neither of our voices, and both echoing. Mary. There is only her. She is out, yet me. We're within. He is nowhere here.

I will never, never leave her, and I know this: My mother is dead.

Chapter twenty-four

We Depart

The auks are come again, after their long season out to sea. I wonder if there's a special land they take to, or if they only seek out any point in warmer waters. They went so soon after the hatching that their young were scarce able to shed the spray. They swam desperately, with some gray down still puffing through bright black feathers. But though their choice of time seemed perilous, it's sure they do know well the turn of the year; for it had not been long after I watched the last auk paddle toward the stone teeth, my belly beginning to increase under the padding of many garments, that the first snow had begun to fall.

Then, when the melting began, every crack become a flowing spring, the first birds returned. At first the most of them held to sea, but a few came to shore, waddling about, scouting. They slipped on the last snow, left prints in a few stubborn, slushy patches.

Spring, I thought when I saw them. Spring, I said and shouted, hands over my head. The season spread before me, and if it was not as green a one as I was used to, it held no less promise for me than in a place of planting and harvest. The birds are my harvest, my good

Lord's storehouse. The joy I'd had from melting snow was an eager one, but not so much as that from the homecoming of agile life. They are life for us, paddling and diving for silver fish—and it seemed to me when I saw them that we'd a good plenty of life left us.

I thought of purple crocuses, that each year were the first sign that my labor must move from the Jacobs' house and into the garden. That pleasure was a mere glimmer when measured aside the auks' sunbeam. And it could not have fallen better, for I'd feared my milk was begun to sour—I'd nothing to sustain it but smoked, dried bird. What I had left of that I've thrown out onto the shore. A few auks pecked at it, then let it alone. They are no cannibals.

Fresh meat's better, I say aloud, and hold my Mary close. Fresh meat has blood in it, and that's the stuff of life. But Mary's yet dissatisfied. She gives me only cries.

I stand, stretch. These skirts I've made to rough breeches, cutting down the middle with a knife, tying off half to each leg. There might have been lichens higher up, perhaps a different sort than those I found near to the base, and I needed something to wear in my climbing; I would not wear his clothes at first, and now all of those are gone, thrown to the waves.

The lichens are cleansing. I think them a great gift, perhaps as much as are the birds, for I don't know we'd have survived on naught but rancid meat.

After the last climb, I needed lay and rest quiet for some hours. My heart beat hard in my chest, my stomach felt wrecked as after a long run. I lower my arms, look at my hands. The skin seems somewhat gray to me, the fingers dry, chapped, the nails near ragged. There's a bloody spot at the edge of my mouth, that it breaks open every time I yawn—a few days past I thought it healed, and yawned, and again broke the tight skin open. Worst, I am constant weary. Even stretching drains me.

Mary cries; I bend to her, take her up in my arms. She's gained only a few pounds, perhaps, in the months since she was born. But I feel each ounce a triumph. Were we at the village they would likely force another nurse on her. My milk, they would say, must be fouled so soon after birth. Perhaps they might offer me churching, then, I think—but stop myself, to stop the screaming in my head. They are gone from here, from us. I will give her my milk. I know it good.

I rock my daughter—back, forth, murmuring quietly. It's this she wanted, for after a while her eyes drift closed, and she sleeps.

She is passing small. I never thought it a wonder, holding other children, that a person should be so small. But she is mine, I know each bit of her, and it's in thinking of each little bit that I know her tiny; her eyes are beads, her fingernails a poppet's tin money. She looks like me, I tell myself, thinking of the mirror. Her eyes, that were blue, are melting to my own brown. I think she has my nose. I'm sure she doesn't have his.

Now that she's sleeping, all's quiet. I've a mind to clean our home, but that can wait, at least a while. I told myself I'd do it no less than every third day, that I may remember we do not live in our filth—and Mary learn that we do not.

What we'll do the coming winter, when she'll be barely able to take first toddling steps—that, I don't know. The weariness I feel in my thighs, in my back, rears up behind me. Perhaps we'll never see another fall of snow; perhaps she'll not see her first. When she was born all had already fallen, and lay melting. And oh, if I should feel myself dying before her…. I push away the fear of what I'd need do. I try to take the good moment, to taste it and cradle my daughter.

So early in the season the auks are not yet fat, nor have they taken any great number of the nesting holes—thus it's near impossible to heat water. The lichens must sit and steep, making a cool infusion that's not so good as hot potion, and takes a week to make besides. But that is what we have, and what we need. So when Mary's slept soundly for a while I rest her carefully against my shoulder, and walk a short way around the mountain. The fog is salty, thick as gruel.

The lichens I want are flat, pale green, like flower petals pressed careless in a book. Higher up they go to purple, and are sweeter. But it's the bitterness of the green that heals us. I won't try to climb again. Once, gathering some score of feet up, a gannet stabbed my hand. If it'd been the one I was holding with, sure I would have fallen. Breaking even an ankle here would likely be my death. I had better keep to the ground.

With the back edge of my knife I scrape off a good clothful of lichen, from the underside of a boulder, where no filth can cling. Though I'm careful some bits of stone come off in a fine dust. When the cloth is full I take it to the tiny stream, hold it by the edges, and fill it full of water. Most of the lichens float up, then, and stone dust settles. I rock the cloth, rest it in a depression in the ground. Then I sweep the floating lichens up with one hand. That little stone as still holds to them will come off during infusion, whether hot or cold.

When we return to the shelter Mary is full awake, and again crying. This time she wants feeding; I am happy for it, for I hope her growing want for milk shows it is becoming stronger, and more pure. And my breasts are past the harsh soreness of the first feedings. There is nothing now to keep me from being as eager for the nursing as she. When done, she again sleeps. I want to murmur to her softly—*my love*—but I would have her rest. Instead I shift, crossing my arms to give her better bed. She has been sleeping more, I think. I will let her do, and not challenge her wants.

Most of the Saints would stop her. They have no mind to let a child dispute them, not even before she may talk. Mary's now some three months old, a month older than the last snows. Fortunate her birth was not sooner. She could, for a time, suckle direct from my inward blood.

I lower my head to her mouth, listen to her breathe. Between each breath, there's a pause; then, when at last it comes, a tiny whistle. Beyond it is the hiss of the surf, and the cooing of auks beginning to nest.

Woman and man are one.

The voice is in my head. But I know it well. It is sandy, adamant. Master Stradling has followed me here; or I have carried him.

They are one, he says, save for heat. Heat boils blood to semen, a simmering condition woman may never know.

I shake my head, listen to the waves and the cobbles rattling beneath.

The affectionate meeting of moist women is incapable of breeding heat. The meeting of men has heat in plenty, that consumes what might have been new life.

There was order when Sarah kissed me goodbye, I think furiously. That kiss was sincere, sweet as chestnuts.

Fortunate, then, that we left you…without diligent enclosure, women may willfully overgrow their boundaries.

I will not have this. I will not be filled with the echoes of old sermons, spoke by a man who, if my wishes fall true, is rolling at the bottom deeps. His bones are froze by depth, I pray, thus not ever washed clean. Or, even if he came to ground, maybe he's found his grave.

"Not nearly…"

I freeze, the quiet of my baby's sleep letting my ears open wide. There is wind, and the ocean, and the birds. But beyond that, I would swear, I did hear a man's voice, and outside my head. I stare down the shore, toward the cold breeze's source, toward the water, into the fog. There's nothing I can see—but then, I can't even see the ocean.

"…many"

I did hear that. I heard a man say many, and I am to my feet. I turn aimlessly—to the shelter, the mountain wall, the source of the voices. If they are there, in truth, who might they be? If they are not, then death is near to me, for madness has come apace. I think, *Jenny Sherwood…*

Jenny Sherwood talked aloud to her departed husband, and in public, at the crossroads. For a time many feared his spirit—but later she took to talking with toads, and to the ragged-man set in Midge Thomas' dooryard. Then we knew the weight of her mind was fled. She never needed labor again, with packets of bread and eggs oft left by her doorway. But there were none who would speak to her, save Sarah. And Sarah would end frustrated, and sad. She never told me what Jenny Sherwood said. Finally Jenny hung herself by the neck from the summer beam, and Sarah needed cut her down.

Well, if this is madness, I had rather take it by the throat. And Mary had best come with me, for unless she lives to eight or more she must be always tethered to me, and to my strength. I gather her up. Then we walk downshore, into the salty fog.

I see them first as shadows, like fish feeding in a pond. They are yet beside the water, dim and without feature; they are only shades. One strides upshore, swings overhand. I cannot rightly see but I think an auk falls dead.

Stupid as hair—nothing like the ones at sea, the man says. Those are the first words with sense I've heard spoke since before the winter. They fall on my ears like oil.

Now the other shadows move up beside, with clubs and sacks. They go killing through rank after rank. At first the birds are most still near by to them, but then I see a stir as some of the auks begin to fall back. The auks waddle between nests but the shadows are coming, becoming men. The birds' panic builds; they tumble over rocks, nests, each other. Their hoots turn screeches. The first man I see clearly wears no hat. He has a long, tangled beard, braided hair that falls over one shoulder, eyes only for prey. Some of the screeches are cut off quick. Birds defend their homes; with thick sharp beaks they attack those fleeing, slowing the retreat. Fortunate for them that most of their number holds to sea, and that most of the nests are yet empty. For even with that, soon the band of nests about the men is a frenzy of swinging clubs, birds fleeing and fighting, tumbling, dying. Those around me yet sit still and curious.

They kill and kill. I had rather wait and come to them in quiet, but it seems the men will never weary of their harvest, their sport. After a while I tire of waiting. I walk for them, hands tight on Mary.

To miss tripping I need brush an auk from my path, then another. The second jabs my ankles—I kick at it absently.

The man closest brushes his arm across his nose. I name you Funk Island, he says grandly.

Your ass you're smelling, says another.

Jesus Christ. But he is not insulted; he has seen me. He stares. I have forgot the way that staring eyes may pierce.

Oh. His partner looks to me, club in hand. I hate the prick and probe of their eyes and I look to his club. It is specked in blood. It is not like a knife, that should have by now gone all red. I look at the club but I know now that all have seen me. It's a good while since I've felt myself the center of a crowd.

Another man steps before the rest. He was down by the water, and took the time to get himself a musket. He holds it across his chest. It's the kind that needs burning match; he has a sourly smoking coil of it.

We want no trouble here, he says. There's plenty birds for the taking, for both our crews.

So there would be if I had me a crew, I say. It feels delicious to speak it; for he is a man, a person, who will speak back. He will say something. I need not drop my words useless to the ground.

Then Christ Jesus who are you, says the first man.

I laugh, and keep laughing. There is something funny here. I laugh and laugh, and no man comes close to touch me, or asks about the jest.

The man who held the musket is Miller, and he the captain of a fishing vessel. His cabin is cozy, windowless, filled with maps. The single small table is quilted with them. I know how to scratch a line in the dirt, showing which forest path is best. These are something different; as though string was spilled out onto each sheet, traced in blue and black, ruled in red. I have seen a paper map only once, at Sarah's, and that in an illustration. There are some dozens of them. These are wealth, I know. Those who own maps may prosper. Miller pushes them aside, then puts out two cups, and a pitcher of small beer.

They rowed me here before going on with their harvest. The auks are near as thick now as when first I came here. The launch's sweeps tore crescents through the flock—I watched the island fade in fog, like a sinking valru. Then I turned and saw the ship.

It is smaller than *Neptunus*, or the *Joan*; I thought it black, but it was only darkened by fog. A sorrow for my humiliation came upon me, and rage for things lost and taken. But when I cried I did it quietly, holding all curtained. My laughter on the shore shamed me—or I felt it should have. I'm heavily aware of men.

By the time we were on the ship they had a mighty fire going on shore; I could see it, a distant glow, though I could no longer see land. It is not so easy to boil water or fat, for the birds are thinned by last winter, their main lard long ago consumed by cold. But the men make up with numbers what they cannot find in quality. They'll render down their birds, and bring the oil to sell.

Miller asks me, first, how I came to be there. That is a mighty question. For a time I don't answer. A great long while, since I've seen walls. I walk from one to the next, holding Mary in one arm, forced to stoop by the low planks of the ceiling. I knock on one wall; I knock on a second, on the third. They were made with near perfect craftsmanship, that no draft cheats. They make this a close, comforting place. The sounds here are of tapping water, not wind. I lean over his hammock, knock on the last wall. There is not even a window to let air. Or rain.

Captain Miller is not like the sailors of *Neptunus*. He has an overcoat, made of a kind of skin I don't know. The others left themselves open to sun. He's more sedate than they, and less shriveled. But his hands are worn and look stained by fishblood.

He is cautious; he looks at me searchingly, but without a probe. I feel at ease with him. But some of that is disbelief—this morning I was a thousand years from rescue, six months perhaps from death. I lean, again knock on a wall. It thumps, delicious.

He has pulled a wooden stool out from under the map table. I sit, and take from him my third cup of small beer. It's so wonderful, wonderful good—the sugars bittered, the foam light. True, I might think it good even were it soured to piss. But this is surprising fine, for a ship. I drain my cup at a draught and clutch Mary happily, thinking the goodness of the beer must soon filter through my body, to my milk, thus to her.

How long have you been here, he says again.

The last of spring, I say, and smack my lips over the drink. Summer fall winter, spring again. A year, certain. Perhaps the bit of another.

You were here through more of a winter.

And how else? I think it's likely early, for ships to've passed this year. Though of course you are here.

It's early, true. He looks at me warily. Did you lose all your vessel—all those on it?

I did.

Horrible.

It is, I say, and dab at Mary's mouth. I much wonder where they came to ground.

He looks at me strangely. You hope they might've been found?

Well, they might've, I say. I see he thinks that light-minded, and realize he thinks them all drowned. For the first time it comes to me that I'll be thought stranger even than a castaway. For now I'll not tell him what passed with me, with them—what I did, and they did. I'll keep that story for my own; for a while.

Some might've been buried, I say. I think to myself that by now that's true enough.

If I was the first man to such a place I'd have turn and run, he says, and chuckles. For the noise and the stink of it. I'd never have known what store of good things might be taken here.

Birding islands are precious, I say.

They are, but oft perilous. Our watch spoke the Lord's Prayer the whole while in.

He chuckles again, hums himself quiet. He meant only to encourage me, not to turn the talk to his own fears or lack of them.

What was he afraid of? I asked.

Shoals. Demons. A mistaken wind, another birding crew. Perhaps the last most of all. We are not birders by trade, ourselves. Those as are customed to the trade become most jealous. I met a man once had his teeth taken by a musket ball. It blew them through his cheek. Even after, they decided to split the take, and him harvesting with a bloody rag at his face.

He hears himself going on, the aimlessness of it.

What is his name, he says.

Hers.

I beg pardon…

He looks some stricken, as though his mistake's of great import.

At her age one couldn't know. It is Harmony.

The name's out before I think of saying it; I find myself mocking him, holding back. But there is no point to such: It is Mary, I say, and that God's truth.

He cocks his head at the change in my answer. And how old would she be, he says.

She is near three months. Eighty days yesterday.

She seems a lusty infant. He means it for a compliment but I feel a twinge. He cannot know her health, or aught of her strength. Since we met she has yet to make any sound beyond a raspy breath, and sure I have not let him hold her. She is strong. But I will not take empty words, as did Frances Jacobs—she clung to frayed ropes, and for that fell all the harder.

There's strength in her. I've known babes more lusty, I say.

He shifts uncomfortably; he must have an uncommon fine ear for what's behind plain words. She has her a strong mother enough, he says. I should not have believed that any should survive winter here.

Are there not savages, in like climes?

I mean it for a true question but it comes out mocking. I've oft imagined meeting one who might rescue me; never did I think to find in myself such bitterness that I should make my rescuer taste it.

I should not have credited that a Christian should live, he says.

Well. I did not think we'd live through the snows, either, I say, forcing myself to gentleness. Did you ever make a snow cave, in youth?

I did, I think.

And longed to live there, until dragged out. A snow cave's a warm place.

Mary bubbles. I wipe her mouth clean with my sleeve. As clean as I can, with such a sleeve. Her face is tender as a mild burn.

Once our old place was polluted, I'd no longer sleep there, I hear myself say. I dropped in a blanket over the whole and on that piled rocks to fill the cut. Later I broke the launch apart into pieces and built what I thought a proper shelter, right against the side of the mountain. Then the mountain itself could form one wall. I leaned boards there, tucked in blankets as best I might. The mountain itself was some shield from winter. What did fall made a better bastion than aught I could've built myself.

There's a knock on the cabin door. A man comes with a steaming bowl of dried, boiled beef, and some kind of hard bread broken up and boiled into a paste. A wooden spoon. I balance the bowl in one hand; I raise it to my nose, breathe in deep. I wonder whether to give Mary to Miller, just for a moment, only while I eat. No. I will hold her, and sup as best I can.

The first bite makes me feel I'd forgot what warmth is; it eases me down to the bones. I eat and eat.

Like a horse once my father had, the sailor says. I look up sharply, searching his face for goodwill and for lust. I find a measure of both.

Leave us, Miller says.

Aye, he says. And now that he must go there is perhaps more lust.

I think you need no defending, Miller says when he is gone.

And why should you say that?

The look upon your face when he likened you to a horse. I sent him from the room for his health and surety, not yours.

I laugh a bit. Already I'm scraping the bottom of the bowl. It is mere mush, but it's so very fine to taste any thing of flour. I am afraid I showed him little courtesy, then, I say.

We did not come here for courtesy.

Or for its lack, I guess. Only a fool would come for either.

That's true. It's a hard, empty land.

Not so empty.

Did you fear spirits, here? It's for that my watch spoke his prayers. He claimed to hear demons in the fog.

No spirits to fear. Why should you fear the ghost of something so easily murdered?

I would not call it murder, he says. He is some shocked, or offended; he thinks I'm speaking of the birds.

Things you can so easily kill, I say with emphasis.

Would you care for more of that?

I would, I say. But then my stomach turns over—it is eager for more remembered food, but rebellious about turning from what's become familiar. Not yet, I say.

I am begun to feel warmer toward this cautious man. There was never reason to doubt him; and now the cups of beer are run to my head. What manner of man are you? I ask.

An Englishman, he says confusedly.

Would you name yourself Saint?

He is quiet a moment. An Englishman, he says. I am no lover of Rome; and there are none I know of would call me saint, though I do not think myself an over-wicked man.

And at that something breaks into my mind, like a chest of cobwebs opened to sun. He has no notion of Saint or Stranger. He's lived all his life, and knows nothing of the name they gave themselves and that they gave to all the wide world. They thought themselves the bridge, and the rest the river. I smile and I smile, and tears come to my eyes, until I must hold Mary 'gainst my face to hide them.

Part III
Cupid's Cove

Chapter twenty-five

I Mark a Destination

Stitching, stitching; Mary sleeping quiet. They have a goodly bit of cloth about the ship. It's been some months, a year, since I've held a needle in my hand. It has been longer since I've made clothes.

I'm determined to make clothes fit for a woman. When I come to shore, I'll not have any think I lived as a savage. Those I wore on the island are thin, near torn. If ever I wash them they'll likely come apart. They're good only for being pressed to felt. Well I'll do that, I think, and use the felt. But until I do, and until these are done, all the old things must be kept, hid, in a leather bag. I cut and stitch.

They have more means for sewing than they do good variety in cloth. The most of what I wear will be plain, undyed, the stuff of sails. It will hang stiff from my waist, my shoulders. And loosely, for I'll make it so, ready for muscles to again fill my skin. I know not how much thinner I am now, but it's plain that my body is some lessened.

I breathe out work's tension, look up to the other needle, the one in the roof. Now that he no longer sleeps here, Captain Miller must oft hold to the deck, for unless he can see this needle he is blind when below. It's hung to swing freely over his bed—or, rather, hung that the ship may turn around it, for the iron point holds always fast to North. A neat, craftsmanlike, eight-pointed star's carved into the wood above. Should this point hold over the needle, we sail east. Should that one swing over, southwest. Lying in bed he could know he held his course, that no drunk or careless man had let slip the rudder. Now he often holds it himself. Or stands that he may mark the sky, and any land breaking our horizon. Though he's not said so, I think he carved the star there himself. It has his care—his foresight.

My fingers are red and raw. The motions, the nip and draw of stitching, have returned to me. But my skin's gone tender in my fingers, even as the most of my hide was loosening, toughening. Still, the pain is a delicious one, a return to old ways and fashions.

The cabin is small, clean, sealed, and ours. It holds us like a jug of apple wine. Such wonderful, uncommon leisure, to have a bed and not a blanketed rock! My back bones were become bolted to each other. Though it's been a mere few days, already I feel them loosen. I'm growing stronger. Holding Mary, sleeping with her, the both of us surrounded by wood, feels like falling into a dream I'd forced myself not to have. Drowsing there, our cabin seems a place of light.

But when he's here, Miller darkens it with shadows of rumor. Kindly, he yielded his quarters to me. Of course that's led to talk. I've not heard it myself, but I see its echoes in our host. That I've not heard the rumors openly doubtless says a deal about how much I've stayed to myself. Though this boat, the *Half Moon,* is smaller than *Neptunus,* the crew oft speaks in shouts. Still they've minded their tongues when I'm about. What I hear from below is only muffled bleating. I've seen the rumors, more than heard them—in the way Miller most always keeps from his cabin, and stays but a little while when he does come, and leaves the door open.

That will do no good, I want to say to him. Men will think what they will think. If you stay so short a time, they will only doubt your potency—they'll think you can take all you want of me in a moment here, two there. If you leave the door open, they'll say they saw it shut.

But I've said nothing to him; if he cares so much, I'll not steal his hope that we're not thought lovers. He shifts from foot to foot. He is curious delicate.

He's taken the maps away, and his chests. Save for a candle set in a nook, the table is most often bare. But sometimes I take out a packet of worn blanket, bound about with string. In it are the remnants of my Book. I unfold the blanket carefully, for the binding's wrecked. Many pages are loose. All were wet in winter, when an unsuspected leak dripped close to the door of the shelter. I smelled the paper before I went to see. And oh, I cursed myself—clutching at the damp sheets, turning pulp, desperate to separate them, holding myself lest I tear what was left. I spread the separate pages out as well as I might, and fanned the rest to dry. Now the Book's scarce better than an incomplete, sometimes clumped packet, that I ruffle through to find if a passage I want yet exists. It's easier here, with the table. But I burn with shame to think of Sarah, and her gift. She would understand. But I am shamed, and furious at myself.

If I were here alone, I should much prefer to be on deck, and often am. But it is good to have a snug place for Mary. She is better out from the wind. The cabin is a blessed gift.

Stitch, stitch. Finally the last is done, and tied. I hold the skirts before me. It is a plain garment, the color of cream. I stand and hold it before me. It will serve well enough. For a while I rumple it into a ball, opening it and again crushing it, taking out the stiffness. This cloth was never yet used to sail; I'm grateful for the gift of it. Finally I put it on, folding the top down to conceal the rope I must use for a belt.

Now it comes to me to take to the deck, and talk to him. Though I hold to myself, speech is sometimes welcome, and Miller always willing for it.

The sky is a calm blue, the wind near dead, the ship waiting. I step carefully from the ladder. Even after a week, treading on the neatly hammered boards makes me feel unreal as once the island did. To be on something so solid, and yet open to the sky, is dizzying as though I'm spun blindfolded. I'd become used to the treacherous cobbling of the island, of taking care lest I fatally turn an ankle.

The sailors stand about as though abashed. Some are fishing.

They hang lines over the side, waiting for them to go sudden taut. Every fisher wears leather gloves. They pull their catches on board hand over hand. They fish without joy, but with satisfaction for their catch. Gannets dive about us, drawn by bait the sailors drop, and fish they pull flapping from the sea. As they dive the birds turn, as though following the threads of long screws with their blue beaks. Where they strike, they leave brief chutes of bubbles.

Bourne is the man who brought me the bowl of meat and pasty bread. Now he cuts up the catch. He must have lost some gamble—of dice, of cards. He readies each side of flatfish, so that when a man's done fishing he needn't take up the knife before his dinner. As he labors, Bourne oft swears. He makes something of a mess of the job. Oily blood slicks the deck around, and the sides of fish are ragged, even more so than those of river perch Patience would cut. In the center of the deck is a low stove of bricks, bolted into place, monumental heavy. I've no idea of its regular purpose. It seems too big for a ship's cooking stove. Now it's full of hot coals, and two men squat by, each holding a bit of fish on a long, delicate trident. Miller stands by the bow, staring at a windward point of rock. He wears the same brown, strange-hide coat, that reaches near his knees.

Nothing changes openly when they become aware of me. The fishers fish; the cooks, cook. Their meal hisses over the coals. Bourne swears sharply as he cuts his hand. But I see in the whole some small alteration, as a few tightened threads will wreck a woven pattern. Every man attends his task; there will be no idle talk while I'm on deck. This fellow hums, watching his line hold stubbornly slack. That one plucks at his, as though to tempt it—another goes to the bucket that Bourne's slowly filling with tongues and cheeks, and baits a hook. One of the cooks touches a finger to the fish, licks it, holds the trident back over. No man will look up.

Do you find yourself hungry, Miller says from beside me. He must have felt the change. Even more than before, I feel the intrusion I make here—the eyes that hold to me even when looking away. I hold my Mary close, against my breast as though to feed her, tightening my lips. There is no threat in these men, I tell myself. They but wonder that I lived.

Or fear that I did? The thought comes like an owl. I am as strange to them as they could ever be to me. Stranger; far stranger. They are only men of odd profession. I am a marvel; maybe a portent.

I am, a bit, I say. I should be satisfied with beef.

There's a plenty of fish. He motions me toward the stove.

I stand behind the men sitting on their haunches beside the stove, cupping Mary, suddenly wondering what to say. I'm not so comfortable here as to demand food.

She would eat fish, Miller says.

You can take this here when done, says a yellow-haired man. The other stays intent on his cooking.

It will be a little time, I see—the one who spoke only just replaced a piece he's gobbled. I near refuse it, then consider. These men that treat me with such caution—they show the respect I wanted. Why should I refuse it, even if it's offered to my history rather than to me my own self? I'll thank you for it, I say.

But a moment, the sailor says, and turns the fish diligently, as though better flavor's born from the rotation.

I cast about for something to say. Tell me about birding islands, I try.

Miller looks at me strangely. You should know enough of that—more than ever I did.

I know one well enough, true. But was that a common one? Are there many such places?

Not so many as they were. Some of the ones in the outer reaches've emptied in recent seasons. Nothing on them but shells, now, mostly. 'Tis thought the rest've removed further in.

Or were killed.

Sure, we could not so deplete the Lord's plenty, he says with a quizzical smile.

Not altogether, I think to myself. We are not so strong as to weaken all the world. But to kill all in one place? I have seen these fishers at their work. I hold silent.

These sailors are froze about me. I feel myself joining their play, holding myself proud, powerful, the woman they think I must be. I have survived a hideous place. I must have mighty strength—or witchery.

'Twas in hope of finding where they remove to that we came further in, Miller says. It's not usual for fishers to come looking for birds. I told you something of birding crews. In themselves they're enough to keep many from looking. We're none of us been naval pressed, or not recent—Bourne's spent his time under Queen's sail. Hence his delicate way with a knife. He claims to've practiced on Spaniards. From the look of it, he's better suited to working on men than fish.

Even Bourne laughs a bit at that, and tosses a cut to flop by one of the cook's feet.

We didn't come for combat, Miller goes on. Still, the owner of the vessel had a notion that there were islands yet untouched. He thought newly arrived auks might swell the ranks of those as lived there before. Having seen it, I confess I think him right. It'd be a rare place that could hold such plenty of birds, unless some'd come recent.

He seems to ask for my judgment on the matter. I've none to offer. What's this hide? I ask, and touch my fingers lightly on the shoulder of his coat.

Though it has fur on it, there's less than on a summer deer-pelt, and in patches all's worn away. The warmth it gives must be more from the thickness of the skin—near half an inch.

Seal-skin, he says.

A seal, so great as this?

I look for seams, but find them only at the sleeves. The seals I've seen are slick, gray tubes. It should take four of them to make such a coat.

Well, there are all manner of seals, he says. Some bark like dogs, others're near small as cats. This one would've been a bloated thing, with whiskers and tusks.

I've seen one, then! I say. A valru seal. I'd never forget the horns.

I know it by the name walrus, he says, and smiles at me. I reach out and feel his cloak, wondering. That beast that brought me such terror, made a simple coat. It seems a poor, homey use for such a thing. But I don't know that I think it entirely diminished. The coat gives Miller a look of savage repute.

Around us, men work. They listen.

I thought the one I saw should kill us, I say. It rose below our boat.

I've heard of such. Those tusks aren't likely made for digging clams.

I rub the coat where there's yet some bristled fur. A much-worn, perhaps much-loved garment.

Here. It is from his shoulders, and on mine.

I thank you, I say. It's brisk today. I shift beneath, feeling the weight. It falls close to my feet.

I don't mean to have it back, he says awkwardly. I look my question at him. You're much taken with it, it's plain, he says. You'll be in need of a coat.

I thank you for it, I say, astonished. It is cut as a coat for a man, but he only saw that I wondered at the skin, and was in need of a coat. He would never keep it from me as a man's thing. Now that it is mine, I feel better the weight, drawing each lip around Mary. Even without fur it is warm, holding out most all of the air. With it and my new clothes I feel a new woman, and a strange one. If they should see me garbed so, they should think me true lightminded, or wild. I smile at the thought. So heavy, I say.

This was a young one. So the man said—I've never hunted them, myself. The hide from an old bull's thick as an inch. The leather from it may stop a fired ball.

There is an awkward silence. Now, if you want the tusks, those you'll have to hunt yourself, he says finally. We laugh, and are closer for it.

Will you eat fish? says the man who before offered it. He holds his small trident by the metal near the haft, cautiously offering me the wood handle.

I will and gladly, I say, and take it. In the man's eyes I see distance, as though he cannot quite look at me straight. I would have your name, as you've fed me, I say.

Dawkins.

Then thank you, Dawkins.

Aye. He nods acknowledgment. Why will this man not look at me straight? It cannot be only awe. They will spread rumors of the captain and me. Yet this is a ship of men as will not look to my eye.

By God that is enough, a sailor says. A gannet has snatched his bait-tongue, and by some miracle missed the hook. The sailor goes to a line, pulls a dripping plank on board. He ties one end of a cord to a bit of smelt, the other end to the board, and throws the whole back over.

I thought you might be sated with fish, Miller says. You must've had it to gorging.

I didn't, I say. Though I don't tell him so, the only fish I had was that I took up from where an auk had choked it out on the rocks. I was hungry for it, and thought nothing of the filth. I imagined river perch, and ate it. Now I take the side of fish, still spitting from the flame. I break it up with a spoon, eat it as fast as mouth will take it without burning.

Where do we sail to, I say when I'm finished. Where exactly? Will you show me on your maps?

I will, since you care to see, he says. Follow.

It's a request not an order, and I do. But before I head below, I look to sea. The board's soaked through, hanging invisible below the surface. A gannet dives for the floating bait; it hits the smelt clean but crushes against the hidden plank. I near cry out. The gannet floats beside the bait with broken neck. Another dives after, and plunges past the wreck of its fellow. I go below before I see it broke.

He has brought the maps to the cabin. They're precious. I can see that much from their very substance; a care was given to the drawing that I've never seen given a woodcut. Perhaps not *care*—more a determination that each line must be so, exactly thus, not a shade nor hair slipped, so different from the exaggerated, floppy, chapbook lines of sketched chickens, or paupers, or a city minister's mouth. And though the maps were strewn on his table in a way I thought careless, when Miller moves them he does it mindfully, from the edges, never leaving a smudge. These are his safety, I see—our way home. He lays them with the care I give the heap of my Book.

There are some charts as must be destroyed, should your ship be taken, he says. And to sell them abroad carries penalty of death. There was no more precious thing taken by Drake than maps. The crates filled with Spanish gold were but a pittance; for the charts were like the table in the tale, always filled with a great feast no matter how gluttonous the owner. These are nothing like those, of course. Just charts to the fishing grounds that every country knows. Portuguese, Dutch, Spanish. French. Christ. Even some from Newfoundland, now. Getting right crowded on the banks.

I can't read the charts, I say. Mary's sleeping soundly, on the bed, and I bend over the table, leaning on both hands.

Well then. Here, this line, is the coast of Newfoundland. And here, this great confusion, is a maze of shoal and rock.

His finger drifts over the pale cream paper like a water-skater.

And here, this blank beyond, he says, is you.

It was.

It was, he agrees.

He looks at me soberly.

You were lucky, he says. Most of the islands do not have such shores—often they come straight from the water, like small cliffs. It takes much labor to get the boats up onto the flats, and that only at high tide, if then. Yours was likely a burning mount, though it slept when we came. Those slip more gradual to the sea, from what I've seen and heard. Lucky that we found you before it sparked again.

I smile lightly. I don't want to speak of what he takes for good fortune. Then where is England? I ask. And how big, measured against...

Newfoundland. Yes.

He steps out of the cabin, holds the map flat.

Now the bed is England, near about, both size and distance, he says. Of course that's but a notion.

I look at the bed where Mary slumbers. She seems buried in it; a tiny bead. Do you have a map of America, I say carefully.

I do. He looks at me closely, and I think sadly. He's sure I'm thinking of lost companions, who hoped to reach those shores. And so I am.

Might you show it me.

He nods, steps back to the table, carefully ruffles through the paper. Here, he says finally. This is only a sketch, no true chart. But it shows the coast well enough.

A strange thing, I say quietly.

What was that?

A strange thing…

The mapped coast is narrow as an eel. Most is colored red as a wound, but there are black lines, and some tiny yellowing that makes the wound look turned.

What's the meaning of the colors? I say.

The red is savage places. The black is rivers, mostly. The yellow, English settlements.

The yellow bits cling to the rivers, like weed on fishing line. So few? I ask.

Fewer than are shown, most probably, Miller said. Adventurers pouring money into the settlements prefer to look successful. More are likely to join them, so. There is not such a plenty of Hundreds as are shown, I should swear to it.

Hundreds, I say. He said the word as a title, and I've never heard it used so.

A plantation, with food and treasure to support a hundred armed men. Here in Virginia is Bacon's Hundred, here Martin's. Flowerdew Hundred…it'd shock me to find threescore men between them. He smiles cynically.

Above and below? I fan my hand, thumb pointing to the green south, last finger toward the great blankness north.

Below, the Spanish, and there for true. They've had forts there a hundred years and more. Above's New England, and empty coast when matched against Virginia. A few fishing stations, or whalers. Few that mean to stay.

As he speaks, the blank land seems to grow before me. What's past the black line of the New England coast? Cold mountains, green fields? Savage armies, readying assault? A second great sea?

Poachers, he says.

There may be poachers there. But, looking at the space, I know there is more. There is one plantation, at the least, whose people mean to stay. There is one with men who seek to profit soul over purse. This is where they were bound—they should not have chosen Virginia, a land filled with men-at-arms under the King's law, even were there many fewer than claimed by adventurers and the crown.

New England is hard land, he says, seeing me stare. Hard. I've never seen it. But it must be, that most men should choose a Virginia seasoning over it. Few choose to try a life so far north.

He looks at me closely. I was further north still. He must have some notion that we were never permitted to sail where we were bound. There could be no other cause for us to slip off of the great sea lanes, that are marked out on his charts as plain and tenuous as dewy spiderweb.

But I give no mind to the hinted question. I am seized with a sense of possibility, that has dodged me during the wonder of finding myself again among society. I may go here, or there. Until now, the only time I thought of going else but England was that first day, when I asked, absently, where we were bound. Then he said that we would sail north and through the shoals, and when clear of the shoals we would turn east. Eastward lay a new colony where he plans to summer, resting and drying his catch of fish.

East, I said to him then. East is good as west. I was careless of destination, wanting only to be off from the place where I'd thought I must sure end my life.

But one is not so good as the other. I will go west, if I need first sail to England to do it. I will go to the new land, and find him there. They cannot so simply claim the blankness before me, telling tales of the mighty wickedness they shed from off their storied ship.

On the island I thought of Adam, of butchering. Can I hold such a killing rage for so long a journey west? I look to Mary, and think, I can.

Chapter twenty-six

We View a Glass

O*n Neptunus* I dreamt of landfall, craning for a glimpse

Island of Newfoundland, Canada

of darkened horizon, thinking myself a manner of bird. Now we pass from open sea and into the long, narrow bay that ends in Cupid's Cove.

> *As I was a-walking one morning in May*
> *I met a pretty fair maid and unto her did say*
> *I'll tell you me mind, it's for love I am inclined*
> *and my inclination lies in your cuckoo's nest.*

The voice is Bourne's, his throat surprising sweet. And, save for a drop in the last two words, it is a tune I know. I sung it, sometimes, with Anne. But I've forgot what words we used, and cannot recall them for so long as he continues.

The sides of the bay gradually narrow, until it seems we're sailing up a steep river valley. The walls begin with weed-covered rocks, quickly rising to slate heights. They're crowned by pines that stand out black against the high blue sky. In spite of the day's fresh color, the breeze feels damp.

There's one other lonely boat, a square-sailed skiff. Little wind finds its way over the ridges here. It seems enough for this small craft. Before we may hail, they see us. Then they tack, sailing away as quickly as they might.

Fearful men, Captain Miller says.

Cowards, Dawkins says.

Hmm. Miller's less sure of that. He walks to the starboard bulwark, watching the shore slip by. He's concerned, I think, about what the skiff's caution hints at.

The small boat has slowed. It keeps pace with us until it reaches a great bend in the inlet, a half-mile ahead. There it turns upwind, pauses. One man waves what might be a shirt, though I cannot see to who. Another points back at us.

Miller seems not to notice. He beckons me, and gestures toward a tussle of logs. One squirms, disentangles from the rest. What I thought part of the wreck of birch timbering is only a seal. There are many on the logs—gray, speckled, limp, taking the sun. Miller watches the first with me as it flops to the water and swims submerged, only sometimes breaking surface. He watches until our sails flap and luff overhead. Then he orders them furled, and the launch lowered.

Dawkins, Bourne, and two others labor at the launch's sweeps, towing us in. A line to them grows briefly taut with every pull. When we're within a hundred yards the skiff spins and slips from view.

I pull the valru coat closer around my waist, leaving a small v below my neck for Mary. I've made a neck-sling that I may easier hold her, and keep her beneath my coat. That such a sling is needed to better bear her weight seems a great victory; even sleeping, even hid under my coat she grows, taking strength from the milk she drank this morn. My own stiff, faint weakness seems a paltry price for such triumph. I place hands on valru hide, feeling her breathe beneath.

Over us the long roots of pines edge through shale, and sometimes spill out into the air. Newfoundland. Silently I test the word, then break it to pieces. New-found land. Spoken so, it makes me imagine myself being the first to see this place, as Miller did with my island. That was my own found land. No matter what mass of men may come there, no matter how they empty it of its auks and gannets, its glory and fleshpot stink, it will always be my place. I know it in ways that no other ever may. To know it so, you must be silent. The winds take on voices then. You may listen to their argument, if not unravel it.

Though it was in a manner mine, I'm furious glad to be shed of the place. A plenty of gulls swirls, trailing us. But when Mary cries out she may cut through their voices—they are not such a barbarous mob as on the isle. Mary swallows the last bit of her cry. I draw her up out of the coat, pat her on the back, hum her quiet.

Slowly, we round the turn. I lean forward; the inlet and valley gradually broaden, becoming a quickly curtailed bay. Cupid's Cove, Miller says beside me. A newly established place, and a useful one for fishers. English fishers, he adds.

But I say nothing; I lean on the bulwark, thankful for the neck sling, my weakness sudden welled up enough to make my eyes swim.

For on the fan of sand and earth, descending gradually toward the water, are houses. There are half a score of buildings there, some of them doubtless dwellings though just now there's nothing to choose between one and the next. To me they seem oddly shaped, and uneven placed.

But there is woodsmoke. And, there cannot be—but I think I detect the steam from bread. Surely I cannot smell it. We are yet too far away, even from the piers were there is an oven. But the scent seems to fill my nose, doughy, near painful, full of remembrance. My mouth fills with water. Bread, I whisper to Mary, though she's much too young to eat such unless it's soaked in milk.

The houses have wood roofing. This must be a younger place even than I realized; they have no surplus of pasturage, no source of thatch or straw. Though I'm most filled with clear longing to come to them, I feel also a scathing mix of scorn and fear that the houses are made so like to those we left behind. A new land this may be—but the housing looks as though it was carried from afar, planted here. I no longer remember what I thought a village should look like on this new earth. Sure I did not think it should look so familiar.

A pretty place, I say too loudly.

Miller looks at me. It's his turn to be silent.

Above the houses is the beginning of a palisade of sharpened logs, a circle left incomplete before it ringed the side nearest the cove. Above the palisade's highest curve are the plantings. The people here have planted poorly, shoddily, I think, though why I think so I could not say, from so far off as we are. But I do know it; without seeing clearly, I feel the fields disorderly.

Higher still the trees have all been cut, leaving naught but stumps.

They wait for us at the pier, below a great hoist tilted on its piling. Much of the crew's already there. Dawkins bows low, sweeping off his hat as though he's governor, and we royalty. Beside him are two boys. A half-dozen men with muskets look at the boys with some contempt—they are the pair from the skiff, I realize. A woman with red hair peeks from beneath a cap like a muffin. She stares at me, curious. I give her a smile; she returns it, her face a daisy. And there is a great fat fellow, with a nose round as a mug handle and a labored way about his breath. He heaves himself up and over the side.

John, he gasps.

Sam. Captain Miller smiles broadly. A pleasure to see you here.

Forgive our sentries. Sam nods toward the boys, now shame-faced, the older of them perhaps fifteen. They're newly arrived, he says, and had no means to recognize you.

No shame to it. Though I confess I worried. Wondered what might've happened, to deserve such alarm.

Well. Sam smiles wryly, rubs his nose. It's red and chafed, as though he's recent taken cold; that might also account for the strange, choked note to his voice, which I think he'd rather let flow free. They are not entire fools, he says.

Miller looks questioning at that. It seems they had some cause for caution after all. But he'll not pursue it now.

But if he will not, I will. What cause had they for worry, I ask.

When Sam sees me he near starts, though he is quick to hide it. I had thought it was the island that so shocked the sailors. Now I wonder what I look like—how my face and body have changed. I know myself much thinner. But that alone cannot be enough to cause such agitation.

And who is this, Sam asks, his head cocked that he might look casual.

Melode, I say. Well met…I cast about for a title. I don't know his station, and had as well be courteous.

Lord will do, Sam says.

His jesting manner has returned to him, and he speaks as though I'm any common passenger. But he does not look at me direct. Without thought I move to touch my face, but catch myself. Instead I draw my coat a shade more open, that Mary might have air.

Slave, and cur, would as well, says Miller.

Sam laughs a bit. Goodman, in truth. Goodman Lasher.

An odd name, I try.

Aye and a prophetic one, he says, drawing himself up. Many's the lazy man who's learned so, to his sorrow.

Miller blows out, mocking him, flapping his lips.

I didn't know you'd taken to bringing women on your voyages, Sam bears on. Some might say that'd help explain your damnable poor luck.

If there was any luck, it was hers, and none of it bad this week past, Miller says. He's only bantering, but glances at me as though he's said more than he should.

You did not come so quick from England, Sam says. A week—I see no wings to your vessel.

We did not, Miller says. He waits. Sam squints at me, at him. Not my tale to tell, Miller says. And she'd best tell it to Sir Guy, afore any else.

He pauses, looks to me. Or to whoever she will, he says.

Sir Guy'll have an interest, that's plain, Sam says.

He winks at me—again looks away, as though to judge the soundness of the sails. Let's to him, then, he says. There's much to talk about.

The fishermen have set a plank for a ramp. Miller and Sam are first to the pier, and raise their hands to steady me as I descend. Though I let them, I lean no weight to either.

When I reach her, the muffin-capped woman smiles. Well met. Your name? she asks. If her face is a daisy it's a plucked one, its petals some shriveled. Perhaps that is her common look; perhaps she has only seen in me what Lasher did.

Well met. Mel. And yours?

Jenny Harrison. Your babe'll be the youngest one at the Cove, by some fourteen years. Oh she's a honey-looking thing.

Jenny reaches to touch Mary, but is too rough; her fingers press her face as though testing a sleeping-mat's firmness, and I draw back. Jenny looks stricken—then perhaps insulted, or angered. I smell a plenty of ale.

I thank you for your words, I say. Then I go to the base of the pier, where Sam and Miller wait for me.

This place has few women; perhaps one in four, one in five. That's all I note of the people here. For though they all come down toward the water, they give me no greeting; instead they hang back, the length of a dusk shadow away. I feel their eyes on me, hear sawing cease. They know nothing of where I was found, I think again—they cannot yet think me as strange as did the fishers. They must see it in my body, my apparel.

I force my mind elsewhere. Only half of the houses have properly dried and seasoned timber. The oldest have begun to buckle under sun and rain, and that after what can be no more than three years. There is not one proper, blooming dooryard. And with only gray gravel between, each seems set too far from its neighbor.

Though the sight of the houses is a balm, it's one with a hot emollient—I want to take them for my own, possess them, but a part of me cries out in panic. A smaller still longs to see them burn. This feels a foreign place.

In answer to your question, Sam says. Our main cause for caution's rumors of Portuguese piracy. Our palisade's not well equipped to defend against such, though our tower might give them pause.

It's a squat thing of four sides, a dark iron hole marking each like a frown.

Or the guns within it might, I think. I thank you for the news, I say.

Rumor, more than news. Hard to think how the truth of it could've reached us. Still, we hold ourselves ready. I'd feel a fool, waking up to a Portuguese blade. Though at least not for long. And here are our grand flakes.

Between the two rows of houses are dozens of racks, line after line, filling the space that might otherwise have been a sort of commons. The racks are uneasy things, squares of stripped boughs bound by thongs. A few are covered with slabs of dried and drying slabs—the first slab I see seems as long as me, as broad. The smell is like the ship, but more aged, more desirable.

Oh, salted fish, I say. Miller must hear my longing, for he goes without pause or question to the first rack, and with a pocketknife cuts off a good hunk.

And when will you pay me for that, and how will you, says Sam.

From the scores of barrels I've ready to cure, Miller says, and hands me the fish.

I thank you, I say.

The first nibble recalls John Jacobs to my mind. It recalls Frances, and her sorrow. Must everything here recall to me some vanished piece of life? Stockfish was not our common board at home, but some did find its way to us. All much loved the sparkle of the salt.

No need. How would you talk to these men? Miller leans a bit closer as he asks. Lasher has already started on, and his question is meant only for me.

Plainly.

I speak lightly, but I feel a growing weight. It's born of familiar play on my taste, my sight, my nose and ears. Together my senses return me to the village, dragging me to old patterns, commanding that I act in like manner as I did there. I must take care, they say—I must show deference. I struggle against the soul of this place. Most of all, against those parts of it I recognize.

No. I mean to ask would you speak to Guy alone, or with me. And first, or after he's some notion of your coming.

This Guy has no hold on me, I tell myself. He is no head of congregation, nor master to me. He is leader of a small place, and cannot command me long held. Miller can bear me where he will. At the thought I feel sudden lighter. I might drift from earth—I want to take Miller by the shoulders and laugh, looking to his face, telling him I no longer have aught to fear.

But the urge itself is frightening, for it shows my thoughts precarious, wild—utter low, then flighting high. Mary hangs like a bauble at my breast.

After you, I say. *And*, I think, *I thank you for asking.*

Soon after they leave me at the glass-house, and disappear through the door of the last, the largest, building. I know the one beside me is the glass-house because they told me; else I'd see a mere plain lean-to with a low furnace of stone. There are no broken shards of glass about, nor any tools.

The house they went into has carefully joined, well-conditioned wood, and windows barred with lead caning. But I cannot see what passes within. The windows are small; it's yet something upslope. I twist the toe of a flatshoe on the ground. It feels gravelly, loose. How deep they must set their foundations, to stop such houses from sliding down and to the sea.

I sit by the cold glass-house, waiting for Sir James Guy. Guy, Miller's told me, is the adventurer behind this place. What fortune he had from his family has been poured into the two piers, the sawpit, the glasshouse, the smelting-room and racks—all that goes to make this colony more than a bunch of lost cottagers. The gold's all wagered on the future. James Guy himself is a second son.

The fish is salty, delicious. Were we home, I'd soak it in water, stew it to soften, perhaps spread it on bread. Here, I chew some for Mary. She sucks my finger where I've coated it. When that's gone I heft her, go to the next building, run my fingers along the wood. In the village we'd have one new house a year, if that—perhaps a barn, a few sheds. The most of our walls were old, grayed by age, older than Elder Saints. Here all were built within a year or two of each other, and are of timber alone, without the clay that caked and held our dwellings. Strange that some should seem so aged. Still all here feels brief, no matter that they mean to stay.

But there, beside the house, is a shock of spiny green. Rosemary! I lean to it eagerly, pluck a sprig. I roll the needles to crush against a palm. Holding all to nose, I am sudden in my old door-yard—sitting on a stool, the cousins to this plant growing lusty above my shoulders. I drop the needles, and run a finger beneath Mary's nose. Rosemary, I whisper to her. A pot-herb, a delight. Remember the scent, for it's fine and wholesome.

It matters not at all to me that this is no very strong plant; its needles too light a green, without right luster. I wonder if it will last a single hard season. Likely not. Does it speak of hope—that someone here thought it might prosper? Or only of ignorance of this country's turf?

It does not matter. It is rosemary, and smells of spice.

Here's our new one, Jenny says behind me. She sounds excited, and has brought two more along with her. The first would be right lovely if not for a twist to her upper lip. The second reminds me, uncomfortably, of Patience. She has that same glint about her, of hope and resignation mingled, and carries a basket in both hands before her.

These're Hester and Shannon.

Shannon could be Patience, plus ten years. The houses, the smells, the lone herb. And now this woman with the lines at her eyes—perhaps from smiling, perhaps from morbid history. Much of the latter awaits my Patience, unless she should escape the Jacobs' house. This, here, is how she'll look. She'll have the same pretty face, that all can see has been hard worn. I hope I can yet picture her in my old garden, and not place Shannon there instead, fresher and more clear. Inwardly I draw back from her, and from fear she may invade my memories.

Courageous, to bring your child, says Shannon. I'm much relieved to hear her voice, for it has an uncommon lilt. The strangeness of it strips away the horrid likeness to Patience. As does her smile—when she offers it, tentative, her face changes as though seen through pink glass.

I had little choice in it, I say, and force myself to my feet. I'm Mel.

Welcome, says Hester. I'd expect her lip to mar her talk, but she speaks easy.

These are just back from gathering clams. I hope you are fond of clams. There is a plenty of them, says Jenny. She may be mocking me. It may be only enthusiasm that casts her from her balance.

I've no notion of what clams are, and look from one woman to the next.

No jest. I'd never seen them either, says Shannon. She opens the basket, showing it packed with tightly shut gray shells.

Oh clams, yes. And lobster, says Hester.

Sarah had lobster shells. They were dry, empty, two great claws. One was spiny as a tanner's scraper, the other round like a nutcracker. Sarah said that some poor folk must eat so, on the coast, when work is gone and there's nothing else. They must lay them by a fire to roast, then suck the meat. Once that thought was wretched; it is less so now, after my season to sea.

It must be a fine dish, I say.

It makes a change, said Shannon. It mustn't surprise you if you miss them, if lacking once customed.

We've come to hear your story. No holding away from us for here we are as sisters, says Jenny.

There's an impatience about this woman I could much mislike; she pushes at what interests her. Of course they want to know my origins. I've just met these women, and would rather not lie. But the truth must lead to questions, and sympathy. I have longed for companionship—yet after less than an hour here I feel intruded upon, the women here seeking to trespass into what is only mine.

Calm, Jenny, says Hester. You talk like she's strange as Dema. Who's that?

Our Beothuk. I want only to hear where you hail from. We've no secrets between us here.

Before I need decide what to say, or insult Jenny further with an excuse, the door to the great building opens and Miller comes to us. He did not change his garb for his audience with Guy, I realize; perhaps he only has what he labors in and its like.

John Miller. Has been a year, Shannon says when he's close.

Shannon, he says, and smiles to her. You look to've wintered well.

And so I did, without your like about to sully me.

Well, I've no doubt there were others enough, he says mildly.

Not so much. She reaches and takes his hand, smiling. You'll be summering here? she asks.

We will, or until the fish's proper cured. Of course we'll make some passes to sea.

A plenty of time, then, says Shannon.

Ah, get you to your bed, says Jenny. Making such eyes.

Sir Guy will see you, Miller says to me. He seems reluctant to take himself from Shannon. But I've heard another note in his voice. He wants her, that's plain, and yet did not seem entire happy to feel her hand's grip.

Sir James Guy is thin, red-faced, magnanimous. He wears a dusky orange ribbon around the brim of his hat. At bottom his beard curls, but neatly. In the corner's a bedstead, with a silken coverlet; on the walls, gilt-framed portraiture of him, his son, his ancestry. Everything here seems fine—thin, with steadfast color, likely to break. I should never have expected such in a ragged colony, nor the abundance of tapers that fill the air with melting beeswax.

I make you welcome, he says, and rises, gesturing me to a chair across from his table.

I thank you, I say.

But I do not take the offered seat. For now I see, on his wall behind him, between a portrait of an elder man and another of a woman, a hung looking-glass. It catches some bit of light and casts it to table, over a shallow green bowl that holds a pair of tongs. I walk to the glass, without care for discourtesy. He may watch me curiously. For now, it makes no mind.

In a small market mirror, what seems long ago, I looked fed, and content, and desirable. But this woman in the glass—her cheeks are worn, from within and without—from want of food, from wind. I put one hand to my face. The hand in the glass moves up, and touches this woman. She looks my elder aunt.

In her arms is a babe. The babe is beautiful. I hold my own up high, turn her that she may see. In the glass, the little one blinks. Mine blinks back, blinks blue eyes. She smiles an empty smile, and a whole one.

The mother's body is diminished, near gaunt. But only from emptying out to make the dear daughter, a pitcher poured into a cozy cup. They fit like pieces of broken plate. From between the portraits they look out at us—thin, complete, satisfied.

A rare fine thing, a looking-glass, says Sam.

Chapter twenty-seven

I Letter Tidings

When I am away from the looking-glass we sit in silence. The chair he gestured me to has arms the thickness of coppice handles, but burnished, and with an artful curve below where one's wrist is meant to rest. Such a fine thing I've rarely touched, and he has six of them. Six, and in one room.

But I take no pleasure from the polish of the workmanship. I have my Mary with me, and the wooden arms seem less to curve to my form than to cup us together, as in a clumsy cradle. That is the most dear thing about this seat.

The five of us sit in silence. Finally, I wonder if Guy waits for me to speak. Perhaps he is annoyed that I would greet a looking-glass before attending properly to him. If he wants an apology, he will wait long. It may not have been my best courtesy; he may have thought me preening. But any man who'd bring so great a looking-glass to the settlements, and one with a carved, gilt frame, must become customed to those who'd wonder at it. More, he must want them to. I look over his shoulder to the glass' surface. From my seat I see nothing in it but the roof.

It seems a great while I sit waiting. But Guy is not greatly annoyed; his mind is only elsewhere. When he rises, takes up a shallow green bowl, and goes to the hearth, his questions come in easy voice. He asks if I bore my babe on the isle where I was found.

I did, I tell him. He has startled me, for I'd expected him to ask first what I'd been doing there. But to my great surprise and pleasure, our talk only briefly touches my history, rebounding after each touch to Guy and his beloved colony.

Stooping to the hearth with a brass shovel, he scoops a child's fist of coals up and into the bowl. I have his pity, he tells me, for the circumstances of Mary's birth. Bearing a babe alone should be mighty difficult. Even at Cupid's Cove, there are as yet no infants. Or none save for when the Beothuk come trading, which they will doubtless do again one day. Does not a cousin of Dema's have herself a son, who she oft brought in the days before they forsook the plantation? She does, Goodman Lasher agrees. Dema is an admirable woman, says Sir Guy, if a red one. She yet haunts the pale when she has a mind.

Was there a plenty of food on the island that gave me succor? Birds only, I tell him, and a remnant of hard, wormy bread. Guy says I have come to a grand country then, for here there is an abundance of good provender.

At the table he produces a pipe, packs it full, takes up a coal with thin tongs to light it. Once it is smoking well he holds the pipe strangely, thumb and first finger making a "U" beneath. Thus I see the bowl is a man's face, grimacing a grin, smoking from his brains. I remember a vanished spring. Sir Guy is showing it me, I understand, for such a pipe is unusual. While making his smoke, he lists the board to be found in this good land.

There is found here heaps of shell, and eels and finfish in abundance—capline, launce, salmon-trouts.

On Boxing Day they had steaks of porpoise and of herring-hogge whale. Both were trapped by ice in the harbors, and so taken.

At all times, cod and herring. In springtime, netted smelts.

There are ellans fallow-deer, hares. Have ever I eaten beaver? Their tails hold a delicate fat.

Once or twice, they have shot bears. When he says that, I

wonder what shade the bears were. Surely not white, for there is no pelt on the walls. Doubtless he would display such a fine thing for his own.

They are well provided with goats, boars, chickens, sows. No cattle, he says regretfully.

The pipe-tamper is also shaped for a man, who smokes his own pipe, long as his arm.

There was a plenty of birds on her island, Miller says suddenly. A pity it's so deep within the shoals, and treacherous of approach.

Though he hides it well, I think Miller embarrassed. Likely he finds it unseemly that the talk is not all of me. It's kind of him—he cannot know I'm happy enough with the way of the afternoon.

To myself I wonder what tale I'd tell if truly questioned by them. I search within, and am amazed to find a seed of shame. I'd thought it burned to ash by rage—and love, that'd oftimes felt the same. The shame is yet there, hard as a nut, ready to sprout if proper tended. But I'll leave it parched; I'll let it sit thirsting in the eager sun.

True, it was some distance, I say.

Sir Guy has no doubt of it. Cupid's Cove is surrounded by rich land, plentiful in surprising things. Have ever I seen a squid? It squirts ink, and has a beak like a cooney. He coughs into his hand.

Virginia, he says sharply, scornfully. The seasoning there is harsh, that country being unfit for English bodies. Seasoning carries off every third man, every second. Guy waves dismissively. Two women in three. There are savages there in a plenty like to gnats. How are settlers to hunt, to fish, to farm, to do any of profit when crammed within their palisado, woefully surrounded?

He finds his pipe empty, taps out ash, takes up the tamper. A sultry country, and marsh, he says. Merrymount is yet worse, scarce more than a cavernous and deadly coast.

Cupid's Cove holds a superior situation. It is a mere half as far from England. The journey has been made in a scant twelve days coming; going, in fourteen. The fishing grounds are blessed of God. Goods can travel as fishing ballast. There are few savages, hence fewer bowmen. Wars should bring no fear of capture or ruin—fishers are a hearty breed, and likely to defend their grounds.

Sure, Miller would, Goodman Lasher says. Miller nods. But I think him not very happy at the thought of battling Spaniards from his small ship. Even *Neptunus* should have utter destroyed him.

Have ever I worked in a glass house? I have not. That is a pity—they have the right accoutrements, and he thinks the sand here, washed, should serve well. But that bastard-whoreson-ravenous bitch Tom Cowley drank unclean water against Guy's command, and so took sick and died. He'd never once blown glass, as he'd offered word and bond to do. Have ever I helped at a smelter's? No. Ah, well. They should need more than an assistant, to make either iron or glass.

Mary sneezes, squeezing her face tight. I brush her forehead to ease her, and think of when I dripped water there. That was the only baptism I'd thought her ever to have. On the island I was glad enough even for that, and that there was no man to refuse it to us. But, though the water was as clear as I could devise, it flowed from between the rocks. It was touched by the offal from birds. I can yet do better by her, for her.

Her forehead looks perfect clean. But it might, I think, be cleaner. Have you a church? I ask.

We do not, he says.

Nor no bishop, says Goodman Lasher.

There is a worship house, Sir Guy says reproachfully. Or a house, at least, where Sabbath service is oft held.

He's discomforted, seeming unsure of what I might want from the church. Perhaps he fears a funeral service for lost companions—an unreasoned show of grief. He cannot know that when I step into a place dedicated to the King's notion of worship I will break a lifetime's strictures.

You have never worked a particular craft, Guy says, casting about. What can you do, then?

For the first time I'm annoyed. What can I do? I can live. Better than ever he might, without entire holds of gear for his succor.

I can labor, I tell him, as well as any of my size and station. I can name herbs, and their uses—better than many, not so well as some. I can read, and write.

He blows out smoke from a fresh pipe. You can read and write?

The house where we will sleep is down near the water close by to where the new hall is raising. We call it Star Chamber, Jenny says as she leads me, for here there're no secrets.

I think that another probe at me, and it makes me close my mouth still tighter. If asked about myself with kind interest, perhaps I will speak. But such a prodding is never a means to trust. I will not speak to entertain.

But I see when we enter that she only spoke the truth. The Star Chamber will allow for no secrets, for it is made with a curious design. It was first built with two rooms, hall and parlor, the first some greater than the second—common enough. But, Jenny tells me, the five women there took and drew rope across each room, then draped down blankets, and so made two rooms four.

Only whispering will be hid, I realize. And then the shushing of quiet words must itself speak of secrets, breeding distrust between those in one room and another. I imagine most talk here will be spoke louder even than needed.

Every room a sleeping chamber, Jenny says, every one a store-house. They are named for planets as a flourish on the play of Star Chamber.

She guides me through the rooms, naming them and their occupants. Entering, one turns left to Mars, where are Cadence, Shannon, rudders, crossbow bolts, shirts, and a barrel of pitch. Or right—to Jupiter, Hester, breadboxes, and rendered seal-train. Behind Jupiter's blankets is Venus, where dwell Jenny, and Humility, with a barrel of candles, and a few scythes—a grindstone, and a cage for pigeons.

When I enter Mercury is empty, save for a stack of hides. My weakness doubles under the day's confusion of voices and smells and sights; many of them remembered yet painted with different light, dusted with the drifting smells of salt and pine. I drop to a sleeping mat, a mason's tools around me.

Mary sleeps beside me. I listen to her whispered breathing. Below us the earth is strong. I think, We are found.

It's night when I wake, the little window swung open into black. Mercury shares a hearth with Mars. The draped blankets between the two are pulled back far enough to avoid sparks and yet give some privacy. I sit up, stretch.

Hester sits before the fire, her back to me, close enough to the hearth that the blankets fail to screen her. She rubs her hand beside the flame. There is no container by her, but I smell cooking grease and leather, and realize it is from the stack of hides.

Have I taken your mat? I ask. I thought this was where Shannon'd pointed me. Or are we to share it?

We're not. But Shannon'd have some solitude, just now.

She turns, sits at the base of my mat with knees drawn to her chest. From Mars I hear a cry, soft as felt.

Ah, I said. The men are returned.

Shannon's favored one is, she says. Your babe looks right content.

Well, she is sleeping, I say. Then: She is often sleeping.

No need for worry, I think. My brother was so. He grew to fine stature, and a sharp heart. Might I take her up? She looks to wake.

She will sleep better left quiet, I say.

Though I strive to make my voice easy, I fear Hester hears it clench. Her fingers are lined red. How'd you so scratch yourself? I ask.

Picking gooseberries with Shannon, she says, seeming eager as I to move away from what could breed discomfort between us. Or looking for them, she says—they were not ready, as we'd heard they might be. At least I've found good patches for later. Would you like to help me net them? Songbirds'll have them otherwise. There's a seine-net I think past repair. We might use it to hold one patch, at the least.

I would, I say. Do you have no fear of savages?

I think of the logged hill, the plantings, the horizon above. I wonder who might come over it, what weapons they'd carry. Savages have a deal of beast to them, I've heard, and need no spears to do wretched murder. I needed nothing like, an inward whisper says.

But Hester, lightly, near thoughtlessly, says No. So little! she says, her mind back to Mary, quick to excuse me for not giving her over. A true plantation babe, this one, she says. Sure she will have no memory of England, once grown.

I hold my breath. Sure she will not, since she's never seen it, I say, and the words bring some release.

Never for a day?

Nor even within me.

Hester watches me steadily.

What do you know of where I came from? I ask. Surely they've not been so silent.

Not entire. They found you on an isle…is it true? And you bore her there?

Yes. Yes to both.

The blanket swings open—Jenny slides past it, carrying a small brass kettle. This is Cadence, she says, and waves back toward a black-eyed woman.

They walked straight through from Mars; behind them the cries are lower, more urgent.

Well met, I say. Will you sit a while?

We will I think, Jenny says. We've brought some supper.

The kettle is filled with fat and fish, a hearty mix of earth and ocean. We lean to it with spoons, and in turns eat from it eagerly. I imagine myself warming, my weakness driven away.

Though all seem to like the stew well, they mock themselves for it. They'll not long remain Englishwomen, they say, eating such savage fodder as salmon and seal. Soon they'll need smear red clay on their skin, and take to wearing their hair combed and greased. Hester's voice has much empty regret at the notion. I see it for a frequent jest. When we are done, Mars holds silent.

Jenny throws a log on the fire. It pops and snaps. So much lost, I think. And now we're come to shore.

When Mary cries I open my bodice, lift my shirts, hold her to my breast openly and without a thought. Under the island's cold, the soreness of her suckling lasted much longer than was right. At last we're out from it—and from the wind that chafed all my body, whether or no I was clothed. At last I may ease and heal.

No common cloth, Hester says, fingering my sleeve.

It was a sail, or cloth for it. Mine own would no longer serve.

And such a coat. Of sealskin?

Valru. Walrus.

I cannot abide this, Jenny cries. I must know more of you. The Star Chamber—no secrets—I *told* you.

That's more from how the chambers were laid, than our own choice, Cadence says.

I think there's a last woman I haven't met? I say. If I ask where they are from—how each has come to such a place—then sure I will have to tell them my own tale. I am not near to wanting to do.

That's Humility, Cadence says.

Sleeping, I think, says Hester. She's often so these days, while waiting for her babe to come. She'll be startled to find yours here, she'd thought to have the colony's first babe.

Aye she was James Guy's prize, afore this one came, Jenny says. But from where *did* she come?

You push too hard, Hester says sharply. Maybe you shouldn't choose to dwell on such a thing, either.

Here, then, I say.

But though I mean to continue, and tell them there was no shipwreck, the words will not come. *There was no shipwreck.* I cannot tell the tale that may lead to. My tongue seems to thicken. I cannot tell them of Henders, or of reasons.

Why, Jenny says, in reproach for my silence. But I am crying, hands in my lap, looking past them, to the fire Hester fed. The logs are birch, and burn like paper.

Hush, Hester says softly. I think to Jenny, maybe to me.

It's all right, I say. We're here.

But it is not all right. I hold Mary close as though never to release her. Certain never into another's grasp. There is no reason to do. I am her mother, she my daughter; she is only mine.

The blanket swings aside and Shannon comes in, some flushed, smiling.

Goodman Miller's done his work, Jenny says.

True it'd been a while, says Shannon. Is there more food?

Does he come here regular? I ask, wiping my eyes.

When he comes to Cupid's, Jenny puts in quickly. They all laugh, Shannon among them. I among them; at least sitting near.

The next morning a cock's crow starts me upright. I sit in the darkness, amazed—then I cup my hands over my ears, slowly fanning them away, gorging as I hear the cry more fully. A cock's proud challenge. Like the smell of smoke indoors, once it should have passed unnoticed. But how fine to hear it, after being deprived! Against the mindless, confused auks, the cock's a clear fountain.

Part of me wants to go outside, that I might take the full strength of his throat. But I only sit, then lay back, listening to him trumpet. Somehow it seems a greater pleasure to hear it dimly, through a wall.

To the right WORSHIPFULL Sir John Scott of Scott-Torcet, Knight &c., SIR,

It may please you to understand the progress and strength of this our settlement, lately founded here by Grace and for glory of God; the methods of husbandry here used, of fishing, of commerce, and c., and c.

There is now here a glass-house, that wants only servicing by one with knowledge of the glassman's art; there is a foundry, awaiting the mining of slag, and the arrival of the bloomer-man. I write in trust that you have labored to procure such fellowes, that we may soon and justly find them here among our Company…

Our houses are made strong in timber, set well on the bones of this land. We have us a palisado of great logs, made to encompass the whole of our settlement as today it stands, but which will one day be as a mere fortification, or watch-tower, in the midst of the greater township. This land is wholesome, and may support a plenty of fishers and men-about-arms.

The last will be more useful for the defending of our home country, and will so do, in like manner as a palisado that encompasses a settlement.

We have found here no need or cause of fear, but only of great joy in the gentleness of the red Indians who name themselves Beothuk. Our palisado is made more for the distraction and discouragement of Christian peoples...

My fingers are far from at their best practice, and still raw from sewing; my letters spill and tumble, the old hood I use for blotting soon grown black. Guy cares not at all. Even when my lines run crippled, they are laid more truly than those any else at the cove can make.

Guy burns tapers without restraint. The windows are cross-barred with lead caning; the light from the tapers denies the day, filling the room with false light. I force my fingers about the quill, striving to ignore the cramp in my wrist. There are no arrivals expected here until the coming of the *Fruitful*, ship of Plymouth, which will come with full lading of English provision and folk. But if new men may be written into being, then so they shall be—I write letters to all those Guy has partnered with in his chance and varied life. I write to their friends, their cousins, to the man who made and sold these chairs. Guy talks and talks through the days, building a castle with words like sun-baked bricks. And the letters stack higher, waiting for the fishing season to end.

But more than once he bids me tear up a sheaf of letters, concerned that they did not so truly reflect his endeavor's glory. The paper shreds in my hands, precious, more paper than I ever thought to hold tearing in my grasp.

It is not mine, I tell myself. It makes no matter what he does with his pages.

Now I pause, stretch my fingers. Guy waits for me to be ready; but something in his talk must sooth Mary, for when he stops she tosses her arms and begins to cry.

I'll to the workers, Guy says, frustrated. Were his desire for children at the colony not so deep, I think he could scarce abide Mary or her interruptions.

I stand at the window, Mary at my breast. Guy strides for the water and the saw-pit beside it. Men drag felled logs with chain and glove, cut them into order in the pit, stack them that they might dry before the frame of the new meeting house is complete. Nearby are some loose beams that will make the last of its bones. Its model is an ancient hall, built around a middle hearth, in Antwerp, where Guy went with a mind to try trading peat. The one here will be a heart for his colony—and a light of his church, which is the church of England.

This morning I stood with Miller for a small time beside the arched, open-gabled cover of the pit, watching boards slip from beneath like tongues. The muddy earth around was powdered with pine-dust; before it settled, the dust blew about the square in whirls. Miller told me he would return soon. I bantered with him reflexively, from near-forgotten village habit, and said I was sure he would. He followed my eyes to Shannon. God be with you. I'll see you on return, he said, and went down to the pier. I watched him go, curious. Did he think I cared at all that he was with Shannon? Perhaps he some hoped I would.

I thought of calling after him, asking how long he would be. Instead I wrapped Mary tighter in beaverskin and watched the sawyers work.

That was this morning, before I again dragged myself to this house where I write and write and am held away from true converse. The flakes are blanketed with fish Miller took before finding me, that soaked in salt the whole while they were birding. He will be gone for so long as the cod require of him. There was no purpose to my asking.

Guy has given me an old pipe, plainer than his own, with a short stem and a belly bowl. Drinking the smoke between letters restores me from the constant scrawling, restoring my mind, my hand, even making his dreams seem not deception but looming prophecy. Sometimes it so fills me that I make to rest my head on the table, and am only held upright by fear of marking my brow with ink. So clouded, so cleared, I think I am not held here away from the rest, but hold myself away. If I am a prisoner I'm a dubious one.

Tobacco, Guy has said, is his sole regret. Virginia's heat does have that lone blessing.

Beyond the saw-pit, the *Half Moon* tows from harbor. Were I outside I could hear the curses of the rowers across the water, the growl of the saw, the sweet breath from off it. But seeing Miller's departure does not give my thoughts an anchor, as writing does not. I try always to leave my mind behind, casting myself into the letters and accounts. But I'm harried, swarmed, by thoughts of mainland America.

That lone word holds a host of hopes and dangers, that I see more vividly than the distant labor through this wavy, barred glass. Are the Saints safe? Are they plagued by savages, or swept ill? Do they speak of me? I wrestle, laboring to lose them, furious at myself that I cannot.

Chapter twenty-eight

Dema

On the second night in Cupid's I laid awake. The curtain blanket was some pulled back, the fire high. I lay on my side, arm softly deadening beneath my head, and watched without thought as Shannon sat on her side of the parlor, in Mars, murmuring. Mostly I saw her shadow, the fire built up in her corner of the hearth. But she held her hand out, and something dropped. Maybe I smelled it burn—but it seemed at one moment meat, another fish, then smoking dough. Before going to her sleeping mat, she leaned forward and glanced around the blanket. Perhaps she saw the glint of my open eye. Of course I said nothing. Speech might frighten off the grima or household spirit she meant to feed—or worse, anger it, and without hope of forgiveness. He might spill our beer. He might gnaw away the foundation posts. He might bring his bride to Mary, and bid her offer suck to my babe.

When Shannon was gone, sure asleep, I thought of Enry, and I whispered: Are you here. Are your cousins.

But if they were, they were silent to me.

❧

Yarrow.

How's that? Shannon asked. Though Hester is kept at home by illness we go to net gooseberries, and between us carry a rolled, half-rotted seine by the ends.

We climb a small trail winding through a multitude of grasses and a goodly number of stumps. Mary is slung over my shoulder in her harness. By her particular weight I can tell her awake, quietly watching the land pass. I never thought of leaving her behind. Shannon seems to think it safe enough, and I will not have Mary apart from me.

Yarrow—here. And here. All about us!

I squat, gently pinch a sprig to cut it, hold it to my nose without touching. It does not summon the past so well as rosemary—but it's a familiar thing nonetheless, and as common here as thistles.

Smell this, I say. But no touching; 'twould make your nose to bleed.

Then of what use's it? She dangles it away as though a sniff might start her nose dripping red, and looks warily at the herb brushing at her skirts.

Well, it can make your nose to bleed, I say seriously.

She laughs, relieved. In truth.

It's sometimes useful, when such a cleansing's needed, I say. And it's purging when boiled and drunk. I'd guess it'll aid Hester and the rest.

There are a number of ill. One of the boys who took us for a roaming pirate crew has the worst of it, and for a week has bled from the gums. I thought of yarrow, and of mints, but had had no hope of finding them. When on the island I'd have given a great deal for a bit of either. It seems a great blessing to near fall on yarrow in such plenty. I wonder what else there is in this land, that none among the settlers have known to take up and use.

Among the women I feel easiest with Shannon, for she seems quickest to forgive my clutching of Mary. Not all have such goodwill. I see the looks that pass when I draw her away. They feel it an insult that I'll not let them lay hands on her, and won't give me much more time and deference before taking offense. That only makes me cling to her the harder. Mary is mine, and my word enough to hold others away. If they want to hold a babe, to feel themselves mothers, then let them have their own or else wait for Humility. Mary will not be the only infant for long—before our coming all were breathless, waiting for Humility's babe, the first that might be born at Cupid's. Humility herself is cold to me, jealous of my child. My legs labor dutifully, the climbing makes my weakness plain. But I am in fine spirits, feeling, in the glow of such good fortune, that my strength must soon return. When we near the crest of the hill Bourne's tune returns to me. I smile to think of it, and sing out:

> *Five husbands have I married at the church's door*
> *Two were old and rich, but the others young and poor*
> *But the last one is the one that I will love forever more*
> *Both a scholar and a master of his cucumber.*

When I finish I am gasping with the effort. But Shannon laughs, and returns:

> *Some like a man who will open up the door*
> *And some like a man who goes marching off to war*
> *But give me a fellow who knows what his weapon's for*
> *At the bottom of the barrel stands a cucumber.*

I'd never heard that verse, I say.

As I know it, 'tis the chorus.

And a good one. Let's pause here for a look, I say, for we've reached the top of the hill, and cannot turn comfortably with the seine held between.

Some of my happiness has drained with the last of the climb. Singing was far harder than it should have been, and my thighs burn uncommon weary. Likely I'll find standing painful, tomorrow. But I have reached the top—and thus a wondrous prospect.

Below us the logged slopes are like gently cupped hands, gloved in yarrow, and thistles, and grasses thorned and feathered. Throughout them are stumps. Lower still the plantings, that we passed through worrisome quick, a mere fine band of what those here hope will one day be barley, and wheat. Most of our provender comes from the water; Guy once bade me write that an acre of Newfoundland sea should yield as much provision as a thousand of English pasturage, and I dearly hope he is right. Besides the corn there's a general plot for the testing of pumpkins, and carrots—radishes, turnips, and an array of young, limp salad-herbs. Then the palisade, which I now know to be a mere slot-fence and no great fortification. Beside that, a brisk stream; within the pale, the settlement. I think I can just hear the rap of a hammer. But most striking is the cove itself, for it's shaped much like a fallen goblet—the harbor the cup, the inlet the neck, beyond that the waved and slightly foggy sea.

Guy knows his choice of site, if naught else, I say. I turn to my side, that Mary might look around my shoulder, if she will.

He does. Has writing for him been tiresome?

I moan with mock pain, stretch out my hand. Not so very much, I say. It's good to learn something of the place.

Sure he is honest in each detail.

I laugh. You're right, I'd choose to see something before swearing to its truth. But he gives me an idea of what might be here, at least. Or what he hopes for. How many fishing vessels are like to come, in a summer?

Last year, a bare few. Most from England, though we had one from the greatland Americas.

From so far, I say. I think I speak easily. But, though the day is warm as soup, the air moist, a chill has found its path to me.

It's not so far as England, she says.

We take up the seine and begin picking down the trail on the far side. Here the trees have not been so plentifully taken, and the trail jogs between stumps and whole pines, the tallest perhaps twice the height of a house.

I comb my hand through a splash of needles, drag the branch, let it snap back. In spite of the steady distance between me and the others, Shannon's charity toward me and Mary almost made the cove seemed a place I could stay, and be happy. But with news that there might come fishers from the west, that pleasant picture has vanished. We might not winter in this safe harbor. I might never see the hall completed.

No, I think. It is my choice. I can stay, if I choose, no matter who comes to harbor here, and where they are bound for.

But still there came a picture of a vessel bearing to the pier, steady as a tower, come to take provisions, readying to beat back west.

Well, as long as there's Miller, I've a notion you'll be pleased, I say.

And that means.

Sure, you seem to have a particular friendship.

Her back stiffens somewhat. We have something like.

I know I've erred. I meant nothing by that, I say.

'Twas nothing to mean, she says. But her voice is spiked by anger. And perhaps more, a hint of sadness that many would not recognize—to me it seems more familiar than my twin in the look-ing-glass. Probably Miller is not the only man she takes to bed. It's a long year, and must be a lonely one, with him gone more than half of it. If the men think less of her for taking more than one of them, or of Hester for her several companions, I've seen no sign of it. Likely that will change when more women come on the *Fruitful*. Holding back judgment will not be so easy then, for jealousy may grow when the need for such uncommon accommodation lessens. But I think now that Miller's the only one Shannon would take, if she had a choice—beyond being alone, which oft seems no choice at all.

And perhaps it is not her choice to make. Miller's awkwardness when he left seems weightier than I'd thought it at the time. I wish I'd bitten a piece from my tongue rather than jest about him to her. Suddenly it feels a great while since I've wanted a man.

Where are we going to? I ask.

To the berries, she says shortly.

Well I know it, I think, but follow her in silence.

We make our way through the lower pines, where not a one has been cut. None are very tall, not near so much as Guy claimed. To him there's not a one unfit to serve as a mast. Even watching the short planks cut at the saw-pit, I hadn't realized his speech so gassy—I'd thought perhaps they cut the greatest trees first, wanting to make them timber while the weather was proper, and finished them afore I came. But these trees will make boards no larger than those I saw. Their branches whip back, stinging my hands. In this proper wilderness, Shannon gone silent, I much regret bringing Mary—or, rather, that I came at all. For I would not leave her alone.

We are quiet through the pines, and through the mossy ground where the earth's gone soft. The trees shrink down. The cover turns to scrub-pine, then bramble, and finally fades into reeds. Beyond the last is a soft, green pond. We're quiet as we reach it, even when mosquitoes rise in torrents seeking necks and hands—quiet while we unroll the seine, and throw it wide where Shannon thinks the gooseberries best. We are silent until a bird falls to my feet. It's bright blue, a jay, and dead.

Without thinking I look to the branches above, as though it might've died on its perch. A second jay comes flying, hits me in the face, leaving a bit of soft down in my mouth. I drop my end of the seine, coughing, brushing myself.

What ails you now?

Do birds die in the air, in this place?

The next bird is flung straight as the horizon. It strikes Shannon on the back of the head, knocking away her quizzical look. Then I see, beyond the brambles, a face.

It is red as rust. The hair is true straight, open to the air, greased to either side. It is a woman, and beaming a smile. I draw back, one hand fumbling for my knife, the other wrapped behind to shield Mary.

Ah, Dema, Shannon said.

Her name, in full, was *Demasduit*. Or something like it—we stood beside gooseberry bramble, trying each other's names, tripping over our tongues. At least I tripped over mine. She laughed to hear my tries. I came closest when I lost the 'D', thickening it to something like a 'th'. That was near, or as near as most English'd come. But there was no need for the tries. To those at Cupid's Cove, she was Dema.

Her own tries were better, her English surprising clear, if some ragged in form. She also had, Shannon told me, a few words of French from fur traders come to the southern lands, where the Beothuk went for crab. Dema was practiced in mimicry. Many of her folk were so. She held up a dead jay, and whistled, with a certainty that left me no doubt I might recognize one singing in the pines.

Dema could not always put the right words together. She placed those possessed in pairings, and triplets, and hoped you could mend them and think of her meaning. But considered alone, each word flowed easy as water. *Melode*, she said, and again she laughed.

Of course I could not readily sit with her in comfort. She was stained all in red. Her smile, that might have looked pleasant in a Christian face, seemed at first a snarl—it stood out stark as lightning. She was young, her teeth good. When first I saw her I felt for my knife, thinking to fight, or else flee through the bracken—whichever she would force upon me. I'd not felt so since the day I first saw the white bears. Dema was crowned by brambles; she'd crouched below to hide when first she saw us coming. I expected the bracken around her to fill with fierce, rising heads.

But Shannon knew Dema's name, and laughed at her toss of the birds. If not for that, I would never have stayed. But the jest opened a crack where goodwill could flow, or, at the least, where raging fear could drain away to naught. True, my laugh was forced, hesitant. But through it I loosed my breath. I stood with Shannon, feeling shy as a child, listening to them try to talk.

And what should you do with these things, Shannon said. She tossed a jay in the air, made to catch it, missed. She was not entire comfortable herself. So small, she said.

Skins, Dema said.

Dema never hesitated over her words. She would stand quietly, ordering them, then let all come. Oftimes, strangely, that helped make her speech the more clear to me—it made all seem more directed, the clumsily-matched words aimed at her meaning like a dart. But, that first time, I could not imagine what she meant to say. It sounded something like *skeins*. I thought of thread. Then she plucked at the back of one hand, and my wonder then was that any should take birds with a thought to using their skins. A picture came to me of Mary clad in blue feathers, or in a down red as sunset. Once, that should have seemed a horrid thing, something to try only to see if it might draw and cure out damp illness.

But if I'd stayed longer on the island, it might have come to me to try taking auks for coats. What would I not do, to dress my daughter? The thought warmed me to Dema. There was no cause to fear. Shannon did not, or not greatly. Even Jenny had spoken of Dema in passing, as she might of a sweet spring, or boundstone.

Poor woman, I thought, so near to beasts that she must dress her children all in bird.

I was much shaken by her quick appearance, thus foolish. For she was clad all in skins herself, from leggings up, and in a great variety of creatures. Some looked like rabbit. That around her neck was too sleek to be, though I could not name the source. Except for the fringes all was tanned to leather, unless it was worn with the fur on the inside. Every bit was rubbed with the same stuff that colored her face. She was as red as she could contrive. Only her hair was black.

Her main garment was a kind of deerskin, several of them cut and sewed into a square, then slung over her shoulders. It seemed over-warm for it. But then I slapped my neck, my hand coming specked with blood and bugs, and I thought she was wise to so cover herself. My own valru coat was at the chamber, as always since we came to shore.

Still, I could not think of how she would use birdskins, until I saw the mittens she wore when taking berries. When Dema came close, I smelled her—grease, perhaps blood, rancid as the island. I glanced at Shannon, and found her breathing through her mouth. It was not much worse than the stench of a fisher, I told myself. But I could not deny its difference, nor the quick loathing it raised. Dema smelled like an animal; she was a pagan. Yet I sensed a kindness in her, that I might've been faster to open to had my daughter not been there.

The mitts were decorated cunningly, with designs in raised gut of some small creature spun 'cross the palm and back of the hand. The wrist was fringed in a delicate skin.

The jays! I said.

Clothes and bird skins, Dema agreed.

How are they taken?

Dema had her a bow, short but thick. She had a bag filled with arrows, with knobbed heads. Club and club, she said. The first club from the arrow, I gathered. The second, after the jay fell stunned to the ground—when she twisted the head, or knocked it with a smooth stone. The skins made a fine fringe. I imagined the care it must take to remove all the feathers, without leaving the skin riddled. It must take a sure hand, to tan such skin to leather.

It seemed I couldn't see past her garb to her body, nor even her face. But she wore all naturally—skins, fur, the ochre about her face and on her hands, the grease in her hair. She was entire covered.

Chamber people, Dema said.

All are well in it, Shannon said. We've moved once more. Humility's time is harder upon her—she's growing full large.

Sure, she cannot understand you, I said.

Her listening's above her speech.

Is, Dema said.

Would you speak something in your tongue? I asked, greatly curious.

She thought a moment, then spoke like a low flute. I couldn't tell if the melody was from her people's general tongue, or only her own throat. Whichever it was, I liked it better than the jabber of the Lowcountry brothers who crewed on *Neptunus*. Before Cupid's, they were the only ones I'd heard speak foreign.

What did you say? I asked.

What desire and say?

I realized that, were our places reversed, I'd have said exactly that—*What should I say?* Dema was stranger than I'd thought pagans could be. For, if no Christian, still I'd always imagined meeting men first—towering stoic, clad in wolf. Meeting Dema, I thought I knew nothing of pagans; their look, their speech, their smell.

Though she found Mary entrancing, she made no move to touch her. More, I thought she'd have refused that contact had I offered, which, certain, I would not. But she seemed to hold away from more than courtesy. There was nervous caution there, something like fear of poison. Whether she feared giving it to my daughter, or taking it from her, I could not have said.

It was near to evening, a flight of ducks cutting the surface of the pond, when we made to part. Dema gathered up her things; Shannon set the seine more solidly above the gooseberries. It seemed to me something more was needed, a token of the day. I thought of the knife. I'd taken it from the chamber stores; now I held it out to Dema, by the blade.

She took it, suddenly expressionless. Here, she said with finality.

She means for us to wait, Shannon said. Dema turned and walked back around the pond. Behind the bramble she soon disappeared, surely as though she'd left a house.

Why would you give that? Shannon asked. 'Twas a fine knife. They need nothing so fine, for trade.

I didn't mean it for trade, I said. And now she was gone, I wondered if I'd done the right thing. I'd expected gratitude, or at least courtesy. But when she saw I meant to give her a gift, her face had changed like a trunk shutting.

When Dema returned she carried a wide strip of white bark. She folded it, here and there. Then she bit it, precise yet forceful, starting at the middle.

Can it be eaten? I asked.

Watch, said Shannon. This's a curious thing, if you've not seen it.

Dema bit and bit, working her way to the edge of the small white packet. Finally she handed it to me. When I'd unfolded it, I saw she'd bitten in a picture—of stars, of the moon. Of two moons, opposites.

Oh, the sky in a lake, Shannon said. Lovely done.

Or in this pond, I said. Thank you, Dema.

I held the bark with both hands, above my heart. But I thought she seemed still dissatisfied as she left us and went off around the pond, brushing through reeds—holding her knife, her bow, her bag of jays.

Chapter twenty-nine

How We Pass Midsummer

T here was a savage from New England, Guy tells me, named Tantum. Before ever a Christian town was planted on his native turf, Tantum had passed years in England; he'd been a slave in Spain. While in England he was admitted to court. He was the talk of London adventurers. While in Spain, he was owned by Papist Fathers. A remarkable tale—and a great thing for those colonies now near his first home, Guy says slowly, perhaps wistfully. Then he bids me take up my quill, and write of Dema to his cousin.

The Beothuk are Red Indians, their skin colored in a red like to good brick. Among their number is Demasduit, a woman of fine parts. Mayhap she had better now be numbered among us, for though variable of temper, and much given to wander, she oft returns and does at times choose to dwell here among Christians. Though I had rather claim this solely from the pleasure she takes in our company, and her generous desire to aid our people, honesty bids me write in other wise. She dwells here in part from rank misfortune, that struck her upon one visit to us. And struck

her husband more strongly yet, though here I may mistake, for I think
she loved him well. They are a tender people in temperment and in body.
At a whim they may be killed, and are readily took deathly ill.

The bell rings three times. It tolls a fourth. Though the morning's
muggy, the bell is clear as air.

Bells, I've been told, are treacherous—Papist temptations. The
bemused oft think them meaningful. A bell's a useful thing for calling
parishioners to worship. And only for that. It may not be blessed, nor
ever serve for more than a signal.

These codes no longer make any matter to me, I tell myself.

And here, it seems, they do think a bell a blessed thing. Hester's
stuffed a rolled deerhide under her bodice, about her stomach, mocking Humility's swelling belly. Humility pretends to anger, and makes
to douse Hester in beer—I think she's glad for the tease. She enjoys
anything that calls our minds to her coming labors. Though I'm
outside the play I watch like a cat watching kits as they stomp about
Jupiter, Humility's feet heavier than needed, Hester's mocking hers.

Again the bell rings, sounding stubborn. The women sigh away
their laughter; the deerskin drops to the floor. We make for worship.

It being a warm day, we'll worship at the cold glass-house. It's
a wonder to me that Guy should call us to the glass-house, a place
where the failings of his colony are so utter plain. Until a craftsman
comes, the glass-house is but an elmwood lean-to. Cod-drying flakes
shade the ground on three sides around it. We are the last ones to
arrive and Lasher pulls the bell-clapper, gives a final ring.

Sir Guy has cast a cloth across the squat base of what was to
be the furnace until Tom Cowley died. Sir Guy removes his hat, leans
on the furnace, and speaks of duty. He speaks of Providence. He puts
us in mind of hopeful mornings, and ships come full of goods from
England, that'll go away heavy with our treasures. He speaks less of
the Lord than I am used. But his speaking makes this place useful,
and no mere shell waiting for a glassblower.

He speaks steadily, and sure. My own mind is hard to hold. I
could fill that firebox with water, I think, I could dip in my Mary's
head. But I did dip her in the spring. She's known the Lord's

waters—my goodwill, and love. What need of a firebox? Of any but me to hold her head, to bless her heart?

Now the settlers shuffle about, form a line. Most must stand without the roof. There's been some signal, though I never heard it. Sam Lasher is first in line. He kneels before Guy. He will take a Host.

My mind goes stony. This, I never thought to do. There was a time I should have liked as well the thought of eating dog. Jenny is next; she squats, drops lightly to her knees. Her head falls back. I cannot see her mouth, nor any of her face. I imagine she thinks herself looking godly.

This bread cannot have been blessed, I realize. All Papist bread must be, or any for the Church of England. Here, there's no man for the task. Blessing, at least, Guy should not presume to. He only breaks off crust to place in each waiting mouth. Well, I've longed for many things forbidden us. Some of them I yet think right.

I take my place in line. That I've never done this is my own secret—no one here knows so much of my history. The fellow before me yet wears a floppy workman's cap. They're all uncommon subdued.

After a while I kneel before Guy. I accept the offered Host; it's stale, the crust sharp on my tongue, and tastes like bread.

As those behind me kneel I leave them, go outside the glasshouse. Though it was not near so momentous as I'd imagined, that itself harries me. I feel no plague taking hold in my blood, no corruption planted in my bones. Yet I feel myself defiant, as though I must justify myself to those Saints that raised me and will follow me until I find final means to shed them. The melee in my mind is real to me—so much as to fill my ears.

But that last is real, and not from me. From close beside the palisade, where there's oft a guardsman, a steady barking has begun to tear.

Lasher steps beside me and stares toward the hidden gate. There's no watch this day. All are bound to attend worship, and there's never yet been a cause to raise alarm. But the barking draws steadily closer.

Sure, it's naught but a coney they're after, a man says.

Return to us, Samuel, Guy says.

We've guests, Lasher says sharply. Quiet yourself. He looks to Guy for pardon. You, Jason, I mean, he says to the first man who spoke.

Finally Dema comes visible from behind Guy's house. About her dances a bevy of sholt-dogs, gray as burned ash—quarrelsome beasts, but more desperate of voice than true angry. They dodge and skid before the Beothuk, crying from their throats. Guy brushes past me, goes another few paces to stand beside Lasher.

As she nears, I see Dema is clad as she before save for the great square she'd used for a cape. She carries a staff that I think some sort of club.

A rare visit to us, I hear Guy say. He says it as one parent to another, when amusement at a child's antics overcomes the desire to offer reproach or punishment. Soon Dema stands before him.

New people and here, she says without introduction. She has seen me.

Lasher looks over his shoulder, to see what stayed her eyes. You've made a friend it seems, he says.

It may be, I say. Though I've no notion of why I merit a visit.

Nor I, Lasher says. Well, come to us.

Lasher looks expectant, as though I might serve as messenger between him and the Beothuk. Though at first I wonder what to say, it comes to me that I need not say anything at all. Instead I fold the fingers of one hand against its palm, and quickly nibble along it as Dema did the bark. Dema nods seriously, and hands me her staff.

It's polished smooth, and carved out on top like a cup. It wasn't a stick, but a larger piece of wood that'd been carefully cut down, now too short to use for walking.

I thank you, I say. But she is not done—she reaches into the folds of her clothing, takes out another piece of bark. This is bitten yet more cunningly than the other, that I gave to Mary for play. The toothmarks make a woman standing in a long, low boat. There is a sun overhead.

I look at her gift, and smile. I hope for one in return. But Dema is yet serious, nearly grim in her satisfaction. I wonder if I will ever understand what has passed between us—if there is anything to understand.

Whilst raising the second frame of our great hall, there came among us Beothuk in a small party, being no more than Demasduit and Nonosabasut her husband, both seeming very grave and yet like to laugh at no purpose or object. We traded with them well, and had a multitude of skins, some very good. After our truck Nonosabasut made sign that he would help us with the raising. He took hold very willing on a staff, and readied to hoist the next rib, that was made in fashion like an A. But though Samuel Lasher my foreman had made good preparation and even set silver coin in the posthole for best surety, there was during the raising some general err. The frame did fall, doing no damage to itself but leaving three men hurt, and of them, Nonosabasut wounded much the sorest.

It being summer, and their people dispersed for many months before their gathering at winter camps inland, Demasduit determined they must remain within our pale while her husband strove to heal. In truth there was little else she might have done, save altogether abandon him.

The smokeroom was built hopefully—there are only four shoats at the cove. But Lasher built the walls of stoutest timber, to keep beasts and thieves from the ham. Thus it served well for a while as a small armory, guarding butts of powder, muskets, halberds, a blunderbuss...now there's naught but a few ancient, close-faced helmets, that Guy says came from the London Tower. Lasher will not leave arms with a Beothuk, whether or no he knows her friendly. For it's here that Dema's husband died, and here they let her dwell when she comes within the pale.

The room is close with horrible, beasty smell. The hearth here was made to smolder, and fill the room with smoke. Dema did her best to widen the chimney hole, even climbing to the roof with a loaned hatchet. Still the room's murky. When I opened the door, the draft tossed inner air, a rock in swampwater.

I've brought her a jug of weak beer, and a rasher of fish. Dema

Strange Saint

goes to the hearth, throws on another branch. Its twigs flame quickly, and some sharp smoke twists through the moulder of old fires. My eyes sting and water. I much wish I'd left the door open; I kneel beside her. Dema sings softly, indifferent to me, her voice lovely as a marsh-pheasant. She smells most of butchery, the blood of a lifetime's hunt and slaughter.

Guy bade me come here with food. Though the room's fogged hot as August, I shiver. Most of Dema's blankets, her bedding, are woad blue. The mat they've given her once belonged to the glassman. If she knew it for such, I think she'd refuse a dead man's rest. The room's crammed with her—with rotten blood, muddy ochre, with the murk left in the chamberpot made for a grinning fool's head. Though she sings right sweetly, I much wish Dema silent.

Finally I leave the food beside her bedstead. The blankets were once colored plain blue—now ochre has stained them, or her sweat. Savages have furnace bellies, a man told me, and no need for a living hearth. But the fire's dutiful hot, and Dema at home in the swelter.

Mary is perfect. I cup her in my arms at night, by the light of our low, clean fire. Mary's perfect nose is chafed, for she has taken a small chill. I pray it'll not take to her bones. Sure it will not, for she is perfect strong.

She'll battle off all maladies and those she can't, I'll shield her from, using what herbs we have here. There is rosemary, and basil, though that's not yet above a sprout. There are fields of yarrow and will one day be woodruff—wide leaves I'll weave, and layer to a shield.

All but the yarrow are poor. But all have some memory of Eden's strength. That's enough to shield her, for Mary's perfect strong. Her hair's come thicker now, darkened like thatch after a rain. Her eyes have lost their blue. They've come the green of marigold stem. Just now, they are closed.

She whispers when she breathes. Her hands lay open, soft in sleep. My milk is grown stronger, here. It's flush with eggs and meat. Mary is perfect as she may be. I'll weave the herbs, make them armor. I'll hold my body as a rampart.

Oh you'll be a careful one, I whisper.

❧

On the island the smell of birds and their filth draped me, and covered that of the fishermen. Now that Miller has returned from the Banks his fishy stench is plain, far worse than that of the drying-flakes, where breeze brushes the cod. Besides, that on the racks is only flesh—once sweet, now salted. Miller is steeped in oil, blood, bile. But when he greets me on the pier, my surprising pleasure overtakes any dislike for his smeared look or smell.

Perhaps it's the memory of being found that sparks me. Whatever, I do feel it, and take one of his hands between mine. I loose it when a boom swings overhead, ready to lower a firkin of greencod.

Will you go coasting? he says abruptly. I wonder if he thinks that his presence is not soft for landsmen.

I don't know that I'm asked to, I say. I stand firm by him.

I think you will be. Your herbery's been a boon, I've heard. He rubs his beard. Who better to pick out new and useful things?

Sure, Guy should like more plants to write of.

And we will find pearls, maybe, he says, and smiles. Later that day he stands on the pier, and dumps over himself two quick pails of seawater.

Come away, come away,
Come with me, and quickly,
Across the honeylake...

Bourne's voice is cream. If his mind was not so turned, and more like to the tune he makes, he'd be a handsome man.

The shallop is a fine, small craft that takes eight rowers and four more besides. I'm not needed for rowing, nor would they likely let me. So I sit and watch the cove drift by, the palisade and houses diminish, finally the mouth of the next bay as it slowly opens.

Miller stands at the rudder. Often we've no need for the oars, for a kind breeze bears us well. Sometimes spray jumps to my face.

Left there, it strengthens the sun. The rest of me's covered by my valru greatcoat, where other water beads.

Sir Guy let me bring Mary. Luck, he said, and smiled.

Now I kiss her, leave my lips atop her head.

In the afternoon, Miller says Mamateek, and points to shore. He smiles to me. Above a shore of white shells, at the edge of a meadow girded by black pine, are three huts, as rough as those the cottagers built.

Sir Guy is pleased at the sight. Our coasting's done, he says.

Outside the mamateek, a stripped bough is stuck in the ground. On each of three branches hangs a pelt. Miller tells me they are beavers, and a ferret. The beaver fur is dense as moss. Inside the first hut are seal skins, a fishing reel, a single copper kettle kept very bright. Sir Guy doesn't like finding that last—from helping with his letters, I know he prefers thinking himself the first Christian on this shore. I wonder what he makes of Dema's French.

We will take the seal hides, he says, and leave in place some amber beads and biscuit. He leaves the pelts on the stick outside, unsure of whether they were meant for gift or holy offering.

In the other huts there's naught of great interest, only some bark vessels filled with venison. The mamateek smell of river-reeds. Beside them the meadow's covered in bare strawberry. The sun plays brightly on the leaves and pink buds, sometimes cast to quick shadow by passing clouds. There're occasional stands of another plant. I take it for a cousin to angelica, and gather it in bunches. I'll ask Dema if she drinks of its sap.

As I wander the meadow a game of corkers begins behind me, three men to a side. The heat here holds back some of the flies that Guy calls Russian. One man cups the ball in his hand, punches it toward the others. Another catches it, punches it back.

I often played at corkers, when a child, Miller says. He leans to pluck up some of the angelica, and tosses it with that I've already picked.

I never did, I say. We were more given to archery. I see he thinks that strange, and add: It was demanded by the crown. So I heard from Frances Jacobs.

To my great pleasure, I don't stutter over *Frances* in tongue or in mind. She's no longer any mistress to me.

Men practiced at it, I say, and loved the habit.

Unlikely a prince'd demand such a ball-game as this, he says.

Past him, by the huts, Guy runs sealskin through his fingers.

Or stop me from joining it now! I say. I make to hand him Mary—but stop as though my arms are checked with rope. Miller's gentle, most probably worthy of trust, and I find something in him freeing. Still, I put Mary on the ground. She may nestle among the strawberry.

I'm to the game before any realize I'm coming. Through happy chance the ball flies toward my path. I go fast as my skirts will let, stretch out—the ball strikes my hand, bounces. I fall, roll, catch it just above my face. Without standing I punch it toward the other side, and listen to the laughter. I stand, and give a jesting curtsy.

Bending so fills my head with air; for a moment the world swirls. Running has recalled my abiding weakness. Horrible, that I may so readily spend all my strength in play.

Ware, a man cries out. Men! Indians.

All go to the guns, but without hurry. Perhaps they go more for the form of it—sure they'll confess no fear. But I've no such luxury; with a shock of guilt I fight my light head, rush to Mary, snatch her up. Once I have her I feel safe. We walk with directed step toward the mamateek. From there I watch the maw of pines. We wait, as men arm.

The timber here is higher, thicker, than that by Cupid's. For a while I see naught but shade, behind the branches, beneath the boughs. Then there's one place darker than the rest. There are three, like holes in the night. One shade, maybe, is a woman. But when I squint again they vanish.

Perhaps I never saw them. Perhaps they were truly Beothuk, the owners of this place—perhaps only ellan. Or shadows.

Near to dusk, we do see an ellan plain. Each horn has five noble points. The lone shot misses; the beast sinks away through evening's pines.

That night we sleep by the lapping shore, near a fire that turns the meadow orange for six houselengths. A weasel could not pass without our knowing. No one says they fear the Beothuk. The mamateek are empty, the fire high; the guns loaded, ordered, black.

Miller brings me a clam he's opened with a knife. It is sweet, he tells me, though it holds no pearls. He is right—it is sweet, and tastes of surf.

Later, a wolf howls. I've never heard anything at once so cold, and boiling.

Miller whoops back. Beside the wolf, his howl's cool.

Nonosabasut dwelled in our smokehouse and there died, and not better than a fortnight after his coming. It seemed a strange chance that even so grievously broke a limb as he had him should bring death. We after talked much talk of savages, and the doom the Lord is like to visit on them in our presence.

Demasduit was in that little time bound to us, though whether through bonds of affection or fear of her people is a matter here disputed. For my part I think her here for love of us, also from honest fear, being that she has spent more hours here than is thought by her people dutiful or right. So much we have gathered through long converse by means of signs, but are much hindered by her lack of Christian speech and ours of pagan.

The salmon are running. At night they fill the cove, thrashing upstream past the palisade. Lasher has set torches—the light makes the fish pause for a moment, that they may be speared. We can take them with pikes. Their coming's true astounding, their flesh pink, red, like none I've ever eaten, luscious good.

The water flashes with fish, with torchlight. If there were neither, the stream would yet flash—for the sky is gone wondrous, swirling silver. There is among the sheen popinjay blue, purple, a glimpse of dandelion dust. Were I here alone, I'd think the lights a sign of death. But the Cupid's folk saw them last year—and, after that, came the salmon. Now they think the lights a Lord's blessing. They spear fish, and toss them flopping on shore.

I stand with open mouth, watching the sky deepen, go shallow. Then I realize that the stolid woman beside me is Dema. For a while I'm quiet. Perhaps she wants silence. Colors fold, shimmering like luffing sails.

Death and men dance, she says.

It sounds an explanation. *Dead men dance.* I stare wide-eyed at the horizon. She's given me new sight—where there was a sign now there's a host of spirits, hid behind the air, dancing. The flashes are where they push carefully against the sky, the clouds, seeking to crack through. Do they mean harm? From Dema's voice, I think no—they'd only see the world as do living folk.

I shake my head—such a wonder! The world holds more than I dreamed, more than I dream now. But Dema sees things I do not, as I must things hid to her. She has no notion that though the Saints are a long voyage away, hid in a different wilderness, the stars oft look as eyes to me.

Dema is quiet, watching. She might be here alone. It is no horrid thing, I think, that she may see the world differently. Hawks must see the world differently than do whales.

Will others not come to you? I say.

That, she seems to hear. Slowly, she waves her hands about her. They take in the shore, the moist air; the slipping, flashing salmon, and the vault of the sky.

Spring, she says.

Summer.

She nods. Summer and no people and bunch.

Guy told me something of this, or at least told me to write it in one of his letters. The Beothuk, he said, band together when the snows come. Then they live in the higher inlands, where there is a plenty of wood, and the beasts have generous fur. But I don't believe they're so dispersed that Dema must now despair of coming upon them. If we saw Beothuk accidental, certain she could find some herself. Certain they must have their regular tracks. There must be someone she could go to. There's something else that keeps her here.

Dema sits. Now she's watching only the fishing, hands clasped before her in her lap. Can I ever know this woman, I wonder. Once, I should have thought it past belief that a pagan and Christian should meet, and speak, and be friends. Now I much wish it.

But there is something stiff between us. Some of it's our foreign tongues, but that'd be easily breached, if we would. There is something else. It's wider than speech, deeper than the ochre staining her skin.

※

The frame of the great hall is up, if yet naked, and the salmon run is over. Sir Guy called for a feast to mark both. Thus Lasher has brought out tables, and placed them within the empty frame. There's a mighty blaze of pinewood where the hall's hearth is to be. The heat's too quick for beef or fowl, but will serve for fish. Outside, the beams cast barred shadows.

Sholt-dogs skid, yelping for salmon. I tear off a bit of crispy skin and toss it. The dogs scrabble and nip. I understand, for it's as good a fish as I've ever eaten—I lean to the bowl with my spoon, gulping. Across from me's Jenny, her pale skin gentled by firelight. She is the only woman to have joined me; since my time coasting I've felt the others colder, and wonder what Shannon's jealousy has led her to say. It takes only one voice to mark a woman as thinking herself above the rest.

I eat better here than ever I did in the city, Jenny says. Save for the first winter. But that was not very much worse—we'd killed a mighty heap of ellan. Some ducks, as well. Fat ducks.

Did you live in a city? I say wearily, my mouth full.

Always Jenny wants something from me; I'm a puzzle to her, to all of them. By now I would have spoke to them of my past. Perhaps I would have let them touch Mary. But they push, and they prod, and I trust them the less knowing their minds so envious. Mary is mine, wholly mine, not even a living father to make a claim. I will not place her in grubby hands solely to have better household peace.

In the city and in the lands about and in the city again, Jenny says. We ate raveled bread when there was any crumb or crust to be had at all. I lived here and there and some places you've not heard of. I say fuck England.

I should have known more than to ask a question of Jenny—her talk's a gaggle even when not encouraged. Well, I've not heard of most places, I say.

Mary gives a despairing wail; I take her up from her rest on the table, cuddle her close.

Sure she will never lose her cry if comforted, Jenny says. My eyes snap to her. She said it absently—still, I could bash her from the bench. The Saints would have spoken so to me, harrying me and my means of care. I struggle not to lash out at these reproaches, which the Cupid's women aim at me for not releasing my child into general congregation.

Mary bubbles onto my shoulder, slowly quieting. Jenny goes on and on. She's lived here, she's lived there.

Dema's nailed a fish to a plank close to the fire. She's intent on its sizzling; she squats beside. Now I watch her through passing legs. She pokes the salmon with one finger, licks it. She's solid as a stone—one would think her captive here.

This is the house as wounded her husband. Perhaps it's for that reason she will not look about, never think of aught but her cookery. It must be harder with the beams yet naked, and the one that crushed Nonosabasut's leg somewhere among them. Though the timber is clean I think the beams stained, and wonder if Lasher changed the silver coin he put beneath before the mishap. Surely the first one he set brought little luck.

Miller sits beside me, puts down two mugs of beer with a greeting nod. Times as these, one can't much miss England, he says.

So Jenny was saying. I miss it not at all, I say. And I wonder to myself if that's a jest, or a lie. Perhaps both; perhaps neither.

Certain all can see that there's a plenty to keep you happy here, Jenny says. She hides her smirk and takes a single great bite. Miller looks away.

It's a pleasant place, I say, as easily as I can.

Ah, the dancers, Jenny says. She stands from the table, leaves us alone.

Miller looks at me straight—I think he must force himself to. Do you find yourself glad here, truly? he asks.

You saw where I was before, I say.

He nods. But there are other places less deathly than that. You need not stay here always.

I'm warm, awkward, and his last words twist me. But there's something to distract me from him—Sir Guy's called out his Morris dancers. These, he confided to me, might hold our minds. The *Fruitful* has not yet come, and some now think a savage dying in our town a woeful sign. Coming before a silver, turning sky, a worse.

And now a piper eases from the dark, playing at a tune. Behind the pipe's the thump-and-jangle of a tamber drum. The breeze carries in the ocean, bearing wisps of fog, yarrow, the forest on the point.

Shannon stands watching behind the fire. She slips away, hid behind the light, a frog slipping into a pond ablaze with sun.

When the players reach the hall something bursts before them into the frame. There are two heads; ribbons, and bells. Flanks of ape's-laugh scarlet. It's a boy dressed for a hobby horse. He prances, leaps, grins like a court fool. When he comes to the beams he dashes against them, as though they're a cage he can't escape.

The sawyer joins him, garbed in scarves and laces, handkerchief over his head. He has a particular grace—some from strength, but even more from long practice. Each step has a force. He spins, steps twice. Spins, steps thrice. With every turn, there's a change in the form and manner of his steps—he dances the part of both man and woman.

Dema smiles. At that I feel a rush of love for her, for the dancers. And, though I think this was all for our distraction not hers, I feel a rush of sisterly love for Sir James Guy.

The night before the *Half Moon* first went fishing, I was in Mercury when Jenny called out, *Change*. And so all began moving from one room to another, in a flurry I heard then saw, as I peeked, amused, into each room. All seemed in good spirits, changing quarters and those they'd shared them with. Each moved some of the gear stored with them, and left some behind. When all were finished we nearly had ourselves a new house. Only I was left in my own place, wondering at the practice.

When the call came again Hester came in without warning, dropping her blankets to the floor before returning for her chest. The solitary space I'd earned as the newest arrival was no longer to be mine. Later she dragged some of the ellan skins from the corner, and returned with bellows from Mars.

The next time the call went out, I thought, I'd move myself. I'd begun to sense the wisdom hid in what at first I'd thought mere play. Hester had quarreled with Jenny; I'd no notion over what, but there was no doubt that something was gone ill between them. When Jenny was at the saw-pit, Hester turned manure; while Jenny boiled wash, Hester cooked. But it was Humility, with no part in the quarrel, that called out *Change* as we were drifting to sleep. Then Jenny moved to Jupiter, and Humility with her.

Wise, I thought, though perhaps it'd started as a winter's game. If Jenny or Hester'd called for the change, then it would have been plain to all, most of all to them, that the call was born of burgeoning dislike. True, the bad blood was still plain to any who'd look. But coming from a woman left alone in the last change, the cry could seem more a call for companionship than a method to avoid another's company. I wondered how many go-rounds it would be before Hester and Jenny again stayed in the same room, and if they'd need some gesture of peace before so doing. I'd have to watch closely, I thought, to learn the methods of the house.

Now I sit in Mercury quietly nursing, listening to talk softly thud through the walls. The speech beats peacefully. At Cupid's, I little care what they are saying. So different from the village, where Patience and I would grasp for any word or sign from John and Frances Jacobs about what our days might hold. I've shed a great good deal since then. Of course, the place is different. But much of it is me.

Change. It's Shannon, calling the turning of the Star Chamber. I should have joined in this some before—switching rooms when called, sharing chambers with someone different, helping keep our household new. Though I've little part in the life of the place, refusing this custom would serve no purpose. I stand, resigned to the game, and go through the blanket to Jupiter.

Hester brushes past me into Mercury, likely hoping she might have it alone. Humility goes the other way, toward Mars. Jenny's the first one to join me—but Shannon's hand catches on her shoulder, draws her back. I'd share this place with our newcomer, she says.

The trouble I felt at the feast returns, takes hold. And welcome, I say.

No need for welcome, she says. You're newest here. If there are any in this room to offer welcome, it had best be me. Of course you are welcome.

I thank you, I say.

I bend, lay out my bedding.

I hope we've made you as welcome as you may be, Shannon says.

I straighten the corners of my blanket, sit down, and open my breast for Mary. I will not make it easier for Shannon, whatever she's leading for.

It has been harder, knowing so little of who you are, she says. Of your lost companions.

Mary draws a steady stream from my breast. It's calming—so different from the hazard I feel growing in the air.

Surely you must have lost some dear to you, Shannon says.

I give no answer. All must hear me, whatever I say. Jenny and Humility laugh in Mars. I nurse in silence, pressed by Shannon's growing bitterness.

And lost another this morn, she says.

I look at her, say nothing.

Aye, she walked out this morning, Shannon says. Her voice threatens to flee her, lashed by envy and hate. She knows, without knowing why, that Dema's leaving will hurt me. I shake my head a little, look to my nursing daughter.

Your blessed time here is done, Shannon says. Holding yourself above us because of a shipwreck. We all had our troubles behind us, and left them there. I'd four brothers when young, and no living family left me when I took passage, none of them.

I am taken with an urge to leave, to walk, breathing, cleansing my mind, and would if that did not mean abandoning the room. I have no friends among these women. I am smothered—tested. But I will not play at this, asking them for news in private, sharing secrets as a means to companionship. I am done with that.

There was no shipwreck, I say.

As I say it I stare at her, and without moving strive to grip her as strong as ever I might—that she might know me true unknown. That she might know me to be no common castaway wrapped in grief.

She squints, suspicious. But soon her face is leavened by belief. She knows I speak truth. Maybe none of those listening will know so. And comforting doubts will return to Shannon—inner surety that I am lying, and that I was borne on a boat from a sinking ship. But for now there is fear in her, and confusion. I think both of them good. For now, at least, she must wonder if I was birthed screaming from the isle's rock.

That we must sleep under one roof does not make us sisterly, I say before she may speak—I say to all of them. Nor any of you aunts.

With Dema gone, Guy bids me accompany to him to the smokehouse to examine her gear. There are woman's things there, that I may better recognize than he. And we will look at what Nonosabasut had, he tells me. We do not know when Dema may return.

Though I left the door wide the room is near dense as before. Sweat drips to my chin. Most of the smoke's from wood, the little fire Guy insisted on. There's also a mingled waft of tobacco from his pipe. He holds a coal-tipped stick over it, and draws in. The bowl's shaped for a face. The weed glows where the brains had better be. I should have said that there's no insight I can give to their possessions. Does Guy suspect that I'm at all like her? I know not whether this is a scraper or the blade of a fishing harpoon—and this, is it a clumsy comb or a device for tanning pelts? Now I curse Dema for leaving us.

Sir Guy goes to the corner, looks at the shelves. The helmets are arrayed like iron slugs. Useless, he says. Credit fighting in the forest with those. You should not see more than an inch to a side. You should not anyway, in the pines, he says, and chuckles.

Hmm. I make as though to lean over Nonosabasut's gear. But it is rolled in a skin, tied with hide ropes that have been soaked to make them locks. There's no seeing this without cutting in—and that, Guy will have to do himself.

He did not last long, Sir Guy says, and blows out tobacco.

I pull in my cheeks, unwillingly imagining Nonosabasut where lies the rolled ellan hide. In the close air I can near hear him breathe. What was in his leg, that the breaking loosed to course through him? What poison? Such a strange, horrid destiny, that men may carry their poison in their bones. Where did it lodge? The lone blessing is that it's not so easily freed, but needs the fall of a house or other calamity.

Poor fellow, Sir Guy says.

There's no true pity in his voice. He's calculating what to bid me write.

They are fragile people, he says. Before even we came here, there was a horrid death among them. There were a score of mamateek not half a league from here, and some yet filled with the dead. One lady was dead outside. Whatever the sickness, it touched us not at all. Well. The Lord did leave enough of them for trade.

I would that he'd never asked me to watch over this man, or would at least stay away himself. I've nothing to stop the poison loosed here. I hate this place and of thinking of Mary in it.

He has often so provided for the English, Guy says. Then he adds, as though yielding an argument, that He has even done so at Merrymount.

Once I longed for death of any kind for Adam. But such a death as was found here—so slow, so tenuous, so sure—that I would not wish on any man, nor the witnessing of it.

Sir Guy stoops to place a helmet beside Mary. She smiles at the sight, reaches out—the visor rises, clinks back into place. It has mere bars for eyes. It should take a cunning arrow to harm the wearer, one with little barb.

Will you smoke, Sir Guy says.

Though I long for it, I nearly refuse—it is too like a reward for being here. But in the end I yield to the desire for relief. I would pleasure to, I say. The tobacco rushes to my chest, my head. My head sinks down. All's warm and blurry. Mary giggles, lifts the visor. Clink.

At last the manure's well rotted. They didn't know to turn it, for many of those here are city folk, that thought it might rot in place. Well, it would have, if we'd a deal of time to wait. But I showed them how to mix in straw from last year's scrabby wheat, and then turn the whole. We carry it in buckets to one of the gardens, Mary in a sling on my back. Of course the manure's not full ready. But we may layer it above the salad, and let the rain wash the strength down. Likely we won't wait long for that—the sky's gone dark, and blowy.

Someone staked a sholt-dog here, with enough play in the leash that the hound might keep away coneys. As we spread the night soil, the first drops fall on my neck. Then more on the earth around, warm, pulsing.

I take off the sling and put Mary on the ground. Then I put one of the pails beside her—on that a hoe, finally my valru coat, making a sort of tent. Thunder growls across the ridge. Behind us the bell rings furtively. The ringer seeks to hold off thunder, and shield us from a falling sky.

That's a pretty charm, I say, though I'm doubtful it'll help as he hopes.

Likely not, Hester says resentfully. Doubtless she hates that I know aught of growing things here, more than they have learned in their time on this land. She's dumped the nightsoil out in a small mound, and pushes it rapidly, unevenly, with her hoe. I walk slowly along the row, dropping out mine as even as I may. It's been a great long while since I've done anything like this. Still the labor makes me feel secure, even if the beans are lacking. The stems are yellowed—so soft that I think rain may lay them down.

A poor place for crops, I say absently.

And why's that? She's some offended I would judge them wanting.

Well. I point to the dampening earth. Already it's begun to go slick—it's plain to see how the slope will let it form rivulets, then small streams, and those bear away the dirt we seek to better.

Aye, she says, so dejectedly that I must laugh, and do. I think she holds back a shy smile at herself. But my laugh catches—for when I turn to fetch the second pail, I see Dema passing over the ridge.

I recognize her from her garment of ochred deerskin. Soon

she nears. Then I see her face has lost much poise, as though a score of years have fallen on her. She uses a rough bough for a walking stick—she comes to us and says, Good Day.

She's taken a slat of white bark, and holds it over her head. I think it's more habit than a true desire to keep the rain from her skin. Certainly she doesn't seem to care that the rain strikes her hand and runs from it slightly red, darkening the jayskin fringe at her sleeve.

Good day, says Hester.

Dema, well met, I say.

She looks at me and at Hester. Thus we may know she has looked at us, and think her less diminished. She walks past us, swinging her stick, planting it heavily, taking little care against a slip.

We'll to the palisade, I say. Here.

I lift the walrus coat from Mary, wrap her in it.

I need carry the pails, I say, heedless of Hester. Will you help me with my daughter?

Dema nods. She drops the bark. Now the rain hits her greased hair. She holds Mary carefully against one shoulder; we go down to the pale.

What could they have said to her? I ask.

Dema has boiled hot water, and cast in dogwood bark. She has taken a pail of it to the smokehouse, and closed the door tight. For an hour we've seen naught of her.

Sure, I've no notion of savages' thoughts, says Miller. He's working, ordering a crate of lines and hooks, the last large as his bent elbow. Of course he has no answer to offer, and of course I push for one. There's no one else here whose opinion I'd want.

What could she have wanted? I say. What could she have asked, that they'd refuse? Are these people at all?

He looks out to where the *Half Moon* lies at anchor. The second load of fish is near dry; he won't stay long. Sure, I've no notion of that, he says.

Finally the door opens. Dema is clean of ochre. For the first time I see her skin. Though darker than me, with the red washed away she looks pale as a babe cleansed of birthing blood—youthful, as though she's washed away wrinkles. Her hair is yet straight, black, greased, groomed. She goes down to the shore, and under the pier pours out her pail of brown water.

The Red Indians here are gentle, curious delicate that are struck down, killed at slightest mishap. Though this is cause for grief enough among them, it redounds to our Advantage, for they are the less like to War on us.

I write as clearly as I may. Yet I had rather blot away these words, and leave the pages blank. Guy strives to make Dema heroic—more robust than her people, a survivor of their general death, sympathetic to Christian folk. He strives that the English may be delighted to receive her, should she choose to go.

I sit by the shore of the cove and watch the sky turn upon itself. This I could never tire of, I think. A heaven of mirror-faced playing cards, their suits of cups and swords and coins catching a sunset's ghost. If there is ordered rhythm to the dealing I don't see it, nor very much wish to. I watch it from the end of the pier. When my neck tires, I look at the gently rocking *Half Moon*. Soon, it will go.

How many fish and they catch, says Dema from behind me.

A great many, I say without turning. But different from the salmon—else they could stay here and take so much. Some go and catch whales.

Walus? She comes up beside me.

I hold one hand over my head, burst it open as I blow out.

Walus and here, she says. Small boats and—she thinks—ice.

I nod. Sir Guy told me they had herringe-hogge whales for Christmas. The thought of that day of resurrection recalls to me our old burying ground within the slot fence, under the oak, where there were gravestones with moss near deep enough to hold a thumbprint. Each was carved with a Death's-head skull, with flesh slipping from the bone. Eyes round, or like hearts; hair flighting in waves; teeth in even, paling rows. Each stone faced East. On the Day of Judgment the Saints would rise, hands gripping footplates, backs to their rotting portraits, eyes toward the Glory to shine that day above Jerusalem.

On the *Neptunus* a man told me savages would hollow out a mountain, and there lay their dead. It would be something. Will you hold general rites for Nonosabasut, I ask.

No.

She means, I think, that there will be no farewell from any but her. Is there no one who will come to you? I say, and there's as much anger as wonder to the question.

Here long. And time? she says. She hesitates as she seeks that last word.

I've been here too long. And it begins to come clear to me.

She touches her cleaned face. Not find me, she says.

And I understand, or think I do, that those in the sky need ochre to see their children in the world. Without it, Dema is invisible to them. The lights must look different to her now. Before, I imagined the spirits hovered that they might see life. Now, away from her living people, she hides also from the dead. She will hide while yet struck with grief; for so long as she feels herself in trespass, and shamed.

I would give much to know how long within the palisade was too long, and what it is the Beothuk fear her taking into herself. Do they fear illness, or treachery?

I don't know, and maybe never will. But at the thought that her people may call her criminal, or polluted, a spider of dread hatches. There were those dead Guy found in the mamateek. Whatever this land was before Christians came fishing, now it's most made of corpses.

The moonlit ridge turns a row of glowering faces, and in my memory the shadows through the pines go bleak. Here the Lord brings death for uncertain offense. Do the Beothuk know that touch between us must always kill? My dread's not for Dema's soul, nor Nonosabasut's. It's for all of us, and now.

Chapter thirty

I Hear a Companion's Tale

How many will there be? I ask, and with my curved first finger whip a stone into the cove. It skips four skips before beginning to slide, finally to sink. The spreading circles make an arrow. They point from Mary, sleeping by my feet, toward the cove's open mouth, and to a pair of launches laboring to haul in the newly arrived ship. Though I cannot make out the name I know it to be the *Fruitful*, that the settlers have waited weeks to sight.

Dema squats beside me, carefully sifting sea-stones, searching for one flat enough to skip. She is sometimes awkward at our common tasks. But she has readily shared her wisdom about this whole land, and recent showed us a kind of starchy root that might be dug from the sandy soil just aside the pale, where it grows firm as carrots. A great wonder, to find such toothsome food growing abundant, and so near. Perhaps, eating roasted roots, Dema pretends she lives other than in exile. If so, she must keep her eyes fixed to her bowl. There are none about here with garb like hers, surely none with her religion or faith.

James Guy thought the root delicious, and ordered a plenty laid up in baskets. Hence the three of us have come digging—Dema, and I, and Hester, who is the only chamber woman who will yet willingly work beside us. Besides that Hester is shy, and has no desire to greet the *Fruitful* when it comes to dock. Now the coming of the ship has distracted us from our work, and prompted this play.

Perhaps a score and a half, Hester says judiciously. She spins her own rock. It goes further than mine, skittering a long line of rings—but then, hers landed farther from us to begin.

We need count the number of skips, I say. So many of them? They'll near double the numbers here. They'd best bring a plenty of stores.

For themselves and for us, she says. I'd give a plenty for a milk-cow. It's a long while since I've tasted white cheese. I loved that at home. Curds, fresh from whey. A drink of whey itself—curds or whey, I loved either more than the final cheddar.

Ship's stuff is nothing like to it, I say. What would you give, for the cow?

I'd give my bed.

A great prize.

True. Maybe not, —not *my* bed. I would give Shannon's.

I laugh at that, enjoying the companionship the momentous day allows between us. In the cove a skiff bobs from the pier to join the launches. This new boat is filled with Cupid's men. Today is a near holiday, for this is the first arrival of new settlers since the place was planted. From today Cupid's Cove may feel itself a destination, a prospect where Englishmen choose and desire to dwell.

Sure, there is reason enough for that desire. This place has seen no great death of Christians, as we've oft heard lurks waiting in Virginia and the rogue greatland settlements north of it. There, sickness and scant board kill as many as one man in two. Here most have survived, their humors yet sound, no more death come to them than would strike in the normal turn of a midland year. Most thank a fat country. I think they should as well thank luck.

Finally the skiff makes a stern-line fast to the ship; together the boats tow the *Fruitful*. It masses behind like a fresh-killed whale.

Dema skips a stone. It jumps twice, sinks. She waits then, watching us carefully to catch the motion as we flick our wrists. There's much confusion about her since she washed off the ochre. Before it was as though she was scarcely a woman at all. Doubtless, the men thought of having her. But idly, jokingly, as they might think of being with a sheep, or their sister—with curiosity and revulsion mixed. The truth of her was hid from them. As we English are hid from her spirits, who have eyes only for those who cover themselves in ochre.

Now Dema is clean and a woman, a comely one. Were it sure that she will one day leave the palisade, there would be a plenty of men to take her. But even those who might risk fathering a bastard in the wilderness will not chance a red Indian son of their own here, at their own home, where all must know the parentage whether or no it is confessed.

I look at her, and think, Tantum. Guy would greatly love to send back a Beothuk as a trophy. I shake my head.

Humilty, Dema says, as I toss my next stone. It slips a bit beneath my knuckle, strikes with an ignoble *plop*.

I proclaim myself winner, Hester says. She grins crookedly.

Our best of five tries, I say. Humility's well enough, Dema. She's begun her lying in, and most likely won't come to open air 'til after the birth.

Soon and come, Dema says. The *Fruitful* has begun a slow turn toward the pier.

It will be, Hester says. Sure Humility's ready for it—last night she told me she felt ready for the child to burst out. The kicking wakens her at night. She's constant weary, though she rarely leaves her bedstead. There's a proper sight.

Now that it's closer I see the *Fruitful* is painted gaily, a sky's-blue, the ship a moving festival. The Cupid's folk would feel it so whatever its hue. From the tip of the pier they give a shout, then another. Rowers in the ship's launches wave hats and a striped scarf.

But the men in the Cupid's skiff seem less happy. Though they pull resolutely, they have none of the joy I'd thought to see. After a moment I see why. For as the ship finishes its turn toward the final docking, the name scripted black near the prow comes plain—and it is not *Fruitful,* but *Elegant.*

In a few moments one of those on the pier sees his mistake; a moment more, and he believes it. Then the news passes quick, as though the grim knowledge jumps direct between their heads. The cheering on shore dies; but those on ship have not yet noted the change. They still feel themselves honored and welcomed, and are taken up with pure delight.

Now the sky-blue seems meant to mask the *Elegant* against the horizon, turning its sails to clouds—though, seen at sea, it might yet show only as a bulky shadow. Against the steep rises that make the entrance to the cove, the color seems rather deceitful than joyous. But that's naught but fancy.

A great disappointment to them, I say.

It is, it is, Hester says.

There's far more distress in her voice than I feel myself. This is but a brief moment of peace, of friendship—I am far without the life of this place. I see it like an old woman peering through her fence.

Shall we go to them? I say without enthusiasm.

Well, I will, Hester says. I'd know who these are, even if they've no notion of staying.

She leaves us; soon the *Elegant* bumps to dock. A ramp goes down, and the first arrival descends like a cock to chickens.

The skipping game over, I sit beside Mary, draw up my knees, and wonder what the coming of the *Fruitful* will mean for me. One is always marked by the place she comes from. Here, I must always be from the bird island—always suspected of performing rank and unworthy charms. How else might I have survived such wilderness? I am not so godly that they might imagine I lived through the Lord's blessing. Perhaps their attention to me will fade amid the excitement of so many come with their own stories. Or perhaps tales of my misfortune and evil disposition will grow, a means to draw the newcomers close. In any case I've no intention of joining the greeting party. That should mean taking on the airs of a Cupid's woman. But as they descend the ramp, backs to me, among them I catch a slim shoulder-line.

No, I say.

What and not.

It cannot be, I say. I am to my feet.

What.

Dema laughs a little, for my wonder is transparent. Commonly I'd be joyed that she's smiled, that the metal helmet has dropped from her even for a spare moment. But for now I've no mind for aught but that passenger.

When her feet touch the pier she turns, feeling firm wood beneath her, smiling a particular sweet, sharp smile. I take one step, another. *Anne*, I say.

How ever to come to her? I run toward the pier, feet pushing pebbles into sand, for once heedless of Mary. Though I hold her tight before me, the running jounces her until she cries. Strange, for my haste comes from a picture of handing my babe, careful, to Anne. Of seeing her hands upon her, as it would have been had we never parted. But when I reach the base of the pier I slow, drawn back as by a bit. I stop beside pilings; they seem the legs of a troll's table. How can I be certain it is her? It cannot be, I know. How would it be her?

Half clutched by haste, half by misdoubt, I climb past pilings to the base of the pier. And indeed when I reach the planking and can see the crowd she is gone, vanished.

But she steps from behind a stack of crates—smiling broadly, happy to be on solid ground, playing with her arms for the balance of it. I stare, drink her in, though still uncertain. This woman is heavier than Anne, her manner less contentious. Certain it cannot be her.

But she sees me. And when in the next, frozen moment she looks to me again, I know that Anne has somehow come. She shakes her head a little, stares into me. Then she gives a little cry—a laugh, or my name.

I hasten, I sidle through. But when I'm close Anne's face changes, covered in slight horror like a dusting of pollen. She looks over me, past me, looking here and there as though she thinks the cart a dragon—every barrel a beast.

Of course, I think.

It is only me, I say. It sounds a reproach. I try again: I am alone here.

Alone? she says. Then she looks at Mary, and she smiles with blessed relief; with wondrous surprise, and affection. I am beside her and with her, arms around, Mary close between. Anne's arms are around me and we cry, hard as with grief.

I never thought to see you again, I say.

And you. And you, she says, hand on my face.

So thin, she says.

So fat, I say. For in drawing her close I feel her swelling stomach.

And who's this? she says, her voice as familiar, as near-forgot, as the savor of mother's milk.

Mary, my daughter.

And her father?

On her face is joy for me, for my babe; unbelief that I am here that she may ask her question; most of all fear of my answer.

Oh there's a deal to tell you, I say.

But I would hear her story first, and that she may not press me, I say only that, like her, I would not accompany the Saints. She will doubtless think my story the mirror of hers, who abandoned them in England. But before I hear her tale comes the storming wonder of all the company that I should here meet a companion—a true marvel of God that you may so replenish dear friendship, Guy says. And I meet her husband, a thin, worthy-looking carpenter whose name is Gil Crackston.

I take one of his gravel-rough hands in mine. He lets me, leaving it there clasped, watching me close as though to match the curves of my face against those of another. I understand—he has heard of me. Wherever Anne has been, she has not forgot where she came from, nor the names of her friends. But I know nothing of what she's told Gil of her origins—how she's masked them. Perhaps, in her telling, I'm her servant; perhaps she's mine. There have been times when either should have been true—we were long each other's masters.

Finally we beg that all may grant us space and peace. But that'll not happen in the Star Chamber. Instead we make for the smokehouse, where I beg Dema's leave that we may have her room for a time. Here none may hear us, for there are no windows—and certain no passel of women waiting aside a hung blanket for gossipy words to pass. We sit in the center of the room; Anne is first to speak. And though the stories best for listening are oftimes those most miserable, this one is sweet to hear as aught ever in my life.

That night I left I never slept, she says. After you took from us, our gathering soon splintered—the joy'd gone from it some time before.

She smiles slightly, wryly; I take her hand.

We broke and went our separate ways, she says, or at least the others went theirs. I told them I'd follow after in a moment's time. I was angry, and torn, shamed for my words—and then I was angrier still. And my face hurt.

She grins.

Well. When all'd left I sat fuming. Though my head was full of ale, that clouded me less than did my thoughts. But one thought drove off the others, clean as soap skimming grease from water. What I'd thought was that I need not go back. With that, all was clear. You won't know why…

Isaac, I say quietly.

She is startled, then softens. Isaac. Well. You do know me.

I thought of it after, I say, when we missed you at the shore.

Yes. I think I'll not say any else of that. But I wouldn't travel with him. That seemed so simple—so plain and true—my only wonder was that the thought'd not come to me before. To be born serving such a household's one thing—it's another to choose freely to accompany it.

For an instant she looks stricken. She spoke careless, before thinking that I made just that choice. But I smile regretfully; she relaxes. *After all*, she must think, *Mel did leave them in the end.*

Once I thought I need not return to the Rowes, she says, I couldn't have bid my legs carry me to their house if I'd spent the night at it. And I passed scarce a hare's leap trying. Instead I took myself up, and walked north. Not through the village—I went through the fields. Leaving the road at night felt a bold crime. I walked past the flanks of the houses but felt myself already gone. With the moon it was bright as dusk. I felt alone, and at terrible hazard. Certain there were spirits about, and my basil was fallen away from behind my ear—from the breeze, or some fall I'd had.

Though she passes over it lightly, shame twinges me; I recall the feel of my hand against her face, and the joy the blow brought.

But when I stepped into a plot I knew recent seeded, she says, my fears fell away. It seems a poor prank, now. There were many stayed behind who I loved well enough, whose crops I'd not choose to injure when my head was straight. But I was not in the most joyful or forgiving of minds. At the thought that I might leave footprints in the plots, that there were none to catch or chase me, I felt stronger—without either fear or the need for it.

Once, I did trip. Though I caught myself at the last, I bit dirt. It jammed between my teeth; I spit it out. That seemed a proper farewell to the place. North, I told myself, then west. My lone regret was that I'd not thought earlier that I might go. If I had, I might've said a proper farewell to you, and not left bitterly. Or at least stolen some food. In truth, it was a horrible thought that I'd left you in hate.

She looks at me steadily, and I swallow. Never fear it, I say.

Nor you. But, oh it was awful. Perhaps I make it more so now, when I've none of the anger I had then. I had never asked you to go with me. But I was still furious that you were not. I would be truthful, now. Many times I've wished I spoke more honest to you before all broke apart. I thought you blind and willful.

I was hopeful, more than true blind, I say. Though there's slight enough difference, when hope's strong. Enough. Where did you take yourself to?

North, along the road, when I again found it past the burying grounds. As near I knew, that was the least likely path for any other to take. I wanted the emptiest road. If not for the cottagers I'd have took through the forest.

At night?

I feel immediate foolish for asking, for I know she would have. I would have.

She laughs a bit. My humors weren't arrayed at their best, she says. Travel at night feels faster than it is in truth. I thought I near ran—but by dawn I'd scarce reached the northern crossing. I watched the sky turn purple. I'd at least have good skies for my flight.

I remember, I say. I think back to eager Saints, scanning the horizon for signs of cloud.

Ah, you would, she says, and reaches to touch me. At the crossing I turned west, she says. When the ale dried in it, my head felt like to split. I struggled—it was like walking through flax. I'd nothing at all with me. Only my clothes. Having nothing might've been freeing—but after a while it seemed a greater burden than a full sack. There was nothing before me, nothing to return to. I sat by the side of the road and let hopelessness drown me. I felt a stringed poppet, like those we'd see at market—it may be they resent the cords, and wish to move themselves, but cut them free and they're naught but a heap of wood.

But it was not so very long before I heard a cart clacking behind. I might've hid. But just then being taken up seemed not the worst of fates, I was that tired. I only sat and waited. The cart was filled wood cut to make chicken coops. The cartman walked aside his horse to guide it. They stopped before me; the cartman held the reins short, and asked if I had not rather ride. I looked to his face. The man was Gil Crackston.

That was Gil?

Anne nods, and her smile turns bright. She lays her hands on her stomach. And he now my husband, she says.

I cough a laugh. It's the beginning of a shaking torrent; I laugh until a cramp near stitches my side. I drop my head between both hands.

And what is so funny in that? she says—puzzled, and, from old habit, mock-offended.

If I could speak, I'd say it seems to me the Lord's jest that she met her a loving man, and near before the rest of us'd pulled from the village in caravan. That's the tale? I'll say when I can. The whole of it? You decided to go, and did, and there was Gil Crackston—God's bounty cast to your feet. I laugh not at her but at myself, my old self, and at my hopes and prayers that once seemed so possible and real. I laugh, for that is all there is to do—and then I hug Anne close, my arm tight about the back of her neck.

Are all houses here so built? she asks. I smile, for Anne's asked it bravely—I realize she's held back from the question since first we came to the smokehouse. Now her asking it's a kind of courtesy; she won't push me to talk.

This is the smokeroom, I say. The only blot's that there's not enough meat to merit using it. Or not enough homey meat—I think in autumn we'll smoke us some venison.

And never a warden to call eating deer a crime, she says.

Sure, it takes some getting used to, I say.

But that's a lie, I think, at least as regards myself. When first I came here my world was already spun, toppled. That we might hunt deer at pleasure seemed the smallest of things. Had there been a warden—*that* should have seemed the greater wonder. The thought recalls to me the vast leagues between the road Anne took and that I did.

How can you be here? I ask. Of all places, to come here.

How can *you* be? she says. That *I* am seems not a wonder at all to me.

It seizes me pleasantly to see her confident in herself as ever she was. Of course I've a slight waft of doubt at her easy manner—I know now it once masked Isaac's sins, and her anguish at them. But she's a delicious balm to me, the warmer for being so unexpected. Any doubts I have only show her more tender, thus more dear.

But here, of all places.

Where else might we have stopped, she says reasonably.

Of course, I say. There's not so much else between here and England. There's nothing at all. What caused you stop?

A sail, and broken barrels. A few days ago we spied a far distant sail. There'd been rumor of Portuguese pirates. The *Elegant's* swift, so I'm told, and we might've made for a northern passage, or hid us behind an island. But either'd have taken more time than we could spare, for we'd lost three barrels of beer. So instead we made straight for here, straight as we might, in hopes of both shelter and hops. This is only what I heard, though I think shipboard news passes quicker even than in the midlands.

Well, I say, I think you'll be well provided, whatever your wants. Sir Guy'll be much flattered that his colony's thought a place of solace. Ask for silks or gold—he may offer them.

Now, Anne says. We've spoke only of me. When did you choose to leave the Saints behind, and how'd your path lead here after?

I take a breath. The door is slightly open; through the crack warm wind passes, bearing in the ocean, putting me in mind of hopeful sails. I take up Mary, hold her close.

Tell me, Anne says.

I tell her.

Chapter thirty-one

I Drift Aboard a Pleasure Craft

I follow Dema from the pond where first I met her, and up a watercourse as feeds it. First we circle the pond, brushing aside rushes, muddying our shoes, sending unseen, frightened frogs splashing. Then we follow the brook through the forest. I wonder why Dema did not go straight to its banks. It seems important that she chose to follow it from the end.

We follow it an hour, then two. To my eyes the forest is always the same; the slow rise, just steep enough to loose the brook to flow, always the same. It's like a dream to me. I wonder why she asked me to come. Then it seems she did not, that I asked her. I think about that, whether it was her or I that wished me there, until she stops at a bank that raises sharply from the edge of the brook. Aside from one particular, gnarled pine, it's the first thing I've seen I would take for a landmark. But to Dema it's no mere bound marker. She plunges in, two hands, grabbing at the earth. When the first, dark layer is broke and spilling, I see that the soil beneath is a dried-blood red.

Dema takes a gourd from her sack and she fills it, packing it tightly, eager for ochre. When the first brims, she fills a second. I stand stupid, still unsure of my purpose, now some wishing she had not called me to come. Or was it I that first wished to do?

Behind us, across the cove and through the gorge of night, comes music—a soft, glad clamor. In the rowboat we sway softly under Miller's pulls; on shore bonfires burn high, draping silks, dragon-red and tawny, over swells colored Judas-sin velvet. I lean back, trail my fingers in the water. When I stretch my arm I may ripple the lights.

All those who have them a means of music have brought it forth. Now there are lutes, drums, a single horn. Men who have no proper means beat on metal pots, or they dance. They sing, shouting their songs.

Though we're close enough that I might hear the words, I let my ears go dull. The bright music blurs then; becomes a murmur.

A joyful night, Miller says.

He gives a final pull on the oars, lets the boat drift. It was he who suggested coming here—that we might see the festival as a whole, he said. That I might know what it is to take leisure or pleasure on a boat. As he spoke he laid in cheering stores under the gunwales: a sack of dried apples and pears, bottles of ale. He handed me a stoneware lamp with candlelight shining through cuts and tiny circles in its clay.

It feels a right luxury to be on the water with no other purpose than pleasure, without even the excuse of herbery that permitted me go coasting. Here there's naught to do but sit with him, and watch four fires blaze. Miller's beard is dimly half-lit. The most of him I see as though from starlight, off stars I must squint past our lantern's glimmer to see. There's no moon, only the light of our lantern on the gray rowboat planking, and the light of the bonfires on a circle of shore and the creased fronts of houses—and in one of those, Anne cuddles Mary, in a room curtained off from Humility's birthing.

Between the flames of lamp and those of shore a path of light stretches. Outside those bounds the night is black as ravens.

One they'll remember, I say. And those as live here after—doubtless Guy'll see it writ in his history.

Miller nods. And his letters, he says. Must be few in England without one meant for them by now.

Writing's given me fingers of iron, I say in agreement.

The folk on shore are distant, dancing finger-shadows; some are naught but shades cast on sand. A clear, throaty cry lays out from the gentle general tumult like a single fish flighting from its school. Straight below us the water is dark, untouched by fire. The rub of oar and lock has ceased—else I'd be unsure that Miller had let us stop. I must look behind if I'm to see the holiday.

They have much to celebrate. Finally the *Fruitful* is come. Its stores now swell the colony's stocks, its women swell the populace. But the great joy is for Humility's babe, who is now birthing in the Star Chamber.

When the word came to us I was sitting aside the stream with Anne, and Gil Crackston, and Miller. Even Dema had come to join us, being much taken with Mary's newfound skill at crawling. We sat against boulders, watching her drag herself along, a handsbreadth at a time as though to find the stream's source, gnawing toothlessly on dried ellan, salted fish, a bit of bread and dried ship's cheese. On so soft a day, with company so dear, I could near pretend that I had come to rest in a place I'd choose to live. But then came Elizabeth, a shipboard friend to Anne, calling to us that we might witness the birth. Only Elizabeth had thought to call us. She yet knew nothing of the women of Cupid's, of their fast contempt. None of us went with her to the chamber.

A chance moment of quiet in the music fills with half-heard calls for another song and, quieter still, the invisible, creaking rig of moored ships. Though shrouded they must be closer than I had thought; else I could not hear them at all. Even so they're subdued, and would go unheard if they did not fill a more cavernous hush.

Though I stare gape-eyed, I cannot see the ships. Heard but unseen, their quiet hints at stalking.

The ship I imagined beating west, to the shores where went the

Saints, has come. Wisps of thought have turned sail and timber. It has a name—it is the *Elegant*. My staying here is no longer something I'm forced to, a decision made by the Lord when he brought me to rest, choosing here of all His world after my fortunate rescue. Now that the passage west lies clear and possible, it has turned fearsome, a black hole sudden yawning beneath my feet. It might be a tunnel. It might be a den.

Anne waits hopefully to hear that I will go west. I have not yet spoke my intent to her; since the coming of the *Elegant* I have not spoke it to myself.

For a time we sit in silence. We've drifted even with the shore; thus we may look at both fires and each other. Water calmly taps on timber. Something in the quiet holds me. Here I feel balanced, steady between the cove's mouth and the birthing town at its heart.

Once, a mob of fish jump. They doubtless flee some scaled, toothy hunter; maybe a shark.

> *For to see mad Tom of Bedlam*
> *Ten thousand years I'll travel,*
> *Mad Maudlin goes on dirty toes...*

Some chance eddy of breeze carries the verses; as I take a bite of dried pear they fade again.

The fruit brings perry to mind, I say. I sometimes liked that over cider.

Miller blows out softly; his sigh wavers, falls briefly into cadence with the shore song. What do you intend do? he says.

What will you? I say, finding refuge in the tease. And I at your mercy here.

But he shakes his head, as though sudden angry. I do not mean this for play, he says. Will you go to Merrymount?

I had rather not think on that, tonight.

He sits quiet for a moment. It is an uncertain place, he says.

So Gil told me.

But he's never seen it, Miller says. He's only met Morton, and Morton has a troubled name, whatever Gil's measure of him.

I think to myself that Gil's measure was a full one. He told me this of Thomas Morton, founder and chief man of Merrymount: that he is gifted in tongues, and insists he'll add red Indian to his store of Latin and Greek. That his own seal bears the imprint of a goat's head. That he believes the savages have them no religion, and is himself much given to joy. Gil's words painted a portrait of a men with a scholar's mind but who may stand, secure, within a wild wood, smiling rapacious, as though he would chew the trees for juice—perhaps Morton has him sympathies toward Pan. Certain he cannot be much given to conversion.

But Miller goes on and on—that Morton was once a city lawyer, that many tales are told of what it was drove him from England, and none of those should add to his acclaim. I would take a horrid chance, placing myself with such a man.

I wish he would not speak so. Though I hold away from them, the birthing and the attendant celebrations strike something tender in me. I had rather love this place, if only for a lone night. I had rather tell myself that my time here was other than frail and empty. Thus I might not so scorn the idea of another colony, and so fear the prospect of coming to one. Are not the fires lovely? I say…. Are not the fires lovely?

But Miller cannot stay himself; he is took by some passion of his own. Sure you cannot stay here, he says. That you've come here with me is sign enough of that.

He speaks with force, and unhappiness. The fires begin to look a stilted painting, and the half-heard song seems a mere memory of music. Any joy I've had in the birthing or the sight of the flashing festival drains from head and heart surely as from a tilted kettle.

He is right that there are none on shore I need rejoice with—that I cannot feel this place my own, and have no need for glad riot. And he is right that I have come only to escape from them, and not to be with him. Some part of me does want him to my bed, where I might feel him warm, with me—soft as skin, and hard as skin. But that should take abandon I do not feel. There is yet some dread constraint; smothering chains, heavy as granite.

Suddenly I fear I'll never lose these links. They'll weight my burial shroud. Perhaps he sees them; hears their clang.

Why would you press me? I say.

I must to England, he says. I've contracted to it, and the men will not hold here long. Before we sail I'd know your mind, and where you'll go.

He does not say, *There's room yet with me, on my ship*. But I know it well—the very cot. Living in his cabin would be almost familiar.

He looks to me. Behind him, surprising close, I hear the wooden tapping of feet on the pier. They seem suspended in the night; nothing to hold them where they walk in air.

I throw a scrap of dry pear, making circles in water stained pumpkin.

I take a breath. It comes struggling. Blood lumps behind my brow. I feel I straddle a wall, that I must fall from or leap from.

On the pier the steps have stopped, stiffened into moans. The lovers want a place out of sight. Still, their passion may be known and noted.

I'll go west, I say.

Perhaps seizing the reins of a lusty horse should feel the same as speaking so; in riding one claims dominion, and yet must ready to careen.

Will you, he says.

To myself I think: *Will you not ask me.*

But even in thought that question's a manner of lie. If he asked, I would not go with him. Once I chose me a destination. That coast yet waits for me, even if it be much settled and taken by enemies I once hoped join. And the Saints will know that we have come safe to shore. However many of them yet breathe living air will know it.

After a short, silent while, Miller rows for the fires. He rows wordlessly. I feel in me a great emptiness. But it's a clear one—clean, and ready to be filled.

I will see you again, he says—one foot on shore, the other in the boat as he offers me his hand. The music is swole up, the words come clear and impossible to ignore.

Still I sing bonny boys, bonny mad boys
Bedlam boys are bonny
For they all go bare and they
Live by the air…

It's unlikely, I almost say—but do not, holding back from what might be loose cruelty.

He reads my silence right; shakes his head, and smiles at me. I'd hear the end of this story, he says. Certain, I'll see you again.

At that I take his hand; I let him help me to dry land.

Leaving him, I pass into light, briefly blinded. When my sight is restored me I see a bed prepared for Humility, set on a bedstead between two of the fires. It must be furious hot; though she had better be left within doors, at least she and her child will catch no very dire chill if brought here after the birthing. Breeze swirls smoke between houses and toward the darkened, empty hills. After the quiet of the cove the town seems built of tumult.

How long will they raise you high? I think as I look at the empty bed. Do not imagine this may last—that they'll never cease their honor, that they see the woman behind their triumph.

But I chasten myself. If they must raise them a trophy tonight, they had as well use this.

I enter the Star Chamber. If I were Sarah, with her easy, unthinking force, I'd pull down the blanket walls. I'd yank the cloths that hide Jupiter from Venus, Mars from Mercury. Then there would be naught but hall and parlor; nothing more hid from the eye here than the swirling joy and lust and woe of any common house. Had the *Elegant* never come I might do so, and cry out *Open our house!* But I come here alone, as one who will soon leave, no longer even a chance member of the colony and company.

I push through the blanket into Mars. The fire is built up high, showing Mars made nearly a passageway by stores from the *Fruitful*. But Anne and Mary are not here. Behind Mars is Mercury, now made a birthing room. Mercury must be full of women, settlers and newcomers alike, perhaps a score together. For a moment I wonder if Anne has joined them. But she would not have; she should think that treachery. She must have removed to the smokehouse, and there sought quiet and sleep.

Within Mercury they pray; they hold each other close, they clink together strips of stiff copper ribbon. Perhaps someone has given Humility a length of cord to twist, for the distraction of it. Perhaps she has so done until it loops about her fingers, knotting them within the rope. I know she lies on Guy's fine bedstead—it will be an honor to see it used for the purpose, when comes the gala day, he once said. He will make himself progenitor, no matter who the true and unnamed father.

The copper tinks, tinks quicker. I may hear a crying babe. But Humility yet gasps her labor, her babe yet smothered within; sure I cannot hear it cry. I look to the hearth—I remember Shannon, tossing dough to some sprite or grima. But there's naught there but a fire.

The room is noontime hot, but it is chill to me. I will not go to them. But I will offer one gift that they knew not enough to offer themselves; I will offer it also to myself.

Quietly I move aside a crate of pewter, a small clay still, a brace of bandoliers, until I'm in the corner where I leaned the staff given me by Dema. It is smooth, small at the point, the top thick as a club, the head carved out like a cup. I've no notion of its proper use. Perhaps it was made by a cunning man. But it was given me by Dema, as was its secret intent.

I knock open a barrel of flour, spill some to mix with water in a stoneware bowl. I mix it to a paste, thick enough to roll to a lumpy snake. It will not be of best savor—it has no proofing, nor salt. But it is the best baking I may contrive here, and baking is one thing yet missing from here, from this day. The smell of cookery may embrace and welcome a coming babe. I roll the dough around the thin end of the staff. Then I hold the staff above the fire; I toast the dough to bread.

A brown crust begins to come. I turn the staff. Is this cruel misuse? Does Dema think this carved branch holy? I cast away the thought—no cunning man of goodwill should grudge me using this so, and Dema would not have a staff from a man without such charity. I hope Dema would see what it is I do, and not think it a slight of her gift.

The smell of baking fills Mercury, and doubtless seeps to all our chambers. The wet air is steam from off my bread; the coldness is driven out. The voices in Mercury rise, come clear. He is come. A boy. The air is filled with smell of false baking. The women call their joy to low rafters. Below their cry is another hum, near a howl, below what any should hear—hidden yet sharp, like broken glass hid under stream stones. It returns their call, and shakes me. I listen though I cannot hear the words, and will not unless all fall impossible silent. They will never do.

Enry. Shannon, tossing dough in offering to dying coals. A boy is born, a voice sparked, and Cupid's Cove's become an English place.

When I come to the storehouse, it seems to me an ogre's storeroom—a fortress solid as a cave, windowless against threat of light. But by the light of the fires that flows through the door I see that the newcomers have set barrels of honey, and hung slabs of bacon—there are hams, powder, birdshot. Pipes of train, kinterkins of butter, a stack of round cheeses. Also a crate of black rabbits, that will be kept here waiting for a hutch strong enough to thwart foxes. Amid the clutter, Dema, Anne, and Mary sleep; at least they all lie quiet.

Soon they'll tell Dema that she must take other quarters. But for now the smokehouse is yet filled with the stench of her garb, as though this is the lair of something that weaves bones into its nest. Once I found the smell repellent. Now the bloody dankness is familiar, and in a manner comforting.

I close the door, grope through blackness on until I find the edge of blankets. Outside they've tied a goat to the side of the smoke-house. It kicks the wall, agitated by the revelry.

I feel my way to Anne, take Mary from aside her. Anne stirs in sleep. Dema, I whisper. Dema. Wake.

I feel her roll slightly. Then my eyes begin gathering what light comes from the low hearth. Mary is with me like a gosling under wing.

I bend forward, hug her and Dema together. Dema lies there—does not pull away, nor embrace me back.

I rise to my knees. There is much I could say to her. I think her my friend, and I hers. But that is less from understanding than from mutual goodwill. Perhaps understanding would have come in time. But her unexpected silence, her laughter without aim—Guy was right about some of that, if uncharitable. If she chooses go to England, I will be blind to her reasons.

Will you give me ochre, I say. Will you give it her?

I cannot explain this as seizes me. But I know, without thinking, that if she does go, Dema will again stain her skin. She will not leave without seeing that her spirits will again perceive her walking on earth. I've no notion of how much she'll need. But surely to cover a babe, to stain only a babe's chest, will not take so very much.

Bits of song reach us but all is garbled, perplexed. Again and again the goat kicks the wall, butts it, a muffled knocking.

If Dema does not understand my purpose, at least she hears the need in my voice, that cuts through other jabber. And she need not understand the purpose; she would not refuse my need, not refuse my daughter. *Her* is the password here.

Dema rises, rustles through cloth, unwinds a sheet from about her gourd. She has a second gourd, empty, that she may use for a bowl. Beside the smoking hearth she mixes a pinch of ochre to a paste.

In near dark I dip three fingers gently into the wetness; it is warm, the water Dema used left over from boiling roots for her evening sup. Our shadows block the little light. From feel alone I softly draw back undercloth, touch my fingers to Mary's bare skin. Dema holds the gourd-bowl carefully, with both hands, cupped by her knees. I touch my three fingers to Mary, to her navel, the dimple where we were recent linked.

Here we were joined together. Now the place we were most intimate is stained, colored all about. All is dark; and, but for a song of strained, confused talk, all silent. But the staining ochre seems to me a signal fire.

Now they will see you, dear. You'll be seen by any men I can make see you. Never will you be hid—not from those on the land, nor those in the sky, nor spirits behind it.

Though they denied me, the Saints yet in His world will see her, if I've the strength to see it done. We'll go west.

Part IV
The Seasoned Coast

Chapter thirty-two

I Forsake a Boneyard

T he more I look, the more I like it, Morton says. He leans on a bough, that he may better look with bleary eyes from the Prospect Tree.

It's this sort of thing that makes me like him. He's a true enthusiast, of a kind I'd become wary of. But his passion is of a particular, appealing tenor. He does not seek to carve the land for commerce—or such is not his first, driving intent. He does not seek to force sealed order on those here, making him his own rigid society. He seems rather to love all for its own sake—the muggy, late summer air, the clear, rocky bay, even the mosquitoes that at dusk hum insanely from lowland forest mulch. When we came, he embraced Gil Crackston jubilantly, then each of us in turn, squeezing with such happy abandon that one could not help but return both the embrace and the humor behind it. He vowed eat an oyster for every newcomer. The which he did, though some needed three bites, their shells big as bowls. It's not from failure at trying that he has not gone fat, though he has him well more than twoscore years. By night's end he was roaring from his repast of ale and armored fish. I've liked Morton from the first, and I've liked Merrymount.

The Prospect Tree is a white pine, the sort most needful in shipyards. It's the tallest tree on the hill they call Mount Wollaston; thus they set a ladder at the base, and above that pounded in boards for hand-and-footholds, and finally built them a curved platform on five branches whorled about the trunk. From under the branches overhead one may look out as from a lean-to, but instead of a muddy farmyard the view is of forest, and cornfields, and vast miles up coast. When first we climbed to it Morton brushed the platform free of tiny bits of some hardened foam—he shook his fist in jest, and swore at spittlebugs. He says one day we'll strip the tree overhead, at least somewhat, the better to see both blue sky and coming storms.

Massachusetts Bay is a marvelous bright place at sunrise—blue water but glimmering gold, tempered by a handful of sandy isles. Though they have some trees the isles seem roamers, likely in time to shift and slide, blown by seawind. All about the bay are wet, grassy lands. Clouds of birds may rise from them—ducks, widgeons, fishing cranes like tridents. To our north is a river Morton called Neponset; to our south, the Monatiquot. Between us and the Neponset stretches a wide farming ground set with Indian corn, and squash, and beans.

But the clear land below us, the marshes, even the bay itself are but a pause, a brief hush before the chorus—now whispering, now thunderous—of the forest bellowing behind over some thousands of miles of earth. I seem never free from thoughts of it. All this land is timbered. Wetland cedars, oft taken over with vines—oaks, and chestnuts, the ground beneath them clear enough to ride a horse through, wondering—and everywhere, whether on far, thin peaks or in soil black enough…to satisfy the stingiest husbandman, there are white pines. Morton spoke of the woods during our walk to the Prospect Tree, and well I believe in its extent and abundance. For coming to deck one morning before dawn, before ever we had sighted land, the forest filled my nose and all the blown sea-air around—humid, turbid, rapturous, a world of wood. In the darkness I imagined America green as sunlit ivy. After another day of brisk sailing the watch spied shore, still naught but a brown line, perhaps some hazed by what seemed to me the breathing of the land and its wild arbory. What a destination for those who love good fires!

Not very far offshore we sailed through small, black, spouting whales. Another, alone, and far greater, jumped. I saw only the end of the leap, had only a vague sense of the shocking trunk rising, shedding ocean water in cumbrous sheets—but the crash and foam of its landing spoke of something at once lusty and monumental. I think I'll never tire of watching whales.

The town, for so I think of it, is set in a kind of glade nearer the foot of Mount Wollaston. From the Prospect Tree I cannot see it at all—there seems nothing special about that patch of greenwood. It's as like the rest of the forest as one sea-wave is to the next; and, like a wave, the townsite seems to have no solid hold on itself. From our vantage is it only timber. But I know there are some eight houses there, built in a circle around a common yard, the whole hemmed only by oak and red maple for a paling. There is a good store of chickens. There's a vine they told me will bring blisters if touched; there's a tree hard beside it they swear bleeds sugar, though they have yet to learn from the Massachusetts the proper method of boiling it to a cake. They would have thought the glade made them by Providence, if not for the black, burned trees that showed it an abandoned Indian place. I've no notion why the Indians cleared it, their great open land seeming far better ground for planting.

For September, it's precious hot. Last night, as Morton ate oysters, the clearing itself seemed to sweat.

Merrymount is no tomb, Morton says suddenly, as though he heard my thoughts of Indians. When we came we found no empty roundhouses.

Morton's hair is long, past his shoulders, some curly, and gray has begun salting the black. Once he must have kept his beard trimmed, but he's begun losing the habit. If I'd not talked with Gil I'd think Morton more given to sporting than to study. He seems robust, in ways more like a young bear than a man at middle age.

Indian roundhouses are like to those of the wild Irish, he adds, being made of drawn poles.

It seems you'll have fine provender, I say, looking at the far fields of tall corn.

We will. It is not all of it ours, he says. Seeing my question, he goes on: the Indians yet farm it—their women. Some are there now.

He points, and for the first time I note a few distant, roofed platforms amid the corn, like turtle-shells in tall grass.

The women oft come to pay homage to their dead men, their dead families, Morton said. Some of them to the wives their husbands had before they were themselves married. When they're done they stay a while; in spring that they may bury fish to better the earth, in summer that they may throw stones at the crows.

Do they not resent your use of the place? I ask.

Well, we bargained and traded for it. And some of their people now reside with me. I've not oft disputed with them. If any here are resented, likely it's those good Indian fellows that live with me and so grow fat.

I think back to my arrival—among the Englishmen were four Indians, all of them men. One was dressed only in squares of deerskin drawn up between their legs then tied at the waist. The rest were garbed in a mix of English and savage stuff—a deerskin cloak slung over the shoulders of a green jerkin, a wide-brimmed hat that shaded the wearer of a leather shirt. Three were cheerful, greeting us much as did the English. The last watched more cautiously—dour, or unsure. All had straight black hair. If they had any beards at all they were shaved perfect smooth. I had thought them come as traders, and that they'd soon choose leave. It amazes me that they live there, and go so unremarked upon by either word or questioning eye. Surely there are few colonies that will so admit savages. Their converse with the English, that seemed so easy, becomes near astonishing now that I know it to be intercourse between inhabitants of the same town. Many English should find it easiest to offer friendship to Indians who they know mean to leave.

After the plague, there were never so many as might use the ground, Morton goes on. It's a pleasure for me to watch things growing, and Massachusetts growing them. Else this place'd be a Golgotha, like the most of their villages afore we came.

Those men live with you?

Why should they not? he asks briskly. They are fine hunters

and furriers. Where else had they better live? They and theirs treated me as a worthy guest when I went with them, such is their humanity. All who will live and work with me are welcome to do, Lady.

There's something behind this I don't understand; he seems to carry on an old argument, with me standing for another contestant. Or maybe it is only the residue of his drunk.

I never intended offense, I say. I only wished know the particulars of the place.

Rightly so.

He stretches, ending with arms toward the rising sun. Then he breathes deep, clearing the murk of his celebrations. Even so reduced, doubtless with a painful head, he has a hunger about him. If he could I think he'd tilt the world, drink this country down in gulps—men, women, furs, future.

What a land this is, he says. What a fine place. Even squirrels here make a dish to savor. Though not those living in the Prospect Tree or other white pines—their flesh takes the odor of ship's tar.

He looks through branches at what sky we may see, peering at white clouds hung in the morning.

Zone torrid is healthful for grasshoppers, he says, *zone temperate* for ants and bees. Among which do you count yourself?

When first we met, I asked him if there was any man who might guide me and my babe to other English. I'd reason to think, I said, that some I'd known in the old country were now resident on this coast. Morton looked at me puzzled, and agreed they might be.

He would not hazard a journey up coast for my pleasure or convenience, he said honestly, for good weather's like to turn. Even a well-manned shallop may turn naughty, and flip. But even as he spoke I could see him consider, weighing the dangers and possible gains. Talk may make good neighbors, he declared suddenly—it may temper bad ones. That evening he stood on a stump to announce that it was time a party went north, to learn the health and humor of those living near New France. The humor of those at Plimoth to the south, he said sourly and to laughter, was already known them.

Since such was our first intercourse, I know his question of bugs is no child's riddle. It's rather a probe, of me and my intent.

The ants and bees, I say.

He looks at me humorously, questioning.

The grasshopper lives for today, and so dies, I say. What country is coldest?

Zone frigid. It is less a country than a band that rings the world, alike in north and utter south.

Zone frigid is altogether deadly, I say. For grasshoppers, ants, or bees, any of them.

True, he says, and smiles at me. I've heard something of your history. I'd hear more, when I have a better hold on my head. I make you welcome to zone temperate—New England falls well within its golden mean.

I believe it, I say. You spoke of hospitality—how long did you live with the Indians?

A day here, two nights there. But living in this land you reside with them, surely as though you lie with one within her lodging, on a bed of raccoon. We're far from being full owners of this place. They may have seen great death, but when they gather it's yet a marvel to see such a horde come out the forest. I much wish I'd met them before they were so struck with plague.

What is their worship? I ask, remembering that Gil said Morton believed them godless.

What manner and degree of association have you had with them?

Friendship, with one woman.

For a moment I see Dema on Miller's ship, sorely sick from absence, and from dwelling on a vessel crammed with fish both dry and wet-salted. Surely they must be bearing near on to England by now. But they'll likely still be in open ocean. Dema stands at the prow, taking the air; she struggles for glimpse of land, scarce less alone than I on my isle. The bears were no stranger to me than the citizenry she'll meet will be to her. I pray that Miller watches over her, or at least offers her some aid after landfall. I think he will.

I thought her godly enough, I say.

As I do the most of them. But they've no worship a priest'd recognize. They've no temples, nor prayers. They've no worship but

the whole of their lives; eating or sleeping, they think on God. Even
their sleeping-mats are in some fashion altars. So I believe, whatever
others should say. Let's to earth.

He steps from the platform to the first rung hammered on the
trunk, begins climbing down. I follow hard behind. Though my skirts
billow out a bit about my lower legs I take no special care. He may
look or he may not. There are those who might say this Morton's soul
is uneven, lacking in balance—that he's confused about the purpose of
settlement and about right worship. Very well. I've oft been thought
disorderly myself. He has him passion, sure, enough of that. I think
we may make good companionship.

When we are to ground, and stand where sun warms a mat of
pine needles, I ask if he has met men who name themselves Saints.

I have. To the north, and to the south in Plimoth.

Have you met the leaders of those to the north? I say.

John Stradling, he says. I liked *him* not at all.

My stomach knots cold—to hear that name brings him here,
as though he might step from behind the trunk of the Prospect Tree.
We're in accord on that, I say.

And yet he's the one you'll travel to?

We begin walking the trail—it's quickly buried among chestnut
and black birch, and will remain so until unearthed in the clearing
that is Merrymount.

Him and his relation, I say.

Then why will you go to him?

I tell him, and most of it honest. When I finish, he stops—the
sugar trees and first boards of his town visible beyond him, and he looks
at me strangely. Almost with a start, I know his look affectionate.

The river is wide, slow, sunken as the sea. Surely at high tide the
salty waters must overwhelm the fresh, reversing the general flow
for those few hours. But we come to the mouth at low tide. Water
more fresh than salted slips slowly through a marsh of reeds, then
through firm, mossy mats that Morton says hide mussel beds, finally
to the foaming ocean. Morton takes the tiller to guide us as we coast
through to flat water.

For three days we've sailed north in the shallop; ten men, and Mary, and me. All that while I've watched the forest. There is scarce ever a pause in its solid, torrid reach, and then only for waterways overhung, near overwhelmed, by more juniper and cedar. It is oft fearsome—and, sometimes, has given me the hint of a desire to worship. The woods are like a hot stew, with all the coast naught but the thread-thick skimming atop them; and that last, little skin is the only country where English here dwell. If they could, they would burst beyond the seashore, grow far as where the shallop sails, cast roots through the world—only the ocean, the whale-road, may stop them.

I might have used the forest for distraction. What better to call my mind from coming hazard than sight of a country new, rich, fat, at once generous and deadly? But most of the time we've sailed I've felt placid, as though watching myself from afar. It seemed unreal that I would again see the Saints, that somewhere, behind that thorny wall of forest, they have made their home. It seemed a dream that I was coming to them—those folk who know my name, but expected to speak it again only in a tale of betrayal and godly honor.

At Merrymount Anne asked, as I took up my sailcloth garments, if I would bring Mary with me. I will, I said, almost defiantly. Surely Anne thought it reckless to bring her, and that it was only for my own comfort and satisfaction—that I might confront them with her. She cannot know that Mary is rather a shield for Adam. I do not know what he'll say, what he'll do. But if it inflames me, I'll not sully my babe's eyes with sight of human blood.

An hour past, when the shallop was still cast about by white, spilling spray, a man pointed to shore. In the distance, behind the first row of hills, was a small mount overtopped by fencing. I thought it looked a toy crown set atop an anthill. Then I chided myself, thinking I should not strive to comfort myself through mockery. These Saints are yet perilous.

When we sailed further in, a hillock near the ocean shielded the pale from sight. If we cannot see them, sure they cannot see us. But the view they most wanted is of ocean reaches, where would sail foreign warships. They would think first of defense, maybe imagining themselves likely to be attacked by a mighty host.

Since seeing the pale I've felt helpless, a passenger. Might I row, I say.

Morton is steady at the tiller. Pewter rounds at his belt flash silver. If you will, he says, perhaps some amused, and nods one of his men to yield his place.

Gently I set Mary among bundles of trading goods brought as gifts. When I turn to take my place at the bench, I see, in a small side inlet, half-hid from view by a stand of what looks to be marsh elder, a small, solid dock.

The handle is solid as a sword. Hauling on it brings sweat to my cheeks, my chin. Rowing through marshland I need not imagine their faces; the changes, sure as mending, that a year of seasoning will have brought each one.

I lean into the oar. In this way I face the breaking sea. There is a road across those waters, away from this place. There's another place I may flee to.

Not flee. I may return there. *We are not like to let women be stole from us*, Morton said one day, doubtless meaning to offer solace, and say that they would not see me took by Saints. But I passed by *stole*, took my comfort from the *us*. I think myself included in that. I think I have a place with Morton, at his Merrymount. And the Saints will not keep me, whether or no the men of Merrymount aid my leaving.

As we slip further up channel the marsh smells rank and rich—full of the murk of fish, of sulfurous mud, of spouting clams. The breeze bears salt and sweetgrass.

Finally we bump to the dock. From the prow a man jumps to the planks, takes hold of a line. An empty bucket sits on the dock, an eeljig beside it. I stand carefully in the shallop, and with both arms push myself to kneel beside the man. Then I start; my stomach falls away. For each plank of the dock is set with five nails—four making a kind of diamond, the fifth at the heart. So Benjamen Smythe bade us hammer the planks of the footbridge when it was found rotted, three springs past.

Smythe is here. He has brought his manner of building, and Abigail his daughter. They are here, up that path—across the marsh, and through pines that border it darkly. Elsewhere those trees would look like nothing more than did those near by where we went coasting, that hid nothing worse than an ellan and fear of savages. But somewhere behind these is their palisade. Now the pine boughs seem a cloth cast over serpents.

My heart quickens. Still kneeling, I reach that Morton may hand me Mary. For a while I do not stand; I hold her, looking past the shallop, and under it, into shallow waters. There's some curious manner of crab swarming. They're shaped like horseshoes, with spears for tails. One rides another; four more feed on a ragged dead fish. Finally I stand.

We will wait here for you, Morton says. He must think my hesitation born all of fear. Sure, much of it is—though it was my choice to come here, I know now how a baited bear's heart must thrum. But within that melee is another, wrenching excitement.

They are here. *But I am here.*

I thank you, truly, I say. It should not be so very long. An hour.

We'll go after, and make our parlay, he says.

I raise Mary overhead, lower her backward into a sling. It's more difficult than I'm used. She's growing well. She is growing better than ever the Saints should credit, if they knew her place of birth, I think fiercely; she is growing stronger than ever I could have hoped.

These Saints're not so diligent, says a man in the shallop says. Never took aught time to mend a sodden weir.

Following his gaze I see a set of fences in the water, a bit upstream from the inlet where lies the dock. The fencing is disorderly, most probably useless, whatever the first purpose was.

Nor so wary, Morton says. That we might come from open sea, and no party to meet us.

They're trying to fill the silence while I prepare. I'm grateful. But it is time for me to go. I take up Dema's staff. Already, under my sling, I wear my valru coat for a cloak. Around my neck is the charm of sidley root, of grima pot, and now a few folded pages of Sarah's Book. I've assembled those gifts I find meaningful. I wear a biggins-cap, and clothes I've made. I'll come to the Saints with my own talismans, my own protection, bare of devices they would recognize or endorse.

An hour, I say.

If longer, we'll come.

I think there'll be no need, I start to say.

But Mary weighs heavy on my back. I am not here alone; I must not act so. She may shield him from me. But first, I must shield her.

I thank you, I say. Then I turn, and begin the path to what I think the Saints will have named New Monkshead.

It is near to noon, the day hot. The dock was set in the only place possible—the trail from it is on a long land bridge through the marsh—a dry, raised berm—that might have been mounded for the purpose. In the heat, the valru coat seems an affectation. It is one; but one with meaning for me, and I had rather sweat than disrobe.

If this was dusk, doubtless the place would be entire mobbed by mosquitoes, by biting flies. The grass here is plentiful but looks sharp, stiff, almost hard. But after a while the grasses end, leaving the path on proper ground, and me among the pines.

I walk through the forest. All is strange in this country—the bird bright red as a carnation that lands to pick at a dandelion, the stuff like warped cabbage that fills the lowest, wettest ground. Near a patch of that last I catch a glimpse of what I think is a deer. But when it takes another step I see it's bigger than a horse, its horns like horned shovel-blades. It meanders clumsily, and is soon from sight.

Another time it would be cause for thought—what was that beast? What else takes shelter in the woods, or finds damp sustenance amid the marsh? Today it is only brief distraction from the hard beating of my heart.

After a short while, the ground on both sides rises in hills. But they soon descend again, and more sun can reach near the path. Then there are maples with gnawed, pricked leaves, their branches netted with the nests of tent caterpillars. I swing my staff higher than needed, the better to spear it to ground.

I pause, gathering myself. I am draped about in charms; I hold another in my hand. That last might serve for a weapon. But the one most important hangs at my back. I need these things for my own protection but more, perhaps, that I may know myself here in truth. All is strange in this country. But strangest of all is us—that we are here. I feel us alone as never since the island. Without my charms I might forget myself, my history, my name. Already I think I might forget my purpose. Why will I bring us into hazard?

Mary coughs, as though waking. She slaps at my ears.

We need not stay there long, I say to her.

But inwardly I think that we must go. I must see them here, and know their condition, and they must know mine.

I walk through the last slope of flanking hills that fall away like curtains. Then there is the last hill, the greatest, and atop it their pale. I cannot see it clearly, for the slope below is yet overgrown with forest—maples, and oak. But from this vantage the pale seems harder than I'd thought, its roots more firmly set, more like a warlock's keep in a tale than a fence for livestock, or even defense. The path splits before me; one of its branches, old and packed as that I stand on, leads around the hill and then, likely, to the west. The other angles like a snake-fence through the trunks uphill.

I climb. This trail, at least, is new—no inheritance from the Massachusetts, or whatever Indians here name themselves. There are still some branches at the edge, not yet trained to grow away from the Saints' passage.

This is not like the boat—the labor of climbing gives me no release. Adam. John Stradling. Abigail. All wait for me, unknowing. All will be shocked to silence by sight of me. Perhaps they'll think me a ghost. Perhaps they'll be comforted, relieved of the guilt that they set me in a boat, and so rid themselves of me. Could giving us muskets have truly comforted them, let them think themselves no murderers? But maybe they feel no guilt, and never have. Certain I feel none for Henders; he never haunts. Maybe they think I sinned against them as he did against me.

I climb the path that's in places still loose and spilling, the ascent not yet tamped and set by generations of feet. Before it seems possible I am in pure sun, by the pale, near enough to lay my hands on the wood.

There is a shut gate. I lean against it, catching my breath from the climb. Then I push. It's barred, and seems solid as I'd thought below; there is no give, no play in the doors or sideposts. But on each corner of the keep is a bastion tower, projecting some four feet out. Were I to assault this place they might stand there, shooting lead balls along the wall I tried set fire.

My breath has returned me, or all that fear and excitement will permit. Still I lean, now resting. I am all blank, with no notion of what to say or do when I do find entrance. I think of calling out. But there must be another way to pass inward; they must have some better route to the fields where they labor to sustain their congregation.

I walk alongside the palisade, near brushing the wall with my right shoulder, until I'm to one of the bastions. It seems right curious that they sweated so in raising a rampart, and yet left their best vantage unmanned. The tower abuts a bluff, a drop of a man's height into a thicket below. My steps begin to crack. The ground here is mussel shell, clam, lobster. I kick up horrid smell, and a cloud of buzzing flies. As I circle the watchtower I most hug the planking—such a fall should not likely injure me, but Mary's on my back. Shells spill to join the greater heap below. Some hang on the thick, thorny vines until they're knocked free by those falling after.

After the tower the ground is more level, and clear, the wall angled inward. They have not built perfect true. Once, I think I hear a hammer blow. But it's only the first rap of a woodpecker's drilling.

Finally I'm around the second tower. Grass grows to my knees. I am at the true front of the keep, where is set an open gate. But I do not make for it; I am come to the burying ground.

Now I know these among the dead:
Katherine Gardner, who was dear to Patience.
John Hamilton.
Mabel, his servant.
Abigail Smythe, who plagued her.

David Merchant.

Midge Thomas.

Jonathan Hooker, who was the first man I held, though then a boy.

Joseph Flynt.

Master John Stradling.

There are more dead than that. I wander the burying ground, reading news of ruin in names carved on walnut. There are no other devices, none of the skulls and wings and flesh found on English stones. Disputes are turned bone, those I thought deserving and undeserving laid dead in indiscriminate congregation.

On the island, thinking of Abigail, I imagined shouts. I imagined a tearing combat, a desperate fight. This is only quiet, strange, her name writ absolute. It's been some months; the mould of the grave has sprouted its own briar, near matching that of the surrounding ground.

It is late summer, the dandelions here gone naked under wind. The place seems older than is possible. We have not been so long absent from England. It is the weeds that make it feel so aged—the Saints yet have no stock to chew the ground trim. Once I need brush tall grass aside to read a widower's name.

At some names I am grieved; there are a plenty enough of dead that I am often so. When I come to Midge's name I think of Sarah, and lost friends, and for a time I weep. Under my grief I become dimly aware that our coming may not be so stirring a thing as I'd thought.

From the palisade behind me comes coaxing talk. Now that I no longer view it from below, it looks less imposing, if no less hard-set—it is more anvil than monument. About its edges and those of all the burying ground are vines, creepers, blackberries, all grown lusty under unfamiliar sunshine. From the open gate comes a woman. She leads a small boy, and in the other hand carries a hoe and a basket slung over her elbow. When she sees me, she stops.

Susan. Susan Porter, I say.

She wears a wide work-hat, and midland clothes—a long underskirt, a coif, an apron like a tanner's. She squints at me, threescore feet away. Then her face opens with amazement, becomes a dry flower. She walks to me as she might to a cow ready to bear—judging whether or no its time has yet come.

No, she says.

It's Melode, I say. Mel.

No.

Seeing her in her common midland garb, I feel my own stranger than ever yet before. For this is how I might look myself—this is the home I thought myself bound for. Her condition might be mine. I might wear her wool and leather, and never think I had the choice of sailcloth. This is like seeing a looking-glass for the first time, with that same crossed sense of both familiarity and first encounter.

A ship, she says. You were found by another ship, soon after.

Not very soon after.

I never imagined my first encounter to be with one like Susan. If not true friends, we were always friendly. Though she was not born a servant, we lived in like condition—and she took her station with greater humor than me, though that might have masked bitterness. Certain, she felt no joy at my casting out. But she stands across the graves amid dandelions, and thistles, and will not come to me. She might stand atop a watchtower, and I beyond the barred gate.

So many dead, I say, and spread my arms to take in all the ground.

It were a long winter, she says. She grips the boy's hand tighter. He calls protest. He cannot be hers; he is too old. I do not recognize him. But then he would barely have taken first steps, when last I saw him.

How many live?

More than half, by Grace of God. How...how have you come here?

By Grace of God.

Where do you come from?

From Merrymount. Where are the rest now?

In the corn fields, or else mending barrels, she says.

I've not seen all the markers here, I say. Is Adam alive.

He is.

When Susan says that, her look changes. She's no longer a wary almost-friend. Now she is more guarded than distant, ready to call down Saint soldiery on my head.

And his condition? I ask.

An Elder, a well-honored man, she says, and my husband.

She leans to the boy, whispers to his ear. He runs off with the stumbling youth's gait that is nearly as much falling as advance.

It were a long winter, she says.

I am scorched hollow. I say: That boy cannot be yours.

He is now. That is Kenelm Stradling, Kenelm Hamilton until the passing of his parents. I am now Susan Stradling, and his mother.

You have a measure of courage, I say.

Maybe, she says sharply. I will not hear ill spoke of him.

Then I'll not speak so to you, I say.

A long winter, I think. That's likely all the explanation I am to get. Though I should never have thought so, it seems near enough. How much must have changed for them while imprisoned by snow, by illness, by hunger, by dread. I can see only a little through the open gate but that pale looks most empty, the few visible houses clustered like marbles in the corner of a jug. They had better have built shelter from the sky than from savages. Death from winter is death from winter, whether it comes on an island or a hilltop keep.

How died so many? I ask.

From want. From illness. John Stradling died in battle.

She tells me how he and others dug them an Indian mound, the sort where they'd oft found good store of corn. In this one they found a mordant man, not very long dead—also an unstrung bow, and arrows. While in conference over their next act they were overtook by Indians, who stood aside the clearing. John Stradling made to string the bow. Other Saints discharged their pieces, and were soon answered by shafts. John Stradling missed his footing. He fell upon the stone head of the arrow he had sought to notch. He died not very long after, the wound in his leg having festered and gone sore black.

I listen; I've nothing more to say to Susan, who must of course defend her new life, its situation, the man at its heart. And he, the man I want to see and speak to, is behind her, coming from the gate with Kenelm at his side.

Standing so, walking so—as a father—he looks a different man. Perhaps it's the burdens of that duty that have stiffened his awkward gait, making him seem ten years older. In spite of winter want he is some stouter, his beard much thickened. But he is here. He carries a butcher's shamble hook, whether for defense or solely because he had it to hand when called I cannot say. When he looks to me there is a moment before recognition strikes him—recognition, thus doubt in the soundness of his own eyes and mind. I have rarely seen doubt in him. Its coming pricks the confidence I always thought at his heart. Strange, that in seeing his conviction challenged that I should best recognize it, and him.

Once I thought that on seeing him I should raise any club I could contrive, swing it as from the open sea—swing it whining shrill until it struck him in the head, crashing him asunder, leaving little to mark him as once a man but brains and blood on the thistles. So I once thought I would.

But there is Mary, an anchor on my back against the gale. My fingers on Dema's staff are white, my feet are set as in sticky clay. That last should not stop me if it was my true will to murder. But Mary is my anchor—my spring of better will. I take a step. I walk to Susan, and thus to him.

Now I know these among the living:

Rachel Hooker. Isaac Rowe. His daughter, Fight-Faith. Sam Harper, who I once saw whipped for swearing. Daniel Williams, who is given to jest, and calls Adam dearest friend. James Patters. Alice Manning. Joseph Butler, and Temperance his wife. Benjy Butler.

They harry the edge of this ground, where Adam has bade them wait; they'll not approach without a gesture from him. They have formed a bowed line, where they may whisper to each other and yet watch us.

I sit, legs crossed beneath me. My back aches from my climb. But I'll not lean on a gravestone—such might show me too needful of gaining a mocking triumph. Mary has begun to cry. I loose my bodice, untie the shift beneath, free my breast to feed her. Of course all the while I watch Adam; I look at Mary but I watch him.

Oh, he looks different. If he is made uncomfortable by my quick nakedness he will not show it. His scar leaves a weak line in his beard, but you must know to look for it to see. He seems strong, and I imagine that the Saints have been more plagued by illness than by winter want—or else this summer has been generous to them. Adam seems to have slowed, masking his awkwardness. His eyes are much the same. They hold the cold watchfulness with which once he saw his father sermon. His clothes are blue, they are yellow. They are rusty red. But all are dull, none refreshed by spring's general dying.

Near-frowning, he watches me. Besides the watchfulness there is a hint of wonder, perhaps interest—there is no shame. None of it is stark as I thought to see, or hoped for. I wish to see him stunned as by lightning. Instead he looks at me as he might at a star that flashes across the sky, then hangs firm for long moments before withering. I am a portent. Of good or ill, he is unsure. But I do not strike him with fear.

For a moment I feel myself ridiculous, draped with signs that have meaning only to me. I recover myself. For it is true: these signs have meaning only to me. Soon Mary draws milk.

You've lost the best of your people, I say.

Those the Lord chose call, he says. We honor them, but think more often on those He left here to do His work.

Still I can't say He's blessed you with prosperity.

Mary nibbles on my breast as she drinks. I shift, give her my thumb to pull. Such has oft relaxed her in her nursing; it does now.

Adam crosses his arms, then looses them to rest on his hips. He draws in his upper lip, bites it, squints. You are come from Merrymount, Susan tells me, he says.

From his voice I might be a visitor from that plantation, a woman he has met but knows not at all well. He will be as courteous in showing me about this place as he would to any. And it comes to me that this is no pretense. It must seem as long to him since we've met as it does to me. A long winter—one filled with coughing death, and wasting death, and the black-leg death of his father. In all that time I was no concern to him, to them. They had enough to do with the dwindling of their congregation, the stacking of the dead as they waited for earth to thaw. Perhaps there were those that at times thought me fortunate.

I am.

A disorderly place, I think.

It is, I say. I know his notion of order.

Is it true that savages dwell there?

Some Indians do. Some labor in the fields aside it.

An unusual practice, he says. He speaks as though prophecying doom—that any who so countenance savages will not long survive this land.

It is, I say shortly.

He will not ask me how I lived, I see; their judgment, his crime, will never be spoke so open. You have a surprising old child, I say.

We must look to our own, he says. I think him my true son.

He fingers the shamble hook. It is two feet long, the straight end sharp as a nail, meant to be pounded into a tree to hang pigs during butchery. I have no notion of what he was doing with it before he was called—they have nothing to butcher, even were it the proper season. Where is the sailor? he asks.

Henders. Dead.

He looks at Mary then. I know he thinks of parentage.

His, and she a bastard, I say.

Perhaps I speak too quick. Though he would quickly realize she is too young for it, he must wonder for the moment if she is of his blood. I could let him suffer so. But I would here speak plainly, without the fear of rebuke hinted at by a lie. They may do with my history what they will; I know what happened.

The sun is past its noontime arc, and shines brightly on the palisade wall. Those Saints without broad hats must shield their eyes to see us. I think them beyond ready hearing.

I've recent seen Anne, I call. I call as though to Benjy, but my words are meant for Isaac. He must know that Anne lives, near enough to be recent seen, and yet is beyond him, away from him. I will not expose her by speaking to him straight. But his face turns a dropped stone.

I shift, giving Mary better suck. You had better have spent time growing food than building such a strong-barred place, I say to Adam.

We had cause enough to fear savages.

Or clumsiness. I cannot mourn your father, I say.

I've sparked some pleasant anger. I will mourn him enough for ten of you, he says.

I'll rejoice enough to match it, I say. The world's richer since his passing.

If I was standing he might strike me. If he did he would be grateful for the shamble hook, for I would strive to send him to his father's embrace before any else might aid him. But I sit nursing, and he collects himself. Not for you to say, or me to say, but only Him to ordain, he says. Why have you come here?

He tosses the hook to the side; it sticks like an arrow.

To see you.

And then?

Some Saints have gathered on the watchtower. I see the face of one small girl, younger that Patience, who I knew and liked. I cannot recall her name. All but her forehead drops from sight; she must have been standing on toes.

I thought of murder, I say. I had enough time alone to think of that.

It was never my intent to see you left, he says.

He does not mean it for apology. It is only the truth.

Rather, to keep me, I say. In your fashion.

Do you yet think of killing?

There might be a thread of mockery there. But I ignore it, and think only of my answer. For even if he thinks it scarce more than play, it is one that matters to me.

Mary bubbles a bit, spits. I run a hand across her head, her yellow hair, the place at her crown where once her head was soft and without defense. Now I think the bones well fused, and growing stronger yet.

I rest her on my folded legs, begin tying my shift. I can no longer think so much of killing. I think I could not, even were Mary not here. Killing is itself a manner of keeping. Henders does not haunt. But killing him was done hotly, and a manner of shield. Violence here would be coldly thought; wretched, vengeful, a lading I'd always bear.

No, I say. You are useless to me. As much as I am to you. That I ever dwelled with your folk was never more than accident.

He looks at me closely, and sees I mean it truly. I am what he first spoke to me as—a woman of Merrymount, come with men of that plantation in their parlay and visitation. There is no longer aught more between us than that.

You cannot have come alone, he says.

The men will follow after, in a while, I say. Thomas Morton would speak with you.

At that name, his face shows brief disgust. But it passes quickly.

Will you come inside the pale, and wait for them? he asks.

Not today.

I stand, sling Mary back over my shoulder.

Mary's feeding's done, I say. There's a place we find ourselves more welcome, and easily at home.

I turn and walk from him, away from the half-circled Saints.

Mel, he calls.

I look back. My skirts have left a path lightly pressed in the weeds.

You are a damned, strange woman, he says. You should be welcome at Merrymount.

Though he has dropped his hook his words are meant to match it; once they should have twisted me painful, maybe goaded an attack. Now they bring comfort—relief.

I'll pray thanks tonight for all of that, I say.

We're bound for a place that may yet, one day, see no less death than this. Still I feel, for now, that we are leaving death behind.

We pass around the keep in the same manner we came. When

we reach the path this time eyes fill the watchtowers, both north and south, eager for a final glimpse. This time, if they call, I'll not turn.

Adam smirked at my last words, confused, never sure why being damned, and strange, and a woman, should ever be cause for thanks. Well he may wonder.

I clamber down the hill, along the sharp turns of the path. It seems much shorter on descent; the sun is now to our backs. Soon we are out from it, between the hills, among the maples and oak and blackberry bracken.

Freedom is accord with the will of God, they say. Perhaps on that they are right. But who to know His will? They may think what they will think. That freedom I thought of before was fetters.

We leave the new trail, begin the ancient path through the pine forest. Mary cries in her sling. Not crying—crying out. She punches at my shoulders. I know she throws her arms high between the raps. I walk the path through the pines, my steps falling, from happy chance or sympathy of blood, into cadence with her dear fists. She yelps, happy and senseless.

Through a long tunnel of pines there is light on the water; a distant egret skims the grasses, flying wondrous white. A second follows—a third. The trail leads to the marsh. Thus to the boat. Thus to the ocean, and thus to Merrymount. Merrymount. And I feel—oh, I feel marvelous.

March! I call to Mary. With each beat of her hands, each step of my feet, a link drops, leaving me lighter. I feel I fly the path. Surely my feet must scorn the earth. But if I could fly in truth I would not, from fear the loss of beating steps should weaken our accord. My pace, my staff, the palms of my babe on my shoulders, thrum together like heartbeats, they ring like triumph-drums.

I thought that Morton wished to drink in all this country. Now I feel myself party to his wish. For every needle on every pine stands out clear—I could not see one more distinct were I to lay it on my palm, peer at it as a Lord's marvel. I might stop and dig, clawing past brown needles and into the loam, so close and loving do I sudden feel to it. The wind carries the ocean, the provender of feeding crabs, fallen wood. Birds chirp and quarrel on high branches—their argument looses a twig to fall, or a cone. Punch, step, cry, punch, step, step, then cry! Together we chime, we are blazing bells.

But I do pause, and breathe, so much do I desire to hold this time and feeling. There is in the world such abundance of the Lord's fine needlework, His forge, His husbandry yard, His wonders. I want to shout and yet hold perfect silent—to feed, and be fed from. I know I cannot understand nor keep even this one, fine moment. But for an instant I feel close to tearing all aside, to seeing something great, a glimpse...

I haul me a chest of air—green air, and new. I ready myself to shout. But there is too much to say, my head too full. And I breathe out, that I may once more inhale this company of abounding wood, and salty marsh, and sea.

Selected Glossary

adventurer—a person extending capital into a risky venture, such as establishing a colonial settlement. Sometimes they were reimbursed through total profits from a settlement for a set number of years.

berm—a long land bridge.

bandog—fighting dogs, often bound with ropes or chains.

bill—pruning saw

blod cloak—blod: archaic color name, dark gray.

brachet—hunting hound

bugle—herb related to mint.

changeling—sickly imp or fairy infant left in the place of a stolen, healthy child.

cheat—wheat bread, of decent quality but less desired than that made with white flour.

chine—backbone, or cut of meat along the backbone.

churching—an old ceremony or ritual, performed to cleanse a woman after childbirth. It was thought necessary before she could return to worship in church.

coney—rabbit

crucks—buckets. Also used to refer to a kind of roof framing, composed of pairs of naturally curved timbers.

dewlap—loose skin beneath the neck of a cow or other animal.

dirk—dagger

eeljig—fishing tackle used to bob for eels.

ellan—elk

facking—end of a piece of rope.

flux—diarrheic illness, often deadly when water was scarce.

grima—Old English, used to describe a goblin, ghost, or spectre. Also linked to the word "grim," when used in the sense of "bogey or haunting spirit."

hundred—a plantation or settlement capable of supporting a hundred men-at-arms; sometimes also applied to much smaller outposts to give impression of strength.

husbandman—class of farmer, above laborers, below landowners.

jerkin—sleeveless jacket, with extended "wing" shoulders.

kermes—natural red dye

killframe—variation of kill, a type of low-fired kiln used to dry malt during beermaking.

King Bee—or Master Bee. The largest bee in a hive, widely described as male until the eighteenth century.

kinterkin—barrel of about 18 gallons.

league—measure of distance, varying between 2.5 and 4.5 miles.

manchet—fine grade of white bread, above either raveled or cheat.

molespear—garden tool, used to kill moles in their burrows.

nightmare—supernatural being (often associated with a witch), who could bring terrifying visions or crush a person to death in sleep.

perry—pear cider

pinuins—corruption of "penguins"

poppet—doll

Prester John—legendary figure, believed to rule an ideal Christian kingdom somewhere in Africa or Asia. Crusaders fantasized that he might one day march his armies west, meeting them in Jerusalem.

rapes—heaps of straw left to dry after threshing.

razing—sexual metaphor, typical of the period in its aggression.

Saint—any of God's chosen people following the "true" tenets of congregationalism, rather than a sanctified individual as in the Catholic Church. In actuality, probably used more in a general sense than as a self-reference.

seine—drag-net

shoats—young pigs

slag—metal residue from smelting.

speanes—cow's teats

stempost—the foremost timber of a ship's keel.

tarn—small lake or still pond.

truck—term for negotiations or trade.

trencher—wooden platter, sometimes used as a single general plate by a group.

tyg—cup with at three or more handles for easy passing between drinkers.

weld—yellow dye taken from "dyer's rocket" plant.

woad— blue dye from a relative of the mustard plant.

Writs of Passage—legal requirements for leaving England, refused to Catholics and other religious dissenters.

yard—penis

Afterword

Notes on History and Sources

Readers who have come this far with Melode may wonder how much of her story is rooted in fact. The religion and community of the Saints is based heavily upon accounts of the old Plymouth Colony and the people later known as the Pilgrims. These Separatist Congregationalists were not, as is often said, Puritans—they had no hope of reforming the English Church from within, instead resolving to live "according to the simplicity of the Gospel, without men's inventions" in congregations bound to one another by attachment to basic principles of worship rather than hierarchy. Their refusal to pledge their faith to the official church was as much political as religious, and accounts for the hostility of the state to their continued existence.

After fleeing their English home at Scrooby in Nottinghamshire in 1608, the "Pilgrim" congregation spent eleven years in Amsterdam and Leyden before leaving for the Americas in advance of a feared Spanish invasion. They were a literate group, and concerned with justifying themselves to posterity as well as to their contemporary

European detractors. Like many groups that (rightly) believe themselves the targets of persecution, the Plymouth settlers were capable of both measured justice and great communal crimes, both disinterested verdicts and violence toward those (within and without) perceived as threats to the whole. The conflicting tendencies were probably exacerbated by a feeling of deep isolation, following a journey of some 3,000 miles across the Atlantic and a first New England winter that killed fifty of the original 102 passengers. In any case, the books that best conveyed these contradictions to me were William Bradford's *Of Plymouth Plantation, 1620–1647,* Edward Winslow's *Good Newes From New England* (1624), and *Mourt's Relation* (1622). They were all extremely useful, as were the twelve volumes of the *Records of the Colony of New Plymouth in New England,* and Thomas Morton's *New English Canaan* (1637), which provides an alternative, and often scathingly funny, view of the community.

The broad story of Mel's abandonment is based on that of Marguerite de La Roche, which Farley Mowat recounts in *Sea of Slaughter,* his disturbing account of Canadian, European, and American hunts for everything from cod to mink to auks. In 1542, Marguerite took a lover en route to Quebec, and was abandoned with her lover and a maidservant on the "Island of Demons," where she bore a child. At last she was rescued by fishermen, her companions and son having died during the previous two years. Moving the story to the English Midlands during the reign of James I was prompted by my studies and interests at the time, as was the change in Mel's station—I was at the University of Virginia studying the Plymouth Colony through the lens of historical archeology, a discipline which tries to locate illiterate (hence voiceless) people who are too often absent from existing records.

The historical chronology in the novel has been considerably compressed. Though the descriptions of Melode's Midland village, the island, Cupid's Cove, and Merrymount are as internally accurate as I could make them, the settings were not actually contemporaneous. For example, for the action of the book to occur in actuality, Mel would have to leave Cupid's Cove in 1611, but not come to shore at

Merrymount in New England until 1626. New Monkshead is entirely an invention.

Those familiar with other portrayals of the early seventeenth century, whether in England or the Americas, may feel that the picture of life given here is too "early," the physical environment and worldviews in places closer to medieval than Jacobean. But it is the pace of modern change, with ideas, objects, and practices enthusiastically adopted seemingly days before being just as enthusiastically discarded, that traps us into thinking of physical surroundings as so transitory. Thus I have tried to avoid focusing on the "leading edge" of physical and intellectual change. To use a material example, the bearded, bellied jugs known as bellarmines first appear around 1550, but it took the better part of a century for them to become prominent. My assumption is that the same slow spread was often true of the social and religious attitudes familiar from the writings of the time. Certainly even apparently uniform groups such as the Plymouth settlers (a bare half of whom were actually practicing Congregationalists), would have included a much wider range of belief and practice than that propounded by the colony's religious leadership.

Two exceptional books by Keith Thomas were invaluble when constructing Melode's world and her view of it. In both *Religion and the Decline of Magic* and *Man in the Natural World,* Thomas assembles a wealth of fascinating and often surprising details that highlight the vast distance between us and the early settlers—as well as the wildly diverse, and often contradictory, beliefs of the time. The combination of slow, spotty communications and, as more and more individuals found themselves traveling between distant countries and even continents, surely contributed to conflicts between folk and theological beliefs. Even in supposedly staid Plymouth, a "naughty" canoe was tried, found guilty, and destroyed after two of its passengers drowned—and a jar that archeologists found buried under a doorway was probably once full of needles and urine, a charm against the entrance of witches.

When writing dialogue, both internal and external, I have aimed for something more plausible than strictly accurate. Though I tried to avoid demonstrably anachronistic words and phrases, when writing of a period before recording devices it is simply impossible to claim that one has accurately represented the vernacular. Some of the dialogue is drawn from or based upon the writings of historical figures—for example, Thomas Morton's *New English Canaan,* which documents his 1624–9 stay in New England, and John Guy's 1611 letters to England, partially compiled in the Hakluyt Society's *Newfoundland Discovered*—and I was heavily influenced by readings of these and other period documents. But many are so stylized and formal that nothing in them can be taken as a true representation of speech. Even contemporary film dialogue only rarely approximates modern tones, and I would argue that, if we could somehow access a recording of a four century-old conversation, translation might well be necessary.

The specific profanities used were almost certainly present in vernacular speech. Though the written record contains only spotty—sometimes punning or ciphered—references, this simply indicates the broad taboo on curses being written explicitly; at the same time it attests to their presence in spoken English. The earliest reference to the verb "fuck" dates to 1535: "Bischops...may fuck thair fill and be vnmaryit" (unmarried). Names as elaborate as "Fight-the-Good-Fight-of-Faith" are also accurate.

Many of my specific physical details are drawn from the archeology of seventeenth-century sites, in the form of published summaries, field reports, or conversations with archeologists or historians. Many more come from one of the world's extraordinary (and today, extraordinarily difficult to find in its entirety) books, Randall Holme's *The Academy of Armory.* Holme's stated intention was to draw everything in the physical world, often with accompanying lists of terms. He filled several thousand pages with fantastic details—his *Sounds Made by Men* includes details like "When *Tortured,* he *Howls*". Much of my terminology—haying, naval, fishing, and more—as well as the physical architecture of Melode's world, relies heavily on Holme, who composed his first drawings in 1649, and probably continued through about 1680. In spite of the "medieval" tone, therefore, I am in these instances, erring on the side of anachronism. Also useful as both a check on Holme and a source in its own right was William Harrison's

The Description of England from 1587. The nature of some of the tools, practices, and beliefs derived from these and other sources should be clear from context; others are listed in a partial glossary.

Historical reenactors are often as engaged with the particulars of dress and speech as any novelist or academic, and provided me with a wealth of great detail. The research done by reenactors on the names of colors, appropriate fabrics, songs, folklore, and more—all the things long vanished from the archeological record—was invaluable, whether by professionals such as the wonderful crew of interpreters at Plimoth Plantation, ADD in Massachusetts (the living museum maintains the period spelling) or by enthusiastic amateurs. In particular, the hospitality and dedication of the Plimoth Plantation interpreters were inspirations throughout the writing.

One person, in particular, was more important than any dozen texts. I was fortunate enough to study under Jim Deetz both at the University of California, Berkeley and as a graduate student at the University of Virginia, and to experience firsthand his contradictory ability to perceive systems within the odd and idiosyncratic in human life. Most important for *Strange Saint* was his insistence that our common, staid view of the Pilgrims and of Puritans in general owed more to the Victorians, who projected an "idealized" view of a deeply repressed and monolithic society, than it did to what we knew of the people themselves. Jim's *In Small Things Forgotten*, as well as the account of the Plymouth Colony that he wrote with his wife, Patricia Scott Deetz, were essential and inspiring resources—as were my memories of the field schools at Flowerdew Hundred Plantation in Virginia, and the course in which we intensively dissected the twelve volumes of the Plymouth Colony Court Records. But the many evenings I spent at their home were more important and precious to me still. Jim died in 2000; I very much miss him, and his all-encompassing humor and intellect.

Acknowledgments

Many thanks to all the students and faculty at the Spalding M.F.A. program in Louisville. Mentors and friends Robin Lippincott, Kirby Gann, and Julie Brickman were enormously generous with their time and insights. I'm deeply grateful for Crystal Wilkinson's guidance in and out of workshop; thanks also to Connie May Fowler and Mary Clyde for their early enthusiasm and support. Special thanks to Neela Vaswani, who cheered me on from first to last, and to Sena Naslund, whose dedication to craft infuses the program she founded and sustains.

Thanks to Leslie Daniels, who is as fine a reader and editor as an agent. Thanks also to Don McQuade, whose close reading of an early draft was kind, on-point, and continues to be much appreciated.

Many thanks to all the wonderful people at *The* Toby Press, especially Matthew Miller for his vision and steady hand, and my editor, Aloma Halter, for her alert, graceful, and generously critical work.

Thanks to my parents, Richard and Carolyn, and three sisters, Michele, Jenny, and Suzanne—their suppport never wavered.

Thanks to all my friends, especially Jerris, Dave, Karin, Miranda, Sean, Cameron, Stephanie, Ellen, Derek, Susan, Greg, Angela, and Mike.

Finally, my wife, Elizabeth Windchy: this is as much her book as mine.

About the Author

Andrew Beahrs

Andrew Beahrs was born in 1973 and raised in Connecticut. He studied Archeology and Anthropology at the University of California, Berkeley, and at the University of Virginia, where he received his Master's. He later earned his M.F.A. in Fiction from Spalding University in Louisville, Kentucky, and has written articles on subjects as various as the California abalone fishery and capoeira, the Afro-Brazilian dance and martial art. He lives and writes in Berkeley with his wife and son. This is his first novel.

The fonts used in this book are from the Garamond family